GODSBANE

LINDSEY RICHARDSON

AUTHOR'S NOTE

Godsbane is an adult fantasy romance, and as such, contains darker themes, explicit language, and violent and sexual content that may not be appropriate for all readers. Reader discretion is advised. For a full list of these themes, please visit www.lindseyrichardsonau thor.com.

Godsbane is book one in a series.

PRONUNCIATION GUIDE

Places:
    Corinth — *cor-in-th*
    Amale — *ah-muh-lee*
    Synal — *sin-al*
    Synalian — *sin-ah-lee-an*
    Eida — *eye-da*
    Gathe — *gay-th*

Gods & Goddesses:
    Nobus — *no-bus*
    Mikais — *mick-eye-is*
    Bastin — *bass-tin*
    Drayca — *dray-cah*
    Arcasia — *ar-cay-zee-uh*
    Aevus — *a-vus*

Northern Sea
Amber Port
Topaz Region
Quay
Coronal Peak
Facet Mountains
Alloy River
Kingswood
Western Sea
Amale
Port of Gems
Coronet Isle
Diamond Region
N
W
E
S
Southern Sea

The Jeweled Kingdom of Corinth

RUBY REGION

GODSWOOD

GATHE

EIDA

EMERALD REGION

MYRA

BAY OF JEWELS

SAPPHIRE REGION

EASTERN SEA

ABALONE INLET

PATHAN

BEZEL

For anyone who has ever felt poisonous.

PROLOGUE

The cold, gray depths of the Eastern Sea threaten to swallow the girl whole. The rip current tugs relentlessly on her flailing limbs, every breath pulling more and more of the salty water into her too full lungs.

The Dark God of Death encroaches.

Leathery skin in blackest night flits across her peripheral—a glimpse of the creature of myth sent to collect her. Fire erupts from within as the sea beast grazes its serpentine body across the girl's spine, forever marring her porcelain skin.

Something long-slumbering awakens in her veins, power not in or of this world. Snippets of fate flash before her as the creature spurs her onto the shore.

Onyx hair.

Crimson blood.

A burning throne.

A name the soul knows but the mind cannot understand.

Shadowy death.

Blood-tinged water pours from her mouth in violent coughs as oxygen tries to fill her lungs again. Vines spring up from the dunes with each slide of the girl's frail hands as she crawls across the beach. Shadows wash away the blinding light of day as the sun vanishes from the heights of the noonday sky—an illuminated crescent on the sand the only evidence of its continued existence.

Time halts with the eclipse as reality shatters into two.

There is what was before and there is what will be. A child entered the sea, but something ancient and powerful emerged from the watery depths.

Touched by a god and destined to rule.

CHAPTER 1

he King is dead.

The single sentence hastily scrawled on a strip of rolled parchment lays on the center of the council room table. Its jagged edges echo the urgency in which the message was written. Torn from the blank margins of a larger document, ink smeared from the rain.

It was well past midnight when the messenger collapsed on the front steps, the missive gripped tightly in his curled fist. The occupants of the manor were fast asleep—everyone except the night watchmen and me.

I watched from my window as the guards dragged the man's soaked body inside, setting off the chain of events that has taken up the past sixteen hours of my life.

The King of Corinth never married, never sired an heir before a mysterious illness took the life of a man we were all made to believe was divinely blessed. The second king in less than three decades to succumb to the same fate, and yet these men still have the audacity to believe our nation is beloved by a pantheon of gods who could not care less about us.

"Without an heir to the throne, the constitution demands an Ascension Vote. It's the Governor's responsibility to attend," Lord Yarrow declares for the fourth time.

"And yet we've already established that my father cannot make the journey," I say, snapping the shaft of what remains of the last quill in my pile.

The dark wood table is littered with the mangled white barbs of the feather, one plucked from its stem each time I forced myself to stay quiet when one of the Governor's councilors said something ignorant.

"The capital city is too far and his heart isn't strong enough. It's my duty as the heir to the Emerald Region to attend in his place."

The Lord of Treasury flares his nostrils in restraint. He has never believed me fit for the title my father bestowed upon me. The first and only female who has ever held the title of heir in any of Corinth's five jeweled regions—and I've been rebuked ever since my father acknowledged me as such.

When my mother died and left him without a male successor, the men that now sit around this table judging me with unforgiving eyes urged him to do what his predecessors and peers do—appoint a noble lord to the role until he remarried and sired a boy.

"Lady Ivy has a point," Lord Bartlett sighs. "If Governor Fellows' health was good enough to travel, he'd be with us now. His condition worsens by the day. He'd never survive the two week journey."

A muffled prayer ripples through the room from the lips of the Emerald Council, each offering a whispered plea for my father's health to gods who won't answer their prayers.

They never fucking do.

"Why should we send a petulant girl in his place?" Yarrow demands, crumbling what restraint I have left with his venomous question.

"I haven't been a girl for over a decade, Yarrow, and I have

4

spent every one of those years trying to better Corinth for all who live here."

"Corinth is already great," he scoffs in dismissal.

"Great for you. You have fair skin, gold-lined pockets, a willingness to worship gods that are forced down our throats, and a cock between your legs. Should we ask those who don't look and think and worship like you if Corinth is great for them?"

"See what I mean?" Yarrow raises his voice in address to the other councilors who surround him. "Poison Ivy doesn't care about Emerald. She only wants another chance to spread her vitriol and publicly humiliate us all."

"Yarrow," Lord Barlett warns, "Ansel would not stand for this and you know it. Give Ivy a chance to explain her vote. Preferably in a less ... *spirited* way, my lady."

The father of my best friend and a man who has been more like an uncle to me than an advisor glares at the Lord of Treasury until he finally yields. Every eye pointedly descends on me as I rise and move towards the head of the table.

Before the seat reserved for the governor, a worn map of Corinth spreads across the wooden surface, large gems sitting on each of the five regions.

"As the commander of our national military and the king's closest advisor, Lord General Marks will vote on behalf of the Diamond Region," I say, picking up the sparkling jewel and tossing it lightly in my hand.

"Two kings have sat the Amethyst Throne with Marks controlling their strings. Those kings did nothing but bring war to our shores in the name of the Golden Pantheon. But those gods have done us no favors, and those kings divided more than they united."

"My lady, if I may. There are those who will say that you only wish to keep Marks off the throne because of your ... *history*. What do you say to them?"

"I say to them, Lord Adler, that placing the Lord General on the throne condemns the realm to more of the same fate. Corinth deserves someone better."

My father's Master of Arms dips his head in a single, solemn nod. I've made more enemies than friends with the council, but Lord Adler's honor demands he follow my commands regardless of his personal feelings towards me.

A quality I wish more of the men in this room possessed.

Setting the diamond back on the table, I pick up the egg-sized red jewel on the opposite side of the map. "Ruby will vote with Diamond."

"The only thing you can count on Governor Charles Rollins doing every time is the thing that best serves him," Lord Bartlett chimes in agreement as I set the ruby beside the diamond.

"The nation of Synal decimated a large portion of Sapphire when they invaded. Porter won't vote for the Lord General who orchestrated the holy war. He is our only ally and the best chance we have at a fair and just king. That leaves Topaz as our swing vote."

The golden yellow gem feels heavier than the others, the fate of a nation resting in the palm of my hand while the men in this room weigh my worthiness.

"Wilson will never agree to side with her. This is why we must send someone else!" Lord Yarrow rises in a flash, the clanging of his wooden chair echoing as it smacks against the stone floor. "If we send Poison Ivy to the Ascension Vote, we might as well place the crown on Marks' head ourselves."

"Call me that again, Lord Yarrow, and your counsel will no longer be needed."

A muffled gasp ripples throughout the room. They feign surprise at my outburst as if they haven't poked and prodded me like a caged animal for sixteen godsdamned hours. As if I haven't allowed them time and time again to call me the slanderous nickname courtesy of the man we seek to keep off the Amethyst Throne. The name meant to demean and degrade me.

Something forbidden sizzles under my skin, a deadly secret that I've spent eighteen years concealing. Unexplained magic that would find me at the end of a hangman's noose or worse—as a weapon under the command of Lord General Marks.

I will my power into submission, forcing it back into the crevices within me as the door to the chamber opens.

Every member of the council is on their feet in an instant, waists bent and heads bowed in reverence. My father stands in the doorway, hands braced on the wooden frame. Even in his current state, his appearance demands the respect they've withheld from me.

"Councilors," my father dips his head in acknowledgement as he pushes off the frame and makes for his chair. He stops before his seat, eyes locked on the map and scattered jewels laid out before him. "I trust you've spent these long hours advising your heir on how best to win Topaz's vote."

"Ansel," Lord Yarrow says, my father's hand coming up to halt him. "Governor," the Lord corrects. "It is this council's wish that you send someone else to the Ascension Vote. Someone who isn't … *her*."

He spits the word like a curse.

My sex has always been a convenient excuse for their dislike, and had I not opened my mouth and spoken out against our king's forced religion, it might very well have stayed the only one they had. But I made an enemy out of the most powerful man in our nation with my words, and he made sure the country hated me because of it.

My father's voice slips into the familiar low timbre of authority as he makes his decree. "Lady Ivy is heir to the Emerald Region of Corinth. She speaks for me—and she speaks for all of you. She will attend the Ascension Vote, and that is not up for debate."

The council doesn't roll their eyes, huff their breaths, or murmur disagreements out of respect for the Governor. Their disapproval, made crystal clear, will now follow them quietly out of the manor and into their homes where it will take root and spread like a diseased vine hellbent on strangling me.

"Now, if you all will make your way to the dining hall, the staff has prepared a dinner for us, and your spouses will be arriving shortly."

They don't stifle their groans at this command, however. It's not like a dinner in my honor is ever high on their list of fun activities, but it's dropped even lower after spending all day sitting in this room.

"Dinner isn't necessary, Father. I'd be fine to spend time with just you."

"Nonsense, Ivy," he says, taking my hand in his as the last of his advisors exit the room. "It's your birthday. We can't have the ball you deserve, but we can toast to you and the future that awaits."

"A dead king does suck the merriment out of a good ball," I joke.

I don't much care for noble balls, but they bring him joy and there's nothing I wouldn't endure for him. Especially when we only have hours left together.

Tomorrow, I'll set out for Amale, the heart of the Diamond Region and the capital city of Corinth. But it's not just the Lord General and his band of angry governors who await me at the palace.

No, something tells me that the Dark God of Death waits for me too.

The nightmares, left behind by the creature who must have been his creation, have gotten so frequent that I can't remember the last time I slept through the night. The visions have only gotten darker—bottomless pools of blood, the Amethyst Throne on fire, and a name my soul knows that I can never recall when I wake. Whatever waits for me there may very well be the end of me.

"Did you see the physician today?" I ask, already knowing the answer.

I've summoned every doctor, naturopath, and spiritual healer that tried to save my mother and they've all had the same answer. There's nothing to do but make him comfortable, and he refuses every tonic they offer.

A violent coughing fit seizes him. We both pretend not to notice the blood that leaks from his mouth before he quickly swipes it away. Fragments of my foreboding dreams flash through my mind again at the sight of the crimson liquid. Snippets that I have been trying to forget all day.

"Say a prayer for your father, will you?"

He jokes as he dismisses me, but his humor is misplaced. The gods never heard our prayers when my mother lay dying, and they've done little for us since.

Neither of us are pious, but in a country that claims to be the favorite of the gods, nonbelievers are shunned or killed. So we attend temple services and erect statues in their honor despite holding no love for the gods who abandoned us long ago.

False devotees for false gods.

I scoff at their stone effigies that adorn the courtyard gardens as I avoid the dining room. The ground is barren around them, just like Corinth under their watchful eyes. Their prized jeweled nation battered and scarred in the wake of a holy war. Our determination to convert the people of Synal and the island nations found us on the receiving end of an invasion—something entirely avoidable and entirely orchestrated by the Lord General.

My magic is primed, itching to be used after hours of sitting in an uncomfortable chair while listening to minuscule men debate my ability to sway a vote. Here, away from prying eyes, I can finally release it.

No one will notice a little more ivy mingled amongst the already thick vines that crawl up the stone tower or a few more blades of grass along the flagstone path. I'd like to disappear deep into the Godswood and use my magic until it's depleted and I fall asleep under the stars, but there's no time.

A quick detour through the garden to my favorite patch won't be the same, but it'll satisfy my magic for now. A right past the fountain, a left at the bust of the God King Nobus, and another right past the holly bushes leads me to my destination.

The gardeners planted the seeds of godsbane at my insistence. Their hesitance to add something poisonous amongst the wholesome blossoms further fueled my attachment to the flower. If it wasn't crucial that everything be intentionally placed by them first in order to hide my powers, I would cover every square inch of this garden in the death plant I've become so fond of.

I pick a small bundle of the deep-purple, nearly black blooms, carefully regrowing the missing flowers that surround the northern base of the faceless statue of the Goddess of Light. Her name and likeness are both lost to history. There's barely a mention of her in the sacred scriptures and holy texts, and not a single portrait in the temples depicts her certain beauty. All that remains of her is a stony, featureless face and a lithe, marble body draped in flowing cloth resting across a crescent moon.

A sliver of light from the setting sun peaks through the graying dusk illuminating the statue's outline on the still pool at its base. I kneel, pausing at my own reflection on the water's glassy surface. Pushing the tangle of brown waves from my forehead, I scrutinize the green eyes that stare back at me. Eyes that mirror the color of a region that holds barely any love for me. Eyes that don't match my mother's no matter how much I wish they did.

A spark snakes down my spine at the memory of her, magic

emanating from the tattooed bloom between my shoulder blades. Ink painstakingly added to hide the ghostly patch of skin left behind by the primordial sea beast who simultaneously saved my life and damned me, leaving me with strange power and even stranger dreams.

Ripples disturb the smooth surface as I trail my fingers through the water. I linger here, wishing to hear her long silenced voice but nothing comes. The dead don't talk and the gods don't grant wishes. Magic that shouldn't exist in this world sings within me, always drawn to the water since that day.

There is no explanation for the secret power that I possess. The more my magic has grown, the further inward I've retreated. I use my anger-fueled words to distract people from looking too closely, staring too long. Even the few people I've let behind my defenses don't know what runs in my veins.

"IVY!"

Eileen's voice echoes through the garden, snapping me from my introspection and causing me to drop the flowers into the pool. The sky opens as the matronly woman rounds the corner, fat raindrops pelting her head as she swats them away.

"There you are! I've been looking everywhere for you. Dinner is starting and you look like something a cat would drag in from the Godswood."

"Please, we both know cats hate me," I joke, ducking under the now open umbrella in her outstretched hand. "And I look fine."

"You'd look better in a dress. You would have had time to change into the special one laid out for you if you hadn't wasted so much time in the garden. I swear, sometimes I think you prefer plants to people."

"Plants don't tell me to shut up," I mumble as Eileen ushers me to the covered walkway at the edge of the garden. For someone whose job is to attend to *my* needs, she sure is opinionated.

"Was it Lord Yarrow again? I don't know why you still associate with his son. The way his father treats you is abhorrent."

"Miles isn't like his father," I say. "We aren't our parents."

"I think you're more like your mother than you remember," Eileen offers with a knowing smile. "I also think the gods have big things planned for your future, Ivy. Try not to miss it."

"How could she miss something that looks this good?" Miles Yarrow steps out of the archway that leads back into the manor's main hall, arms outstretched as he turns in an exaggerated circle. "Come on, Ive. You're going to miss your own birthday dinner."

"You'll never find a husband while you associate with him," Eileen chides as she takes the umbrella and departs for the dining room.

"Good thing I'm not looking for one!" I call after her.

My father would never dream of betrothing me against my will, but Eileen would have me married off before sunrise if she was governor. A fact that she has told me many, many times.

Miles, son of the man who is a perpetual thorn in my side, is an integral member of the trio that is the subject of much of the Emerald Region's gossip. Made up of an unruly, unwanted heir and the oldest children of powerful nobles, Miles Yarrow, Quinn Bartlett, and I have a knack for igniting rumors that spread like wildfire through the circles of the elite.

"Well … aren't you going to tell me how good I look? This is a new jacket." Miles smiles, puffing his shoulders and tugging on the fabric like a preening bird.

The rich embroidery of golden thread across the emerald lapels is a perfect complement to his sandy blonde hair. He's an irrefutably handsome man. Women fall over themselves for a single night with him and he is more than happy to oblige. He's an absolute rake and the brother that I never had.

"Not until you tell me how good I look." I smile, already

knowing that 'good' isn't an adjective I would use to describe myself at the moment.

"Let's see ..." Miles circles me as he takes in my disheveled appearance. "You haven't slept in days, you've clearly been tugging on your hair ... likely out of frustration over something my father said ... but *damn* your ass looks good in leather pants."

"Thank you for finding at least one nice thing to say about me," I joke, swatting his shoulder as finishes his assessment. "I'll consider that my birthday present."

"Oh no, I've got a much better birthday present for you. A piece of scorching hot gossip fresh out of the oven. You'll never guess who—"

"Whatever piece of undoubtedly scandalous information you're about to share with my daughter will need to wait, Lord Miles."

My father, now dressed in his finest suit, steps out of the archway. The emerald velvet jacket is cut perfectly to fit him and I can nearly see my reflection in his overly polished shoes from across the way. He stifles the same cough with a new handkerchief, fresh crimson spots bright against the crisp, white fabric.

"I'm off to rearrange place cards." Miles winks at me before bowing to my father and disappearing down the hall.

Lightning flashes overhead in the sky. The thunderous clap that follows hides the clack of the wooden cane my father uses to close the distance between us. Something he has refused to use before today.

"I don't like leaving you in this condition, Father."

"You worry too much, Ivy. Death comes when he's ready, not when we are, my flower."

"I believe you're right. And I believe our guests are also ready, Governor." I wrap my arm through his, squeezing gently to savor what may very well be one of our last memories together.

I don't tell him that I believe Death is ready for us both, because to tell him that would require the true story about what happened that day in the sea. Divulging the secret of my power is an unnecessary complication that would serve no purpose but to ruin the limited time we have left.

If he suspected that I had magic, he never once mentioned it. I walked that harrowing journey alone, just as I will this one.

CHAPTER 2

The walk down the hallway to the dining room takes twice as long as it should. We both pretend not to notice when the cane snags repeatedly on the plush runner that covers the stone floor.

When a member of the staff brushes past us with an empty tray, my father thrusts the cane into her hands, mumbling swears about wretched walking aids and curses from gods. She has barely departed with his cane when a drunken man decked out in full Corinthian military regalia stumbles into our path.

Lieutenant Williams reeks of whiskey and stale piss. The gold accents on his gray jacket are tarnished, his shoes scuffed and muddy.

"Gov'ner!" Williams calls out much too loudly. "I want to …. to wish … birthday. Happy birthdaaaay … to youuuu."

"It's my birthday, Lieutenant. And you are drunk … *again*." I lift a hand to flag down two approaching guards.

"I'm sssssssorry that it's not me. Orders and … what not," the lieutenant slurs, swaying on his feet.

Gods, how much has he drank?

Williams is notoriously bad at his appointed position, but this is a new low for him. Emerald needs a new military liaison, and if I can somehow convince the governor of Topaz to vote with me, maybe our new king will finally relieve our region of this insult.

"Can you please escort the Lieutenant to his rooms?"

No sooner have the words left my lips does Williams' body involuntarily pitch forward toward me, the guards barely catching him by the arm before he faceplants.

The drunk continues his mumbling as they haul his half-conscious body down the hallway and away from the party.

"I guess this is as good a time as any to tell you." My father turns to face me, placing both hands on my shoulders to steady himself. "You're not going to like this, but … the Lord General has sent a soldier to escort you to Amale and I've agreed to accept his request."

"You're right, I don't like that," I say flatly. "We have plenty of soldiers who are loyal to Emerald. You can't possibly trust one of Marks' men with my safety."

"Normally, no, but this is different. There's more at play here than you know."

"Like what?"

He slowly shakes his head in dismissal, his eyes cutting to the crowd that lingers in the open doorway.

"You can't expect me to leave without all of the information, Father. Failure dooms all of Corinth."

"I can and you will. Some things are better experienced. Trust my judgement, Ivy." He tucks an errant strand of fawny hair behind my ear. A soft smile appears on his face as he slowly trails a knuckle over the dusting of freckles that accent my cheekbones. "Gods, you are so much like her."

I wish I could take the compliment that is so frequently given. I barely remember her beyond her final days—days spent at our cottage by the Eastern Sea, too weak to even lift her head from the

GODSBANE

pillow. I don't feel the light in me that I'm told was so present in her. Only carefully concealed anger and a gnawing, decaying emptiness lives where it should be.

I square my shoulders and stiffen my spine, refusing to let the grief that still lingers in her absence drag me under tonight. I raise my shields and slip on the mask of the polished politician he raised me to be instead.

"I think I'm an awful lot like my father, too."

"More than you know, Ivy."

The Governor pulls me into an embrace before leaving me in the hallway.

With a deep inhale, I step into the dining room and the sea of green that surrounds the banquet table.

Among the Corninthian nobility, clothes are akin to currency, even the color of clothing is a statement. My brown leather pants and olive shirt are starkly out of place amongst the formal gowns and dinner jackets worn by the noble guests.

A bell rings denoting the start of the meal and I spot a smiling Miles holding out a chair for me.

"Why do you look so giddy?" I ask warily as I approach.

"Oh you'll find out ..." he says, scooting my chair up to the table before taking his own, "... in three, two ..."

As the last of the nobles take their seats, the ocean of green clothing parts to reveal a single hulking figure clothed in blackest night. Leather pauldrons, wholly unnecessary for a court dinner, bracket the man's muscular chest, making him appear even more menacing than the stories of his battles. My breath hitches, a tingle racing down my spine at the sight of the fabled warrior amongst us.

"One," Miles whispers.

The Captain of Corinth, commander of Lord General Marks' troops and the only person in our nation with a larger reputation than me, sits at the far end of the table. Marks didn't send just any soldier—he sent *the* soldier. A man rumored to have wiped out an entire legion of Synalian soldiers single-handedly.

As his gaze moves to me, a defiant smile turns up the corner of my lips. The deadliest soldier in all of Corinth must have really pissed off his commander if he's been sent to escort Poison Ivy to the capital.

"Oooh, I love it when you get that look in your eyes," Miles says as the first course is deposited in front of us. "I've asked around and all my sources agree that you will either find Captain Murphy incredibly irritating or completely irresistible."

Conversation strikes up around me and fades into an indistinguishable hum. Try as I might, I can't fight the strange pulling sensation in my chest. The invisible rope wrapped around my sternum demands my attention be wholly focused on the deadly creature in our midst.

"Lady Ivy, did you hear me?" Lady Adler's voice breaks the spell on me. "I was just saying to Lord Miles what a shame it is that you won't be able to attend the wedding. Lady Quinn will be a stunning bride. Can you imagine how beautiful my future grandson will be?"

"A truly breathtaking sight, I'm certain." The words taste bitter in my mouth as I force them through a fake smile. Miles' fingers grip the top of my knee under the table in silent support.

My eyes drift down the table to my best friend. Bubbly and bright, Quinn is a comical contrast to the Captain of Corinth who is strategically seated beside her. Things have been strained between us since her betrothal and I don't have nearly enough time to make it right.

"Lady Adler, is it true that Nick will take over the daily management of the forge after the wedding?" Miles expertly directs the conversation. "I have been meaning to visit him and commission a new sword ... one that's very sharp."

The rapping of a spoon on crystal halts the prattling as every eye turns to my father. Governor Fellows rises slowly from his seat, his voice booming in the quieted hall as he speaks.

"Esteemed nobles of the Emerald Region. Tonight is bitter-sweet. Not only do we toast the memory of a king, but also the continued longevity of our heir and the promise of a better Corinth." He raises his wine-filled goblet, his soft brown eyes finding mine in the crowd. "To our future."

"Here here." A mumbled chorus echoes from the nobles. Pursed lips and soft sighs accompany the toast they half-heartedly make. The beast of their disapproval never takes a day off, not even on my birthday.

Their chatter resumes as the staff begins to serve the second course. The King's death is the topic of the evening. I listen as my father boldly promises the one thing he has no power to control: that he won't be following our former monarch's steps anytime soon.

As if any of us have a say in the timing of our own end.

Through each course, my attention drifts to the dark presence at the end of the table. The ridiculous armor he wears to dinner, the slight dishevel to his hair, the uncomfortable way he shifts in his seat when Quinn bumps his arm with her overly-exaggerated hand motions.

I chase carrots around on my plate, prod potatoes with my fork —anything to keep my eyes off the source of the strange pull in my gut.

"You're avoiding making eye contact with our guest, Ivy," Miles says, dipping his head low so only I can hear him. "It's a long way to Amale. You could have a little *fun*."

"I have fun."

The blatant lie falls flat. Only on rare occasions have I ever allowed myself to let loose, too afraid of the secrets that I might spill or the certain rejection that would cut deeper than any blade.

"Feast Week doesn't count. Everyone who's not a priest has fun then. I mean *real* fun... without a mask on."

"What's the rule about Feast Week?" I narrow my eyes at him in warning. What happens during the debaucherous celebration is never spoken about aloud, a rule that Miles himself instated.

He waves his hand in dismissal as if the entire fate of a nation doesn't rest on the success of this mission.

"Just enjoy the adventure! He could be a good ally to have on your side."

Miles' call to revelry falls on deaf ears. This is a political mission in which every move must be carefully calculated. But perhaps the Lord General's highest ranking soldier could be a valuable weapon to have. The electric power within me forces me to steal one last glance at the ominous man.

"You're considering it, aren't you?" Miles chuckles as the staff synchronously clears the now empty plates from the long table.

"About as much as you're considering settling down with that redhead I saw you with last night," I quip.

"*Ivy*," Miles says through clenched teeth. "Unless you want a duel over dessert, you should probably change the subject."

"Oh, Lady Powell," I call out, wiggling my fingers to get the attention of the woman sitting across from us. "I love your necklace. Is it new?"

Lady Powell's gloved hand touches the thick pearl choker that barely covers the purple marks at the base of her neck before pulling her auburn hair over her exposed shoulder. "It is, Lady Ivy. Thank you for noticing. My darling husband brought it back from his travels."

Miles stomps his foot on top of mine and I bite down the urge to grimace. The tinkling of a bell sounds again signaling the end of dinner. Chairs scrape across the stone floor as the nobles stand to make their way into the various sitting rooms that occupy the first floor of the manor. Staff members carry trays of port, brandy, and frosted strawberry cake through the meandering crowd.

"I will get you back for that, Ivy," Miles calls out playfully as I slip past him and into the swirl of departing ladies in green gowns.

A flash of golden hair against seafoam green catches my eye and I rush after my best friend. "Quinn!" I call out over the crowd.

Quinn turns, her honey eyes finding me as I sidestep past her father and future in-laws. Lords Bartlett and Adler pay me no attention, their focus fully trained on the black-clad man lingering at her elbow. A strange ache stabs at my chest and I grab a glass of port from a passing tray to calm my racing heart.

"There you are!" Quinn says sweetly as I deposit the empty glass on the table. "Ivy, do you know—"

"Everyone knows the Captain of Corinth."

The tan hand extended to me retracts to his side at my interruption. My gaze trails up the broad expanse of black leather until it locks onto the storm gray eyes of the deadliest man in Corinth.

"The same way they all know Poison Ivy."

The captain's voice is thick and heady, every word laced with the promise of danger. We stand there in pointed silence, each sizing the other up. The first moves in a deadly game that I must win. He may bring armies to heel, but he has no power over me.

Quinn clears her throat. "I'm going to grab us some cake. Don't … run away, I guess?"

Captain Murphy takes a step closer, looming over me in our continued stare down. Squaring my shoulders, I let my power rise to the surface of my skin. I wouldn't dare use it here, but just knowing that it's ready and willing steels my resolve.

His eyes flit close momentarily, reopening to reveal something more akin to pools of molten silver. "Are you planning to run away?"

"I don't run away. Not from anyone or anything."

The captain dips his head, black hair falling over his brow as the heat of his breath warms my ear. His low, whispered words brush against my skin like silk. "Your reputation precedes you."

Time seems to slow at his words, the sounds of the crowd around us fading as thunder booms outside the large floor-to-ceiling windows. His figure is haloed in a flash of white lightning as he steps back.

"Any enemies besides the Lord General that I need to be aware of before we leave, poison?"

"Anyone who calls me poison is my enemy. Does that clear things up, Captain?"

Captain Murphy nods, a sly smirk on his face and a twinkle in his eye as he says, "See you at dawn, my lady," before disappearing like a phantom into the crowd.

"Thank you, Lady Adler," I say, taking the plate of strawberry cake from Quinn's waiting hand when she finally reappears. "Took you long enough."

"Ivy, don't. I'm not fighting with you on your birthday."

"It's not a fight," I correct. "You took a long time … and you insist on following the archaic tradition of betrothal that absolves you of your agency."

Quinn snatches the plate from my hand and deposits it on the tray of a passing servant. Heat colors her fair cheeks as she grabs my hand and half drags me from the dining room and into an alcove off the main hall.

"Is it too much to ask for my best friend to support my choice?" She finally asks when we're away from prying ears.

"Is it too much to hope my best friend would marry for love instead of some family alliance?" I counter.

Quinn's anger dissolves in an exasperated sigh, a sad smile forming in its place. "I know your anger comes from a good place, but you have to understand. I am trying to love Nick."

"Even with that monstrosity on his face?" Quinn lets out a half laugh at my attempt at a joke. There's an unmistakable sadness in her eyes that stabs like a knife into my aching heart.

"Quinn," I start, "you don't *try* to love people. You either love them or you don't."

Her fingers move to her golden hair, twisting and twirling the strands as she avoids my gaze. "I don't think love is that simple. I think … if you really want something … well, I think it grows."

"Hopefully it grows better than his attempt at a mustache," I joke again, a single tear leaking from my eye to mirror hers. "Listen, maybe you're right. What do I know? I can count the people I love on one hand."

"I count myself lucky to be on that hand." Quinn cups my cheeks as she continues. "And I won't let you leave thinking I don't. What happened … it's in the past. We have futures to look forward to."

We stay like that, basking in the moment as the disagreement that settled between us this past week dissolves. I don't tell her of my fears of never returning or the strange feeling that eats at my seams with each passing moment. We simply relish in the present until it stretches thin, popping like a bubble and forcing us into what lies ahead.

"There you are!" Miles calls out as he rounds the corner, three glasses of amber liquid in his hands. "Who wants to get into a little trouble on Ivy's last night in Emerald?"

"Haven't you found enough trouble," I tease. "Actually, I think I saw Lady Powell alone ..."

"Perhaps I should go get Captain Murphy," Miles quips back. "I don't know what you said to him, but he looked as if he wanted to devour you. And I did promise to pay you back, after all."

"Miles," Quinn chimes in, taking a glass from his hand, "I think we'll need an entire bottle of whiskey for that. You know Ivy prefers her men in a mask."

"That's enough, both of you."

"Did you *see* those muscles, though? Absolutely terrifying … and delicious," Quinn adds.

"If you two are finished, I have actual things to do before dawn. Things that do not in any way involve the Captain of Corinth."

I pull them both into a hug that lingers past our normal good-byes. I have no idea if I'll ever see either of them again and I'm not ready to let go just yet. "Promise you'll take care of this place while I'm gone."

"Don't worry about us," Quinn says as Miles adds, "Give them hell, Ivy."

I smile, planting a loving kiss on each of their cheeks before stepping back. "I wouldn't dare give them less."

And I won't.

CHAPTER 3

My footsteps echo in the empty hallways of the governor's manor. The leather strap of the traveling bag catches on the broad sword sheathed at my back, both thumping against me as I march towards the courtyard and the captain waiting for me.

It's always quiet in the hours before sunrise, but even more so today. Bundled in cloaks of green to fight the chill of the late winter air, every other noble in the Emerald Region has traded in their comfy beds for the plush pews of the Grand Temple.

Sunrise on the twelfth day—the only time the Golden Pantheon deems their worshippers worthy enough of their attention—is a required day of petitioning. But I have no time for prayers that consistently go unanswered or gods who turned their backs on me years ago.

The bell tolls announcing the six o'clock hour and the start of their sacred service. With each ring, dread washes over me in a wave, causing my steps to slow. Somehow I know, deep in the recesses of my soul, that the woman who returns won't be the same one who leaves today.

If I return at all.

The Captain of Corinth stands across the deserted courtyard beside two saddled mares, his focus on the temple that looms outside the manor walls. I move slowly, assessing him before he notices my presence.

Sunlight peeks through the clouds, the first light of day ringing his head in a regal, god-like glow. He tightens the straps of the leather pauldrons that span his broad shoulders. There's a slight tremble to his hands as they skate down his sides, visible even from here. His lips move in a soundless, murmured prayer as he turns to face me. Magic tingles under the surface of my skin, the weight of his gaze heightening the power within me.

"Morning, Captain." I hold my head high as I step out from the overhang and make my way towards my horse. "No desire to go to temple before we leave?"

"I have little love for those gods," he answers matter-of-factly. "From what I hear, neither do you."

"I have little love for those who take away the choices of others. It makes no difference to me if they're kings or gods."

"I know you didn't choose to follow me..." he starts.

"Follow?" I scoff. "I think you have the wrong impression of this dynamic, Captain. I don't follow you."

"Maybe not yet, my lady, but it's a long road to Amale." The corner of his lip hitches up in a smirk.

"We'll see who follows whom, Captain."

I pluck a dagger from the saddle bag and casually flip it before sliding it into the sheath strapped to my thigh. I've dealt with plenty of men like him before, and it's best to show yourself as a formidable opponent early on, asserting dominance like you would with any dog.

I pull myself up with the saddle pommel, swinging one leg over and mounting the caramel-colored mare "Oh, and drop the '*my lady*' bullshit. As you pointed out, it's a long road to Amale so let's not pretend that you've been ordered to respect me by a Lord General who certainly doesn't."

His eyes narrow at my directness, a quality that the other rulers of Corinth don't possess. But political niceties matter little when everyone already hates you and I much prefer to see the shock on their faces than waste time with fake pleasantries.

"What would you have me call you?"

"You'll figure something out, I'm sure of it," I shrug.

Bitch. Poison. Cunt.

I'm not going to recite the ever growing list of names that people find synonymous with mine. He seems more than capable of picking one on his own.

"You seem to have a fondness for sharp things."

He points to the broadsword strapped to my back before lifting a knuckle and quickly rapping the side of my boot. Steel knocks against the round knot of my ankle and I have to swallow the reflexive bite of pain. Amusement gleams in his storm-gray eyes. "Are you trying to send a message?"

"Never underestimate the power an appearance holds, Captain." I smooth my sweaty palms down my leather corset, the faux boning within concealing thin blades. An appearance is something I know how to wield even better than a blade.

Captain Murphy nods once, slowly and deliberately, before turning to mount his own horse. My magic sparks again, ever so slightly, urging me to watch him intently. Urging me to pay attention to his appearance. Not just the outward, overly handsome soldier, but the barely perceptible sliver of who lies beneath. The person I have to uncover if I'm going to figure out how best to use him.

I spur my horse towards the iron gates, taking one last look around at the stone manor and its ivy-covered towers now fully illuminated by the shining orange hues of the morning sun. A cool breeze whips through my hair as it sweeps past, its path the same as mine: away from home.

The holy day means no foot traffic in and out of the capital city of the Emerald Region. We pass no merchants pulling wagons of goods or traveling bards to entertain us as we trudge through the dirt road that cuts through the Godswood.

The absence of any noise besides the sound of our horses' hooves quickly becomes the soundtrack of our travels. Trees, trees, and more trees blur into a mass of greens and browns as we pass. My eyelids droop, heavy from the hours of sleep stolen by restless nightmares. The steady, rhythmic swaying of the horse lulls me closer towards unconsciousness with every step.

Captain Murphy's gray mare stops suddenly, snapping me to attention. He lifts a single hand in command, the forest seeming to still around us. A low, foreboding growl echoes through the trees, the noise causing the horses to take a cautious step back, anxious to run but held in place only by each of our firm grips on their reins.

Another bated second passes before the source of the noise makes itself known. A large brown bear, nearly the size of my mare, prowls from between the trees, stopping and rising to stand on its hind legs in the middle of the dirt road. The animal's beady black eyes are trained on us in warning. The air is charged, thick with anticipation of what comes next.

Instinctively, I raise my hand to rest on the hilt of the broadsword sheathed across my back. I have no logical reason to kill the bear. The Godswood is its home, after all, and I am the trespasser.

But something deep and primal within me wants to eliminate it. The dark side of my earth magic calling for the balance that I always deny it. I grant it life but never death, growth but never decay.

"I'm sure you know how to use those blades, but I doubt you can take down a fully grown bear." Captain Murphy's voice is stern but low so as to not disturb the animal before us.

I don't take my eyes off the bear, choosing to stare straight into its black irises. There's a war raging within me, a quiet battle between my head and my power. He's right—I can't take it down with my blade alone.

My mind races with a thousand solutions, all impossible without using at least a small part of my magic. If I'm going to tempt the bear to leave us alone without any bloodshed, I have to distract the captain.

"You're right," I concede, dropping my hand slowly from my blade. "You're the highly-trained swordsman, not me. Do your soldier thing and run it off."

"My *soldier* thing?" he scoffs. "You're a princess. Can't you talk to it or something?"

"I'm not a princess, and, in case you haven't noticed, this isn't some child's fairytale story."

"I disagree," he says. "You're an heir who sleeps in a godsdamn tower. That's definitely princess shit."

"While I'm touched that you've been thinking about where I sleep, you should probably focus more on the bear."

Playing right into my hand, two brown heads peer around the corner of a tree.

"To your left, Captain. Just past the second birch tree. Are those cubs?" I whisper.

Captain Murphy turns his gaze away from the bear and scans

the tree line. I seize the only second I might have and let my magic escape with a gentle flick of my wrist towards the thicket on our right. Red winter berries spring to life in the bushes several yards off the path.

The bear watches me intently, following the motion of my hand before giving a loud snort at the sight of fresh food. The sound draws the captain's full attention back to the road and my only chance to use my magic without detection is now gone.

It'll have to be enough.

"Go on now. Eat," I urge softly.

Two balls of brown fur prance out from behind their hiding places and head straight towards the bushes, the mother bear following closely behind. When the animals disappear into the thicket, I finally exhale a small, shaky sigh of relief.

Captain Murphy shakes his head, murmuring as he urges his mare in slow, steady steps. "Fucking princess."

CHAPTER 4

The common area of the inn is abuzz with patrons finished with their day of praying and eager to make offerings to Bastin, the god of revelry who delights in drink and pleasure. A fire roars in the corner hearth, enveloping me immediately in a sweet, welcomed warmth as I cross the threshold. I ache to shed my thick wool cloak but I don't dare remove it.

Hidden underneath the hood's emerald fabric, I am faceless—and I need to remain that way for as long as I can. Soon, word will spread that I'm traveling with the infamous captain rather than with the expected carriage and full entourage, but until then, I can simply be another unknown Emerald noble. The less I'm recognized, the better.

I make my way across the crowded room, carefully zigzagging between the tables to avoid swinging mugs of ale, when a hand reaches out to grab my wrist.

"You."

My head snaps to find the owner of the hand, a man dressed in the cavalry uniform of Corinth, gray fabric trimmed in deep golden cords. I try to yank my hand from the asshole but his grasp only tightens. He leans in, pulling me closer towards his body, hatred etched into every line of his face.

Captain Murphy steps into view over the man's head, the sight of the black-clad warrior causing everyone around him to pause.

"I wouldn't do that if I were you."

Instead of cowering, a defiant smirk blooms on the soldier's face. He rises slowly, readying himself for a fight he won't win. Before he can swing, he turns his head to see the face of his competition. The realization of who stands behind him cuts through his anger-filled haze and hits harder than any punch.

"Captain!" The man drops his hold on me and steps back, palms skyward in submission. "My apologies, Captain Murphy," he stumbles.

"Don't apologize to me." Murphy grabs the man by his collar and forces his face towards me. "Apologize to her."

The soldier glares at me again, eyes even harder than before.

Shit.

He's about to make sure everyone in this place knows who I am.

"I'm not apologizing to that poisonous bitch," he spits.

"Soldier."

A single barked word sends the entire tavern into silence, even the fiddler stopping mid-song. Murphy's hold on the man's collar tightens, his toes just barely brushing the floor under the captain's grasp. The man's face, already reddened from drink, begins to turn a shocking shade of purple.

"Apologize to her or I'll stand by while she runs that sword through your heart," the captain commands in a near growl, his eyes flashing black before returning to gray.

A drop of blood leaks from the corner of the man's mouth as he struggles to breathe. Seconds tick by like hours as the realization of who stands in their midst settles amongst the patrons.

"Sssss…sor…sorry," he finally squeaks out.

Captain Murphy drops the soldier to the floor and callously steps over the heap. The soldier gasps for air, a dark spot creeping across the front of his gray breeches as he writhes on the floor.

"Carry on," Murphy's voice booms to the crowd, motioning towards me with a sweeping hand. "Your heir commands it."

If they didn't know for certain who I was before, they do now. I lower my cloak hood and lift my chin as a familiar scene unfolds.

Men throughout the common room openly scoff into their cups. Women turn their faces as if a single look in my direction will blind them. No one bothers to bow, salute, or clap. Not for the poisonous heir who is destined to ruin their beloved region with her hatred for their gods.

Whispers turn into chatter, filling the tavern again, though I'm positive the topics are different than when we walked in. With Poison Ivy and the Captain of Corinth present, there are better things to gossip about now.

"Both gods-cursed if you ask me," one scoffs.

"Nobus save us," another prays.

"Why did you do that?" I chide as I follow in Murphy's footsteps towards a small table in the back of the room. "I could have handled that myself."

He hails a serving girl with the lift of a single finger and three of them nearly fall over themselves in their haste to serve him.

"My soldiers, my responsibility." The rickety wooden chair groans as he sits.

"At least they respect *you*."

"They fear me," he corrects.

"What's the difference?" I ask, the trio of serving girls arriving before he can respond.

Each carries a single item so that they can justify their presence. One flagon of wine. Two cups. Three giggles.

Captain Murphy never acknowledges them, pouring wine for

both of us as he speaks. "There is a big difference. People do not fear you, they fear what you represent … a world that looks nothing like the one we live in. These men, they fear me and what I'm capable of."

"What are you capable of, Captain?"

He lifts the glass to his lips, gulping down the red liquid as I brace myself for the bragging that's sure to follow. Bragging about the legion that supposedly fell to his blade, his renowned battle strategy, his female conquests, or maybe some sick combination of all them. The typical stuff cocksure men choose to flaunt.

"I'm capable of shouldering the burden of being their villain until a better one comes along," he says, wiping the wine from the corner of his mouth with his thumb. "They need someone to hate, so I let them hate me."

It's not the response I expected, but his non-answer provides a sliver of hope. A chink in his armor that I can exploit.

"And if you had a chance to change their opinion of you … would you take it?"

"Would you?" he counters.

"Not if it requires bowing to someone who doesn't deserve it," I reply.

There's a gleam in his gray eyes, a spark of something that wasn't there before. Captain Murphy reaches under the leather armor and into his shirt pocket, dropping a folded piece of blank parchment on the table.

"Then make sure they deserve it, princess."

The messenger owl leaves just before sunrise, my missive gripped tightly in its claws. With the Ascension Vote three weeks away, there's still a chance my letter can get to the Topaz heir before his father departs for Amale. Though his father cares little for the woman I became, Silas Wilson still has a soft spot for the girl he used to play games with at the annual governors summits. We might appear to be rivals publicly, but ever since his mother's passing two years ago, Silas has drifted further and further from his father's oppressive rule.

Maybe he will be willing to convince his father to at least hear me out—especially since my letter claimed that I have Captain Murphy as my formidable ally.

A claim I now need to solidify.

Turning the Lord General's commander against him will prove to both the Topaz and Sapphire governors how serious I am about keeping Marks off the Amethyst Throne, but in order to do that I need to be less poison and more ... *Ivy*.

Whatever the hell that looks like.

A decadent smell wafts from the kitchen as I wait in the common room for Captain Murphy. A petite, older woman emerges a few moments later with a pan of fresh pastries, their golden brown tops and bright red filling calling me toward one last indulgence before the journey ahead.

"I'll take a half-dozen, please," I say, placing a few coins on the counter. Her eyes lift from her creations and I know she recognizes me. "I'm sorry for the disturbance last night."

"No matter. There's always a fight on the holy day. Bastin prefers his offerings that way," the woman replies as she loads up a paper bag with the crumbly tarts.

Heavy footfalls pound down the wooden stairs and a smile blooms across her thin lips as the captain strides across the room. She leans across the counter, her eyes scanning me up and down as she muses, "The best way to a man's heart is through his stomach, you know."

"Actually it's between the fourth and fifth rib." Captain Murphy, voice gruff from sleep, takes a pastry from the innkeeper's outstretched tongs. "Thank you, Suzette," he winks, vanishing out the door nearly as fast as he appeared.

"He's a charmer, that one," she giggles.

"Him?" I ask in disbelief. "Do you know who that is?"

"Oh yes," she replies, placing a bag of pastries in my hand. "The captain has been stopping here for years and he's always just the sweetest young man."

The old woman turns and disappears behind the swinging kitchen doors leaving me standing with my mouth agape. The Captain of Corinth is a *sweet, young man,* who apparently has a soft spot for kind old ladies.

Maybe I can use that.

Captain Murphy waits outside the inn, mares already saddled and ready to depart. He holds their reins in one hand and a half-eaten pastry in the other.

"Between the fourth and fifth rib, huh?" I ask as I approach.

"It's the most efficient way," he says, handing the reins of my mare over to me. "But I think you already knew that."

"Oh these blades are just for show. Princess, remember?" I joke, lifting myself up into the saddle and settling in.

A chuckle escapes from his lips. "You're funnier than they make you out to be."

"Laughing in the face of the gods requires a substantial sense of humor, Captain. Jokes are all you have when there's likely to be no afterlife in the Eternal Meadows for you."

A slow, knowing smile spreads across his face as he swings a muscular leg over his mare. "And here you thought we'd have nothing in common."

"Ah, but the real question is: do you also want to stop Marks from taking the Amethyst Throne?" I ask, biting down the nerves that skate under my skin. If I've misjudged, this could all blow up in my face.

Sunlight fills the streets as merchants and tradespeople begin their morning routines. Murphy circles his mare, turning around to come up beside me and leaning down so only I can hear his hushed words.

"Let me make my position very clear. He may be my commander, but I want Lord General Marks on the throne even less than you do. If you think you hate the gods now, well … let's just say that hatred would only deepen with him as your king."

There's an ire in his gray eyes when he pulls back, a fury that burns for only a moment before he blinks it away. He spins his horse and spurs it ahead on the dirt road that leads back into the Godswood.

I can't imagine what the holy war was like—what the captain must have experienced leading our armies against an invasion entirely of our own making. Something like that could certainly cause someone to lose their faith in their gods and their commander.

I urge my horse ahead until she catches up with his. Only once we're safely under the cover of trees and away from prying ears do I say, "Marks is not the kind of man who would stop at king. He wants worshippers, not subjects."

"You have no idea, princess," Captain Murphy says, extending his hand.

"Enlighten me then," I say, passing another tart his way and plucking out one for myself.

Surely as second-in-command he's been privy to something that can help me convince the other governors to vote with me. I'll take any information that can guarantee Marks never sits his horrid ass on the Amethyst Throne.

"In time. Why don't you tell me who you're planning to put on the throne first?"

"Why don't you tell me why I should trust you?" I counter.

"Marks hurt someone I love, and if he becomes king, he'll continue to hurt them. He must be stopped and we're going to have to work together to do it."

One look at Murphy's face and I know he's telling the truth. The anger that flashed in him earlier is replaced with a sadness that etches deep into the creases around his eyes.

"How's that for a confession?"

"I'll take it. But if you fuck me over, Captain," I warn, "I will have to take you down too. And you don't want to be my enemy."

"Noted," he chuckles. "So ... who are we putting on the throne?"

"Sapphire is my first choice. Governor Porter openly rebuked the crusade on Synal and the war that followed, which Marks repaid by ensuring that it was his shores that were invaded instead of Diamond's. His heir is also strong. Micah could rebuild the region and their capital city of Pathan while his father fixed Corinth."

"Smart." Murphy's brow creases in thought, a smirk forming on his face echoing the idea forming in his mind. "Why not you?" he asks.

"I'm not an option. My father is still alive ... for now." Images of his bloody handkerchief and bone-rattling cough fill my mind. The ache in my heart must be evident on my face, because Murphy wastes no time changing the subject.

"Sapphire is a good choice. I'll do what I can to help you win Topaz's vote. Governor Wilson is a dick, but he can be reasoned with or ..."

"...bought," I say.

"...killed," he says.

The difference in our answers is stark, but it lays bare the unspoken question. I know now how far Captain Murphy will go to keep Marks off the throne, but how far I'll go remains to be seen.

"Why do you hate the gods?" I ask, placing another tart in his waiting hand. "Rumor says you worship the Dark God. Do you have any love for Death?"

"Do you?" He returns my question with a pointed glare. "If we're believing rumors, you're his creature too."

I don't tell him how much truth actually lies in the heart of that piece of gossip. While the story was intended to slander me, I am his creature in a way. I have been ever since the sea beast touched me and cursed me that day. The dreams of my demise left behind in its wake have only increased as my secret magic has grown. Images of blood, burning crowns, and running after someone I can never remember—a name I know in my soul that disappears from my memory as soon as consciousness returns.

"Eat your tart," I snark, trying not to notice the infuriating smile that pulls at his mouth. "I would have bought more if I had known the terrifying Captain of Corinth was planning to eat so many."

Captain Murphy eats half of the pastry in a single bite. He wipes the filling from the corner of lip with his thumb before cleaning it off with his tongue.

"Should have planned better," he tsks. "That guy's a real pig."

"Wow, we really do have so much in common. I feel the same way about him!" I fake a smile, batting my eyelashes exaggeratingly for added effect.

Murphy grimaces. "That is a truly disarming facial expression. Try not to hurt yourself."

"Okay, asshole," I start, righteous indignation flaring to life. Men telling you to smile is bad enough, but being told *not* to smile might be even worse.

Something soft hits my cheek. I raise my hand to touch the spot and my fingers pull back red and *sticky*. Is that …. *holy shit*. That's raspberry pastry filling.

"Did you just throw a tart at me?" I ask in disbelief. Surely I'm imagining this.

"You were being a tart," he teases.

My chin is practically dragging the ground in shock. I've had a lot of things thrown at me in crowds before, but I've never had a grown man throw a pastry at me in jest on horseback.

"I don't know what kind of backwoods hovel you were raised in, but those of us in the civilized world don't throw food."

"I may not have grown up in a tower, princess, but my home was plenty civilized."

"And where exactly did the Captain of Corinth grow up?"

"*He* grew up on a battlefield. The man he was before was raised in the Diamond Region."

The man behind the murderous reputation has barely crossed my mind before, but he's suddenly all I can think about. I know who I was before Marks made me, but who was he? And can I use that to ensure he can't revoke our alliance?

"Does that man have a first name?"

"He does." Captain Murphy's eyes meet mine in contemplation and my magic tingles oddly. A smile blooms across his lips, maddeningly white teeth flashing briefly. "Maybe one day I'll tell you what it is."

Without another word, the captain spurs his horse into a gallop and disappears over the cresting horizon.

CHAPTER 5

As the sun dips low in the evening sky, Captain Murphy steers us off the road in search of water, a task he accomplishes with an unnatural ease.

I make a mental note to watch his tracking habits more carefully in hopes that I might learn something valuable. Surely being able to find water quickly is a skill that will prove useful at some point.

While the captain pitches the canvas tent, I set out to find a secluded place to expend my magic away from his watchful eyes. It tickles relentlessly, like an unreachable itch that can only be scratched by growing life.

Despite the late hour, what remains of the sun is warm. It's the first day that has truly felt like this winter might be coming to an end. I shed my cloak and wool sweater, letting the rays dance across my shoulders, now exposed in the thin cotton tank I wear underneath.

This area, ringed with evergreen trees and holly bushes, provides the best chance at privacy. I drop to my knees on the ground, eager not to pray to the gods who demand penance from

41

this position but to connect with the life force that runs under our feet.

Eyes closed, I breathe in deeply, feeling the warming sensation of my magic just under the surface. I call to it on the inhale and let it trickle into my waiting palms. Pushing all the air from my lungs, my earth magic flows from my fingers in delicate green rivulets, gently waking the dead grass that lingers under the pine straw floor of the forest from its seasonal slumber.

I search the clearing again to make sure the captain isn't lurking between the trees, and satisfied with what I find, I tilt my face towards the sunlight streaming through the canopy of leaves overhead. With my palms planted firmly on the ground, I close my eyes and imagine my fingertips extending deep into the dirt and becoming roots and vines searching for water.

In my mind's eye, my body becomes the trunk of a tree, sturdy and strong, weathered and steadfast. My brown hair blows in the warm breeze like autumn leaves clinging to thin branches before they fall to the earth.

I am rooted.

I am grounded.

I am the earth.

Concentrated clusters of magic form dormant bulbs under the barren ground as power seeps through my fingertips and into the soil. In a few weeks, when the last dregs of winter disappear, snow white crocus and deep-purple godsbane will bloom in this spot. In this moment, under the sun's rays and connected wholly to the land, I am at peace.

"What are you doing?" Captain Murphy's booming voice startles me back to reality.

I jump to my feet, quickly trying to swallow down the panic that clenches my chest. "Meditating."

"Meditating," he repeats skeptically. "If you're not careful, someone might mistake that for worshipping."

He stalks towards me in long strides until he's close enough that I can feel his breath. The woods seem to go quiet around us— the only noise the pounding of my heart and the rushing of blood between my ears.

"There's no god I would ever get on my knees for," I defiantly declare.

Gray eyes scrutinize me, boring into me as if he already knows my darkest truth and he's waiting for me to reveal it. I force myself to breathe around the darkness that threatens to overtake my vision. I've come close to being discovered before—much closer than this—but no one has ever peered into my soul the way this man is right now.

"Meditating…" he repeats. The last syllable lingers lazily in his mouth, eyes still intently focused on my every move. "Why?"

We may be allies, but we are not confidants. Some secrets, especially ones as damning as mine, are better left unsaid. The magic in my veins, the power that aches to be released into the world, the way I feel when I make the earth bend to my will— those are truths that I've always believed will only be exposed when Death takes me at last.

But the way he's looking at me right now makes me want to offer an infinitesimal piece of a confession, to unburden myself of the tiniest fraction of the insurmountable weight that gets heavier with each passing year.

"It calms my mind," I concede, "centers me … like I'm connected to something larger than myself."

The corners of Captain Murphy's lips turn up in an unexpected smile. "I feel the same way about swimming."

His feet carry him backward, his eyes locked on me until he's several steps away. Turning and walking towards the nearby trees, the captain calls out over his shoulder, "Find us some firewood, princess."

A heavy sigh leaves my body. That was entirely too close for comfort, and yet a part of me grieves the loss of that sliver of safety, the brief moment that was entirely too good to be true. No such safety has existed for me since that fateful day in the Eastern Sea—the day I was swallowed whole by the water and ended up on a beach, lungs filled with sea water and blood filled with magic.

The black serpentine beast flits through my mind at the thought.

"I'll get firewood when I'm ready," I mumble, as I make my way back to our campsite.

My caramel-colored mare wanders over and I begin the process of unsaddling her for the evening. Minutes pass without a quick-witted quip from Murphy for my blatant disregard of his command. My head swivels to locate him, eyes scanning the trees until they reach the waterline.

There, on the bank of the small pond, Captain Murphy stands with his boots, armor, and shirt casually discarded at his feet. My eyes roam up slowly, taking in his low-slung black leather pants, the large hands planted firmly on his hip bones, the expanse of scarred tanned skin that covers his back, and thick rippling muscles that carve out his broad shoulders.

Holy gods.

As if on cue, my horse snorts, drawing my attention away from the half-dressed man in front of me.

"You're right, girl," I whisper, "it's not polite to stare."

But as I unbuckle her saddle, I can't stop myself from peering over her back for another glance. Murphy is wading into the pond now, eyes closed and face turned towards the sky.

My gaze lingers, watching his aqueous movements. It's as if he *flows* in the water, as if he is composed entirely of droplets that morph into ripples surrounding him as he submerges.

Another second passes before his head breaks the surface again, rivulets of water streaming from his onyx hair as he ascends. His shoulders rise and fall with each breath of the now chilly air. He turns towards me and it's there, across his honeyed skin, that I find my doom.

Tattooed in raven ink across his sculpted chest is the perfectly replicated image of the primordial sea beast. The leviathan of my nightmares twines through cresting waves of ink, its mouth open as if it's poised to strike the captain's neck with one wrong move.

"If you're going to stare, you might as well join me."

His gruff voice forces my eyes away from his body, snapping to a pair made of molten silver before I turn and run.

CHAPTER 6

My feet pound against the hard ground, but my racing heart moves faster, causing me to stumble over fallen branches and overgrown thorny bushes. My knees hit the earth in a thud that rattles through my bones. The force of the fall and the weight of my circumstances crash into me at once.

There is nowhere to go, nowhere to run.

"It's just a coincidence," I lie to myself over and over as I try to catch my breath.

Maybe if I say it ten times, a hundred times, it will be true. But coincidence is just the gods' way of remaining anonymous. Their handprints cover everything.

I've scoured text after text, questioned priest after priest. There are no stories of the sea beast, no fables or tales written or spoken of the creature that haunts my sleeping hours. No sketches or drawings that depict the menacing jaws or razor-sharp scales that are so perfectly hewn onto the captain's chest.

No, if Murphy knows about the sea serpent, it's because he's seen it too. And if he knows about that, what other knowledge does he have? As if on command, my magic streaks a burning path down my spine, the very place the beast touched me all those years ago.

What have I done to be so egregiously cursed? It's not enough for the gods to simply force this magic upon me. No, they have to send me omens. Dark signs of certain death that are incredibly clear now in the light of this revelation.

In light of my connection to *him*.

Crazed, half-maniacal laughter echoes through the trees and it takes me several seconds to realize that it's coming from me. My magic knew he was important before my mind could piece together the puzzle that seems idiotically obvious.

I see it all clearly now, the images from my nightmares replaying in a loop.

Water dripping from tendrils of onyx hair.

The Amethyst Throne burning.

A loud hoot startles me and I turn to find a large horned owl, the symbol of the King of the Gods himself, resting on a tree branch directly overhead.

"So it's decided then?" I yell at the bird. "I'm just supposed to follow him to my death? Is that all I was made for?" My voice trails off as hot tears break loose from my eyes. "Did I ever have a choice?"

I openly weep into the forest floor, mourning the loss of a future I had only dared to dream of.

There is no question in my mind that the Dark God of Death waits for me in Amale. And the Captain of Corinth, a man whose shadow is rumored to be a reflection of the soul reaper himself, is his harbinger.

"Fine. Have it your way," I boldly declare to the sigil of Nobus, wiping the tears from my cheeks, "but if I'm going to die, I'm going to take them all down with me."

Captain Murphy looks up from the small fire he's built in our makeshift camp. My eyes have to be red and puffy, but if he notices he doesn't mention it. I have no doubt that he probably heard my wailing, but he doesn't draw attention to my moment of weakness.

We wordlessly stare at each other across the fire until the loud hoot of an owl breaks the tension. It's only then that I notice that Murphy still hasn't found all of his clothes.

"Did something happen to your shirt, Captain?" I ask, unceremoniously dropping the few measly twigs I collected so that I didn't return empty-handed.

"I didn't want it to snag on the firewood I had to collect or to get wet while I caught dinner." He motions to a large bass lying dead on the log beside him.

"If you think you're going to sit there while I cook it for you," I start.

"I don't," he interrupts. "I know how to cook, but you're going to help me."

"Help you?"

"Yes, princess. Help me." Placing two large hands on his knees, the captain stands and starts towards me. "I saw you earlier. The problem is, I can't tell if you were staring because you wanted to put a knife through me or if you wanted to—"

"Yes," I quickly interject before he gets the wrong idea. "Fond of sharp things, remember?" I tap the dagger sheathed at my side for added effect.

"In that case..." He places the handle of his own dagger in my hand.

I examine the sharp point and look up to find him staring at me, eyes ablaze. "I'm hoping you'll gut the fish instead, but it's your choice."

"You're under the assumption that I want to stab you, and yet you willingly hand me a blade?" I ask incredulously.

"I'd have you on the ground faster than you could raise that blade. But like I said," he says, palms raised, "I'm hoping you'll gut the fish instead."

"Awfully trusting of someone you barely know." I sit down beside the flat rock that will be my cutting board. "Bring me the fish."

Captain Murphy's eyes take on that storm-cloud quality again, flashing briefly like lightning as he smirks. I'm hyper aware of his movements—every stride of his powerful legs, every flexed muscle across his obsidian tattoo, every still-wet strand of onyx hair.

He drops the fish atop the rock before moving to kneel behind me.

"What are you doing?" I ask a little breathlessly.

"Helping, princess. Unless you're intimately familiar with gutting fish."

His breath is hot against the column of my neck as he nearly whispers the words. The world around me spins and I nearly lose my balance in his orbit.

My throat is thick as I force out my reply. "Not …" I clear my throat, "*intimately.*"

"Hold it just above the throat."

His scent envelopes me and I can hardly focus this close to him. Murphy smells like a mixture of salinity and worn leather. Like the old tomes in the small seaside cottage of my youth. My hand slides against the fish's slippery skin as I try to follow his instructions.

"Take the tip of your knife and insert it here." He grabs my wrist, directing the blade to the underside of the fish's gill. At the slightest touch of his hand, my magic jumps. It skitters, erratic and frantic, echoing my thundering heartbeat.

Captain Murphy leans in closer, bracketing my body with his. His tattoo sears into my back like a brand, his exposed skin scorching the ink-covered scar across my spine.

I've never been able to put into words what it felt like when the sea beast touched me all those years ago, the electricity that sparked in my chest and lit up my bones. I've never felt anything close to it again … until now.

Wild magic courses through me. I'm wholly consumed by its allure, a deadly siren song tempting me to forget.

Forget that my magic must stay hidden.

Forget the foretelling of our deaths.

Murphy's nose scrapes the shell of my ear, his body tense behind me. Every fiber of my being yearns to lean in closer to him and I'm close to giving in when I hear it.

Another distinctive hoot of an owl snaps me back into reality and forces me to remember.

Remember who I am.

Remember who he is.

Remember what this isn't.

I jerk away from him, forgetting completely about the sharp blade still in my grasp that nicks my palm. Bright red blood bubbles up from the wound.

The captain is up and digging through his saddlebag before I can yell the curse currently on my lips.

What in the gods' names possessed me just now? What was that feeling … and can I get more of it? It's a traitorous thought and I banish it the moment it crosses my mind.

"Give me your hand," he commands, dropping a small medical kit on the rock.

Before I can protest, he takes my bleeding hand in his and uncorks the canteen with his teeth. Clear, cool water pours from the spout and my body drinks it up as if it can quench some unknown thirst rooted in the depths of my soul. Invisible sparks fly from his every move, like flint striking against stone, and my power burns through me, bubbling up eagerly in response to his touch.

The bleeding stops almost as suddenly as it began, seeming to retreat inside my skin. Murphy slowly wipes what remains away and begins to wrap my hand with a clean cloth.

As he bandages, I study him with curiosity. This feels like nothing and no one I have ever encountered before. My eyes trace the lines of his tattoo, following the open maw of the beast from his neck and across the span of his chest. My eyes cut to his retracting pupils, gray once again coloring his gaze.

Alarm bells peal within me and I know for certain that I'm not the only person in this clearing with magic.

Murphy's deft fingers tie off the edges of the bandage, but he doesn't drop my hand. His eyes linger on the crescent-shaped birthmark at the base of my wrist before his thumb lightly, purposefully traces it. Unknown magic shoots up my arm, stealing my breath as I struggle to contain it.

The last light of day fades into twilight with the sunset. He lifts his face towards mine and time itself pauses. Black flashes briefly in his eyes again before my racing heart begins to slow, the frenzied blood in my veins calming.

"Can I tell you a story, princess?" Murphy's voice is low and soothing. The way one speaks to a spooked animal.

My head involuntarily moves in a single nod urging him to continue.

"When I was a young boy, I used to have terrible nightmares. My mother would tell me a story to soothe me. A tale about a people, the *aevus*, who could wield magic."

Every muscle in my body pulls taut, like a rope seconds before it snaps. I should act surprised, terrified of something that should not exist in this world— something that should not exist in me. But the look in his eyes tells me that he would see through the lie.

"The magic was elemental in nature," he continues. "The *aevus* could control the earth, the air, the water, and even fire. Some say they were descended from the gods; others said they were gods walking amongst the mortals. Either way, the *aevus* were said to have a mark."

Murphy watches me intently, the veins in his neck bulging slightly as if he too is struggling to maintain control in this precarious moment.

His eyes never leave mine as his thumb trails over my birthmark again. The tiny crescent shape on the inside of my wrist.

The same shape my mother had sketched in the worn leather journal I found on my bed when we returned from the shore without her. The book, filled with cryptic information scrawled in her handwriting, gave a name to the foreign power that had invaded my veins and led to more questions than answers.

Murphy's face gives no clues to his thoughts. No indication that he's planning to verbalize our shared secret. Every part of me is silently screaming at him, demanding a confession.

A flash of lightning illuminates the now darkened clearing. The hairs on my arms raise in response to the electric tingle that races across my skin.

Still, Captain Murphy holds my hand in his. The moment is thick and palpable, balanced on a knife's edge. He opens his mouth to speak, his lips moving slightly at the same moment that thunder booms through the clearing and drowns out his words.

The sky opens up, the deluge of rain, sudden and drowning, washing away his certain admission. The timing of the gods is truly unmatched.

There are so many things that I want to say. So many questions I want to ask and yet can't bring myself to voice them now. The gray of his eyes mimics the nimbus clouds rolling overhead and I fight to stay out of their tornadic pull. One more moment in his hold and I will be pulled under, like prey for the beast inked across his chest.

I can't let that happen. I have two weeks to convince Murphy to show me the man behind the persona. The *aevus* behind the captain, the weakness I can exploit. And I need to keep my wits about me if I have any hope of surviving that long.

So, instead, I slip back into the indifferent character of the poisonous heir, yanking my hand out of his before marching into the tent and away from the storm that brews beyond its canvas flaps.

CHAPTER 7

The cobblestone streets of Amale are packed. Crowds of people push past in droves as they file towards the palace. Each of their faces is turned upward at a man and a woman standing atop the palace balcony.

I strain to see who they are, dodging elbows and shoulders as the people clamor forward. I can make out their clothes—a tunic and dress of deep amethyst—but nothing else. It's as if there's a thin, translucent veil obstructing them from the crowd.

A woman to my right wails loud cries of joy as tears stream down her face. A man on my left hurls vile insults and incites men around him to join in. Still I push forward in the crowd, desperate to get a better look at the monarchs.

The crowd is becoming restless, neighbors turning on each other as a heavy rain starts to fall. Shouts ring up from further ahead in the crowd, full of praise and scorn.

"The gods have blessed Corinth!"

"Heretics, the both of them!"

"Long may they reign!"

"Magic has no place here!"

The rain intensifies, coursing through the mortar of the stone streets and soaking my clothes.

Despite my efforts, I'm no closer to the building or the figures standing atop the balcony. I'm shoved hard from behind and I have no time to brace myself before I fall face first onto the wet street. My head smacks loudly against the bricks as the world shifts.

The stones around me turn to liquid, the roar of the crowd replaced with the roar of waves. The cold waters of the Eastern Sea lap around me.

Desperately and unsuccessfully, I try to swim. Something black breaches the surface just out of my frame of vision and panic seizes me.

Death's creature lurks in the murky water.

I call to my magic, grasping for any thread of power to save me. Vines of ivy shoot out from my wrists angled towards the sea floor seeking purchase in the silt. The black shape crests the surface again. With one final breath, I scream a single syllable name.

The leviathan opens its mighty jaws, wrapping around me and sending the entire world into pitch black.

I wake in a panic, gasping for air. A thick layer of salty sweat that feels too much like sea water coats my skin. The crackling fire calls to me and I step cautiously out of the tent to warm myself.

I expect to find Captain Murphy on watch, but he's nowhere to be seen. Palming the dagger that I keep sheathed against my outer thigh, I creep around the tent, eyes searching the dark for any signs of life—friendly or otherwise.

Murphy kneels at the edge of the small pond, his hands clasped and head bowed reverently. The light from the full moon shimmers across the glassy surface, illuminating his reflection.

As if in response to a whispered petition, a cool breeze cuts through the trees, sending a ripple across the water and a chill down my spine. The clouds above shift slightly, casting the captain's head in a glowy, silvery halo.

If the gods are real, I imagine they look like he does now. Mysterious, radiant, gorgeous. The appearance alone is worthy of disciples.

A childhood spent in religious schooling gave me plenty of exposure to the pious, the devoted so-called sons and daughters of faceless gods. People who are quick to pray and even quicker to judge. Followers who blame the cruelty of this world on its faithless inhabitants instead of the vengeful gods they worship.

The Captain of Corinth is the antithesis of holy, his acts openly rebuked by the righteous, and yet here he is on his knees in benediction.

There's an eerie feeling in the air as if the world itself is holding its breath. My magic roils in my veins, suddenly desperate to get out. My muscles ache in protest as I keep my power locked away. Magic claws at my skin as I stumble backward towards camp.

Slumping down against a log, I try to steady my breathing. The fire cracks loudly, a flame nearly licking my boot before I can pull my knees to my chest. As suddenly as it woke, my power goes dormant again, somehow satiated after a frenzied starvation.

The moon is still high overhead, but I know for certain I won't be sleeping anymore tonight. Not when my stomach is on the verge of emptying itself of the meager dinner of fire-cooked fish and bread that Murphy slipped under the tent flap.

Not when my dreams have already driven me closer to the edge of madness and further from anything resembling rest.

Laying my head back against the log, I chart the constellations overhead. Supposed symbols of the great divine. After today, I expect to find the starry image of an owl, but it's a celestial wolf that greets me instead. The sigil of the Wolf God Mikais, brother to the God King.

The story of the traitorous sibling has always fascinated me. The holy texts conveniently omit the details of the brother who supposedly cast the ultimate betrayal upon Nobus. When asked, the holy priests only reply "The gods didn't see fit to tell us."

I have never been one to take things at face value, not when stories are the currency of reputation. Whoever controls the narrative decides who is a hero and who is a villain. I can't help but wonder if Mikais and I have that knowledge in common, if maybe his actions were warranted, if maybe he rebelled against Nobus' control and was rewarded with a slanderous nickname too.

A cool breeze stirs to life again and I sense Captain Murphy's approach before I hear it.

"My turn for watch," I say without lifting my head from its resting place.

He lingers, watching me as intently as I watched him moments ago. But whatever thoughts are in his head remain there as he wordlessly enters the tent.

When I'm sure that he's not watching me, I let a single bloom of godsbane grow to life in my palm. Five midnight-hued sepals surround a cluster of poisonous nectaries in its center. I flex my power and watch as the almost-petals open and close at my whim.

The power of life flows through my veins, power to create and also to destroy. Power that I have always hidden, biding my time until the right moment to reveal what I can do.

And despite how it infuriates me, Captain Murphy might just be the key to unlocking even more of that power.

CHAPTER 8

There's no bright sun to greet us in the morning, only rumbling thunder in the distance and moisture thick in the air. We ride hurriedly and anxiously, skating the outskirts of the storm that seems to stalk our path.

Our lead diminishes around midday. Dark clouds block out the sun and cast the day into an eerie gloom. The bite of electricity fills the air in anticipation of the storm that's closing in.

We are still a few hours away from Eida, the last proper village before we cross out of the Emerald Region. If we push the horses to run through the howling wind, we can make it by supper. Our meager tent won't withstand the gusts this storm promises to bring, and one look at Captain Murphy tells me that he doesn't wish to spend the night in the elements either.

Lightning flashes through the sky, causing my mare to thrash against the reins.

"Easy girl," I call out in a feeble attempt to reassure her.

"We need to hurry," Murphy yells. A strong burst of wind rattles the trees forcing him to pull his cloak tighter across his broad chest. "I have a bad feeling about this storm."

The signs of wildlife that are usually present in the forest are noticeably absent. There are no squirrels scampering across the branches or rabbits hopping in the underbrush. Everything has taken shelter; everything except us.

We spur the horses onward as the dam that's been holding back the water in the clouds finally cracks. It starts as a drizzle—the steady kind of light rain that embeds itself into the fabric of your clothing, soaking you slowly.

It rains like that for more than an hour before the clouds open up and release the full contents of their stores. The wind relentlessly whips my sodden cloak from my body, removing any shield that I might have from the biting cold.

"We need to move faster," Murphy yells over the roaring wind and rain.

I nod in reply, dropping the hand that I'm currently using to shield my face and urging my cantering horse into a gallop.

We ride headfirst into the worst of the storm in a desperate attempt to close the distance between us and Eida, and the warmth of the inn that awaits there. Magic tingles in my veins as an unsettling feeling swirls thick in the air around us. It's the same feeling from last night—the one that sent my power into a frenzy. I force air into my lungs, hoping the torrential downpour of rain will subdue the fiery spark of power that threatens to break free.

A loud crack bellows through the woods and my horse rears up on her hind legs at the noise. She lets out a frightened whinny as orange flames burst to life in the tree overhead. A thick, large branch dangles, mere seconds away from snapping completely off. I tug on the reins trying to turn my mare, but she fights me. The horse may not want to move, but if she doesn't, I'll meet Death sooner than I'd like.

With one last ditch effort, I swing my leg over the saddle and fling myself from the horse's back. My kick spurs the horse to bolt to the side as I fall face first into the muddy road. I tuck my shoulders in towards my knees, flinging my wet cape over my head.

I brace for impact, but instead of crushing pain from a branch, a deluge of water knocks me further into the mud. Water pours down my face as I gasp for air, my head swimming as calloused hands pull me upward.

"Are you hurt?"

I can barely hear his muffled words for the liquid pooling in my ears. I shake my head to clear it, my eyes catching on a pile of ashes laying only inches from my muddy hole. Smoke still rises from where it burned only moments before.

Captain Murphy pulls a drenched rag from his pocket and begins to wipe the mud from my face, a well-intentioned gesture that only serves to smear the wet earth further.

"What the hell were you thinking?"

There's an unmistakable anger in his voice. He probably thinks I'm an idiot, and I certainly feel like one right now.

"I was trying to save myself."

My words are barely a whisper as the last dregs of my adrenaline from my near brush with death evaporate, leaving me shaking in his hands. Murphy pulls me tightly against his chest in an effort to stop the tremors that overtake me.

That rush of strange power floods my system again and I allow myself a moment of weakness. A single moment to crash into his depthless gray eyes, to drift carelessly in the endless pools of brackish water that stare back at me.

It's a mistake. One that might very well cost me. Because right now, I barely have the strength to fight the pull of his riptide.

A droplet of water runs off the tip of his nose and lands on the center of my bottom lip. He reaches to swipe it away using the pad of his thumb and slowly pulls my lip down before letting his finger drag down my chin.

I suck in a ragged breath and feel the warmth in my veins ignite into a blaze. The heady rush of magic surges and the air grows thick with tension. Thunder cracks overhead again, breaking the spell. I step out of his hold and tighten the ties on my soaking cloak.

Murphy whistles and our horses rush to his side. "Try not to jump off this time, princess," he says on a shaky breath as he hands me the reins.

I take them, careful not to touch him again. I'm still in fight-or-flight mode, maybe even more so now that the realization of my moment of weakness settles in. I can't form words and I'm thankful for the icy chill that settles between us in their absence.

The sun has set by the time we finally arrive in Eida. Everything I own is drenched and my bones ache to be in front of a fire.

Even though it's been hours, we haven't spoken since the incident with the branch, and I'm not sure what I'll say when we finally do. I should thank him for helping me, but I would have thought less of him if he didn't. And I'm not sure I'll be convincing enough yet to tell him that I don't want him to ever touch me again.

I wait at the entrance to the small stable while Murphy gives detailed instructions to the groom. Water streams off the roof's overhang and my hand instinctively comes out to touch it, creating four tiny rivulets that dance as I wiggle my fingers.

What would it be like to command it with my power? Water is necessary for the land to thrive, and while my magic may create blooms and invigorate plants, they cannot thrive without its sustaining force. But water can also be dangerous. A river looks quiet and peaceful at first, but given time it will erode deep valleys and canyons into the land. A simple rainstorm can turn into a flash flood sweeping away anything and anyone in its wake. Water is a delicate balance between life-giving and life-ending.

So are all the elements, really, and perhaps those who wield them are not dissimilar.

"Ready, princess?"

Murphy's rough voice jolts me from my thoughts. My fingers are still intertwined with the water and I don't miss the half-smile that tugs at the corners of his mouth when he notices.

"For dry clothes and a fire? Always."

I grab my bag from his hand and bolt across the small yard that separates the stable from the inn.

The onslaught of the bright lights and warm air from inside the tavern is staggering. There's an immediate welcoming ambience to this place. It's crowded with people sharing drinks and laughing while folksy music lilts through the room. A large hearth roars in the corner with plush chairs pulled up to face it. Cozy booths line the remaining walls on both sides of the small dining room. There's a happiness to this place that contrasts the dreariness of the storm raging outside.

A half door that must lead to the kitchen swings open, and a small, cheerful woman steps out carrying a large tray of steaming bowls. Her hair and skin are the color of pure snow, making the pink flush of her cheeks pop. Small wrinkles pull up at the corner of her eyes and her mouth, the only signs of her advanced age.

"Well aren't you both a sight for sore eyes!" she exclaims, passing off the tray to the young man trailing behind her and wiping her hands on her apron. "Mikel, deliver these and then fetch some hot mead for our guests here."

With a nod, the young man takes the tray and disappears to deliver the bowls.

"This storm is serious business and my old back tells me it's only going to get worse tonight. Always flares up when something bad is a'brewing, I tell ya. The name's Mae and this is my place."

"Hello, Mae. I'm—"

"You need no introduction here, sweets."

Mae dips her head in a curt bow and I instinctively scan my eyes to see if anyone around her has noticed. The patrons, as far as I can see, are still thankfully engrossed in their cups. From the corner of my eye, I can see Murphy quietly surveying the filled tables surrounding us. His lips move silently as if counting the number of patrons filling the tiny space.

Mae's eyes narrow as she studies me and the captain from head to toe before shaking her head with a sigh, clearly disappointed by whatever she was hoping to find.

"I wish I could offer better accommodations for m'lady, but the storm tends to draw travelers in who would normally stay in the woods."

It's my turn to be disappointed. Pain picks the back of my eyes and I know they'll be no beating the princess allegations if I cry over not having a dry bed beside a warm fire. Today has left me near exhaustion and I credit that for my lapse in decorum.

Before I can reply, the matronly woman extracts a single brass key from her apron pocket. "I've only got one room and it's nowhere near what you're used to, I'm afraid."

My hand is on the key before the weight of her words settle in. This has to be a joke.

The realization must have hit Murphy at the same time because he's now staring at Mae as if she has three heads. He opens his mouth to protest but she lifts a single, wrinkled hand to silence him.

"I wouldn't offer this to anyone else, but since you're escorting the heir, I will make an exception." She pauses, seemingly only for dramatic effect. When she's finally satisfied that she has the captain's full attention, she continues. "There's a cot in the broom closet down the hall. It's not a guest room so I won't be hearing any complaints about the condition, but if all you're after is a dry place to sleep, I can offer it to ya ... for a discounted rate."

Murphy reaches into his pocket and places two silvers and a copper on the counter. Mae raises her eyebrows and waits until he slides three more coppers her way before she places the key in his hand and motions towards the stairs that run up the back wall of the room.

"No fireplace in the closet, I presume?" he asks gruffly.

Mikel deposits two steaming mugs of mead on the counter in front of us. "Just rats," the young man laughs, earning a sharp look from the innkeep. "But maybe you can move the cot somewhere warm?"

"That's enough meddling. Go stir that stew before it sticks to the bottom." Mae swats at the man as she shuffles him back through the half door and into the kitchen.

"Come on," Murphy grunts as he shoulders both bags and heads for the staircase.

I grab both mugs of warm mead, the delicious scent of cinnamon filling my nose, and follow him.

There are only two floors—the bottom serving as a tavern and the upper filled with guest rooms. A small "B" adorns the first door at the top of the stairs, indicating the bathing chamber. We walk along the old embroidered runner that spans the hallway floors, the carpet threadbare from years of guests walking along its center. It's drafty up here and I pull the steaming mugs closer to my chest in an attempt to absorb some of their warmth.

Small brass numbers top each door and Murphy halts abruptly at number six, its match engraved on the key. At the end of the hallway, a slim door sits slightly ajar—the broom closet, I presume.

The captain shivers and I suddenly feel guilty that I'll be the only one snug and warm by a fire tonight.

I exchange the mug in my hand for the bag on the captain's shoulder. There's a hard expression on his face and the words spill out before I can think better of it. "You can put your cot in front of my fireplace, assuming there's room."

His gray eyes smolder as he takes an unexpected step towards me and that's when I feel it again—that tiny spark of magic, the bite of electricity in the air before a lightning strike. I know with certainty that I can't give this fire oxygen or the flames will surely consume me.

"Do you offer because you feel sorry for me?"

I don't answer him. Not because I'm playing coy, but because there are too many questions warring within me at the moment.

Do I want him to suffer in the cold while I'm warm? Of course not. I'm not cruel.

Is there a war happening between my head and my magic right now? Yes.

Am I strong enough to fight it? Not in this state.

Thankfully, my silence is answer enough.

He steps back quickly and his voice is nearly a growl when he responds. "Your pity is misplaced, *princess.*"

"Let your pride keep you from a fire, then. It makes no difference to me."

"Liar." He practically spits the word at me.

"I didn't invite you into my bed, *Captain,*" I mimic his tone. "I don't even know why I offered in the first place. You won't even tell me your name."

The captain steps into my space, forcing me to take a step backwards to avoid touching him. He's intimidating but I stiffen my spine, unwilling to reveal an ounce of the strange weakness that I feel when we touch. He takes another step and I follow suit. He doesn't stop his forward assault until my back hits the door behind me.

"Would my name make a difference to you, *Ivy?*"

There's a song often played in the temples whose arrangement is said to bring tears to the eyes of the gods. It's stunning, achingly beautiful in composition and even it pales in comparison to how my name sounds on his lips. And he doesn't just say it, he practically *purrs* it.

"It's a start," I breathe through the lusty, magical haze clouding my vision. There's barely any distance between us but I'm grateful for every sliver of space that allows me to keep my wits. I have to keep them if I'm to have any chance of succeeding at my mission.

He is my ally, nothing more.

"To what end?" he asks.

"To you showing me who you really are." *To you showing me how I can use you.*

One truth I say aloud, the other I keep only for myself.

His calloused fingers grip my chin, forcing me to look fully into his gray eyes. A silver fire burns in them that mimics the scorching I feel in my veins.

"Why would you want to see the real me?"

"Call me a masochist, but I like to know who's leading me to my death." I snap my mouth shut in an attempt to take back the secret I didn't mean to divulge.

"*Death*. Is that who you think I am?"

My voice trembles with each word I speak. "Who you are remains to be seen, Captain."

Murphy drops his hand and steps back as quickly as he approached. The air around us is cold but the tension between us is warm—too warm. He turns to head for his room but stops suddenly, looking over his broad shoulder with a sly smile.

"My name isn't Death," he starts. "It's Callan, but you can call me Cal."

He disappears swiftly into the tiny broom closet, slamming the door behind him and leaving me alone in the hallway.

Callan.

Cal.

I repeat it back to myself slowly. It's not a unique name—in fact, it's fairly common. But something about the way he said *Cal* steals the breath from my lungs.

It feels eerily familiar, intimate almost. Like I've said it a thousand times.

And then it hits me.

I *have* said it a thousand times, maybe more. The scenario and the circumstances always change but that name never does. The face that I never see, the dread that always comes, the name that I always call out in my nightmares.

Cal.

CHAPTER 9

I am completely and totally fucked.

The thought replays over and over in my head as I scrub away the mud that has buried itself under my nails, in the folds of my arms, and on the roots of my hair. The magic and the tattoo weren't omen enough, no, his name has to be the connective tissue in all of my nightmares. The single syllable from his lips is the final nail in my coffin.

"Is that what you all sit around and do for fun?" I taunt the gods. "You just toy with people's lives like we're dolls. Is this all some big game to you?"

I don't expect an answer, which is good because I don't get one. The gods only care about their own amusement—and what better game for them than to bind my fate to the Captain of Corinth … to *Cal*.

Even thinking his name sends a shiver down my spine. I have to figure out how best to use him against Marks before whatever end the gods have planned catches up with us.

The coals under the cast iron tub are embers, the now chilly water cloudy with the dirt I washed from my skin and hair. I grab the poor excuse for a towel and wrap the thin fabric around me before opening the door to the cold hallway. I'm all but running to my room when the sound of a creaking door stops me in my tracks. Out steps Captain Callan Murphy wearing nothing but a towel slung low across his hips.

We're not indecent, but this moment feels too intimate. I saw his tattoo from a distance last night, but it's closer now. The way the ebony ink ripples across his pecs as he stalks towards me makes the beast appear to open and close its jaw. It's tail disappears completely under the towel and, in a momentary lapse of judgement, I wonder where it ends.

I clear my throat and start walking to my door. "Captain," I nod.

He follows suit, face gravely serious as we pass in the narrow hallway. "Princess."

I'm unlocking the door to my room when I hear his footsteps stall.

"Godsbane."

It's not a question, but a breathed realization at the floral bloom inked between my shoulder blades and the thick scar it attempts to cover.

"Godsbane," I repeat without moving.

The captain lets out a low, deep chuckle. "Fitting," he replies.

I glance over my shoulder, curiosity written plainly on my face, only to see him swaggering into the bathing chamber.

"We leave at dawn, princess."

It's still dark outside when a loud pounding wakes me from my restless slumber.

"Give me a second," I groan out as another, louder knock sounds.

I dig through my bag quickly searching for my oversized cotton shirt and slip it over my naked body. The impatient knocker pounds a third time, causing me to completely abandon my search for pants. The hem of the shirt skims the bottom of my ass, but it'll have to be enough for now.

Just before the fist can pound again, I jerk open the door to find a young woman holding a steaming mug and an envelope.

"Are you Ivy?" she asks, clearly annoyed at me for reasons unknown.

"I am."

"I was told to give these to you."

She extends both hands and stares at me. When I don't react quickly enough, she shakes the objects she holds, signaling for me to hurry up.

I force a saccharine smile and take the mug and envelope from her hands. The scent of fresh coffee hitting my nostrils elicits an audible moan before I can snap my lips shut. The mysterious inn employee vanishes before I can thank her.

I take several sips of the coffee while I walk back to sit on my bed, carefully stepping over the pile of clothes unceremoniously scattered across the worn rug that covers the floor. It's hot and rich, a little bitter, but I don't mind.

Despite the perception that I live a life of luxury, coffee is one of the few indulgences that I allow myself. My father always has exotic beans from the island nations shipped in for my birthday and I know they'll be waiting on me at the governor's manor when I return.

Or they will be, if I return.

That *if* feels heavier and heavier each passing day. Another night filled with haunted dreams turns into another day on the road with my fated doom. There's no escaping what awaits me.

I slide my finger under the wax seal and read three sentences scrawled across the parchment.

STORMS KNOCKED DOWN TREES OVER THE ROAD. NO TRAVEL TODAY.

P.S. THE RATS SAY HELLO.

I read, what I presume to be, Captain Murphy's scrawled words again.

STORMS KNOCKED DOWN TREES OVER THE ROAD.

If the storm was powerful enough to uproot trees, there's likely damage to homes, shops, and schools. They can spread whatever stories they want about me because of my disapproval of their gods and their forced religion, but I have never abandoned my people when they were in need and I don't intend to start now.

I down the rest of the coffee quickly and search the unruly clothing pile for something inconspicuous to wear. I leave behind any trace of my identity or status in the small room, choosing to wear the brown of the common folk over the Emerald Region's green. I fix my hair into a simple braid before pulling the cloak's hood down over my eyes.

I don't need or want their recognition. I am not a politician looking to garner favor, just an unworthy heir hoping to help without being turned away.

The rising sun showcases just how much of a complete mess Eida has become in the wake of the storm. Inhabitants emerge from their homes to survey the damage. Branches, leaves, and trash litter the streets. Houses are missing their shutters, wagons are overturned, and the fountain in the center of the village is filled with rubbish.

The elements were not kind.

Few villagers spare a look in my direction as they distribute brooms, shovels, and rakes. Men push wheelbarrows and wagons through the streets to collect the debris. Crews form to start the clean up and I silently fall into their ranks. Hours pass quickly as we work, no one engaging with me except for the occasional directional command to place a limb or a leaf pile in a different wagon.

The sun is nearly completely overhead when the village baker sends a child with a basket to pass out small pastries as a treat. Mae comes by shortly after to pass out cups of water and ale. The heat of the sun combined with physical labor has caused me to ditch my cloak. I know that without it, Mae will instantly recognize me. My heart hammers in my chest as she approaches. If she calls me by name or title, all of the good I did here today will be for nothing. I'll be dodging the very sticks I've helped to clean up.

The cool water does little to extinguish the panic rising within me. Mae offers me a soft smile as if she knows exactly what I'm thinking.

"Another cup, sweets?" she says with a wink.

I nod and she hands me another cup of the cool liquid before moving to the next person in line. That was close—too close. The clean-up effort in the center of town is nearly finished, so I decide to walk around to find another job, preferably one with less attention.

Life in a village is truly something amazing. I always loved the days that my mother would take me into town as a child. The shops, the smells, and the people all coming together to paint an idyllic picture of what life in Corinth could be. I linger in front of the bakery windows reminiscing on a simpler time, a simpler life.

Before I was heir.

Before I had secret magic.

Before I was hated by most of Corinth.

I wasn't Poison Ivy then, I was just Ivy.

"Come hear the word of the gods! Let us beg for penance and praise Nobus for sparing our homes!"

The shout rings out through the village streets. The priest, an old man with a long white beard, herds the crowds towards the temple like a flock of sheep. Blind masses worshipping a god who couldn't care less about them.

I put my cloak on again and slip through the throngs of people moving in the opposite direction. I'm met with a few sidelong glances, but they mostly pay me no heed.

A bell peals through the village, echoing off the stone buildings and calling all to worship. A tingle traces its way down my spine, a pulling sensation settling somewhere deep inside me. I follow the strange tug down an alleyway, across broken cobblestones and buildings worn with age and the elements.

Magic reaches a crescendo in my veins as a hooded figure steps out from the shadows. The body, shrouded in darkness, is female. Lithe and delicate—and completely out of place. Everything about this figure feels as if they do not belong here, as if they're trapped here. Piercing eyes cut through the darkness, a deep shade of indigo that vacillates between blue and purple.

Stepping into the sunlight, she removes the shawl covering her head to reveal raven-colored hair in an intricate braid. Freckles pepper her face in tiny constellations that seem to dance across her pale skin.

"No desire to worship? Have you no love for the gods?"

Her voice is lilting, a haunting hymn echoing through the stone halls of a temple. I open my mouth to form a pretty little lie about being lost or having urgent business to attend to, but each one turns to ash on my tongue before I can give it voice. The hue of her eyes shifts again demanding the truth from my lips.

"They have no love for me."

I expect a sharp retort, a scold for my insolence towards my makers and keepers. I don't expect the chuckle that tips her mesmerizing mouth into an amused smile.

"Nobus has no love for them, but that doesn't stop their prayers or offerings. He doesn't send the storms that plague them, nor does he protect them from their wrath. There's only one reason he hasn't completely forgotten about this realm."

"We'd be better off if he did."

Another unwilling truth offered up to the ethereal stranger.

"How quickly they forget what life was like when they held his favor. Before the Great Betrayer Mikais doomed them all. The air smells of their blood just waiting to spill. Drayca approaches."

The intrigue that pulled me into her turns to skepticism. Perhaps I mistook her craziness for mystery. She's about four years too late with her prophecy of war.

"The Goddess of War already delivered her wrath to our shores. Synal invaded us and cities in Sapphire still lay decimated."

I step to the side in an attempt to distance myself from the strange woman. A pale hand shoots out to grab my arm. Ice floods my veins at her touch, the cold seeping through the layers of fabric and chilling my bones.

A strong breeze whips around us, the clouds overhead blocking out the sun. The woman's violet eyes fade into pools of pitch black. Her hold on my arm tightens, my heart pounding frantically in my chest. Magic goes dormant in my veins as if it cowers in the presence of an older, ancient being.

"The gods of the Golden Pantheon don't concern themselves with mortal maps. Synal, Corinth … your lands are inconsequential to them. Nobus will decimate this realm with little more than a thought. The one with the power to unite us rises as foretold. Are you ready?"

"You have me mistaken for someone else."

Nobus, Mikais, Drayca, Death—they're all the same to me. Gods as useless as whatever lost prophecy she rambles on about. I am not whoever she believes me to be.

"Walk with me," she commands, the clouds parting in a blinding flash of light as she drops her hold from my arm.

Magic pulls me, clawing at my skin in a desperate plea to follow the woman. Her brown cloak flits in the wind as she disappears around the corner of a building. My feet follow her down the cobblestone path, past stores, houses, and gardens.

"Are you a seer?" I call out after her.

"I've been called that by those with simple minds."

The full weight of her indigo gaze lands on me, her eyes quickly transitioning from blue to purple and back again—the violet hue there one minute and gone the next.

"Fate is not something you can read. It's not written in stone, but in the shifting sands of time. One can change it, if only they're strong enough."

I want to believe her words, and I might, if not for the twisting feeling in my stomach every night when foreboding images pull me from my sleep. Haunting hallucinations of swords, crowns, blood, and darkness. What awaits me is as inevitable as the setting of the sun or death itself.

The ethereal woman begins walking again, magic tugging me along gently behind her. Our steps echo on the cobblestone streets, the afternoon quiet after the clamor of the morning clean-up.

I'm not paying attention to where we are walking, only to the mysterious words spoken by the otherworldly woman. I don't comprehend their meaning, but I understand their importance, no matter how ludicrous they might be.

She stops abruptly and turns to face me. "When the truth reveals itself, you must accept it. Trust the power that guides you and you might have a chance to save the people you love. But if you ignore it, Death will keep you."

Her whispered voice caresses my cheek like a warm breeze. One moment she's beside me and the next she's gone. As if she vanished on the very wind that billows around me.

Frantically, my eyes search my surroundings, glancing in every direction in an effort to find the stranger before landing on the stable across the cobblestone street.

Mud coats Captain Murphy from the toes of his black boots to the knees of his leather pants. One foot rests on the wood-planked wall behind him in casual ease, no armor in sight. Hopefully he helped clear the road today so we can leave this gods-forsaken village in the morning.

I walk toward the stable, my fingers still trembling from the strange encounter. My magic is desperate for release. I need to get to the woods. I need to grow something and maybe even to decay something just this once.

Murphy pushes off the stable to stand fully as I approach.

"Who was that?" he asks in a gravelly voice that I have no doubt has made grown soldiers nearly piss themselves.

"I'm still trying to figure that out myself."

Not a lie and probably the closest thing I have to the actual truth.

Heavy footfalls echo behind me as I move into the stable to saddle my mare. I work quickly, shaky hands securing the tack as best I can while he silently watches.

"Where are you going?" the captain asks.

"For a ride."

"I'll join you," he says sternly.

"I'd prefer you don't."

Calloused hands grip my upper arm, forcing me to stop. My magic jumps pathetically under my skin at his touch like a dog welcoming home its master after a long day away.

"It's my duty to protect you."

"Then give me your sword," I bite back.

"Tell me who she is and what she said to you." There's a storm raging in his gray irises as he commands me.

"A woman from the village," I start. "And she spoke nonsense."

The audacity of him to demand such an answer from me. An answer that, if I'm being honest, I don't have. She spoke of the gods, of fate and power and prophecy ... but what did she really say? What did any of it mean?

"Are you going to give me your sword or not?" I ask incredulously.

With a solemn face, he unbuckles the sword-belt from his chest and places the sheathed blade in my hand.

"You spent the day in the village?"

I expected a scolding for venturing into a crowd of people who hate me without being properly armed. I don't expect him to appear awestruck at generosity he surely deems uncharacteristic.

I secure the strap and buckle it between my breasts before mounting the horse. It's only once I am fully seated and turning my horse to leave that I reply to him.

"Did you think I'd spend the day sitting on my ass?" I scoff, spurring the horse forward.

As I cross the stable threshold, he speaks. The words are barely audible, but I swear he groans as he utters his confession. "I'm trying not to think about your ass, princess."

CHAPTER 10

T barely get an hour alone in the woods before the setting sun has me retreating back to the stables. It's not nearly enough time to satiate my restless magic or dampen the strange feeling that still sears my soul.

I thought giving into the gnawing call of death might help, might temporarily calm whatever the stranger lit within me today. But even decaying an entire bush didn't soothe it—the most I've ever allowed myself to indulge. A stiff drink is the only thing that might stand a chance at rounding out the sharp edges of power that still claw and scrape at my skin.

The tavern below the inn is packed with villagers all eager to make offerings to Bastin after a hard day working to clean up what the storm left in its wake. A foreign joy fills the room as the jaunty tune of a fiddle wafts from the open doorway. The musician stands precariously balanced atop a rickety, makeshift stage, two crates propped up in a corner with an empty ale mug placed at his feet to collect tips. Around the room, heads nod in time with the folksy tune, mugs of ales clank together in cheers, and a few daring couples even attempt to dance a gleeful jig amongst the spread of tables.

I scan the room, looking for the captain to return his sword, but it's Mikel, the young man from last night, that catches my eye first. He enthusiastically waves me over to the busy bartop with a wide smile that exposes a grin that's missing more than a few teeth.

"Can I get you something, my lady?" he asks sweetly.

I repress the shudder that instinctively rolls down my spine at his words. I can't decide what I hate more, open disdain or over-eagerness to cater to my every whim. Thankfully, he doesn't notice my discomfort or the impatient way that the other patrons around the bar try and fail to grab his attention.

"Whiskey, please."

When Mikel bends to extract the bottle from under the counter, I spot Captain Murphy over his shoulder. Sitting alone at a small table near the staircase that runs up the back wall of the inn, the muscles in his chiseled jaw are so tense that I can sense the agitation rolling off him from where I stand.

"Better make it two." I place a silver, well above what the whiskey is worth, on the counter and nod at Mikel. A silent command to take the overpayment without complaint.

He places two glasses on the counter, but instead of pouring the whiskey, he slides the entire bottle my way with a wink. Before I can object, he disappears into the kitchen through the swinging door.

It takes nearly an entire song to push past the shoulders of stumbling patrons, avoid the booted steps of dancers who swing haphazardly through the crowds, and dodge hoisted serving trays of tonight's dinner special. When I finally reach the back wall, Murphy is surprisingly absent. Physically, his body is still sitting here, but his attention is locked onto something across the room.

I drop the heavy bottle on the wooden table, the tin cups clinking together before they knock against the glass. The chair scrapes loudly as the chorus of applause dies down, but whatever holds Murphy captive doesn't release him. It's only when I slide his well-made, but too-heavy-for-me sword across the table that he looks my way.

"Your sword, Captain. Unused."

"Where have you been?" he barks out through gritted teeth.

I could tell him that I went for a ride, or a walk, or took a nap by a stream, but I don't bother. Because it's none of his business.

The stranger's words, cryptic as they were, were meant for me. Whatever she knew about my power or my fate isn't for Captain Murphy's ears.

The burnt woodsy scent of cheap whiskey invades my nostrils as I uncork the bottle and begin to pour the caramel liquid. I slide a hammered cup his way before lifting my own to my lips and downing the dram in a single gulp. The fiery spirit floods my system instantly settling the power that sparks and pops in his presence.

"That is somehow even cheaper than I imagined," I joke.

The captain's focus is elsewhere again, the muscles in his jaw matching the white-knuckled fists that rest on the table. I pour another and drink it quickly to avoid the impatient silence growing between us.

I wait for a snarky remark but nothing comes. I expect something along the lines of 'What would a princess know about cheap whiskey?' or even 'Can't handle a cheap poison, princess?' But instead I get nothing.

Fuck this. I can drink alone upstairs.

I push back from the table, grabbing the bottle of whiskey in one hand and my tin cup in the other.

"Running away from me?" he asks, finally turning his gray eyes to meet mine.

"You seem a little preoccupied. Wouldn't want to keep you

from enjoying your night, Captain." The rickety chair smacks the ground as I stand.

"Stop."

One word, a command more than a request. It's sharp, imperious, and maddeningly... *sexy*. And I hate it.

I grab the open whiskey and take a pull directly from the bottle without breaking eye contact. Darkness smokes in his eyes at my impertinence, further stoking the mixture of alcohol and something even more dangerous growing within me. Tiny droplets trail from the corners of my lips as I pull the bottle away and swipe my face with the back of my hand.

Mikel's smiling face suddenly invades the space between us. Gingerly, he sets down a plate of roasted chicken and root vegetables, disappearing back into the crowd. Murphy lets out a slow, low chuckle as he rises to stand. I pull my eyes from the plate to see the bastard smirking.

"If you drink like that, you better eat something. I don't slow down for hangovers, princess."

Murphy slips into the roaring crowd and instantly disappears. My traitorous stomach growls at the delicious scent of the steaming plate. I haven't eaten all day and I've expended a lot of magic. If I don't eat this, I'm certain to puke up whiskey within the hour.

I don't like being cared for. This is now the second time today he's done something like this, and I need to squash the habit now. His actions, regardless of how they were intended, imply a debt that I don't care to owe anyone.

I pick at the food on my plate, stabbing each bite with more force than necessary before bringing it up to my mouth. This chicken could be the most exquisitely spiced dish in all of Corinth and I wouldn't know it. I barely taste it before I wash it down with more swill.

The tavern floor, which saw a slight reprieve when the fiddler took a short break, crowds again. Shouts echo throughout the small room as the first notes drift from his bowstring. A local favorite about a bear and a maiden that instantly has everyone on their feet. There's so much happiness here tonight that the faithful might claim Bastin himself is present.

It's been so long since I've had a single carefree night of fun in a tavern. Before the war, Miles, Quinn, and I would frequent The Royal Jewel, a nobles-only establishment in Emerald. He always denied it, but I know Miles footed the bill for the entire bar on those nights.

'If I did, it would be a small price to pay for your fun ... and their silence,' he would say.

But during Feast Week, the time dedicated to debaucherous offerings to the Golden Pantheon, the three of us would ditch our emerald wardrobe for common browns and ornate masks to camouflage ourselves amongst the revelers in town. With nothing to give away our identities, we lived. Drinking, dancing, and fucking until the sun came up.

It was on those anonymous nights that I truly felt alive. No title, no nickname, no magic. Nothing that made me Ivy, and everything that made me feel powerful.

I'm not foolish enough to think I can go quite that far tonight, but I am in plain clothes and I do currently possess a belly full of liquid courage. Risking a little ire and a solid hangover is worth a night of a little joy, even if it's fleeting.

The crowd parts slightly, a flash of sunfire hair catching my eye as I survey the room for a group of revelers to join. The woman is gorgeous. Flaming hair cascading over her shoulders, pooling above her large breasts that are currently inches away from the broad, muscled arm of a man dressed in all black. Delicate fingers trace circles on the table top as she whispers something low from her scarlet lips.

Slowly, a head of onyx hair turns, gray eyes locking onto mine and pinning me to my seat. Eyes that blaze with the intensity of the sun itself. A sour, sickly feeling starts low in my gut and spreads throughout me. I grab the bottle and try to wash it away, but it doesn't break.

It's not jealousy. I barely know this man. I feel nothing for him … nothing besides the way my magic goes batshit crazy in his presence and the maddening rush that overtakes me every time our skin touches.

No.

No, no, no, no, no.

This is the whiskey and the remnants of unspent magic, nothing more.

A loud cheer from the front of the room draws my attention. There's a long table near the fiddler's makeshift stage filled with villagers deeply engaged in a rowdy drinking game. That is exactly what I need to turn this evening around. And there just happens to be a single empty seat at the table.

I down another gulp of the whiskey to steel my nerves before the bottle and I ask permission to play.

"Room for one more?" I ask as I approach the group.

Most of the participants are too deep in the game to acknowledge me, but one, a large man with a thick beard and warm brown eyes, smiles at me.

"A lady bearing whiskey is always welcome. I'm Garrett." He motions me to the empty seat beside him, pulling it out like a gentleman.

"Selene," I tell him.

My mother's name. The name I give out on feast nights, always too afraid of the weight my own carries.

Garrett quickly explains the rules of the game, but I opt to sit the next round out to observe the players in action. It's a fast-moving game, a singalong with repetitive hand movements and

claps. Anyone who messes up the words or misses the next movement has to drink. This is clearly a favorite in Eida.

Not sure if it's my inexperience, the whiskey, or both that
ensures I am terrible at this game. But even the good players drink.
There are no losers here.

With every round, Garrett leans in a little closer, his hands
linger on my arm a little longer, his breath a little hotter on my ear.
Even over the whiskey and spilled beer, I can smell his intoxicating
scent—burning coal and hot steel, courtesy of his trade as the
village blacksmith. He's saying something but I'm consumed with
the thought of burying my nose in the overly-defined muscles that
are on full display in his thin white shirt.

Garrett's fingers inch dangerously close to my inner thigh but
he remains a perfect gentleman. Another song from the fiddler,
another round of the game, another glass of rot-gut whiskey, and
before I know it, I no longer care that we're in a tavern full of
people. I want nothing more than to feel the weight of his hands
on the rest of my body.

I move closer, readying myself to ask him to do just that, when
the fiddler strikes up a song that sends the rest of our table jolting
to the dance floor.

Shouts ring out at the sound of another local favorite. One of
Garrett's friends is pulling him by the arm, urging him up from his
seat to join the others. His hand grabs mine and tugs as he's
yanked further into the crowd.

"Dance with me, Selene!" he calls out.

I follow, eager to feel the warmth of his touch again.

It's a fast-paced jig and I swing playfully from arm to arm
through our group as we turn in circles. When the music stops, my
arms are hooked around Garrett's midsection. My head spins and
he pulls me against his broad chest to steady me.

I close my eyes only for a moment, leaning fully into his
warmth. Rough fingers lift my chin, angling it slightly. I rise up on

84

my toes, preparing my mouth for what's sure to be a crushing kiss. But as his thick beard scrapes against my cheek, I freeze. I pull back from him slightly, opening my eyes to find a pair of deep brown ones staring back at me instead of the gray ones I crave.

My stomach lurches as a commanding voice resounds throughout the tavern. "Get your fucking hands off of her."

Garrett never breaks eye contact with me as he speaks. "You don't speak for the lady."

"Did I stutter?" The sharp sound of a steel blade leaving its scabbard echoes through the now quiet room. "Get your fucking hands off of her right now or I'll cut them off."

Garrett drops my chin, squaring his shoulders and turning nose-to-nose with the Captain of Corinth.

"What did you say to me?" the blacksmith challenges.

Fuck.

This night is not going at all like I had hoped. I need to say something to defuse this, but I can't think straight. This is simultaneously the most frustrating and arousing thing that has ever happened to me. I should be fuming that grown men are about to duel over me, but I can't stop picturing what it might feel like to be caught between the two of them.

Fucking whiskey.

"That's enough of that!" Mae's voice cuts sharply through the room. "Go home, Garrett. And you two," she points at both me and the captain, "upstairs before I turn you both out."

The entire tavern is holding a collective breath to see what will happen next. Garrett takes a long look at me before reluctantly deciding I'm not worth the fight.

"Only for you, Mae."

The captain doesn't resheath his blade until the blacksmith leaves the tavern, his friends going with him to ensure the situation doesn't escalate. Once the door swings closed, the atmosphere immediately lightens, the fiddler restarting his song and the patrons resuming their conversations.

Captain Murphy shoots me a menacing glare that makes my blood boil before stomping up the stairs. I run to catch up, never one to back down from a fight, especially with this much whiskey running through me.

"What the hell was that?" I snap as I furiously climb the stairs after him. "I don't need you to protect me."

"Clearly you do." His voice is accusatory and angry in a way he has no right to be.

"He wasn't going to murder me, he was going to—"

Murphy turns abruptly, and I don't have time to stop before plowing into his granite chest. I can feel his eyes glaring down at me and I meet them with instant regret. He grabs my arm pulling me towards him, the whiskey serving as an accelerant on the growing fire that threatens to burn us both.

"I know good and well what you were going to let him do to you." His hold on my arm tightens, mimicking the muscle along his jaw as he restrains himself. "Godsdammit, woman. Did you want me to kill him?"

"I didn't think you'd notice. You looked pretty preoccupied from where I was sitting."

Murphy's head cocks to the side, strands of black hair falling across his brow. He drops my arm and takes a step backwards, letting his gray eyes survey me from head to toe. Pearly white teeth snag on his bottom lip as his gaze wanders back to my face.

"You really can pull off every shade of green, can't you?"

"Fuck you!" I call out, turning towards my room with every intention of putting distance between us.

"You want to."

His words stop me in my tracks, my mouth hanging agape. I know my audacity is fueled by whiskey tonight, but I'm not sure where he's getting his.

I turn back to find Captain Murphy walking towards me at full speed. I backpedal, my back smacking the wall seconds before his forearms move to bracket my head, holding me in place.

"Let me go," I protest half-heartedly.

Wow, real convincing, Ivy.

"I will," he promises. A soothing bolt of magic washes over me urging me to trust him. His lips brush against the shell of my ear as he speaks. "As soon as you admit that it wasn't the blacksmith you really wanted to fuck tonight."

The feel of his body pressed against mine overwhelms all of my senses, his words stoking the embers of my magic and my lust back to life. I fight the urge to expose my neck to the heat of his breath, futility demanding the molten heat in my core to steel.

I cannot melt into him.

"You think awfully highly of yourself, Captain." I force the words past my lips. Words that neither confirm nor deny his damning accusation.

He stiffens and my magic shudders as a ripple of emotions cascade through me. Waves of frustration mingled with a deep longing and capped with an indescribable desperation. Emotions that I know don't fully belong to me. He shifts slightly, angling my head upward until our eyes meet.

"Why do you refuse to say my name?"

"Why does it matter?" My whispered words are barely audible over the hammering of my heart in the empty hallway.

The tattoo, the inexplicable way my power dances around him, his name. They're all omens. Dark signs of our intertwined fate. Saying his name aloud doesn't change that; I know that in my bones. But it feels like accepting it. Like I'm giving up my last chance at fighting whatever waits for me.

Murphy's hands move to cup my cheeks. "The only people who use my name are the people who are important to me. Whether you like it or not, *you* are important to me."

"I'm not ..."

"Don't do that." His demeanor shifts, something akin to pain flashing across his expression. "Don't diminish yourself."

His right thumb traces my cheekbone, leaving a trail of sparks in its wake. Instinctively, I lean into his hand, sealing my fate without a thought in my head besides the otherworldly call of his touch.

"Look me in the eyes and tell me that you don't feel that. Tell me that you're not ... that *we're* not important ... that we're not connected. And don't fucking lie to me, Ivy."

My stomach clenches at the sound of my name on his lips. The very world feels as if it's spinning on an unnatural axis. I swallow the thick knot in my throat, fighting back the warring feelings within me.

"The only thing *we* are is death."

My whispered confession burns as it claws its way past my lips. Giving voice to my premonitions feels oddly like carving them into a headstone. Proof of our demise that will last for hundreds of years after the Dark God has claimed our damned souls.

"Death and I are well acquainted." The captain's voice is just as pained. Unspeakable memories must be playing on an infinite loop behind the silver storm that churns in his irises. His hand slides to grasp the nape of my neck, hauling me closer to him until his nose rests atop mine. "I'm not afraid of shadows."

"What about poison?"

A low chuckle shakes his chest as a sly smile forms across his too close lips. "I've waited a long time to be poisoned by you, Ivy."

What little hold I had on my stability is completely lost at his words, his grasp the only thing keeping me upright. I struggle to breathe, to form a single thought other than his name. I clench my fists hard, nails digging into my palms in a futile attempt to restrain myself from falling completely into whatever spell he's cast over me.

I don't want to think—not about who he is, who I am, or the doom that fate has in store. I just want to fall senselessly, passionately into the neverending chasm that awaits us.

"Cal."

His name is barely above a whisper, but his eyes open instantly at the sound. Murphy's demeanor shifts from longing to something akin to pain before settling on resignation. His hand slides down the column of my throat before dropping to his side, a chill racing down my skin at the loss of his touch.

The moment, once far too intimate, is now gone entirely.

"Go to bed, Ivy. You're drunk."

He's right. I've consumed too much whiskey tonight to be trusted to make decisions, but that is not what intoxicates me now. That honor belongs solely to the magic coursing through my body at lightning speed urging me closer and closer to him.

"Don't," I say.

Don't what? Don't go? Don't do this? Don't say these things to me?

Even I don't know what I'm asking.

Cal runs his hand through his onyx hair. Every muscle drawn taut as he steps backwards towards his rat-infested broom closet.

"When you kiss me, princess, it won't be because you're drunk. It will be because you can't imagine living one more second of your life without knowing how I taste."

Cal stalks into his room, slamming the door closed behind him. And once again, I'm left standing in the empty hallway cold, gaping, and struggling to catch my breath.

CHAPTER 11

T here is a horrible pounding in my head that grows louder by the minute. Begrudgingly, I open one eye just slightly enough to find the room awash in sunlight. It's too bright, so I throw the covers up over my head until I'm cocooned in darkness again. But the pounding doesn't stop.

There's a vial of dried feverfew somewhere in my pack, along with other medicinal herbs and tonics. If I can just make it there. With a groan, I muster enough strength to push myself up into a sitting position.

The door bursts open suddenly, and I barely have time to cover my exposed chest before Captain Murphy is standing in my bedroom. There's a brief flash of concern in his gray eyes before they're overtaken with anger. His gaze scours the room looking for … what exactly is he looking for?

OH. Does he think there's someone else in here?

It's only at this realization that the events of last night emerge from the whiskey-induced haze. The memory of his sword, his whispered words, and the *almost* kiss—all of it barrels into me so quickly that I sink back down under the covers before he can notice the red flush that now colors my face.

"It's past dawn." There's a light thud on the small bedside table, the sound of something being deposited with haste, that causes me to sink further down into the bed. "I told you. I don't slow down for hangovers, princess."

"Can I at least have a bath first?"

I can practically feel his eyes boring into me despite the blankets over my head. "Hurry."

It's only when the door shuts and I'm sure that the captain is gone that I drag myself out of bed. A small glass of water sits on the bedside table next to a vial of dried feverfew, gifts from Cal.

I suck in an unsteady breath as I repeat his name over and over again in my head. The name that I couldn't bring myself to utter before. The name that will likely be my doom.

The fate-filled dreams didn't haunt me last night, and I choose to believe it's because of the sheer volume of alcohol that I consumed and no other reason.

Absolutely no other reason.

The pounding starts again and this time it is actually my head and not my escort. I chew the herb and wash it down with the water before I start the arduous process of packing up the clothes that I scattered across the room last night in my drunken stupor.

It takes longer than it should thanks to the liquid sloshing around in my empty stomach, but when I finally manage to stumble down the hall to the bathing chamber, I'm instantly greeted by a roaring fire under the cast iron tub. The clean water inside is gloriously scalding.

Another godsdamned gift.

Whatever this is between us is starting to feel alarmingly uneven—something I need to rectify immediately.

I audibly groan as I slip underneath the hot water. Maybe I can scald off my shame and the memory of the cocky bastard's words.

"When you kiss me..." not if, when.

We're standing on the edge of a cliff now, and as much as I would like to blame him for the shove towards the drop-off, it's as much my doing as his. This connection is a death knell, and we lost any chance of fighting it the moment I said his name and accepted our fate. The fire that burns between us guarantees a blood sport with no winners left standing in the end.

I can fight a lot of things, but can I really fight destiny? Right now I need to focus more on fighting this hellacious hangover.

We'll cross into the Ruby Region today, with its major city only a few days further. While it may be our closest neighbor, its governor is no fan of mine. For that reason, the emerald cloak stays safely tucked away in my pack. I'll wear the browns of the common folk to avoid drawing any additional attention to us, though I'm certain the Captain of Corinth will be recognizable no matter what color he wears. My only hope is that word of his traveling companion hasn't spread all the way to Governor Rollins yet.

I try my best to indulge in one last cup of coffee before leaving the inn, but I end up vomiting both it and the whiskey I consumed last night outside the stable.

The ride is more treacherous than I anticipated. There is entirely too much alcohol still in my system and it sloshes around with my horse's every step. Cal doesn't appear to be particularly happy about our late departure, though he never says anything about it. He never says anything at all, actually.

When he finally decides to put me out of my misery and let me off of this damned horse, I nearly fall to my knees in relief.

There's a small stream nearby, the cold water instantly soothing me as I splash it on my face. I lay down on the bank for a moment and try to soak up a tiny amount of warmth from the sun.

The weather this late in the winter vacillates between warm and downright cold. Spring may be right around the corner but you can never count out a snowfall before the equinox. Today is mild and I close my eyes to relish in it. A shadow blocks out the sun and I groan at the loss of the warmth.

"We need to keep moving, princess."

I pop open an eye and see him standing over me with a hand outstretched. Reluctantly, I take it and let him pull me up. He drops my hand the second my feet are under me.

"We need to talk about last night," I demand. Better to get this over with now.

"There's nothing to talk about."

"There's plenty to talk about!" I call after him as he strides over to his horse. "You forced me into something I was not ready for."

Cal turns abruptly towards me, scowling at my implication. "I didn't force you into anything. Maybe you don't remember—"

"That's not what I meant," I interrupt, pinching the bridge of my nose.

This isn't off to a good start and I am in no condition to go into all the reasons that I didn't want to say his name. Rehashing them won't turn back time anyway. My grave is already dug. Time to lie in it.

Ungracefully, I mount my mare, trying not to upset my stomach again.

"The gods have decided that we're … *something*. I don't know what that is and the only way I'm ever going to make sense of this is if we talk. So unless you want me to spend the rest of our journey talking about the social injustices in Corinth, you should probably answer my questions, *Cal*."

I add his name for emotional emphasis and the flare of his nostrils tells me that my arrow hit its intended mark.

"What do you want to know, *Ivy*?"

There it is again. The fluttering of my magic like the beating wings of an insect, the maddening sensation that happens when he says my name.

"How about we start with the basics?"

"I'll make you a deal. I will answer one question every half hour until we stop for the evening." There's a sparkle in his gray eyes, another glimpse of his hidden, playful side.

"And how many questions will that be?" I ask.

"Four, but you lose a question every time we have to stop for you to vomit."

I roll my eyes. "That hardly seems fair. I can't avoid that."

"Then you should probably avoid whiskey," he says flatly.

"If only you'd given me that advice *before* I drank an entire bottle of what was most likely the worst liquor in all of Corinth," I joke, shuddering at the memory of the first few sips of the burning swill.

"Ah, but then I wouldn't have had the pleasure of watching you turn green."

Nausea rolls again in my gut at the reminder. But truth be told, that verdant hue of unwarranted jealousy was pretty damn evident on both of us.

"I'll take your deal," I say, changing the subject, spurring my horse towards the road. "How old are you?"

"Twenty-eight," he answers matter-of-factly.

"Awfully young to have such a powerful reputation, great *Captain of Corinth*."

"I could say the same for you, *Poison Ivy*."

I've been called that name hundreds of times, but it feels like a punch in the gut to hear it from his lips now. My magic recoils at the sound, stinging as it hides deep within me. A silent moment lingers between us and I can't help but wonder if maybe he hates it too.

Does our strange connection make his nickname hurt more when I say it? Does he even know just how connected we truly are?

"Are you going to ask anything about me?" I ask.

"I already know everything about you."

"Stalker," I tease.

"Maybe," he teases back. "Or maybe I'm a soldier well-briefed on his assignment."

Despite his tone, there's a harsh truth to his words that stings in a way I didn't expect. A stark reminder of what this really is, stripped bare of alliances predestined by gods. He visibly winces before collecting himself, searching for words to soften the growing tension.

"You're not an assignment. You're—"

"I wasn't given enough notice to study up on you, Captain," I interrupt. "So I'm afraid you'll have to start from the beginning."

I don't need whatever backpedaling he's attempting. This is an assignment—a forced arrangement for the both of us. I shouldn't care how his words make my magic retreat or my stomach sink, and I'm not going to start now.

"There are very few people who know anything about me, princess. I doubt you would have found out anything, even if you had notice I would be escorting you, at least not anything with any truth to it."

I'm tempted to ask about the legends, about the heinous acts he supposedly committed to earn his promotion to captain, but I know all too well how rumors grow to take on a life of their own. And I'm not sure I want to know yet if there's any truth to his.

One day I'll have the stomach to ask; I have to, but today is not that day.

"I heard that you were a broody asshole, which so far seems to be true."

Cal lets out a deep belly laugh that catches me so off guard that I nearly fall off my horse. "If I didn't know better, I'd say you talked to my brother."

There it is, the tiniest bit of trust, the start to discovering exactly who the captain is and how I can use him.

"You have a brother?" I ask cautiously.

"Nice try, but it's not time for another question. I believe you have another ... twenty-six minutes or so."

"There you go, further cementing my opinion."

A lie. If anything, I respect his hesitation to withhold information from me. I wouldn't trust his instincts if he didn't. And I have to trust him if I have any hope of keeping Lord General Marks off the throne.

I cannot let whatever this is brewing between us keep me from what I must do: *use him*.

CHAPTER 12

We don't finish our game of questions thanks to my inability to hold onto the contents of my stomach. When we finally stop to make camp, I'm relegated to firewood duty again in hopes that I can walk off the last of the hangover that might finally be leaving my body.

Branches litter the outskirts of the clearing, likely courtesy of the storm from two nights ago, and my arms are quickly full of wood that will burn well into the night.

A litany of chatter echoes through the trees from the direction of where I left Cal to set up our camp. Three distinct voices but only one that I recognize.

I peer around the trunk of a large oak tree and find two men talking to the captain, tension evident between them.

"You don't think I know that?" The captain runs his fingers frustratedly through his dark hair, his voice nearly a growl.

Silently, I set the firewood down, choosing to fill my hands with the daggers sheathed at my thighs instead of logs. I could throw the wood but it wouldn't be nearly as deadly. These men don't appear to be a threat to Cal, but they very well could be to me.

I step around the tree, fists wrapped tightly around the hilts of my sharpest daggers and eyes locked on the strangers. Cal's head whips in my direction, sensing me before I'm clearly in view. The men, startled by his sudden movement, draw their own daggers as they follow his gaze.

"Put your blades away, princess," Cal says calmly, exposing his palms in an act of submission.

"As soon as they put away theirs." I look cautiously between the two men standing on either side of the captain. They're dressed in plain brown clothes, no colors of allegiance on public display.

"You heard her, boys," Cal says with a smile. "I'm not stitching anyone up before dinner."

"She really is as vicious as they say," the man on Cal's left, the larger of the two, says, sheathing his dagger.

"Forgive my brother's clear lack of manners and allow me to introduce us." The other man sheaths his blade and steps forward with a sweeping bow, his blonde hair falling over his face. "The name's Theo, my lady."

He looks up at me, hazel eyes sparkling in the dimming light as the corners of his mouth turn up in a charming smile.

Brothers.

There's no familial resemblance between the men and Cal. Nothing that would indicate that the two of them are closely related to the captain. Maybe that's what kept the knowledge of their existence secret from the Corinthian rumor mill.

A large hand swats Theo across the back of the head, causing him to lose his balance and stumble slightly to the left.

"Shameless flirt," the owner of the hand grumbles.

I instinctively grip the handles of my daggers tighter and hold my chin high as the large man walks towards me. The man sweeps his amber gaze over the length of me and I bite back the scathing remark rising in me. His body is nearly a copy of Cal, the same broad chest and honed muscles that are no doubt from a lifetime of military training, but his face is distinctly different.

"Henry," he says, nodding approvingly with his hand outstretched.

I hold my ground, making no move to lower my blades. The corner of his lips turn up on one side and I get the feeling that I just passed some sort of test.

"My brothers will be camping with us tonight, Ivy." Cal's voice cuts across the clearing but my eyes are still locked in Henry's unrelenting stare. "Oh for the gods' sake. Henry, carry that damn firewood over here before she cuts you."

Henry scoffs as he walks to the firewood pile, never turning his back to me. "I'd like to see her try."

If it's a show he wants, it's a show he'll get. I snarl, baring my teeth at him as he walks by. Theo falls to his knees laughing, his arms wrapping around his midsection in exaggeration.

"The rumors definitely undersold you, my lady," he jokes through heaving laughs.

"Stop calling me that."

"Stop calling her that."

Cal and I say in unison.

Theo pauses his laughing long enough to share a look with Henry before erupting into laughter again.

"I seem to have stumbled into some sort of joke that I'm not privy to." Sheathing my daggers at my side, I make my way toward the tent to fetch my canteen.

Cal sighs loudly, dragging his hands through his already tousled hair. "I'm going to try to catch some dinner. Try not to kill each other while I'm gone. Please."

Exasperation is evident in his added plea. I'm not sure who he's more worried about, his brothers or me.

"No need, Cal. I've got dinner right here." Theo pulls a brown wineskin from his rucksack, holding it out in my direction. "Care for a drink, darling?"

"Don't call me that either."

"Lay off her, Theo. Ivy hit the bottle a little too hard last night, " Cal interjects. "I don't think she'll be drinking for a while."

Never one to back down from a challenge, I take the wineskin from Theo, pulling the cork out by my teeth before taking a long swig. My defiant eyes never leave the captain's as the sweet liquid barrels down my throat, my magic thrumming to life as the barest hint of a smile tugs at his lip.

Another chuckle cuts the tension, this time from Henry. "We're definitely going to need that dinner, brother."

While Cal tries to catch something large enough to feed four mouths, Henry carefully constructs a fire. Logs meticulously stacked in a woven pattern guaranteed to burn through the night. Theo, clearly the more extroverted of the brothers, downs a truly impressive amount of wine while he attempts multiple times to engage in conversation with me.

"I hope we didn't get off on the wrong foot." Theo takes another swig before offering it to me. "Meeting someone at knife-point isn't usually how good relationships start."

"The daggers weren't personal," I say, taking the wineskin from him. "A woman should never walk into a circle of strange men unarmed."

A half-smile quirks up on Henry's face. He slides something from his pocket as he settles against the trunk of a nearby tree. The polished blade of a small knife glints in the firelight. There's a small chunk of wood in his hand that is just beginning to take an odd humanoid shape. Perhaps an effigy to the gods or the figure of a woman.

"Smart," Henry says. "... but you have nothing to fear. Any friend of our brother's is safe with us."

My stomach clenches at the way Henry says the word 'friend'.

Theo clears his throat and exchanges a pointed look with his brother across the flames. There is definitely something they're not telling me.

"And compulsory travel companions? Are they safe as well, or should I pull out my blades again?" I provoke.

The brothers exchange another glance, quicker this time. It's the younger brother who answers me.

"Our brother can be a bit of an acquired taste. But once you get to know him—"

"I doubt that will happen." I sigh, laying it on thick in hopes that his brothers' lips will be looser than Cal's. "Your dear brother has told me next to nothing about himself. I didn't even know his name until two days ago."

Henry pauses his sharpening briefly, waiting to see if I'll press on. But I have nothing else to share.

What am I supposed to say? It's not like I know anything of substance about Cal. Hells, I only learned his age and that he had a brother a few hours ago. It's not like he confessed that he's waited a lifetime to be poisoned by me or anything ... that would be ridiculous.

No, if I want to make any progress on learning Cal's secrets, I need to focus on getting Theo to unwittingly divulge them. If a life in politics has taught me anything, the best way to keep people talking and covertly extract information is to ask them about themselves.

"Are you two in the military as well?"

"I'm wounded that you haven't heard of the famed Captain of Corinth's prized lieutenants," Theo jokes, clutching his chest. "We're prettier than him. You think they'd write songs about us instead."

"They did write a song about you, brother. It's called '*The Lieutenant Who Can't Keep His Pants On.*'" Henry chucks a small rock that Theo barely dodges before it smacks the tree behind his head.

"You'd know all about songs, wouldn't you brother? Tell me, did Marianne sing you to sleep after she was done *playing your flute.*"

Theo takes a small instrument from his bag and tosses it towards the fire. Henry, murderous rage filling his eyes, scrambles to catch it before the flames claim the silver flute.

"Marianne?" Cal approaches the fire holding two dead rabbits by their ears. "I thought you ended things with Marianne, Henry?"

"He did." Theo takes another drink from the wineskin. "And then he un-ended things. What was it your letter said, brother? *All the sapphires in Corinth couldn't compare to the sparkling blue of your eyes.*"

Henry forcefully chucks another rock at Theo with a concentrated effort to hit him. I jump to my feet, barely dodging the rock as it ricochets off the younger brother's head.

Marianne? Is Cal's brother in love with the twin sister to the heir of the Sapphire Region? There's no way her father or brother are okay with her love affair with one of Marks' lieutenants—not after what the Lord General did to their region.

The men seemed primed, spun up from Theo's reckless words and ready to fight. When anger rises, lips tend to loosen. And if they think I'm not around, perhaps they'll spill more than they intended.

"I'm going to go wash up for dinner," I say, excusing myself. "I think it's my turn to ask you not to kill each other while I'm gone."

I'm just beyond the tree line when Henry's voice echoes through the clearing. "Touch my shit and I'll break your fucking nose."

"I'll quit touching your shit when you quit playing that gods-damned flute every night while I'm trying to sleep." Theo snaps back, squaring up to his older brother.

"That's enough, Theo." Cal's voice is commanding.

"I should have known you'd side with him. You're no better than he is," the youngest lieutenant scoffs.

"What is that supposed to mean?" Cal snaps.

"You know good and well what it means," Theo says. "How many years have you been walking around with that godsdamned tattoo on your—"

"Enough!" Henry's booming voice cuts off his brother. "You know what's at stake here, Theo. Don't risk it all because you want to play the cocky, playboy brother in front of a pretty lady."

The strange pulling sensation in my gut returns. I want to stay, to hear the rest of whatever anger-fueled words may tumble from their lips, but its beckoning call is too strong to resist. Blindly, I leave the men to their conversation and follow it deeper into the forest.

The chilly water running over the rocks in the small brook that cuts across my path is crystal clear. My fingers trail through it, my skin numb to the biting cold temperature. My mind is wholly fixated on the mention of Cal's tattoo—the large primordial sea beast swimming through cresting waves, the inky image that appeared to dance across his chiseled muscles, the tail that dipped dangerously low below his towel. Sharp pain radiates from the tips of my fingers, a mixture of cold and magic snapping me back to reality.

Focus, Ivy.

Unlike me, Cal is likely not the sole keeper of his secret. The story of his encounter with the sea serpent was probably shared over a meal or around the hearth—things normal families do when discussing the events of their day.

Nothing like my own upbringing.

I was loved in the ways it mattered, but I was never nurtured. Not doted upon, but rather trained to take on a world that was never designed to accept me. We are not a family that shares secrets, because secrets are weaknesses and weaknesses can be exploited. I never told my father about the sea beast, the ever growing magic in my veins, or the nightmares that plague me.

The more vivid my dreams get, the more I wonder if I made a mistake. It's too late to contemplate what kind of life I could have had if I had told my father. I know in the depths of my soul that I'll meet Death before I see him again.

But what if the fellowship I've always craved is within reach in my final days? The more time I spend around Cal, the more certain I am that his tattoo is a sign of the magic he has yet to openly admit he possesses. An inked hint reserved only for those in on the ancient secret.

My own tattoo tingles between my shoulder blades at the thought. The dark rendering of the godsbane bloom sears the place the sea beast touched my skin with a furious flare.

Giving in to the call of magic, I sink my fingers into the ground and let my power out to play. Small dark purple flowers pop up in a cluster along the bank. If we get a heavy rain soon and this stream floods, they'll die. But they'll live beautifully until then, thriving in the wintery nip of the early spring air.

There's a beauty in the fragility of life. A precarious, divinely-crafted balance between the realms of the living and the dead. The space where our souls are allowed to trod for the briefest moments in time. The world existed before us, and the world will go on without us.

Father used to tell me that it's what we do with those fleeting moments in between that matters. And that's the force that spurs me. The one that beckons me to speak when I want to keep silent. The one that pushes me onward when I wish to stop. The one that drives me forward to face my enemies again when I'd rather stay home. The reason that I'm on this road headed straight into the waiting arms of Death.

The predestined story of the princess and the captain is sickeningly poetic. The poisonous woman and the murderous man, inexplicably linked and impossibly intertwined.

I pluck a newly grown bloom from its stem, closing my fist around it and letting my magic decay it. When my fingers open, only powdery dust remains. Death where beauty once stood.

Hours pass silently by as I repeat the same process. Growing things only to kill them, giving into the dark and wasting magic that could be spent bettering the world if I wasn't such a coward.

The moon is high overhead when I finally head back to camp, leaving only a few poisonous little creations alive in the woods to face the cruel world alone.

CHAPTER 13

The crackling of the fire and the low snores from Theo and Henry are the only sounds in the quiet campsite. A familiar figure sits in the shadows, his broad back resting against the trunk of a tree and a tan forearm draping lazily across his elevated knee.

On the surface, Cal is a picture of casual ease, but I sense a tension in him. Something that simmers under the surface, wafting off of his statuesque body and chilling me.

"You missed dinner." There's a hint of sharpness in his words. "I saved you a plate."

He flicks his fingers towards a plate resting beside the fire. It's not close enough to further cook the meat but it's close enough to keep it warm in the chilly night air. An extra kindness that he didn't have to extend but chose to. Another tally mark on the scoreboard in his favor.

"You don't have to be nice to me," I say flatly.

I'm familiar with people being polite to my face and sneering the second I'm out of view, but I don't know what to do with unexplainable niceties and mysterious motives.

"You're important to me. This is what people do when they give a shit about you, princess."

"See, that's the part I can't figure out, " I start. Maybe if I push him he will finally confess what he is, finally tell me about the magic I know he possesses. "Why exactly do you give a shit about me? Why did you say what you said last night? Make it make sense."

"It will," he says, rising to his feet. "In time."

"When? When you finally deem me worthy of knowing the true depths of who we're up against?" I scoff.

"I told you that I would tell you, and I will ... in time."

"And I'm just, what, supposed to trust that? You're asking me to blindly trust that your loyalty is truly with me and not your warlord, based on some vague story about protecting someone you love and nothing else. What good is the word of a stranger?"

Cal stares at me with a growing intensity as my questions linger in the night air. Flames dance in his gray eyes as he closes the distance between us. My magic jumps frantically at his proximity, subdued only by the stubborn anger that rages within me.

"I will never lie to you." He grabs my arm, hauling my heaving chest to his. "And we both know we're more than strangers."

I pull away from him, eager to put the only thing that can calm my magic between us: distance. Cal's forceful grip tightens, stopping me in my tracks.

"Let me go," I demand through clenched teeth.

"Look at me," he says, yanking my arm. "Ivy, look at me."

My traitorous heart does somersaults at the possessive way my name rolls off his tongue. A chilly breeze stirs around us, shadows dancing in the corners of my vision. I whip my head towards him, fire burning in my eyes as I meet his.

"You can deny it all you want, but denial can't change destiny. I'll tell you everything ... just as soon as you decide you're done fighting the inevitable."

"Fuck you," I seethe, wrenching my arm from his grasp.

"Whenever you want, princess," Cal says with a chuckle as he steps back into the shadows. "Just say the word."

The first rays of light dance across the waves that lap gently against the port's seawalls. Horses neigh and tradespeople shout as day breaks in the capital city. I peer over the large crates that block me from view of the palace guards, the men dressed in Corinthian gray and gold that pace in front of the iron gates. Shadows surround me, further shrouding my black-clad body until the clock tower strikes six o'clock. Magic blazes through my body, sending me into full alert.

Something is wrong.

The tugging in my gut urges me to the water's edge. I start to creep but the tug becomes a sharp pull, forcing me to the dock's edge at breakneck speed. The end of the wooden plank is approaching quickly, but my feet don't stop their hurried sprint.

A guttural scream pierces the air as my body surges into the icy ocean below. I call to my magic and summon vine after vine in a fruitless attempt to grab hold to the edge of the dock before I'm sucked into the watery depths.

Further I fall, much further than should be possible. Bloody skin, now exposed through deep cuts in my pants, stings in the salty water. Desperately, I swim upwards, silently begging whatever god will listen to grant me breath again. My head breaks the surface only for a moment before my eyes latch onto the black beast cresting in the waves ahead of me. A dark swish between the white caps floods my system with a panic so deep that my limbs no longer work.

Another primal scream breaks my lips, but it's not for me. Something inside me in the core of my being rips. My very soul splintered into two. One name forces its way into my head, my heart, and my throat before the world goes black.

Cal.

The night air rushes back into my lungs in heaving gasps. It's too damn stuffy here. Using the edge of the blanket, I wipe the sweat from my slicked brow as I try and fail to steady my racing heart. There's no moonlight in the tent to help me mark the passage of time, no indication if I've slept long enough that the brothers have changed watch shifts. But I'm willing to risk another encounter with Cal for the cool, crispness of the night air.

"You okay?" Henry's deep voice carries low across the flames as I take an unsteady seat on the fallen log in front of the campfire.

"Just cold," I lie.

A flash of something silver catches my eye. Marianne's flute rests in the lieutenant's hand, a soft polishing cloth clutched in the other. The tenderness of the act stark against the large calluses that decorate his palms. Hands capable of both delicate and deadly things.

A common familial trait, it would seem.

I want to ask about the flute, about the should-have-been

Sapphire heir. It's been years since she was permitted to attend a summit. A decade since all the heirs and spares to each region's ruling families congregated in hopes we might naturally form alliances or proposals while our parents decided the future of Corinth.

A decade since everything changed.

"We're soldiers, Ivy. I've seen more than my share of men who are haunted by their dreams." Henry's eyes never leave the instrument in his hand but see into my soul all the same.

"What about premonitions? Seen many men haunted by those?"

"Just one."

He doesn't elaborate. He doesn't have to. The implication isn't subtle, it's crystal clear. Premonitions of death must be a side effect of encounters with the dark creature of the deep. Marked by the sea beast and forever unable to get a good night's sleep again.

We fall into a revered silence, neither acknowledging the stop in conversation. It's only a matter of time before Cal finds out about my dreams, if he doesn't already suspect. And I guess it was only a matter of time before I discovered his, too. Traveling in close proximity to someone doesn't exactly afford anyone a lot of privacy. At least this saves us from what was sure to be an uncomfortable conversation.

"Oh, by the way, Captain, we're both going to die at the end of this journey."

"Spectacular. Let's get going, then."

My eyes roll as far back in my head as humanly possible at the thought.

Inevitable. That's what Cal said we were. Just like death, hunger, or taxes. All things that catch up with you eventually.

"He's not your enemy." Henry's voice startles me back into the moment, his amber eyes now fixed attentively on me.

"He's Marks' man. You're all Marks' men."

"We are Cal's men. And my brother's position is one of necessity, not of choice. Your paths have been tied together for longer than you know. Yes, he's stubborn and infuriating at times, but he's honest and loyal to those who deserve it. He will lay down his life to raise you up and ask nothing in return. But I am not my brother … I will ask the one thing that has never crossed his mind."

Henry stands and slides the silver flute into his back pocket before turning his fiery gaze back to mine. "Do you deserve it?"

I swallow the thick knot that lodges in my throat. My mind urges me to yell at him. I don't even know Cal, and yet I have to answer if I deserve his fealty!

But that's not entirely true, is it?

Cal's right, we aren't strangers. I may not deserve the captain's loyalty but my cause does. We are unlikely allies tethered by a common goal and a fate that neither of us chose.

"A piece of unsolicited advice, Ivy. Acceptance isn't surrender. Destiny may not be a choice, but happiness is."

The loud braying of horses wakes me from my dreamless sleep. Early morning light casts the inside of the tent in a warm greenish hue, a delicious smell wafting through the flaps of the tent door. Throwing my boots on quickly, I step out to the sight of Cal cooking something round and white in the small frying pan.

Eggs.

My mouth salivates at the smell, a small moan escaping my lips that causes all three men to stop what they're doing and stare at me.

"It's been a while since you've gotten that kind of reaction from a woman, huh brother?" Theo winks at me, a devilish smirk tugging at the corner of his mouth.

My own mimics his when I notice Henry walking up behind him, hand outstretched ready to thwop his brother over the head.

"Hungry, princess?" Cal's voice pulls my attention just before an audible grunt of pain sounds off to my right, neither of us paying any attention to the physical reprimand his brother just received.

"Starving, actually." As if that wasn't painfully obvious to everyone by my involuntary reaction.

Cal divides the small eggs between the four tin plates and begins passing them around the fire. Judging by the size, I'm guessing that someone stumbled across a quail's nest this morning. I use the tines of my fork to pop the yolk, allowing the thick yellow liquid to run over the perfectly cooked whites. One bite and I'm barely able to keep from moaning again.

"Oh my gods," I manage to say with a full mouth.

"If she likes your eggs that much, she's going to lose her mind over your venison stew," Theo laughs. "It's truly a work of culinary magic, Ivy."

I look up from my plate to find Henry staring, a dark brow quirked up in a knowing assessment. He believes there's a world where I could have Cal's stew, a world where the four of us share meals over abundant tables instead of sparse campfires. But despite what he may think, that world doesn't exist, at least not in our realm.

There's an unspoken heaviness that grows with each passing minute, clearly signaling that the time for our traveling parties to split up is fast approaching.

When Theo and Henry clear the plates and begin the process of saddling the horses, I excuse myself to the woods to relieve my aching bladder, giving the men plenty of time to say their good-byes in private. All traces of our stop in this clearing are gone when I return.

"Well, darling, I believe this is where we part ways." Theo slings his arm casually across my shoulders, leaning in to mock-whisper in my ear. "Unless you'd rather come with me."

"I'm afraid Amale beckons, *darling*," I mock. "Your Lord General has a date with my particular brand of poison. Wouldn't want to delay that, would we?"

A viciously handsome smile blooms across Theo's face as he steps away to face me. "Gods, I like you."

"Leave her alone, Theo." Henry walks up to his brother's side and extends his hand to me. "It really was a pleasure to meet you, Ivy."

Unlike the last time he extended his hand to me, I take it. "Same to you, Henry. Where do your travels take you?"

There's a slight hesitation, a quick tense of his jaw, there one second and gone the next, before he replies. "The Emerald Region, actually."

"Oh." I try to stifle the surprise in my voice as I ask the question I'm not sure I want to know the answer to. "What for?"

"They've got cargo to secure and a ship to catch," Cal answers.

Ships out of the Bay of Jewels are mostly bound for the island nations or the Abalone Inlet in the Sapphire Region. Will one take Henry to see Marianne? Will the flute he holds so longingly be replaced with his lover instead? Has he ever given her the same advice about happiness and acceptance?

"Well, if you find yourself in need of some culinary magic or gossip as rich as your brother's stew, pop into The Royal Jewel. My friend Miles practically lives there. He'll show you a good time."

"Yes, please do check in on ... *Miles*," Cal grumbles as he walks his brothers to their horses before he embraces each of them. His hug with Henry is firm and knowing, but his hug with Theo is a playful display of their dynamic.

When he walks back to my side, Cal extends his hand to help me onto my caramel-colored mare. Magic races up my arm from the spot where our fingers graze as I take them, Henry's words echoing in my mind as we mount.

Acceptance isn't surrender.

But it sure does feel like it from where I'm standing.

CHAPTER 14

T he tree cover in this part of the Godswood is sparse and the unrelenting sun has me regretting the layers I chose to wear this morning. I stash my brown cloak and gloves in my saddlebag when we stop before quickly emptying my canteen, the cool water doing little to calm the heat within me.

My magic has been restless all morning, something about being in the presence of another magic wielder, even one that has yet to admit his powers, amplifies it beyond its normal annoyance. Gods help us if this is how it's going to behave all the way to Amale.

Cal's black hair sticks to his sweat-soaked forehead as he drains the last dregs of his own canteen before reaching for mine.

"I'm going to refill these and then we can get back on the road." The captain looks almost worried as he does a visual sweep of the area. "Stretch your legs but don't wander far. I have an uneasy feeling."

"In that case, I better take this," I say, pulling the broadsword from its holster tied to my horse's saddle. "You know, in case all my other blades aren't enough."

"Yeah, yeah, the princess who doesn't need protection," he jokes as he walks away. "I got it."

When Cal disappears from the clearing, I let my eager magic guide me off the path. Thorny vines that snake from under the thick trees reignite memories of my nightmares drowning in a bottomless abyss. I've had plenty of ominous dreams, visions filled with dread and doom, but never one that felt like my body was being physically cleaved into two. Now that I know who he is, now that I've said his name, everything feels more real.

Cal thinks I'm in denial. Henry thinks I can't accept what the gods have written. They're both wrong. I know inevitability when it stares me in the face.

Like the wind whooshing through an open window to extinguish a flame, my once fiery magic stills without explanation. I call out to it, but it doesn't answer. Sweat beads down my spine as an utterly powerless feeling kicks my pulse into a frantic pace.

My hand reaches for the hilt of my broadsword as the distinctive snapping of wood sounds behind me. A thick hand covered in coarse white hair presses tightly against my mouth before I can draw the blade, a stubby arm pulling me tight against a hard chest that smells vinegary like spoiled wine with a hint of tobacco.

I can't see the man's clothing, but I know his allegiance all the same. The brown leather bracers on his arms are embossed with a battle axe, the sigil of the War Goddess, Drayca. The emblem, once reserved only for soldiers, has been widely adopted by the band of mercenaries who seek to force belief in the gods by any means necessary. They call themselves Deliverers, and I'm a prominent member of their list of enemies.

"What a delightful little treat," the stranger breathes in my ear, smelling my hair. "Did you really think we'd let you make it all the way to the Ascension Vote, Poison Ivy?"

My stomach roils in disgust as the man lets out a low, sinister laugh and buries his head against my neck. The final straw—his own death sentence, signed. Darkness swirls around the edges of my vision as a cloud moves to cover the blazing sun, casting the clearing in eerie shadows.

Lifting my left foot off the ground, I bury my heel into the man's instep causing him to instinctively lift his now throbbing foot. I take advantage of his loosened grip and momentary imbalance, thrusting my right elbow up and back. A loud crack signals my success as I break both the man's nose and what remains of his hold on me.

"I'll kill you for that, bitch!" He growls and lunges forward, unsheathing the sword hanging at his side.

I spin around, barely dodging the first slice of his blade as I raise my own and attempt to call the earth magic that still doesn't answer. He's slower than me, but still manages to dodge my sword as we begin to move in a clunky, uncoordinated dance.

Another slice, another miss.

If I'm to have any advantage on this man, I need to use my magic. The dark, decaying side of me, the side that exists to balance out the life in my veins, knows he won't be walking away from this encounter anyway.

"You can't run from the gods!" the man yells as he clumsily continues his forward press.

I ditch my sword for a throwing dagger and pivot, stepping back to balance my weight. My foot tangles on the root of a tree— a root I would have sensed if my magic hadn't decided that now was a great time to take a fucking vacation.

Gravity forces me to the ground, my ass landing in a smacking thud before a large, booted foot kicks me square in the chest, knocking the air from my lungs.

"I'm going to take my time ruining you," he snarls, an evil smile spreading across his scarred face as he plants his boot on my throat to hold me in place against the hard ground.

But I'll gladly meet Death before I let him take another breath.

Refusing to sheath the sword, the man struggles to undo his fraying leather belt one-handed. He averts his gaze from me for only a second, but it's more than enough time for me to slide my hands down to the sheaths on my outer thighs. I slip the daggers into my hands, readying my grip. The clouds shift again, concealing my glinting blades in their shadows.

Pants now at his thighs and manhood exposed to the world, my attacker lowers himself to his knees. His focus is so singularly on what he can take from me that he misses the way my arms tense before the steel slides cleanly into his abdomen. He screams, panic overtaking his cruel demeanor as he realizes what I've done.

Using the daggers still buried in his sides as leverage, I twist, sending him toppling to the ground as I scramble to my feet, ripping my blades from his meaty flesh as I move.

"CUNT!" he roars.

Anyone in at least a mile radius now knows where we are, and if he's traveling with a pack of Deliverers, they'll be here soon. My attacker tries to stand, thick red blood pouring from his gaping wounds as falls back to his knees.

Realization crosses his face when he pulls his hand from his side and takes in the color of the blood that coats his pale fingers. Even if I allow him to crawl away from here, he'll die soon. Even a piece of shit chosen by War herself can't live with a punctured bowel.

Using the thick vegetation, I wipe his filthy blood from my blades and sheathe them. The darkness inside me doesn't just want to skewer the bastard. No, I want to make him pay first, regardless of who else might be coming.

I crouch in the shadows, taunting the man with the quick death he now begs for. But I won't grant it to him.

I want him to be afraid.

I want him to beg me to stop.

I want him to feel powerless.

And I'll take down anyone who tries to come to his aid.

My eyes slam shut as power rushes back into my body. I wobble, gulping down air as if I've been deprived of it my entire life until my heart rate steadies. I flatten my palms on the ground and feel the soil rumble slightly under my command.

When my eyes open again, they trail upwards from the toes of two black boots until I meet Cal's onyx-filled gaze. Every muscle in his tanned arm pulls tight as he holds the bleeding man around the neck, his chokehold cutting off what little breath the dying man can manage. Bright red blood trickles from the corners of my attacker's mouth on its journey to join the puddles soaking the ground.

I've seen the menacing flash of black in his eyes before but in this state, with his pupils blown wide and his face contorted in a calm rage, he's barely a man at all. Strange power ripples through me as Cal lets out a low, possessive growl and tightens his grip on the dying man.

"Release him," I command, emboldened by magic.

"Are you hurt?" Cal asks through clenched teeth, never taking his eyes from mine even as the man withers in his hold.

"No." I shake my head, raising my arms in slow, deliberate reassurance.

"Then leave, Ivy. I'm going to rip his limbs off one by one."

He tosses the man into a bloody heap on the forest floor, cracking his knuckles in preparation to carry out his threat.

"The only one doling out punishments today is me."

Cal freezes at my declaration, pivoting his head to me as the black in his irises recedes slightly. A dangerous, prideful smile pulls at the corners of his lips as he motions to the nearly-lifeless man below him.

"Then come take your kill, princess."

I unsheathe a single dagger as I stalk towards him, only needing one for the death I plan to deliver.

Using the toe of my boot, I force the man's slumped shoulders flat to the ground, giving him the same respect I would a piece rotten trash in the streets. Fitting for this scum.

Slowly, I lower myself over him, forcing my knees to press deep into his open wounds.

"Look at me," I command, my voice not wholly my own.

His eyes snap to my face, the last face he'll ever see before he meets Death.

"Your slow, painful death is courtesy of Poison Ivy. Your life is meaningless. There are no gods but me."

I raise my dagger high above my head as darkness blocks out the sun entirely. The Dark God of Death lingers in the shadows waiting to claim another soul. One that I'm happy to deliver to him.

I raise my voice, hoping he hears every word.

"When you get to the Under Realm, give Death my regards. I hope he shreds your pathetic soul."

Throwing my entire body weight behind the blade, I thrust downward straight into the man's heart. He twitches below me but I twist the dagger in deeper, harder until he goes completely still.

The clouds part as Death recedes, illuminating the corpse below me and the blood that coats us both. Strong hands grip my shoulder, hauling me wordlessly off the dead man.

"Come on, princess."

I tear my eyes away from the body and take in the captain. His eyes are fully gray again, a mixture of pride, sadness, and longing written across his face.

The darkness within me, now sated, retreats, satisfied with the scales tipped in its favor. And if I leave them unbalanced ... I shiver at the thought of what succumbing to its call might entail.

Cal uses his thumb to swipe blood off my cheek and I catch his hand before it can leave my face. The mixture of my power and adrenaline with the captain's touch is a dangerous concoction, one intoxicating enough that I can't resist leaning into his hold.

He pulls me tightly against his broad chest, my senses flooding with his salty scent. Cal rests his chin on the top of my head, the nurturing position breaking through my final defense.

Tears leak from my eyes, slowly at first before turning into heaving sobs. But Cal stays unwavering. He doesn't move. He doesn't speak. He simply holds me until I can steady myself.

"Don't tell anyone about this," I say in a soft threat as I pull back from his chest.

"I wouldn't dream of it, princess." He wipes the tears off my cheeks and smiles sadly as the gravity of the situation comes crashing back. "His badge indicates he's a scout, which means there are more Deliverers a few miles behind him. They'll be here soon—."

"I'll get rid of the body," I cut him off.

"I will do it," he refutes.

"Please, Cal." The casual usage of this name halts whatever demand he was about to make, whatever command he was about to bark to get me to relent. I have to do this and I have to do it alone. "Let me."

"Okay," he says, stepping backward. "I'll keep an eye out for the others, but you need to hurry."

When I'm sure Cal is gone, I move towards the drained corpse and plant my palms on the ground around him. The dirtiness of his death requires the creation of beautiful life. Everything in equilibrium.

Plunging deep into the well of my powers, I pull more up than I've ever used before. The earth begins to quiver in slow, agonizingly painful ripples as I tear open the ground around me. A hole opens beneath the body, what's left of my attacker dropping into a shallow grave.

I push harder, diving further into the painful emotions I've hidden away in an attempt to wield more magic. My mother's face. The smell of the salty sea air by the cottage. The feel of her worn leather journal in my small, scared hands.

My arms tremble as I mold the landscape to cover the unholy grave. Thick green grass sprouts from the now desecrated earth, watered by the pools of spilled blood.

But still I dig deeper, focusing on the pain of a lifetime decided by others. The loneliness of being choiceless. Every action or inaction that led to becoming the poisonous thing they created. A lifetime spent neglected by supposedly loving gods. Tiny godsbane flowers burst forth, stretching upwards towards the sun.

My knees give out, collapsing me into a heap on the forest floor. My head swims, black swirling in the edges of my vision and distorting reality. The contents of my stomach threaten to empty themselves, but only dry, painful heaves come.

Foggy and dazed, I stumble to my feet, grabbing trees to steady myself as I force my way away from the magically reshaped earth and into Cal's waiting arms.

CHAPTER 15

The rough bark of the tree digs sharply into my temple, but repositioning myself would only make it worse. I'm barely managing to stay upright as it is. Through slitted, heavy eyelids, I watch the captain secure my broadsword to the sheath strapped to my mares—I mean, mare.

Gods, how many horses do we have? Six? Four? I could have sworn it was only two.

"You okay over there, princess?"

Cal calls out over his shoulder as I try to focus my vision on what I know to be true. We definitely only have two horses—and I'm riding one of them out of here.

Three steps away from the tree, the world flips upside down. No, not the world, *me*. I mentally brace myself for the hard impact of the ground that's sure to follow. I didn't notice any logs but I feel the long, steady press of them under my knees and across my back.

"Look at me," Cal's voice commands in my ear. I force my eyes open to find his face inches from my cheek and my body cradled tightly in his arms. "You overextended yourself. Control like that takes practice, Ivy."

Gods, I love the way he says my name. Even without the current of magic in my veins overwhelming my senses, it's ... *magic* ... wait ... is this Cal's confession that he knows about my power?

My tongue sticks dryly in my mouth, the question dying before I ever get my mouth fully open. Cal sits my feet gently on the ground, his strong arms never letting go of me for fear I might fall over again.

"Up you go," he urges, helping to set my left foot in the stirrup before placing both hands on my ass and pushing upward.

Definitely not how I imagined that contact going for the first time.

Focus, Ivy.

Settling into the saddle, I glance to the left and see two caramel-colored mares with the end of a familiar emerald green cloak sticking out of their saddlebags. My cloak. My mare. Beside me.

The gray mount beneath me shifts as Cal braces a hand on the pommel and swings a toned leg up and over the horse's back, settling in behind the saddle's cantle and wrapping his arms around me.

"What are ... you ... doing?" I force out shakily.

"Getting us out of here before those scumbag Deliverers decide to come looking for him and find you covered in his blood."

Cal takes my shaking hand, covering my rust-stained skin with his as he entwines our fingers and pulls me tightly against him.

The horse begins her forward walk, my own riderless mare following alongside in perfect unison. The swaying motion lulls me closer to the edge of sleep.

Under the full heat of the afternoon sun and wrapped in Cal's embrace, I drift towards the level of unconsciousness I've spent eighteen years chasing. Sweet, dreamless rest.

The wind whispers softly in my ear, granting me permission to fall endlessly into the awaiting slumber.

"Sleep now. I've got you."

"Ivy." Cal's voice cuts through the hazy fog of sleep. "Wake up, princess."

His days-old stubble scrapes against my cheek as he gently nudges me awake. The last light of day filters in through the heavy tree cover as I slowly open my eyes.

We've ridden deep into the woods. Dense pine and spruce crowd around us, seamlessly connecting to the boulders that make up the top of the rocky outcropping no doubt meant to conceal us from unwanted visitors.

Cal lightly squeezes my hand, drawing my attention to our still entwined fingers. Embarrassment heats my cheeks as I jerk my hand from his hold.

Oh gods.

I actually fell asleep in his arms. And worse, I didn't dream.

The captain dismounts rather gracefully considering his awkward seating position. If he's hurting from riding uncomfortably for hours, he doesn't show it. An icy chill runs down my spine at the loss of his heat, prompting Cal to grab my cloak from my saddlebag.

"You're safe here. I promise."

One look into his eyes and I know he means it. I fasten the cloak around my shoulders, ignoring Cal's waiting hand for a few moments longer. My fingers are stiff, still coated in the dried, cracked blood of my attacker. Magic tingles back to life in my veins as the memories come rushing back to me.

"I would have done it," Cal's voice interrupts my spiraling thoughts, "ripped him limb from fucking limb while he begged for death. If he had hurt you, Ivy ..."

His pained voice trails off but the dark, reckless side of me stirs at his violent threat. The dark magic was sated, so why does it wake at the promise of danger on his lips?

Tired of waiting, Cal grabs my hand and tugs gently, indicating that he's not moving until he helps me out of this saddle.

"I can do it," I protest.

If I was a different woman, one who hadn't been discounted and underestimated for years, I might let him sweep me off my feet, might let him carry me to the place he intends to camp. But dismantling my pride is too big a mountain to climb tonight.

"And here I thought you'd at least need dinner before you had the strength to sass me again."

Cal steps back, hands raised in acceptance, allowing me the space to dismount. My knees wobble under the full weight of my exhausted body, but I don't stumble in front of him.

"I can sass you in any condition." My stomach rumbles loudly and I clamp a hand across my midsection to stifle it. "Though, dinner would be nice."

A teasing smile tugs up the corner of his mouth before Cal turns and rummages through his saddle bags. Dried meats and a metal flask fill his hands when he takes his seat beside me on the downed log. He unscrews the lid, taking a deep drink from the container before passing both to me. The woody, caramel scent of whiskey immediately invades my nose.

"Are you trying to get me drunk, Captain?"

"I thought it might take the edge off the day, princess. But if you don't want it ..." Cal reaches for the flask and I quickly press it to my lips and take a deep pull.

The laugh that tugs his mouth into a boyish smile warms me more than the whiskey.

There's no fire, and in the dying light of day, as shadows dance through the evergreen branches of the forest, Cal is devastatingly handsome. Beautiful like the deadly blooms my magic is so fond of conjuring. The more I am sucked into his orbit, the closer I come to falling headfirst into an oblivion from which I know I will never recover.

"How did you learn to fight like that?" Cal asks.

"What makes you think I'm not god-blessed? Maybe I'm a natural born fighter," I tease.

Cal rolls his sparkling silver eyes. "Military captain, remember? I know training when I see it."

I take my time chewing the tough, salty meat before answering, debating how much of the truth I want to divulge tonight. I owe him a sliver at the very least, but allies are supposed to trust each other and he needs to know what waits for us.

"Nick Adler, the son of my father's master-at-arms, taught me. He trained with his father and the Emerald infantry during the day and then we trained at night to keep it a secret."

"He didn't want anyone to know he was training you?"

"*I* didn't want anyone to know," I confess. "Men and women are not permitted to only be sparring partners. You know as well as I do that every noble in our region would have been convinced we were fucking if they knew."

Cal tenses beside me slightly before taking the whiskey and downing a healthy amount. I should put him out of his misery and tell him truthfully that nothing happened between me and Nick.

I should, but I won't.

"It took me weeks of secret meetings to find anyone I trusted enough for the task. It turns out that no one wants to actually fight their region's heir and risk accidentally maiming them."

"But Nick did?" Cal asks.

"Nick has always had a thing for my best friend. He agreed to train me and keep quiet about it as long as Quinn promised to attend the lessons. A win for prideful men, everywhere."

I wonder what the new Lady Quinn *fucking* Adler would think of me now—falling asleep in the godsdamned arms of the Captain of Corinth after brutally murdering a man.

It's my turn to take a long drink of whiskey.

"You've told me *how*, now tell me *why*." Cal's gray eyes lock onto mine despite my best efforts to avoid them.

"Self defense," I reply mechanically. The same excuse I gave my father when he inevitably found out.

"That wasn't defensive," he scoffs. "Nick taught you to kill. Tell me why."

"The governors summits are always a giant spectacle. Really a huge waste of money if you ask me." I take another deep drink before continuing. "It was hosted in Emerald when I was sixteen. At the time, I was head-over-heels for a pathetic boy who did not deserve my affection. We snuck off from the penultimate ball and got drunk on each other … and a stupid amount of wine."

I steal a glance toward Cal, his rage-filled glare forcing my attention elsewhere quickly.

"To this day, I swear I was in complete control … until I woke up on the stairs, my face bruised and bloody and no recollection of the past two hours. I ran straight for my father's study, but I couldn't make myself go inside. The assembly was scheduled to vote the next day to send a joint decree to the King demanding education for girls in all regions, regardless of status. My father was the decree's biggest champion and he had spent every second of the summit trying to convince each governor to vote in favor. I knew that an accusation like this would steal his attention and derail the vote … and the girls of Corinth needed him more than I did."

Deafening silence fills the camp, the very last light of day disappearing completely from view. Cal's eyes bore into me even in the dark. I don't need light to feel the utter rage that ripples off him.

"And this ... *boy*," he says, every word laced with violence, the distinct crunch of metal sounding from his fist. "He's an heir."

With a single assumption, Cal has narrowed every male in Corinth down to three individuals. And with a little bit of thought, I'm positive he'll single out the offender easily.

Just in time for us to ride into his city.

Gods, I wish he hadn't crushed that flask.

CHAPTER 16

It takes more convincing than it should, but I finally get Cal to agree to let me take the first watch. The stubborn man would sooner deprive himself of rest he desperately needs if it meant I could sleep all night, even after sleeping for hours today on horseback.

I'm still not comfortable with this imbalance of kindness, a fact I reminded him of repeatedly. He only agreed to sleeping first on the condition that we didn't pitch the tent tonight. Apparently the thin canvas tent blocks his hearing and he doesn't trust me not to doze off.

He doesn't say that last part, of course, but he doesn't have to.

The night air is cool compared to the heat of the sun today, but it's warmer than it has been since before the first snow fell. From my reclined position, if I angle my head just to the left, the pine boughs part enough to allow me a clear view of the celestial-filled sky.

The stars are the eyes of the gods.

Or that's what the priests say, at least. I've always thought they were more; always imagined them as individual worlds, variations of our reality where we are different people. Realms where our fates are still undetermined.

Imagination can be a cruel and wicked thing.

I've known since I was a little girl that my fate was written, unchangeable by any but the beast who marked me that day in the sea. When I felt the rush of power in my blood for the first time, I thought it was a gift from the gods. But in the same breath they gave me magic, they took my mother.

They took my mother. The supposed gods who hold an unopposed dominion over us. The serpent marked me and cursed me with dreams foretelling my demise, and for reasons only the gods know, they decided to tie Cal's fate with mine.

I could probably run from him, but I won't get far.

I could probably resist him, but I won't last long.

The gods always get what they want in the end—and what they want is entertainment.

Forget our feelings.

Forget our choices.

Forget our plans.

We are expendable playthings in their arena of sick, twisted games.

"No."

Cal's voice is barely a whisper as he thrashes on his bedroll, the sheen of sweat visible on his furrowed brow. White-knuckled fists clench at his sides as he jerks painfully in his restless sleep.

My heart aches in a way I didn't know it was capable of. To live in horrible dreams every night is one thing, but to watch as someone else is trapped in one is entirely another. The urge to soothe him is nearly unbearable.

A scream slices through the night. One single word falling from his parted lips.

"Ivy!"

Every muscle in my body tightens. I know this pain because

I've felt it in my own dreams; desperation so deep it feels as if the core of your being is ripping into two. Cal doesn't just know that we're connected, he feels it as deeply as I do.

My body moves before my mind can command it, my hands cupping the captain's drenched cheeks.

"I'm right here," I whisper.

Depthless gray eyes suddenly stare back at me and steal my breath. In this moment of unguarded vulnerability, I see them in a way that I haven't before. They're the misty color of a brackish pool when the tide recedes; the color of smoke billowing from a fire that's just been doused; the sparkling color of a newly polished wedding band. They contain the multitudes of a life filled with days by the shore, fires in the forest, and bells ringing in the gods' temple.

Entire lifetimes stare back at me.

Words stick in my throat like thick honey. I can't speak, can't move, can't tear my eyes away from his unyielding stare. The longer he holds it, the closer I get to the cliff's edge, the precipice overlooking the depthless ocean where I am destined to drown.

Magic unlike any I have ever felt rushes across the top of my skin and skates down my chest, power swelling into a wave that threatens to break over us both. Together, in this moment with his power commingling with mine, we feel *infinite*.

And, for the first time, I wonder if the fall might be worth it.

My body screams in protest as I push myself onto my elbows on the rocky ground. Cal is noticeably absent from our makeshift camp, the thin bedroll I sidled up against also gone. I ignore the way my heart aches at the memory of his eyes, of the distressed sound of my name on his lips, and of the feel of his fingers lightly resting on my arm as he fell asleep. I sit up and audibly groan at the strain.

The attack yesterday, the amount of magic I used to cover it up … it's been a long time since I've expended that much energy. We're two weeks from the full moon and the Ascension Vote. If things go awry and we have to resort to Cal's plans to kill our adversaries, I need to be ready.

My last training session ended in a brawl rather than a lesson. I brought fury and a blade into the ring, and I lost both my cool and the battle for Quinn that night.

I will never forget the look on Nick Adler's face when I showed up and challenged him, not to win her hand for myself—gods know a love like that is forced into the shadows in Corinth—but to win it for her. One of our many archaic traditions that both Lords Bartlett and Adler would have been forced to honor.

"I would say 'good morning' but it doesn't look good from where I'm standing."

Cal waits at the edge of the trees, arms crossed over his broad, shirtless chest. Droplets of water coat the inky sea beast, gleaming in the early morning sun like scales.

"What is it, princess?" He moves towards me, squatting deeply until he's eye-level with my still seated body.

"I want you to train me." Cal's eyes light up, making me instantly regret my word choice. "I lost my last fight and I don't plan to lose another."

"Considering you're still breathing and he's not, I'd definitely say you won, princess," Cal jokes.

"Not him," I correct. "He couldn't have used that sword to cut himself out of a burlap sack. He was easy. My next fight won't be. I need to be able to take down a formidable opponent. Someone with power."

"Power?" he asks slowly, repeating the word and letting it settle between us.

"Marks won't touch you with a blade," Cal says definitively.

"Why? Because you'll protect me?" I scoff.

"With my life, Ivy."

Cal stands until he's at his full height, seconds that feel more like minutes stretching between us. Only when he's sure that I've felt the full weight of his words does he arch his full lips into a playful smile and extend his hand to help me up.

"Come on. You're going to want to clean up before you get dirty again."

"I don't plan on spending much time on the ground," I quip back, taking his hand to rise to my feet.

"I'm going to ready the horses. Can you wash up quickly?" Cal asks.

"Can you find a shirt?"

"I could..." he teases, tossing my saddlebag towards me, "but now that I know it bothers you, I probably won't."

"Wouldn't want to deprive the ladies of Gathe of a good show, now would you? Might as well put your body on display when we ride into the city. Do a little fishing ... see if anyone bites."

Cal closes the distance between us in two long strides, stopping only when his body is inches from mine.

"My body isn't for their eyes ... and I'm the one who bites."

The captain lays a cotton towel on top of the bag in my arms. His eyes trail over me as he takes slow, deliberate steps backwards, further fanning the flames of the fire he's just ignited in my core.

Thank the gods that whatever water awaits me in the nearby stream will no doubt be ice cold. This is dangerous territory, and I've just asked him to train me, to pin me down on the ground, his hips touching ...

Get it together, Ivy.

Cal's back is to me as he tightens the saddle on my mare.

"I was planning to amend our schedule so that you could sleep in a real bed tonight, but if you stand there all day…"

I turn and dash through trees before he can finish that sentence. Not only do I need to put physical distance between us and douse myself in cold water, but there's not much I wouldn't do for a hearty meal and a night on something more comfortable than a damn bed roll. Even if that inn happens to be in the capital city of the Ruby Region.

Once I'm clean, calmed down, and dressed to spar, I make my way back to camp. I would usually forgo my leather corset as it constricts my range of motion, but it also allows me to hide specially designed blades in the faux boning. And, selfishly, it also makes my breasts look great. An asset that will no doubt work in my favor when it comes to distracting my opponent.

"This one is eager to have a rider. I think she missed you yesterday," Cal says, handing me the reins of my caramel-colored mare.

Thank the gods he's fully clothed again.

The horse whinnies as I mount, clearly aware that we're talking about her.

"I think extra apples are in store for you when we reach Gathe."

Cal and his mare let out a snort at the same time.

"Do you hear that old girl? She gets a day off and extra apples. Meanwhile you've carried twice the weight while I rode bareback for hours."

"Fine. Apples for all three of you. But only if you're on your best behavior today."

Cal's mare lifts her head high as if to show how dutiful she plans to be, eliciting an unexpected laugh from her rider.

"I don't really care much for apples anyway." Cal's voice is low as he spurs his horse ahead into the woods, once again leaving me in his wake.

CHAPTER 17

The clearing Cal has chosen for our makeshift sparring ring is bare. A small stream runs along the edge of the trees, but no other brush or plant life can be found besides a small patch of grass the horses immediately start to graze. No vines or thorny bushes that I can multiply when he isn't looking.

Cal may have acknowledged my magic, but he still hasn't divulged his secret power. For better or worse, today's fight will have to be purely physical.

As if he can hear my thoughts, Cal slips his black shirt over his head, exposing the sea beast inked on his rippling muscles to the sunlight.

"Is that really necessary?" I taunt.

"This is a clean shirt and you're very fond of sharp objects. I'd like to keep it in one piece." He stuffs the shirt into his rucksack and stalks towards me. "You're welcome to take yours off too if you'd feel more comfortable."

A heat flushes up my neck and I open my mouth to make a

snarky comment when Cal moves. Stepping towards me, he uses one leg to swipe both of mine out from under me. A startled yelp slips out as my ass hits the ground in a hard thud.

"Nick should have taught you to anticipate distractions. How many battles has he won?"

I stare up at Cal from my forced seat on the forest floor and roll my eyes. "Just like a man to make everything a dick measuring contest."

Cal grabs my hand, pulling my chest against his as I stand.

"I'd win that, too." He winks before dropping my hand and backing away several paces. "I've seen your defense in action; now show me your offense. Attack me," he demands.

I watch for a moment observing his stance. He's nearly a foot taller than me and easily outweighs me by 100 pounds. He's got more muscles than a god and I'm fairly certain he could take down a house with brute force alone. I will never win a match-up of physical strength, but physicality is only one part of a soldier. Strategy and cunning carry their own weight on the battlefield, and as a woman and a politician, they happen to be my strongest weapons.

"You favor your left side," I say, nodding my head off to the left in an attempt to distract him.

"You couldn't possibly know what I favor."

Cal's eyes are fixed wholly on mine while I approach, allowing me the opportunity to slide my fingers into the sheath hidden on my right outer thigh. I move to pull the dagger and Cal is on me in an instant, grabbing my left arm and twisting so that my back is pressed against his chest. The blade in my right hand now rests delicately across my throat.

Cal is in full control. He could slit my throat with a single thought. My magic sizzles under my skin, searing me everywhere his skin touches mine. Adrenaline kicks in, preparing me to fight despite knowing I'm in no real danger.

Well, at least no physical danger.

"You're going to have to do better than that."

Cal's voice is rough, his stubbled cheek brushing against the side of my neck as he speaks. A shiver shoots down my spine involuntarily as a cool chuckle rumbles in his chest and reverberates through me.

"You like that, princess?"

"I'd like for you to get your hands off of me."

My voice holds surprisingly steady as I speak words that couldn't be further from the truth. There's a low, maddening heat spreading through me and he knows it.

Cal drops his hands and steps away, a mischievous grin plastered across his face when I turn to face him. Stormy clouds fill his gray eyes, a faint electricity buzzing in the air around us. A promise of lightning so hot, it'll burn us both.

"Try again. No blades, this time," he says.

Oh there will be blades, just not the ones he's expecting.

I pull the daggers from my thighs and toss them to the ground. If I was fighting any other opponent, I would think twice about using my body as a weapon. Despite the half-truths and hidden secrets, Cal has made one thing clear today: the growing heat between us is eating at him. And that's all the knowledge I need to know how to take him down.

So what if he puts his hands all over me in the process? Maybe I'm a little hungry too.

I turn and retreat a few paces, swishing my hips seductively as I walk. My hands take their time exaggeratingly caressing the sides of my breasts as my fingers work to slip the dainty blades from the boning of my corset.

I spare a glance over my shoulder, my breath hitching at the intensity burning in his eyes. I catch my bottom lip between my teeth and let my gaze reflect his.

Like a spider lying in wait, I prepare to lure my prey fully into my silken web. One more move and he's mine.

"What a pity. I thought for sure you'd attack me from behind," I say breathlessly.

Cal's eyes darken, the raging storm clouds disappearing into onyx night. His voice is a low, deep growl. "Not here, princess."

A wave of heat floods my lower body again, my heart rate spiking as I struggle to stand my ground. With an unsteady breath, I place the toe of my left boot behind me, spinning and releasing one blade in one smooth movement. It flips end-over-end, grazing Cal's arm as it passes him, nicking exactly where I intend.

A tiny, red rivulet of blood trails down his bicep from the cut. Cal glances down to wipe it clean and I rush him. I go low, dropping my shoulder and using my lower center of gravity to knock him over. As soon as his feet slip out from under him, I lunge upwards. My other blade rests against the soft flesh of his neck as we hit the dirt with a loud thump.

Silver flames spark in Cal's eyes as he shifts underneath me, large hands grabbing the backs of my thighs and holding me flush against him. I lower my head, letting my breath caress his ear as I press the blade firmer against his throat.

"You like that, Captain?" I taunt, repeating his words with his same seductive tone.

With a twist of his hips, Cal flips us, utilizing his size and brute strength and my cockiness against me. My breath comes in a ragged gasp that has little to do with being pinned against the ground and everything to do with being underneath him.

He grips both wrists in one hand, forcing them, and my blade, above my head.

"I said 'no blades.'"

Cal slowly drags his pointer finger up the center of my corset, the third and final blade slipping free from the hidden sheath between my breasts. He lowers his head, my back arching off the ground as his lips brush over the swell of delicate skin. There's a faint flash of silver in the sunlight as Cal lifts his head exposing the dagger he holds between his teeth. With his free hand, he plucks it from his mouth and tosses it out of reach.

"Any more blades I should know about?"

His hungry eyes rove over my heaving chest and back up to my slightly parted lips. The air grows thick, harder to swallow with each passing second. I squirm in his hold. Whether I'm searching for a way out from beneath him or for friction of a different kind, I'm not entirely sure. Pure power ripples over my skin at the delicious promise of him.

"Yield, Ivy," he commands.

The sheer mention of my name is nearly enough to make me crumble under him. Cal presses his free forearm gently across my throat, rocking forward until the hard press of him rests against my warm center.

Thoughts and reactions no longer my own, my head lolls to the side, exposing my full neck to him. There's a rough, warm brush against my skin and I feel his growl echo within me.

"Yield. Now."

Each word is clipped as the captain fights to stay in control of himself. A deep, primal ache floods my senses as strange magic courses through me.

I am an undammed river. A tornadic wind. A raging wildfire. A rolling mountainside. I am light and shadow. Life and death all in the same moment.

Magic flares out of me before I can contain it. Deep purple blooms spring to life in the clearing. Poisonous godsbane littering the ground around our entwined bodies. The anomalistic power recedes as quickly as it appeared, the absence pulling me from my carnal stupor.

Instead of fear or confusion, only pride is written across Cal's face. He arches a perfect eyebrow as his eyes move from my creations to me. This moment doesn't feel like it confirms his suspicions. No, it feels like it confirms something much bigger.

Power of a different sort swells within me as I boldly declare, "I yield to no man."

"And you never fucking will, princess."

CHAPTER 18

G athe, the capital city of the Ruby Region, is abuzz with activity. We are several miles from the city center, but still it's crowded here on the outskirts.

There's an unmistakable sound of hammering in the distance and large carts hauling timber travel towards the noise. A stark reminder of the war and how the people from the Sapphire Region fled here when the Synalians invaded their lands. Many of those refugees have no homes to return to, so they build here instead. Far away from the seas where ships sail, bringing with them the first waves of Drayca's offerings.

Merchants with food carts line the road selling pastries and other baked goods to tradesfolk heading home for the evening as wagons filled with grain clamor down the cobblestone streets. Bells toll in the distance, marking the call to pray. All around us, people pause to offer a moment of murmured petition to Nobus before returning to their tasks. A lot of wasted breath, if you ask me.

Cal sits up straighter in his saddle. There's an air of regality in his posture, shoulders back and arms tense on the reins. His mare leads our single file processional through the crowded streets. From this distance, I have a front row seat to watch as he slips into his persona, something he does with ease.

Everything about the Captain of Corinth is intimidating. In this form, Cal somehow looks larger, like a god statue in a temple instead of a man. Watching him, it's easy to see how the stories of his battles took on a life of their own. He looks every bit the menacing death machine they claim he is.

The city residents pause again, this time to exchange whispers about the living legend passing through their street, quickly drawing the attention of a nearby group of soldiers. They halt, each stopping the task of loading wooden crates onto a wagon to salute their commanding officer. These men aren't wearing the expected red uniforms of the Ruby Region's infantry, but the gray and gold of Corinth.

These are Lord General Marks' men. Cal's men.

A loud whistle pierces the air, the captain's head snapping toward a man in an officer's uniform. He nods his head in our direction before walking around the corner out of view. To my surprise, Cal stops his horse abruptly and dismounts in the middle of the street.

"Take the horses to the stables," he says curtly. "When you're done, meet me at the inn. Don't wander."

There's no warmth in his voice or light in his eyes as he speaks. Whoever this man is, he must be important. I nod tightly and take the reins from Cal's outstretched hands, keeping my head low in an effort to draw as little attention to myself as possible.

I'm not far from the inn, but it takes me several minutes to lead both horses through the crowds of people who are milling about in the streets. The stables are packed. Horses of all colors and sizes crowd the small barn and a frazzled groom is chasing a cat from in between the stalls.

"Shoo, you're spooking the horses!" he yells at the frightened animal.

"Excuse me," I signal to him but he doesn't hear me.

The small cat, a scrawny tabby, darts towards my ankles and I manage to grab her by the scruff of her neck as she runs past.

"Looking for her?"

"Oh thank the gods! Get that damned thing out of here!"

"Can I have a scoop of feed?" I ask, looking at the large bins lining the wall.

"What for?!" he demands.

"She's hungry." The groom stares at me flatly, unimpressed with my answer. "She'll just come right back inside looking for food, you know?"

He lets out an exasperated sigh. "Fine, but you're paying for it."

He reluctantly moves to the bins and trades my horse's reins for a half-full scoop. I snatch it from his hands, careful not to spill the sparse amount and take both the cat and the feed outside.

"I will never understand cats," I say, setting both on the ground. "Eat up."

She purrs, twining her skinny body between my ankles as she starts to eat. Thin sides showcase her ribs, evidence of a life lived on the streets. At least I can provide her one meal that she doesn't have to fight for.

Magic prickles my spine, urging me to squat beside the cat. I follow it, bending down behind the wooden barrels that line the side of the stables right before a husky voice shouts in my direction.

"We've barely been home six months and already he's got us mobilizing again. What's he afraid of? There's nothing but mountains in Topaz."

A second voice chimes in. "Aye, and that's where they'll find your body once he kills you for asking too many fucking questions."

Marks moving troops to Topaz? Why indeed.

With mountains to the east and nothing but the iceberg-filled sea to its north, that particular region is the most naturally guarded in all of Corinth. There's virtually no threat of invasion there, unless of course the invasion isn't foreign. I wouldn't put it past Marks to use the threat of a military raid to secure Governor Wilson's vote.

"Freeman, Sanders! Get back 'ere! You're not done yet!" another voice yells loudly.

I sneak a peek around the corner just in time to see two men decked out in Corinthian gray uniforms walking towards the city shops. With slow, light steps, I follow them until they round the corner of the inn. No sight of the commanding voice, but something tells me its owner is the same man I saw flag down Cal with a single nod.

Like the streets, the inn is also teeming with people. It's standing room only in the small tavern that occupies the lower floor, the loud cacophony of voices overtaking the cramped space. Magic twitches inside, tugging me towards the back of the room.

Each crowded table I pass is covered in a spread of roast pig and goblets filled with the Ruby Region's famous sparkling wine. The free-flowing effervescent liquid sweeps the patrons into a haze Bastin would be proud of.

Through that haze, I see a god of a different sort. The stoic captain leans against the back wall, trying and failing to blend in. His elevated foot rests behind him and he's rolled up his shirt-sleeves to expose tan arms that end in a clenched fist. Dark hair falls lazily over his furrowed brow and he's twirling a room key around his pointer finger. If 'uptight ease' is what he's going for, Callan Murphy is nailing it perfectly.

Anyone who glances his direction, and has had the right amount of fizzy wine, might be fooled into thinking he's a normal man without a care in the world. But to the trained eye, the one that has spent the past week analyzing his every move, the truth is obvious. The real, stripped down man hides behind a deadly persona. To me, he's a hybrid—half-Cal, half-Captain of Corinth. And I'm captivated by his presence.

As if cued by his own magic, Cal stiffens and pushes off the wall standing to his full height. His head turns to find me in the crowd, a mixture of relief and exasperation written on his expression. I push through the crowd, offering him his bag with an extended arm.

His voice is sharp when he speaks. "What took you so long?"

"Saved a cat." I shrug, pushing past him and starting up the wooden stairs to my room.

"You saved a cat?" Cal tugs on my arm, stopping me and twisting me to face him.

"Yes. I gave Death a life yesterday. The scales must stay balanced."

"Waaa....tttcchhh oooouuttt..." a voice from behind me slurs. I don't have time to react before Cal pulls me against his chest and presses me against the stairwell wall. An overweight drunk man barely misses us as he tumbles down the last remaining steps before landing on his face on the floor.

The tavern below erupts into laughter at his fall, but I barely hear them over the sound of power roaring in my veins. The sheer proximity of his body to mine has liquid heat pooling in my core again.

Cal leans in, his lips brushing against my ear as he whispers, "You never cease to amaze me, Ivy."

"Hot soup coming through!"

An apron-clad woman carrying a tray of fragrant, steaming bowls pushes her way up the tight staircase, forcing Cal to press his body impossibly closer. My lower back digs into the wooden handrail but the pain is drowned out by the scent of leather and salty air that invades my senses.

I barely managed to pick myself up from the godsdamned puddle he left me in earlier today, and here I am, melting again in a fucking stairwell. So much for that hot bath I was looking forward to. I hope they have ice here.

By the grace of the gods, Cal backs away and motions for me to start up the stairs ahead of him. Devilish pride swells in me as he tries to inconspicuously adjust his leather pants when he thinks I'm not watching.

Glad to know I'm not the only one affected.

The stairs give way to a hall bustling with people coming and going from their rooms. Cal weaves us in between the passing patrons to a wooden door with a large number *12* engraved on an oval brass plaque, the number corresponding to the one stamped on the key in his hand.

The room is small and the sparse furnishings take up the entire space: a simple bed, an armchair, and a flimsy wooden desk. It's not much, but it's better than a bedroll.

There are more inns further into the city center—larger, nicer inns that are quieter, less crowded and more luxurious. But traveling further into the city means risking unwanted attention from Governor Rollins, a man who only tolerates me because of his longstanding trade agreement with my father. I'd like nothing more than to get in and out of Gathe without a run-in with our reluctant ally.

Cal shuts the door and groans audibly when he takes in the space.

"Not the palace you wanted for me, Captain?" I tease, setting my bag down in the armchair and unclasping my cloak.

"The innkeeper said there'd be a couch in here," he grumbles.

"A couch..."

My breath catches in my chest. The gods must have one hell of a sense of humor to trap us in not one but two inns at max capacity. I'd bet all the coins in Emerald's vaults that there's no rat-infested broom closet for Cal to hide in this time. No, tonight he'll be here with me and all the tension that's been building between us.

I should tell him that we can find another inn, but I don't want to further risk Rollins' or Marks' men discovering me.

I should tell him that the floor looks comfortable, but the scuffed wooden planks don't look like they've been mopped recently.

I should tell him to leave me and see if he can find someone else's bed to sleep in, but a greedy, possessive part of me rages at the thought.

I've always been great at denial, but this … this magic-fueled lust … even I can't deny the primitive part of me whose only care is pleasure. The deep, savage need to be physically claimed by him, consequences be damned. I've never given myself to anyone without a mask or an alias, and maybe just once, I'd like to know what it's like to be fucked relentlessly by a man who calls out my name in his sleep.

"You could have just asked, you know," I tease, turning to face him.

"Asked what?" Cal asks tentatively, his voice filled with a restraint I don't possess.

"Asked to share my bed instead of planning this," I wave my hand around the small room, "elaborate ruse about a missing couch."

"You think I need an *elaborate ruse*?" Cal steps towards me, hunger coloring his gaze.

"Wrong question," I taunt. "We both know what you want to ask."

Godsdamnit. This could very well end up being the worst decision I've ever made. I suck in a ragged breath, steeling my nerves and prepping for utter destruction. *Fuck it.*

"Ask me, Cal."

"What exactly do I want to ask?" He closes the distance between us, continuing his pursuit until I'm forced to take a step back.

"Ask if I can sleep in your bed?"

Step.

"Ask if I can kiss your luscious, poisonous lips?"

Step.

My back hits the wall with a thud, my breath hitching in my chest as Cal moves closer to rest his arm above my head. His breath is hot on my neck as he inhales my scent, dragging his chin roughly across my tender skin, causing me to shiver again. He's a man who remembers.

"Ask if I can strip you down and worship every inch of your body?"

Cal's large hand grips my chin, forcing me to look directly at him—directly into dangerous eyes of molten silver that threaten to swallow me whole. His face is inches away from mine, our shared breaths commingling.

"Which one are you asking?" I manage to ask on a shaking exhale.

His breath rattles in his throat in a near growl. "I'm a greedy man when it comes to you. I want all of it and more. "

My thighs clench at his words, his sinful tongue darting out to wet his lips. Lips that I need to feel on my body. Potent, intoxicating power rushes through me, heightening my growing need for contact. I lean in, angling my lips towards his, but Cal pulls away.

"Not so fast, princess. I told you that when you kissed me it would be because you couldn't imagine living one more second of your life without knowing how I taste."

He leans in, lips tracing my jawline and moving upwards to delicately nip at my ear. "Are you there yet?"

His seductive words pour into me like honeyed wine, making

me drunk with anticipation as he presses on. "Is that how bad you want me?"

I nod my head, barely able to form a thought and definitely unable to form a sentence.

"Mean it when you say it, Ivy. Because one night with you will never be enough to satisfy me."

Godsdamnit this better be worth it because I'm fairly certain he's ruining me for anyone else. I don't just want Cal, I *need* him. I know it in the fibers of my soul and the marrow of my bones. This is the beginning of something so much bigger than I could have ever imagined and there is no way to stop it now. I am already far too gone.

"I mean it." And gods help me, I do.

The words haven't fully left my lips before his mouth is on mine, rough and demanding. Cal drops my face, moving his hand to the back of my neck to pull me even closer. I angle my head and open my mouth, letting my tongue join his in a dangerous dance.

He tastes like salt water and divinity. Like the sea god came down from the heavens to pour life into my parched soul with his salinated kiss. Every mouthful brings me closer to full submersion. I could drown in him and thank him for the gift.

My fingers tangle in Cal's dark hair as I pull him deeper into me. His free hand luxuriously explores my body, trailing over my breasts and down my side before finding my ass and lifting me to wrap both legs around his waist.

My back arches as I feel his arousal pressing into me, only our riding leathers separating us from each other. I break the kiss in a moan, exposing my neck to him again. Every part of Cal is electric and my entire body hums under his touch. Magic sparks along my skin everywhere his lips touch, incinerating me thoroughly.

The fingers of my free hand blindly work the laces of my corset in a frenzied attempt to remove the layers between our bodies. The image of Cal with my blade in his teeth flashes in my mind causing my hips to roll against the hard press of him. Cal runs a finger up my corset, hooking it in the middle of the binding. With a single tug, the laces snap, the leather-wrapped blades clanking to the wooden floor below.

"I'll buy you a new one," Cal growls before his mouth is on mine again.

He tugs on my shirt, forcing the hem out of my pants until his hands can roam over my stomach and ribs. I let him explore, reveling in the feel of his skin on mine as my hips rock against him. I'm wholly consumed by him and yet it's not enough.

"Cal." His name, spoken on a breathy exhale, elicits another desperate growl.

"If you've changed your mind, tell me now."

His body tenses in restraint and I know without a shadow of a doubt that he would do it. He'd set my feet on the floor, lower my shirt, and walk away from the burning inferno between us if I wanted him to. But there's only one thing I want him to do right now and it damn sure isn't walk away.

"Fuck me," I command.

Cal surges at me, our lips crashing in a fervent, passionate kiss. He strips me of my shirt before reaching a hand over his head and shedding his own. My hardened nipples rub against the tattooed serpent on his chest as Cal removes my boots, his mouth never leaving my skin. The sharp sting of his rough bite on my neck forces another pleading moan from deep within me. He wasn't lying about biting ... and godsdamnit, I like it.

Cal spins us, moving to the bed with predatory speed. He wastes no time. The moment my back hits the feather mattress, his mouth moves to my sternum and then my stomach. His fingers deftly unlace my pants as his lips continue their descent, leaving tiny fires in their wake.

"Every man who has ever had you has thought they were a god. They thought they owned you, claimed you, conquered you." Each phrase is punctuated with a seductive kiss, dipping lower until his breath caresses my inner thigh. "But they were too dense to know they were in the presence of a goddess."

Like a devotee at an altar, the great Captain of Corinth drops to his knees before me. His hands grip my hips, pulling me to the edge of the bed until my legs are draped over his broad shoulders. He spreads me wide as his fingers begin to move in slow, teasing circles over my most sensitive area. Pure greed colors his expression as he wets his lips.

"Let me worship you the way you deserve."

My back arches off the bed as his tongue trails up my center.

"Let you?" I ask breathlessly. "I command it."

The last remaining hold on his restraint snaps. Another moan sounds through the room as his tongue fills me, swiping in and out rhythmically. He spreads my thighs wider as he alternates sucking and lapping, the pressure within me mounting as he feasts. I writhe against him urging him deeper, but he doesn't let me. His hand moves, pressing firmly below my navel and pinning me in place. In just the *right* place.

Cal's fingers join his tongue as he beckons me closer to the edge. Sparks fly from his fingertips, boiling my blood. Power ripples across my body, sucking the air from the room as I struggle to contain it.

"Let go. Unravel for me, princess."

His words, hot against my skin, push me over the cliff, wave after wave of pleasure washing over me as I pulse around him. He stays there, working me relentlessly until my orgasm recedes. Air rushes back into my lungs and I'm on him in an instant. We are nowhere close to done.

Lifting his wrist, I pull his soaked fingers into my mouth, my eyes never leaving his as I suck them clean. Both sets are full of lust and hunger. We are both starving, the other the only person who can nourish our famished body.

I lie back, guiding Cal up from the floor. He sheds his pants as he moves and I barely have time to glimpse how low the tattooed sea beast's tail dips below his hip bone before he's on top of me.

"Are you..." he starts.

"Yes." My answer is yes to every question he could ask.

Yes, I'm sure.

Yes, I take a contraceptive. (It helps that I can grow it myself.)

Yes, I want this.

Cal kisses me roughly as he lines himself up to my entrance and presses in. I moan loudly at the intrusion, growing fuller and fuller with each slow, tortuously luxurious stroke. When I am full to the brim with him, he thrusts harder and impossibly deeper.

Our bodies move in perfect synchronicity like waves crashing upon the shore. I claw at his back, desperate for more. More friction. More power. More *him*. In this moment, I need Cal more than I need my next breath—and I'm not certain how I ever breathed before him.

"Fuck," he says against my lips. "You are perfect, Ivy."

Heavy rain pounds on the window, casting the room in a dull light as magic barrels through me. He lifts my knee, angling himself until he hits the spot guaranteed to make me fall apart. As my pleasure builds, the grip on my power slips. If I don't do something, the very walls could sprout flowers in seconds.

I mentally picture the clearing where we sparred earlier today. Casting my power out towards it, I imagine vines of ivy wrapping around the trunks of the trees. Magic erupts from my body as I orgasm around him. I scream out at the simultaneous release, the physical and the magical coalescing into a holy absolution.

Cal tightens inside me, thunder shaking the thin window pane as his own groans of pleasure fill the room. He holds me tight against him as we pant, riding out the final swells of bliss.

Cal places another, wholly different kiss on my lips. It isn't rough or eager like before, but delicate and full of adoration. And, even though I don't want to admit it out loud, I know deep down that we are both thoroughly ruined. Power warms my blood, relishing in the endorphins that flood my brain and aching to be used again.

"Do you feel that?" he whispers against my skin.

We have to talk about the magic we both possess, but I'm not broaching that subject while he's still inside of me. I've taken lovers to bed before, but no one has stripped me of my control over my magic. Whatever I'm feeling in my veins right now, Cal clearly feels it too.

I nod, unable to form a sentence that feels appropriate for this moment. Unable to say anything without giving a voice to the one thing I don't want to talk about. Whatever the gods have in store for us, I fear we have catapulted into an orbit not even they could stop.

Cal moves to grab a small towel from the bedside table, standing to his full height. In the dying light of the stormy evening, I take in all of him. From the broad expanse of his shoulders, to the rippling washboard of his abdomen, to the tattoo of a thick ivy vine that wraps around the top of his muscular thigh.

Without thinking, I reach out, tracing the ink with my fingers. *That godsdamned tattoo* was never the sea beast, was it? I look up to him, desperate for answers to the hundreds of questions that fill my head.

Cal motions for me to lay back, delicately cleaning my inner thighs with the thin cotton towel. He hesitates, clearly weighing how much to divulge in this moment.

"All of it," I say. "Tell me all of it."

"I have dreamed of a woman every night since I was ten years old. A woman who has hair the color of a newborn fawn." He tucks a strand of hair behind my ear as he continues. "A woman of porcelain skin," he says, dragging his knuckles across my cheekbones, "with a dusting of freckles and emerald green eyes."

"Those aren't uncommon features," I deflect. "It could be a coincidence."

"Coincidence?" Cal cups my face in his hands, forcing me to look fully into his stormy eyes. The rain outside intensifies as his words boom like thunder in our space. "The woman in my dreams has the power to make the earth tremble at her whim. Does that sound like coincidence to you?"

I swallow thickly at his admission. My fingers absently trace the tattooed vine again, gently grazing the crescent-shaped birthmark hidden within the largest leaf as I let his words sink in.

"Five years ago, I saw you in Amale protesting on the palace steps. I was buying a pastry from a cart when I heard your voice above the crowd. My heart recognized you immediately."

"That's when you got the tattoo?" I ask.

"No. I've had that for much longer."

Cal's thumb gently swipes away the tear that leaks from my eye against my will. He brings his forehead to rest against mine as if it's always meant to be there.

"I've been waiting for you, Ivy."

And I know, deep in my soul, that he's telling the truth, even if I don't want to believe him. I could grab my clothes and bolt out of the room right now and it wouldn't make it any less true. This man, this fearsome and unexpectedly compassionate man, is mine.

And there's a very real, very scary possibility that I might be his, too.

CHAPTER 19

The inn is quiet. For the first time since we arrived in Gathe, there's no noise. No carts clamoring across cobblestones. No patrons singing or guests shouting. No intimate noises or thunderous rain storms. Nothing but the quiet, steady breathing of the man beside me.

The inky blue sky outside is starting to show hints of pinks and oranges. Dawn, and whatever the forgotten Goddess of Light brings with her, is not far away. In a few moments, we'll have to leave the sanctuary of this bed and face the consequences of what we've said and done. We'll have to discuss our magic and our nightmares—and how the latter seems to disappear when we sleep beside each other.

Delicate kisses trail across the back of my shoulders as Cal pulls me tighter against his bare chest.

"Don't get up yet," he pleads against my skin.

"I would stay, but there's this infuriating captain who commands that we leave at dawn every day."

"Oh him?" Cal's lips trail up my neck. "He'd love nothing more than to spend all day in this bed following your commands."

"All day?" I tease, guiding his hand lower down my body. "Surely we could think of more locations than just this bed if we're going to be here *all day*."

We both know we have to leave. Departure for Amale is as inevitable as the sunrise. But we can spare at least another hour in this rapidly fleeting haven.

A loud bang echoes through the quiet room, freezing us both in place. Seconds pass like hours until another, more forceful knock rattles the door again.

"Stay here," Cal commands against the back of my neck.

I pull the covers higher over my naked body to ward off the chill that hits me when he vacates our bed. Cal grabs a towel from the stack on the bedside table, tying it around his hips and slipping a dagger in the waistband as the mysterious stranger knocks a third time.

"What?!" he shouts, opening the door only a crack to shield me from prying eyes.

Even from this close, I can't make out what the person says before Cal slams the door and turns to face me. An ivory envelope with a ruby red seal rests in his hands. I know exactly who it's from, and it can't be good.

I spring from the bed and rush to grab the envelope from his hand, ripping through the flourishing gold script that adorns the front.

"What does he want?" Cal asks, anger lacing his words as I read.

"He's summoned us to his manor." I read on, shaking my head furiously when I come across *bring your bags* and *guest of honor*. "Do you think the soldiers notified him of our arrival?"

"No, those were Marks' men. They were just passing through. I doubt they're in Rollins' pocket too."

Cal holds out his hand and I place the Ruby governor's missive in his waiting palm.

"I wouldn't put it past him," I disagree. "Rollins only cares about power and the vote is stacked in Marks' favor at the moment. He'll be leaving for Amale any day now so this has to be a last ditch effort to make sure I don't arrive."

I pace the room, analyzing everything I know about the governor that could be useful today.

"I don't trust him, Cal. Hide blades wherever you can. His guards will strip you of your sword as soon as we arrive and we may have to fight our way out of there."

Cal drags a hand across his stubbled chin, the muscles in his arms tensing. "You need to get dressed right now."

If the governor thinks he can *summon* me and I'll come running like one of his subjects, he is sorely mistaken. "The Governor already thinks I'm an impertinent bitch. He can wait."

"How long can he wait, Ivy?" Cal asks, his voice deep and assertive. "Because right now, you are standing there completely naked talking about strategy and hidden blades ... and all I can think about is bending you over that desk and fucking you until you scream my name."

Oh. Well that certainly sounds more fun than whatever Rollins has planned.

"This desk?" I ask coyly, looking over my shoulder as I prowl toward it.

My fingers trail across the writing surface and I give it a little shake to see if the furnishing is as flimsy as it appears. Unconvinced the wobbly legs will survive this, I lean over the desk and beckon him to come closer with a crook of a single finger.

A primal sound reverberates through the room. Cal is behind me in an instant, gripping my hair and pulling my head backwards towards his ear.

"You know damn well I mean *this fucking desk,* you wicked woman."

His free hand kneads my breast in rough, sinful circles. The thin towel around his waist does little to cover the hardness that presses against my ass.

"Do you still want me to get dressed?" I ask breathlessly. "Or should we try that other thing you had in mind?"

His grip on my hair tightens, arching my back nearly to its limit.

"I have many ... *many* things in mind for you, princess. Sweet things. Rough things. Things that would make the god of pleasure blush. Do you want to find out what they are?"

"See for yourself," I breathe out, guiding Cal's hand from my chest down to my slick thighs. He nearly purrs when his fingers slide between them and find me ready to take him.

"So needy." He flicks his finger, taunting me. I squirm, searching for the friction he's denying but met only with a villainous laugh instead. "Not yet, princess."

A second finger joins in, the two working in tandem to strum my most sensitive area. "You get more when I think you're ready for more."

Gods, I don't think I can be any more ready for him than I am right now. What else could he possibly... *oh*. A single finger slides into me and I moan loudly at the intrusion.

"Here's the thing ..." Cal's thick finger moves in and out in slow, steady strokes. Giving me only a little and nowhere near enough. "I've only just started worshipping you, but something tells me that you'd love being treated like a sinner."

His finger slides out of me again, leaving me breathless and wanting. I groan at his absence and he tightens his grip on my hair.

"Is that what you want, princess? To be fucked like it's a punishment?"

Every dirty word from his mouth scorches my skin as he breathes them across me. Magic cascades through my body desperate for its own release.

"Yes," I breathe out on a moan as two fingers thrust inside of me at once.

Cal's tongue moves in a long, sensual stroke up my spine, his breath cooling the fire building under my skin.

"Does it turn you on to make powerful men wait while you take your pleasure?" A third finger slips inside me, joining the others to curl in a devilish stroke. "To know he's clenching his hands while you come all over mine?"

His filthy words fling me to the edge of pleasure. Power bursts through every blood vessel, my veins constricting, my heart stuttering. I spasm around his hand, my lips opening ready to oblige his request as Cal's free hand clamps over my mouth.

"Not yet, princess."

When he's squeezed the last bit of pleasure from me, he moves, one hand gripping my hip as the other wraps gently around my throat. Using his muscular thigh, Cal spreads mine further apart and thrusts into my wet heat. The base of him hitting my ass in a single thrust.

Oh fuck.

The rickety desk creaks with every relentless thrust. Our bodies smack together loudly with no thought other than hot, animalistic gratification.

My entire body alights with power as I near the edge.

The air in the room grows thick as Cal picks up the pace, dark spots dancing at the edge of my vision.

"My name will be the only name you call out when you come," Cal groans. "Do you understand me?"

I nod breathlessly, my grip on the desk tightening. The wooden legs snap out from under me with a forceful pop.

A cool breeze ghosts over my skin as Cal spins us until I'm pressed against the wall. I don't care about the noise or about the destruction that litters the floor. No, all I can focus on is the unfettered power that courses through my body.

I glance to my left, focusing my attention on the empty box that lines the outer window sill. I loosen the leash on my magic letting flowers and variegated ivy spring to life in the dead soil. The tension in my veins heightens, pulled taut between opposing forces.

One thought, one name, consumes me.

Just before I snap in two, the sweet release of pleasure washes over me in delicious waves as Cal's name falls from my lips.

"That's right, Ivy. Call out for me."

I cry out his name again, feeling him pulse within me as I do. Delicate kisses make their way up my neck, sweetly soothing away any pain I felt in his grip.

"What are the odds no one heard us?" I joke through shallow breaths.

"I hope everyone in this godsforsaken region heard." Cal pulls out, spinning me towards him. His hands cup my face, leaning in until his forehead rests against mine, his bold declaration breathed directly into me. "I hope every single god heard you calling out for me. I want them all to know that you are mine."

Endorphins and magic commingle in a deliciously dangerous cocktail. His lips find mine, kissing me thoroughly. This kiss isn't frantic or lustful, but it's claiming just the same. He's laying claim over our fate with every touch of his lips against mine.

The post-orgasm euphoria coloring my senses tries to subdue the conditioned response that builds on my tongue. Magic tries to smother the itch of agitation that starts to rise within me. But even the potency of our shared power can't change who I am, the poisonous creature unable to accept that anything good or easy could come my way.

I step back from Cal, easily breaking his hold with my retreat.

"I do not belong to you."

My words are angrier than they should be. Fire that isn't my own flares to life in my veins.

"No, you do not," Cal says as he steps slowly toward me. "But you belong with me, Ivy. Beside me."

"And if I wish to lead you? A man like you would be okay with that?" I scoff.

"Oh, I very much enjoy being behind you. The view is incredible." A devious smile pulls up the corner of his mouth as he moves to carefully take my hand in his.

"I'm serious, Cal. You are not entitled to me just because you are fucking me."

His eyes darken with a sobering seriousness, quickly replacing the playful spark that colored them moments before.

"I have waited my entire life for you, Ivy. If *fucking* is all this is to you, then … then I'll find a way to live with that. Because I would rather have you for a moment than never have you at all. But if you choose to have me, I will be beside you until every realm in existence turns to dust. You don't have to be mine, but I am yours … and not even the gods can change that."

Cold air douses the rising fire, sweeping my anger away with it. Something inside my chest squeezes at his words, something that I push down into the iron-clad box that contains everything I don't wish to feel.

We are two twisted souls destined to march into death together. We have no choice in how we end. Cal couldn't feel this way if he knew the depths of what fate has in store for us. He wouldn't make outlandish statements about realms and existence if he did.

Or would he?

Cal's never disclosed if his nickname was earned or only legend. But a man capable of single handedly taking down a legion of soldiers might just be cocky enough to defy fate itself. The hard granite gaze locked onto my every move tells me that he wouldn't stop at fate.

No, Callan Murphy would defy the gods to their immortal faces. And the choice to follow him or not is wholly mine.

CHAPTER 20

It's expected that I will be dressed in full regalia to meet the Ruby Governor. An elegant, emerald gown would symbolize my region, my status, and my sex. But Rollins disregarded decorum with his little summons, and I fight better in pants.

I step over the pile of broken wood that litters the floor, digging into my bag to locate a clean pair of brown leathers and a blouse of deep emerald green. There's no mirror in the room, so I rely on muscle memory as I pull my wet hair up into a low, sleek chignon.

There's a sobering sort of dread that's gnawed at me ever since I opened my eyes this morning. It disappeared briefly but came back in full force as I bathed alone in the hall chamber. I try to tell myself that it's only nerves about the impending encounter with Rollins, that it will go away as soon as I fulfill this farce of an invitation.

This room has been a sanctuary, a place where I allowed myself to give in to temptation and desire without thought or worry of the consequences. A place where everything about our dynamic changed. And I am entirely unprepared to face our new reality.

Cal steps into the room with a towel wrapped around his waist, skin still dripping from his bath. Droplets refract in the sunlight pouring in from the small window causing the sea beast inked across his chest to glimmer as if it's covered in iridescent scales. The sight of the leviathan sends an errant chill down my spine.

"We don't have to go, you know," Cal says, never looking up from his bag.

"Of course we have to go. I don't want to be in the Ruby Region any longer than we have to be, but refusing Rollins in his own home is an affront that we cannot afford."

"We..." he stills.

"You're my ally, aren't you?" I backtrack, trying to cover the unintentional usage and implications of that particular pronoun.

"Ah." Cal returns his focus to the bag, extracting leather pants and a fitted shirt in the same shade of deep obsidian. "In that case, Rollins is already our enemy. Marks already has his vote. What more could the governor do if we don't show up?"

Cal makes a valid point. Rollins will never side with me at the Ascension Vote no matter who I put forth. In his opinion, Marks is the only one worthy of the crown, except for maybe himself.

"What if he's trying to steal the vote from Marks?" I ask. "What if Rollins has summoned me to try to convince me to vote for him?"

"I'd say he's wasting all of our fucking time." Cal sits on the edge of the bed and begins lacing his boots. "But go on."

"Think about it. The Emerald Region is geographically cut off from the rest of Corinth. We get plenty of imports from the sea, but all land shipments have to pass through Ruby."

The people of my region would suffer exponentially without those goods.

"I know he's a piece of shit, but do you think he'd really threaten trade agreements that have stood for hundreds of years?" Cal asks.

"I do. There's only one other thing that could buy my vote and Rollins doesn't have the balls to do it."

My people are my duty, my responsibility. But the life of my father? That's one chip I would never bargain with, and one that even a scum like Charles Rollins wouldn't threaten.

"Whatever happens today, we will stop him. I won't let Rollins take anything from you or your people."

"I don't need protection," I remind him, the bite in my words mirroring the ice in my eyes.

"I know you don't need it. Killing him would be for my own pleasure."

Cal slips a single dagger into his armor's hidden sheath that runs along his ribs. He extracts another from his bag, offering it to me by the intricately carved ivory handle. Strange markings scroll elegantly across the alloy blade, my fingers absently tracing them as he continues.

"My reputation will deter most of the guards from attacking, but they will underestimate you. You won't expose your ... *power* ... to them, so you'll need blades. I owe you at least three, by my count."

"That was my favorite corset," I sigh with a half-smile. I take the blade from his waiting hands, testing its weight and balance across my palm. "There's always a few men who think they'll die if they touch me."

"They will." Cal moves in front of me, lifting my chin until my eyes meet his. "If you don't kill them, I will."

Gods, that shouldn't be so hot.

Power prickles my skin at the promise of death. Somewhere deep within me, the dark beast that forever craves decay opens one eye. The required balance for my life-giving earth magic smiles in the shadows.

Whatever happens today will be a test. A prerequisite for what awaits me—*what awaits us*—in Amale. My bones tingle at the thought of the unknown, something guaranteed to further propel our conjoined destiny.

Commotion outside pulls Cal to the window to investigate. Rollins' men, who have been stationed outside the inn since they delivered the correspondence just before dawn, are growing more restless by the minute. Undoubtedly taking to policing the streets in their quest for something to occupy their time.

Cal sighs, dragging a hand through damp, onyx hair.

"I need to get down there and remind them who they're dealing with," he says with an exasperated head shake.

"They can't know, Cal. If anyone gets even the slightest whiff that there's..." I struggle for the right word to describe whatever is happening between us and come up short.

"They have rebuked my birthright, discounted my claim as heir my entire life. I cannot ... *I will not...* give them any reason to further question my authority. You may not wish to see Marks on the throne, but the Captain of Corinth represents his interests. I will not be reduced to another one of the Lord General's puppets."

Cal tries to conceal the wince on his face, quickly turning away from me as he straps the emerald-hilted broadsword across his back.

"The problem with puppets, princess, is that everyone thinks they know who's pulling the strings. Marks thinks he's the ultimate master. A god who tames kings. But even his power has limits and even a captain has to follow commands." He turns to face me again, piercing steel eyes pinning me in place. "And despite what colors I wear or what allegiances I publicly swear, I will follow only your commands, my lady."

Bending at the waist, the Captain of Corinth bows at my feet and disappears into the hallway.

The cobblestone street outside the inn is unnervingly quiet. The menacing sight of a fully armed Captain of Corinth atop his gray mare is enough to cause the townsfolk to go out of their way to avoid his attention. Every soul in this village knows the deadly man who sits in their midst. Those who didn't see him ride in no doubt heard tales of his arrival throughout the evening.

Gasps fill the air around me as I exit the tavern. The unrecognizable, barely noticed commoner that accompanied the captain yesterday now has a face and a name. Chin up and shoulders back, I walk confidently towards my own readied horse, ignoring their shocked half-whispers.

"It's her. It's Poison Ivy."

"She's gods-cursed."

They're never as quiet as they think they are. Or maybe they just don't care. It's not like I'm human to them anyway.

Two red-coated soldiers flank either side of Cal, each atop a chestnut horse. The stoic mask of the captain is plastered on his face, the spark in his eyes noticeably absent when he looks at me.

It's exactly what I asked, or rather *commanded*, from him. So why does it scrape at my heart like a blade across tender flesh?

"Governor Rollins has sent us an escort, Lady Ivy." Disdain is thick in Cal's voice as he looks between the inferior soldiers.

One of the soldiers scoffs as he assesses my approaching form. "Summoned hours ago and still can't be bothered to put on a proper dress."

"I didn't realize Rollins allowed his men to openly mock the heir of a neighboring region." The man pales at the timbre of Cal's voice as a hint of black flashes in his eyes. "Perhaps I should have a talk with the governor about the insubordination in his ranks."

The second man breaks into a coughing fit, trying to stifle his laughter at his companion's discomfort. He looks as if he might soil himself under Cal's domineering glare, the threat of violence lingering in the air around us.

"Our apologies, Captain."

"Your scared apologies mean nothing." Cal's voice deepens, surpassing a threat and diving headfirst into a promise. "Show her the respect you show every other heir or you'll be quickly reminded that she has an army who answers to her."

The soldiers turn to face me fully now with a newfound reverence on their face. I know it's only there because they're scared of the Captain of Corinth, and even though I've said time and time again that I don't need his protection, I need this. Every part of me loathes it, but this is the only currency that these men respect.

Until I wish to wield my magic, this is the only power I have.

"If you boys are done, I have business to attend to and men to poison."

I mount my mare with a wide swing of my leg and immediately push her ahead into the heart of Gathe. I don't spare a look over my shoulder, but I don't have to. The disgust and fear that colors the villagers' expressions tells me that they heard and that Cal follows my lead. Two things that tug at my seams differently than they would have two days ago.

Power washes over me like a tranquil wave, gently eroding the jagged edges of my rage until I'm comfortably numb enough to walk into the den of the ruby-eyed lion.

170

CHAPTER 21

The halls of the Ruby Governor's manor are exquisite. Thick rugs in the deepest shades of red line the white marble floors of the entryway. A giant golden chandelier is suspended overhead, the crystal and ruby droplets hanging from its arms refract the light and cast shimmering shadows across the oak walls. Rollins' guards stand at attention near the large doors that lead to the public receiving chamber—his own version of a throne room.

As anticipated, the soldiers strip Cal of his visible weapon upon entering. The guard holds the captain's emerald-hilted sword with extra care as if it might sprout fangs and bite him without notice. They pay me little attention, never bothering to pat around my midsection to find the alloy blade I have concealed under my blouse.

Shadows dance at the edge of my vision, disappearing behind the thick drapes as quickly as they appeared. My magic hums, beckoning me to let it out to play.

"Well, well, well ... look what the gods dragged in."

A voice echoes in the empty corridor as a flash of red hair steps into view. Russet eyes dance with practiced arrogance as the Ruby Region heir leans against the chamber doors. He isn't a large man, but his presence has taken up far too much room in the memories that have consumed me for more than a decade.

"Keiran," I reply flatly, strength and determination filling my viridescent gaze.

"Is that any way to greet an old friend? I thought you'd be happy to see a handsome face after a week on the road with this brute!"

The governor's son pushes off his perch and pulls me into a forced embrace. I go rigid in his hold, air suddenly too thick to breathe easily. The proximity of our shared titles has forced me to stomach being in his presence, but being touched by him is something else entirely. Fiery power sparks under my skin as I wrench myself out of his grasp.

"What are you doing here?"

A foolish question on the surface, to not expect the heir to be in his own home, but Kieran has a penchant for being anywhere his father isn't.

"Father called me home. He's hoping we can squash this little crusade of yours here and save you the trip to Amale."

Mocking and presumptuous, just like he's always been. Just like he was that night all those years ago. He loops his arm through mine, tugging me against him. I'd love nothing more than to let my magic throw him across the room.

"Shall we?"

Kieran half-drags me through the open doors and into the chamber to face his father. From the corner of my eyes, I see a flash of pure, unadulterated fury in Cal's eyes before a cold neutrality replaces it.

Governor Charles Rollins sits at the head of the room in an ornate golden chair that could very easily be mistaken for a throne. The large crest of Gathe is inlaid in opal and rubies in the middle of the long oak table that separates us from the governor. Servants flank the walls, all women and all dressed in revealing cropped tops and harem pants made of a deep red chiffon despite the chill of the late winter air, a public reminder of how women are treated under his rule.

"Captain Murphy. It's an honor to finally meet you." Rollins stands and motions for Cal to sit.

"Ivy. I trust you remember my son?" His words are as pointed as his piercing eyes. As if we haven't known each other for a quarter of a century. As if his face didn't haunt me for years. As if I could ever forget him. And the bastard knows it.

"Governor, always a pleasure." The words are thick and full of forced saccharine, every lie a touch sweeter than the last. "Your home is as exquisite as ever."

"It really is. If only Emerald could have such riches." A sly smile crosses both of their faces as Kieran sits at his father's right hand.

Arrogant assholes, both of them.

"You requested to see us, Governor?" Cal cuts through tension building rapidly in the room.

"I summoned *her*." Disdain is thick in the governor's voice as he speaks. "But a respected military man such as yourself is always welcome in the home of a loyal Corinthian."

"What can I do for you, Governor?" Both my patience and the leash I keep on my magic are wearing thinner by the second.

"Yes, well, I was hoping that we could discuss this little trip of yours. I hardly think the Ascension Vote is any place for a woman." Rollins doesn't even try to hide his condescending chuckle as he speaks.

"Regardless of my sex, sir, I am the heir to the Emerald Region and I speak on behalf of our governor, as demanded by the Corinthian constitution. The very constitution that you are sworn to uphold."

"Well, that may be, but—" Rollins starts, but I don't let him finish.

"Surely you don't suggest that one of our jeweled regions should not have a vote in determining the next monarch?"

"That's not—" Rollins presses on, but I have to squash this now.

"To do so would be to position oneself as a king. Are you claiming the throne for yourself without the proper vote, Governor? Because that would be treason. Would it not, Captain?" I snap my head to Cal indicating the necessity of his response.

"It would," Cal replies.

Men like Rollins will only ever recognize the authority of another man, and as much as I hate to play that card, I know how to use all the weapons in my arsenal.

"Leave it to a woman to always jump straight to hysterics." Rollins gives an exasperated shake of his head at Kieran who nods in return. "Here I am, preparing to extend an invitation to be a guest in my home and she wants to accuse me of treason," he scoffs loudly. "If it wasn't the Lord General's request, I would see you out on your ungrateful ass."

"What did you say?" Surely I misheard his words. I cut my eyes to Cal, but if he's surprised, his face doesn't give it away.

"You're familiar with Lord General Marks, aren't you?" Kieran adds with a devious grin. "Who am I kidding? Of course you are, Poison Ivy."

"The Lord General has honored us with a visit to Gathe. I am hosting a ball tonight to celebrate his illustriousness and, for some gods-unknown reason, he's demanded that *you* attend. I've had my staff prepare rooms since he's so eager to see both you and Captain Murphy. We can't risk you being late again."

Marks is here.

My stomach bottoms out, my vision tunneling as I fight to stay upright. Chilled air nips at my skin but does little to cool the sweat that beads at the nape of my neck. But I will not show fear in the presence of men who already think me weak.

"Miriam can show you the way, Ivy," Kieran's voice snaps me back to attention. "Captain Murphy, I have something I need to discuss with you in private."

No one misses the sharp glare the governor gives his son. As if it's a meeting of usurpers plotting to overthrow their oppressive masters rather than Kieran trying to schmooze his way into the Lord General's good graces through his trusted captain.

"Lord General Marks has instructed me to ensure Lady Ivy's safety at all times. I will need to inspect her room first before our meeting, Lord Rollins." The casual lie, spoken with commanding authority, falls from Cal's lips.

"Do you question my trustworthiness in my own home, Captain?" Governor Rollins' voice booms through the chamber as he rises to his feet at the insult.

"It's not a matter of trust, Governor. It's a matter of following orders." Cal responds quickly, never missing a step in the dance.

Rollins sits again in a loud huff before dismissing us with a wave of his hand.

"Oh, Ivy," Kieran calls out before we cross the threshold. "I've had the staff place suitable attire for tonight in your wardrobe. I am so looking forward to seeing you in red."

My stomach lurches again at the thought of wearing his color. A noble woman wearing the color of another region indicates only one thing: her intention to take a seat within that house.

As the named heir, Kieran is his father's successor and the governor has made no secret about his search for a suitable bride for his son. Wearing red would be tantamount to accepting a proposal.

Intentional or not, Kieran has just revealed the true meaning behind his father's summons. The governor and Marks are planning to force me into an alliance I would rather die than agree to.

But if it's a symbol they want tonight, it's a symbol they'll get.

Leave it to Rollins to ensure we have to walk four flights of stairs before we're permitted to enjoy any level of comfort within his home.

"Shall I wait for you out here, Captain?" The servant asks sweetly once we finally arrive at my room.

"No, that won't be necessary. I can find my way back."

"Anna will be by this evening to help you dress, my lady." She bobs into a curtsy and scurries away before I can ask her not to call me that.

I turn to find Cal finishing a military-level sweep of the palatial room before I can even get the door closed.

"Did you know?" If he did and didn't prepare me...

"Of course I didn't fucking know." White-knuckled fists hang at his sides, his voice elevated and tense.

I approach him cautiously, careful not to corner him. His eyes bounce around the room, clearly not trusting his initial assessment.

"What does this mean, Cal?"

"It means that I have to play the dutiful, submissive captain while Marks tries to sell you off to Rollins. He's going to publicly taunt you, degrade you, and treat you like something to be bargained with. And I have to stand there and pretend like I don't fucking care. Like we're not connected and like it's not ripping me apart."

Anger that rivals my own stares back at me, but it's the barest hint of liquid in the inner corner that stops me. The single tear threatening to break free from his steel-colored eyes communicating everything I need to know.

One word from me, and Cal would risk everything. He would take my hand and bolt from Gathe faster than the gods themselves could move. He would throw our mission to save Corinth out the window and I can't let that happen.

"I have a plan," I admit with a confidence I don't wholly have yet.

"Of course you do." Cal smiles softly, his hand sweeping across his face as he turns towards the door. "Keep that blade on you at all times, princess. And whatever happens tonight, know that—"

"No," I stop him. I will not allow myself to consider any scenario in which I put my own interests above my people's. I cannot take anyone else's feelings into consideration or else I might talk myself out of my plan. "Tell me later."

He may be a royal asshole, but Governor Rollins does have one of the most exquisite manors in all of Corinth, second only to the king's palace in Amale. And despite his feelings towards me, the guest room I am assigned is no exception to that opulence.

A massive oak bed sits in the middle of the room with heavy, red velvet curtains hanging from the four-posters encasing the thick feather mattress. I don't even bother to remove my boots before collapsing onto the luxurious silk bedding.

The late afternoon sun is barely visible over the horizon when a knock at the door wakes me from my nap. A servant girl enters with a tray of food and lays it on the massive desk that sprawls in front of the floor to ceiling windows. She says nothing, only smiles and nods before leaving again.

My grumbling stomach pulls me towards the desk. A plate with roasted pork and a large heap of vegetables steams in the pale orange light. I eat quickly, watching the last rays of the sun dip below the Facet Mountains.

We're still a few days' ride from the base of the range and the river we'll have to cross to enter the Diamond Region, but from the towering height of the manor, the outline of them is unmistakable. Until now, I've thought of reaching the Alloy River as an inevitable, a small landmark on our cross-country journey. But now … now I wonder if we'll even make it that far.

The plate is long empty when another knock sounds. A different woman enters, the candlelight making her tan skin glimmer against the scant uniform her employer demands. Thick braids trail down her back in gorgeous plaits and I know the fingers that created those will be perfect for the hairstyle I have in mind.

She sweeps into a low bow as she approaches me. "My lady," she says softly.

"Call me Ivy." I try to not sound how I feel—exasperated, nervous, unsure.

"I'm Anna," she motions to herself, standing upright again. "It will be my honor to dress you."

Anna directs me to the open wardrobe, proudly displaying the selection of dresses sent by Kieran.

As promised, a red ball gown awaits in the front of the wardrobe. A taunt, but not a threat. Behind it, gowns made of exquisite silk, tulle, and organza fill the small space. Silhouettes in sapphire blue, silvery-white, golden yellow, and emerald green. Every color of Corinth's jeweled regions.

What are you playing at, Kieran?

I flip through them carefully, bypassing the colors of the other regions until my fingers snag on something wholly unexpected: a simple, silk gown in midnight black. The color of the Dark God of Death—and the color of Captain Callan Murphy.

Magic squeezes my heart, not at the thought of publicly declaring myself a harbinger of Death, but at the look that would overtake Cal when he saw me. I shake my head, clearing away the momentary lapse in judgement.

Behind the black dress, hidden in the very back of the wardrobe is the only color I prayed to find. I pull it out, handing it to Anna before I can talk myself out of it.

"You're sure, my lady?" she asks skeptically.

"Very."

Amethyst is a color reserved only for the monarch. If I was a governor, this dress would signal my intent to ascend the throne. But given that I'm not even eligible to be on the ballot, wearing the king's color is more of a formal 'fuck you' to his apparent successor.

I'm coming for the Lord General, and everyone here will know it after tonight.

Anna slides the gown over my head, my breath hitching as I realize how little silk fabric there is. Two swathes of cloth run over my shoulders, gathering just above the navel and clinging to my curves perfectly. I turn towards the mirror, admiring the low cowl that exposes my entire back.

"One second."

Anna's sweet voice trails off as she rushes back to the dressing table and removes a small box from the drawer. She swiftly pins a brooch at the seam on my stomach—an intricate silver serpent with sparkling diamond eyes.

"This was sent for you."

The image of the leviathan is uncanny, a near-identical replica of the beast that adorns Cal's chest but with a much smaller tail. I still don't fully understand why or how the sea beast connects us, but there's no mistaking its role in our fused fate.

Anna directs me to sit at the dressing table and I let her cover my face with creams and serums and cosmetics until my skin glows and pinks in all the right places. She adds purple and gold to my eyelids before darkening the lashes, accentuating my green eyes until they sparkle.

I reach towards the vase of godsbane blooms on the desk that I grew after dinner, extracting a few and explaining the vision for my hair.

Her nimble fingers move quickly, placing a silver circlet on my head before effortlessly braiding and twisting the hair into something even grander than I imagined. Anna pins the deep purple blooms and green leaves into the plaits until the style takes shape.

She steps back to admire her work and I'm breathless again. She has transformed my tresses into an ethereal crown fit for a poisonous earth goddess.

She secures strappy heels on my feet while I add long, thin silver earrings. Standing in front of the mirror, I nervously run my hands down my thighs, exposed on both sides by twin slits that start just below my hip bones.

Everyone will be talking about this dress and the woman wearing it.

"If there's nothing else, my lady…" she moves to clean up the brushes and pins that litter the dressing table but I stop her.

"Actually, Anna, there is one more thing." I pull Cal's ivory-handled dagger from my bag along with a simple sheath. "Can you help me with this?"

Her eyes linger on the strange letters and markings as she examines the blade. With a single nod, Anna drops to her knees and begins to wrap the black leather straps around my upper thigh. Her lips move silently as her fingers work to secure the buckles.

Curiosity overtakes me and I have to ask. "What are you doing?"

"Praying, my lady. To the goddess whose blessings cover you twofold."

"And whose blessings are they?"

"Arcasia," she says, standing to grip me by the shoulders. "May the Goddess of Protection guard you from the enemies who wait below."

CHAPTER 22

What exactly does one think about in the moments before they overtly declare themselves the utmost threat to a nation's peaceful transition of power? Apparently, they think about the absurd amount of stairs they have to descend in poorly constructed heels.

My hands are slick with sweat and my stomach is full of anxious butterflies by the time I reach the hallway leading to the ballroom. The thick ruby runner that lines the center of the corridor threatens to swallow my feet as I walk across it. Each step feels more like trudging through swampy earth than strolling casually across a rug in an opulent manner.

Music swells loudly from the orchestra that plays on the other side of the large oak doors, but I can barely hear it over the sound of my pounding heart and the magic roaring within me. I take a deep breath and will the power in my veins into submission. Head up, shoulders back, I steady myself and nod to the guards to open the doors.

The music reaches its coda just as the doors clang open. Revelers cease their chatter and turn to look at the source of the unexpected noise. Shock ripples across their faces at the poisonous woman who stands at the top of the stairs dressed in the color of their beloved monarch. A phantom wind flares the amethyst silk behind me with each step down the red-veined marble staircase. The dagger is cool against my skin, drawing a gasp somewhere in the crowd as it catches the light from the hanging chandelier.

With each downward tread, more heads turn, more whispers spread, and more sneers are thrown my way. A deep voice booms through the room, drawing the attention from me to the small dais. Governor Rollins stands at the conductor's lectern, his rotund face the same color as the ruby dress coat he wears, rage written plainly across it.

"I am honored to host several esteemed guests this evening," he begins.

Something tells me that he doesn't count me among that number.

"Our most revered Lord General and the famed Captain of Corinth have honored the nobility of the Ruby Region with their presence tonight."

Claps and cheers erupt through the ballroom as an impossibly tall, silver-haired man dressed in Corinthian gray steps onto the dais. Lord General Marks clasps Governor Rollins on the shoulder in a show of respect that looks almost comical with the extreme difference in their statures, before replacing him at the podium.

"It is always an honor to be among my devoted supporters in Gathe. You truly are the ruby in the crown of Corinth. Let us drink and dance and celebrate the great future that awaits us together."

Golden eyes find mine in the crowd at the word meant for me: *together.*

Magic pulses frantically in my veins under his stare but I don't dare break it. I let my hand drift down, my fingertips resting gingerly on the blade across my thigh. Time itself stills, stretching thin. My vision tunnels until it's only me and Marks in the ball-room; everyone else is lost to the encroaching shadows.

There's a low hiss, and, if I didn't know better, I would swear the silver serpent slithers to life against my belly. The air between us grows thick and cold, my lungs contracting at the sudden loss of oxygen. A wicked smile blooms across Marks' face at my struggling breath, but I meet it with a look of fierce determination.

We stand there for seconds, minutes, hours. Time no longer exists in whatever vacuum of space we've transported to.

With a wave of the conductor's baton, the orchestra strikes up again, and I find myself at the edge of the dance floor. The space around me is crowded but I have no recollection of moving from the last stair. Warmth from the fires along the outer walls of the ballroom warm my skin, the air light and easy to breathe once more. I search the dais for Marks, but the Lord General is nowhere to be found.

My magic flares again as someone approaches me from behind. I grip the dagger's handle in preparation, expecting to spin and find the hard, angry lines of Marks' face.

But it's the rich scent of leather and salt that I find instead.

Noble couples flank Cal, waiting for the guest of honor to start the first official dance of the evening, as is tradition.

"Lady Ivy," Cal says with a slight dip of head. Anything more would be construed as a bow. "As an esteemed visiting dignitary from the Emerald Region, it is only proper for you to lead us in the national dance of Corinth."

"It would be my honor, Captain Murphy."

I can think of few things I'd like to do less in this moment than dance in front of nobles whose faces show their open contempt for me, but society demands I do just that.

I place my hand in his waiting palm, the familiar tingle of his magic warming me where our skin lightly touches. The crowd parts as Cal leads me to the center of the floor. His hand moves to gently rest on my exposed back, careful of the watchful eyes that dissect our every move.

A violinist softly sweeps his bow across the strings, the first notes of the national song filling the ballroom. We move together in perfect time, a slow step followed by two quick steps. Couples join in all around us as the notes rise and fall. All eyes are focused on us as Cal spins me effortlessly to the music.

"Everyone is staring," I mumble through a soft smile.

Cal leans in as we spin again, using the closeness required by the motion to speak softly so only I can hear.

"That's because every man in this room wants to fuck you in that dress and their wives know it."

I cough, nearly choking on the shock of the words as the captain returns to his pleasant, demure smile. The music rises and falls again, our steps in perfect alignment.

"You could have said something more couth for listening ears. Like, 'You look ravishing tonight, my lady.'"

The next move calls for the men to dip their partners and Cal uses the opportunity to brush his lips against my ear as he speaks. "I'd like to ravish you tonight, my lady."

My cheeks flush as I swallow down the heat that floods me with his forbidden words. We are adrift in a sea of onlookers, nothing but casual acquaintances swaying in slow-quick-quick steps to the swell of the orchestra.

"This might be our only chance to speak." Cal's words are clipped and stern when he speaks again, the tantalizing lover's tease gone. "Marks plans to show me off tonight."

"Like a crown prince?" I joke without thinking. It's a cruel comparison to make, insinuating that he's Marks' heir, and I instantly regret it.

"More like a prized stallion," Cal corrects.

If my words hurt him, he doesn't show it in front of the noble eyes that scrutinize us like we're nothing more than a museum exhibit.

Overcompensating in an attempt to cover my carelessness, I joke again. "The women in this room would hand over all of their rubies for a ride on you."

"I'm only interested in amethysts tonight." Cal dips me again in a low, sweeping movement as the music ends. "My mother's brooch looks excellent on you, princess."

He pulls me to a standing position and steps back quickly to join in with the other men clapping loudly around us. I bend my knees in a customary curtsy along with the other women, but my eyes never leave his. There's a wink of his signature smoke—a reminder of the fire that burned between us—before cold steel stares back at me.

I dip my head in a curt nod, eager to make my way off the dance floor quickly. I don't wish to entertain nobles tonight with waltzes and quicksteps.

Serving women dressed in sparse uniforms flit around the crowd carrying trays of sparkling wine, and I eagerly accept one as it passes by. The effervescent wine is sweet, too sweet. How do the people of the Ruby Region manage to down bottle after bottle of this?

"You have some gall, strutting in here like a prized whore in the King's colors." I don't have to turn to know who the voice belongs to.

"Careful, Governor. You wouldn't want to appear threatened by a woman, would you?" I keep my back to him, casually sipping the syrupy liquid.

"You cocky little cunt. Your father should have put you in your place a long time ago."

"My place," I turn to face Rollins head-on now, "is a position of power. And I plan on being there for longer than you'll be alive."

I push past him, forcefully bumping his shoulder as I stride towards the open doors that lead out to the courtyard.

The night air is cold, but that doesn't deter the couples sneaking around in the maze, desperate for a taboo tryst amongst the shrubbery. I walk the outskirts of the plant-lined walls, careful not to disturb the lovers in their act. I trail my fingers along the petals of the winter roses that grow thick in the hedges, wishing not for the first time that I could freely use the power I hide, that I could wrap magical vines around the throats of every vile man who seeks only to degrade and destroy me.

But instead, I hide it. Too terrified of becoming their weapon to become their reckoning.

"Searching for a partner?" Kieran's voice cuts through the dark as his moonlit form takes shape just ahead.

"Hardly." I clench my fist, the rose beside me wilting into dust.

"Can I offer you a drink?" His outstretched hand holds a stemmed flute full of the sickeningly sweet wine.

"The last time I accepted a drink from you, you slipped poison in it. I think I'll pass."

Anger floods through me alongside the memory of that night 10 years ago. The saccharine liquid and heated kisses that led to blood, headache, and heartache.

"Fair." Kieran deposits the glasses on the tray of a passing servant who quickly scurries away. "I can see that you dressed to piss off powerful men tonight."

"I dressed to make a statement. Pissing men off is an added bonus."

Kieran moves closer to me. To anyone standing on the expansive porch off the ballroom, we might very well look like lovers ourselves. I step back, creating distance between us to ensure this conversation isn't misconstrued by any watchful eyes.

"Selene would be proud of you."

All sense of decorum leaves my body at the sound of my mother's name on his lips.

"Keep her name out of your vile mouth."

Footsteps sound rapidly behind us and Kieran moves with lightning speed to cage my head between his strong forearms, pressing my back into the wall of hedges. My hands reach for the dagger, the tip coming to rest against the soft underflesh of his chin.

His voice is low, his lips mere inches from my face as he speaks. "I can give you a way out of all this, Ivy."

"What makes you think I want a way out?" I bite through clenched teeth.

The heir chuckles deeply as a single drop of his blood snakes down the alloy blade. "We all want a way out."

Giggles carry from the other side of the shrubbery, sounds of smacking lips and moans of pleasure following. Kieran searches the dark, pulling me away from the hedges and deeper into the shadows.

"When Marks makes his offer later, you should at least consider it."

I don't have time to ask what he's talking about before he turns and heads deeper into the hedges.

A frozen wind sweeps through the courtyard causing my entire body to shudder and carrying away any ounce of curiosity to follow him with it. Spring is beginning to bloom around us, yet the air lends itself more to snowy conditions, and anyone spending time out here is likely to fall ill. I rush back to the warm ballroom to escape the abrupt change in the weather, my senses going into overdrive at the onslaught of sight and sound.

Sparkling wine spills neglectfully from too full glasses as nobles spin haphazardly around the crowded dance floor. Orchestral instruments play a cacophonous melody that ends with the loud clanging of cymbals. The room appears more like an offering to Bastin than a noble ball.

A crushing sense of dread sours my stomach, like the air is too thin and all of the exits are blocked. My ears ring and my vision tunnels as overwhelming panic starts to attack my every sense. Time moves backward. Reality shifts.

Something is very wrong here.

"What luck to catch you alone, Lady Ivy." The owner of the icy voice needs no introduction. Lord General Marks steps into my line of sight, his gloved hand extended in my direction. "Dance with me."

My heart hammers against my ribcage, my blood revolting at his presence. I would sooner die than dance with him, but my body operates of its own accord. I watch through confused eyes as my hand lands in his waiting palm. The dark leather gloves covering his hands are smooth and warm. Too warm, like fire runs in his veins rather than blood. Invisible vines wrap themselves around my brain and squeeze tightly, forcing me to bend to Marks' will.

I am a puppet, and Marks is the puppet master.

Unnatural shadows foxtrot across the walls as we begin to move. I follow the dark that dances around the edges of my vision, focusing on anything other than the wrongness of living within a body that no longer belongs to me.

Is this how he makes kings answer to him?

A swarm of bodies dressed in ruby red part to reveal Cal's black-clad form. His head snaps in my direction, his gray irises overtaken by black pupils. Familiar power floods my body, mixing with my own until I can breathe steadily again. My feet move in time to the music, but their movement is all mine again. Whatever spell Marks held over me is now broken.

"Interesting choice this evening, declaring yourself as royalty before the Ascension Vote." There's an oily quality to his words and they leave a slick trail as they wash over me. "You never have been one for subtlety, have you, Poison Ivy?"

The barb of his little nickname spears me, injecting me with a boldness that I wield better than any blade.

"I am coming for you, Lord General," I whisper. Marks spins me outward in a sweeping twirl, my face coming close to his when he whips me back into his hold. "And when my poison slows your heart, I want you to look me in the eyes as you admit your defeat."

A foreboding, humorless laugh bellows from his mouth. Dancers around us pause their steps in an effort to hear our conversation. Marks waves them away with a flick of his hand, never stopping our long-short-short step sequence.

"This game goes beyond you, Ivy. Be a good girl and play your part."

"And what part is that?" A barely contained fury barrels through me at his words.

"Willing partner. Subdued paramour. Dutiful wife." He spins me again. "It matters not to me, just as long as you submit and keep your poisonous mouth shut, lest I shut it permanently."

"It's you that will submit, Lord General." I snarl at him, baring my teeth like a wild animal, unable to contain my ire any longer.

The music stops abruptly and the dancers step away to clap, but I'm unable to move. The air in the room is impossibly thin but no one else seems to be struggling to breathe. My lungs spasm in short pants as I gasp for oxygen and find none. My nails claw at my throat desperate for breath as black spots threaten to overtake my vision. My body sways and I can feel myself slumping towards the marble floor.

Strong arms encircle my waist, catching me before I fall. My body rests against a broad chest, the only thing holding me upright and conscious.

I am not supposed to die like this. This isn't what the gods have foretold would be my fate. I am not in Amale yet.

Air suddenly rushes back into my lungs and I gulp it down by the mouthful, desperate for even a hint of oxygen.

"You don't look well, Lady Ivy. Perhaps you've drunk too much wine? I hear you are fond of that." Marks' pointed words scrape against my skin. "It's a good thing Lord Kieran caught you before you cracked that pretty little head of yours."

My stomach clenches at the realization of who currently holds me but I don't have enough strength yet to break away.

"You know, I was just explaining to Governor Rollins how advantageous of a match you two would make," Marks continues. "Especially now that your father is dead."

Time stills again, the entire world ceasing to spin as my mind tries to make sense of what's happening. There's a cracking in my chest and hot liquid spills from my eyes in wordless rivers.

My father is dead.

"Escort the heir ... I mean, the *governor* ... to her room, Kieran. Or yours, if you'd prefer."

"Yes, Lord General."

The wet blur of faces, the garbled sounds of music, the forceful grip on my arm, the gasping breaths in my chest—they're all part of an obscure moment in a new world. A world without my father.

Kieran hauls me forcefully into the hallway, dropping my arm as soon as we're clear of the heavy oak doors that separate us from society. They shut noiselessly and I'm only vaguely aware that he's speaking to me.

No, not speaking to me ... shouting at me.

But I can't hear him. I can't hear anything over the sound of my universe shattering.

"Are you listening to me, Ivy?" Kieran yells.

"No." My voice is barely a whisper, barely a breath.

Kieran pushes me backward, forcefully smacking my head against the hall wall. Whatever the purpose, the collision forces me out of my stupor.

"*What the fuck do you want from me?!*" I scream, my voice raw as magic sizzles at my fingertips. I can't control it in this state, and there's no telling which side will decide to come out when my hold breaks.

"Tomorrow, you're going to accept Marks' offer to marry me."

"I would rather DIE!" I shout at him again and the floor beneath us trembles.

"And that's exactly what you'll do if you don't get yourself under control right now."

Kieran must have slipped the dagger from my thigh at some point during my stupor, its edge now pressing against my throat. Warmth dribbles down the column of my neck as the cold steel bites into my skin. It's barely a nick, but the dark side of my magic rises in response to the iron tang of blood that laces the air. I lean into the alloy blade, my blood trailing down the markings—Arcasia's markings that now glow blue.

"Kill me or get out of my fucking way, Kieran."

The otherworldly voice that leaves my throat isn't wholly mine. Thick vines of ivy trail up the wall behind him. Everything I imagined using my power for in the garden hovers just within reach.

"What the fuck do you think you're doing, Rollins?" Cal's voice cuts through the haze like a knife as it rumbles down the large, empty hallway.

Fury, the likes of which can only be rivaled by the Dark God of Death, drips from his form. His entire body vibrates with power. Thin black shadows swirl around my feet in response, skating over my porcelain skin in a delicate graze. With only a thought, the ends sharpen into dagger-like points, poised to strike.

"Back the fuck away from her, Kieran, or I will kill you where you stand."

Black overtakes Cal's irises as he stalks towards us, power crackling in the air around him like lightning. Is this what he looks like on the battlefield before he takes on his enemy? Is this the last thing the legion of Synalian soldiers saw before they met Death?

"Do both of you have a death wish?" Kieran mutters, his russet eyes burning as red as his suit as he backs away from me. "Marks has eyes everywhere."

Kieran lunges at Cal but only gets a single step before my blade falls from his hands. Blood drips from the corners of Kieran's mouth as he gasps for air, clawing at his throat in a manner that feels all too familiar. Cal's arms shake violently as Kieran drops in a heap to the floor.

The air is electric and my own power screams back in response, more than eager to join the symphony. Magic calls out to me, the siren song almost too strong to resist. Something old and strange shouts at me to release my hold and join whatever ripples through the cold granite hallway. To shake the foundation with only a thought, to kill with the inky apparitions that flit around me.

Shouts and pounding feet echo on the stone floor. Cal's eyes snap to me before barking a single command, every word dripping with violent, unruly power.

"Run."

Shadows flood the room, casting me into total darkness. A scream rings out through the pitch black, a scream that I recognize as my own. I turn and run, my feet covering more ground than should be possible in the short amount of time. I take the stairs two at a time, not slowing until I find my room.

Locking the door behind me, I dive into my bed and pull the silk sheets over my head.

Whoever I was this morning is no more. Whatever hold I had on my power, on my life, is gone. Violent sobs wrack my body, tears flowing freely until my body passes out from exhaustion.

And it's there, in the Ruby Governor's manor, that I die.

CHAPTER 23

Dark envelopes me wholly. I am numb, adrift in a bottomless void of emotion so vast that I doubt I will ever plant my feet on solid ground again. Wave after wave of icy indifference washes me further and further away from the shore.

The poisonous heir to the Emerald Region of Corinth is dead. No black will drape the temples nor will jewel-colored flags fly at half mast.

But the people will grieve.

Not for her, but for the way of life they hold so dear. For the misogyny so embedded in their blood that the very thought of a woman as their ruler turns their dreams to nightmares. For the gods they love so deeply whose names will become curses instead of prayers.

Their longstanding hope that she would submit to the will of a husband or be killed before she was elevated to governor is now extinguished. And in the cold light of a late winter day, we all wake to a reality we didn't choose.

A muffled knock sounds at the door, but I don't bother to respond or even remove the blankets from over my head.

"It's time to get up now, Governor. You're expected at breakfast."

Anna's sweet voice drifts through the layers of bedding and into my covered ears. I can't stifle the shudder that wracks my body at the formal way she addresses me now. Delicate fingers slowly pull back the blankets, exposing my swollen, sensitive eyes to the eerie light of day.

Are the colors of this new world different? Somehow both brighter and wetter?

Prying the matted hair from my face, stuck by the gallons of salty tears that I shed in the dark, I adjust my eyes to take in the scene outside the floor length window.

"It snowed last night, my lady."

Snow? It's not unheard of this late in winter, but it's certainly unexpected in the valley that protects Gathe from the mountains to its west. It's almost as if a god froze the water in the clouds and forced it to the ground so the outside could mirror the frigidness of my heart.

"I need to make you presentable, your Governorship." Anna holds a boar-bristle brush in one hand, her other grasping a cluster of crushed godsbane she pulled from the mattress.

"Those are poisonous." The words are scratchy in my raw throat.

The woman nods, never speaking as she starts to unpin and untangle the mess of hair that clumps down my back. Her brush snags on knots, but I don't feel its pull. She could rip it from my head with her bare hands and I would be none the wiser.

Somewhere in the span of the minutes or hours that follow, Anna strips me of the purple silk gown and silver jewelry. She gasps when she finds the indentation left on my stomach by the silver brooch, the red impression of the sea beast stark against my ivory skin.

This mark hurts less than the first one the creature left on me.

I'm submerged in water, scrubbed until my skin pinks, and then dried with tender care. My wet hair is plaited and secured into a bun at the base of my skull. Clothes designed to fight the chill of the winter air are slipped onto my pliable body. Supple, double-lined brown leather pants, a thick cream sweater knitted in intricate knots, and knee-high brown boots. Across my shoulders, Anna secures my noose: a heavy woolen cloak in my region's color.

When she is done, and I am finally considered presentable for whatever I've been summoned for, Anna steps back in a sweeping curtsey.

"The Lord General and his men are leaving this morning, Governor."

I don't pull my eyes from the pristine snow that covers the ground outside in thick blankets. The door clicks softly behind me but my thoughts are consumed by the glimmering drifts of white below. If we have any hope of traversing it successfully, I'll have to use magic. Unruly magic, life and death commingling into a mass of wild power I'm not sure I know how to control anymore.

"Maybe they'll all die in it," I mutter bitterly to myself, turning away from the windows and forcing my feet to take me down the red-veined marble stairs.

The Captain of Corinth waits for me outside the open doors that lead to the dining hall. He angles slightly as I approach, blocking my view of the room with his broad shoulders. His posture is rigid, his face like stone.

But his eyes—*Cal's eyes*—sweep over me in assessment. From head to toe and back up again, they search for any sign of physical injury. Every muscle along his jaw is clenched, a perfect mirror to the fists that hang at his sides.

"Meet me in the courtyard after breakfast."

Cal's voice is a low whisper, careful not to be heard by the passing servants carrying heaping platters of food from the kitchen. There's an unmistakable tinge of pain in the lines of his face and the tilt of his lips, something even his normally convincing mask can't hide today. His finger brushes against mine in the barest hint of touch as he steps back and enters the hall.

Lord General Marks, wrapped in a cloak made entirely of white fur, sits at the head of the long table in an oversized chair. Rollins must have a throne-like seat in every room of his gods-damned house. Sparkling rubies nestle between the swirling clouds and stiff mountain peaks carved into the dark mahogany above his silver hair. His unnaturally golden eyes watch me as I take my seat, a predator observing my every move.

"So glad you could join us, Ivy."

His voice is viscous, syrupy on the surface to lure in his prey. But I am no easy kill.

"Governor," I correct. "That's my title now, and you will use it when you address me."

"Such venom in the mornings," Marks tsks, turning his focus to his captain. "You could have warned me, Callan."

Cal takes a slow sip from his steaming mug, never breaking eye contact with his commander. When he doesn't give Marks the satisfaction he seeks, the Lord General turns his attention elsewhere.

With the flick of a finger, he waves over a servant girl, her silver platter piled high with smoked sausages. She's still wearing the scant ruby-red uniform, her whole body shaking in the drafty room as she attempts to place the meat on his plate.

"Someone light a fire," I demand more than ask.

"A fire?"

Delight sparks in his eyes as a cruel smile overtakes his face. Marks pushes the heavy chair backwards, his royal mantle rippling behind him as he stands. Gods, it must have taken the pelts of two dozen wolves to make his mockery of a cape.

"Allow me."

The Lord General lifts his thick fingers in the air and snaps only once. Flames explode from the logs stacked within the stone hearth, blazing to life without the strike of a match. Servants scream and run from the room, but Marks never takes his eyes off of me.

His smirk begs for a sign of surprise, a scream, anything that might make him feel powerful. Anything that might make me appear scared or weak. My face shows nothing but a cold neutrality, as if we are three completely normal people having breakfast instead of three *aevus* with hidden magic preparing to battle for control of a nation.

Marks slams his palms on the table, his cruel, low chuckle echoing through the silent room.

"I've sent notice of your engagement to the Royal Clerk. When the other governors learn that Kieran will be speaking for Emerald, well … they'll thank me with their vote. Now run along home lest I use this power on you."

Tiny flames sprout from his fingertips, but they do not scare me. Shadows of my own making flit around the edges of the room as I rise to my feet. Where rage and fury would normally overtake me, a killing calm settles instead.

"With all due respect, Lord General, which is none, you can go fuck yourself." I round the table to step into Marks' domineering space. "The only person with authority to speak on behalf of the Emerald Region is its governor. Whatever your reasoning for committing the treason that gave me the title, it is *mine* now. And yours will be next."

"You are nothing." Marks grips me forcefully by the chin. Soulless black pits stare into me and I meet them with a fiery defiance.

"You might be an heir, but you will never sit on a throne. Now run back to your pathetic little region and wait for your betrothed to return."

Green movement draws my attention just over Marks' shoulder. Verdant vines crawl slowly across the brown stone walls. Vines of my own making come to life without so much as a command from me. Vines with a mind and a power of their own.

The temperature in the room plummets suddenly, the fire extinguished by an icy wind that ripples through the room.

"Down, pup," Marks snarls at Cal, dropping his hold on my face. "You know what it will cost you. But you ..." His attention is back on me now, black spots forming at the edge of my vision. "You have no idea what it will cost you. Foolish girl, daring to play the game without knowing all the players."

Wisps of black shadows swirl over the Lord General's arms, skating across his chest. His head drops, eyes following them as they twist around his massive form. He waves a hand dispersing my misty black bands into nothing as his head lifts slowly.

Preternaturally golden eyes drag up the length of my body until they lock onto mine. The muscles in his face and neck look primed to snap. A wolf ready to unhinge his jaws and rip out my throat.

"Go. Home."

Each word is forced through clenched teeth, his voice a low, foreboding growl that causes the last remaining servant in the room to faint. The Lord General pushes past me, the fur of his cloak flaring behind him as he crosses the room in giant strides.

"Come, Callan," Marks commands.

Cal shoots me a single, unreadable glance before reluctantly following his commander to the edge of the room. Marks halts when he reaches the door, pivoting to face me so quickly that Cal nearly runs into him.

"If you step foot in Amale, Ivy Fellows, I will personally make sure you meet your father. And trust me, Death will have no mercy for you."

The coffee is bitter and lukewarm at best. Between sips of the rich, bold liquid, I admire my handiwork. Thick bands of vines at least six inches in diameter decorate the stone walls. Running both in parallel and perpendicularly are vines of variegated ivy. Forest green leaves rimmed in white tangle amongst the solid, sprawling vegetation.

Magic must have a signature. I recognize mine even when I don't feel its familiar tingle in my blood. The tugging sensation that flares within me every time I use it didn't come, but these plants are mine. I can sense my life in them. The pulsing heartbeat of air, water, and chlorophyll. I created them and they answer only to me.

I've felt Cal's magic and now I've felt Marks'. Each different. Each unique.

I snap my fingers and watch as the plants begin to shrivel, slowly compounding in on themselves until they crumble. By the time I've drained my second cup of coffee, the stone walls are bare again. Piles of dust along the floor are the only evidence that something occurred here. And even though the vines are no longer living, the decaying death that stripped them of their essence is as much mine as the life that coursed through them minutes ago.

Ever since my magic manifested I've kept it hidden, terrified that someone would exploit me against my will. But that deep-seated fear has vanished. I am a weapon, and if I don't wield it, someone else will. I broke my personal blood oath of secrecy and snapped the rigorous reins of my own repression. This magic, both beautiful and deadly, is as much a part of me as my blood and bones.

It's time I started acting like it.

The courtyard isn't far from the dining room, but I take my time getting there. Cal is undoubtedly getting an earful from Marks anyway. I recognized the cold air that extinguished the fire as his, and I'm certain his commander did too.

Soldiers in gray uniforms trimmed in gold file down the large staircase and out the doors, each carrying bags, swords, or furs. I watch them in quiet contemplation, but even as the last of the envoy heads towards the stables, Kieran doesn't appear.

No matter. Whatever happened in the hallway last night was denouncement enough of this proposed union.

Tables made of red-veined marble sit every few feet along the hall that leads to the courtyard, each topped in a vase filled with winter roses. Blooms clipped from the hedges that cover the gardens and stripped clean of their thorns. I pluck one from its urn, trailing a single finger down the slick, green stem. Sharp, brown points sprout from the scarred places where they once protruded. I slide the pad of my thumb across one. The prick doesn't sting or burn; in fact, my nerves barely register it at all. Bright red blood pools to the surface of my skin. Blood that looks the same as it did yesterday, but feels infinitely more powerful.

The sun is bright against the snowy drifts that cover the paved walkway. The green of the hedges contrasts beautifully against the stark white. Four thick hedges, each at least eight feet tall, create the outline of a square. A golden fountain nestled in the center forms the crowning centerpiece of the courtyard. Roses, petals shriveled and frozen, dot the thorny rows. Wilted blooms perk up, life filling them again as I walk past.

I close my eyes, tilting my face towards the warmth radiating from above. With an exhale, I breathe out the essence of existence. Deep violet crocus blooms burst brazenly from the empty, frozen garden beds. Drooping green and white snowdrops, yellow daffodils, pale narcissus, orange pansies, winter daphne, and bold pink camellias join in a color symphony that looks as if it was sent by the Goddess of Spring herself.

Power flows effortlessly from me. With barely more than a thought, I can summon more magic than I ever dreamed possible. I wielded only a fraction of this in the woods, when I commanded the earth to swallow the dead and conceal every trace of the gruesome scene. Using that much pushed me past the brink of exhaustion, but I don't even break a sweat now.

My skin tingles as a warm, familiar power washes over me. I know he approaches before I hear his footsteps.

"Did you know?" I say without turning around.

"Ivy." Pain laces his voice, the single word telling me the truth. But I need to hear him say it.

"Did you know?" I ask again slowly.

"No, I swear it." Cal steps beside me, his shoulder brushing mine as he takes in my creations. "I found out when you did."

My magic screams at me to believe him, and it's that feeling that forces me to push him further. I need to know if I can trust this new, seemingly depthless magic not to lead me astray.

"The soldier that stopped you when we rode into Gathe. What did he tell you?"

Cal's head moves on a silent swivel, surveying the courtyard and the windows that overlook it. He grabs my arm and pulls me to where two hedges meet, the corner providing the perfect shield against prying eyes.

"He told me that Marks is mobilizing troops. Not a lot, but enough to make a statement. Enough to remind the people who is really in control."

Cal offers the information easily, leaving me room to ask the question that will solidify his trustworthiness. It's information that he can't possibly know I have, courtesy of soldiers with too loose lips.

"To where?" I ask.

"Topaz," he replies without hesitation.

In a world of politics and strategy, truth is rarely offered so freely and openly, even amongst allies. He pulls me into his chest, one hand cradling the back of my head as if he can absorb me into him if he holds on tight enough.

"I'm so fucking sorry, Ivy. If you—"

"Is this when you beg me to go back to Emerald?" I ask against the black wool that covers his expanse of muscles. "Tell me all about your orders and what's in my best interest?"

"What?" Cal drops his hold on my head, pulling back to look me fully in the face. Silver lines the edges of his gray eyes, full of shock and hurt. "You think I would do that? Fuck his orders! The only person who commands me is you."

"Until I ask you to do something you disagree with," I scoff.

"What have I done to give you the impression that I would do anything other than whatever you asked of me?" Cal's voice is gruff and agitated. "Turning back never crossed my mind. But do you know what did, princess? Setting up a meeting with an informant so you can know exactly who's warming your chair back home. You need to go to Amale, but you also need to know that your people are safe. Look me in the eyes and tell me that I'm wrong."

I swallow the thick knot that attempts to fully block my airway. His pain shoots out like an arrow piercing through the membranous layer of numbness that covers me. And as his forehead bends to rest against mine, the last of that protective shield slips away. I feel it all; our shared anguish, grief, and sorrow is depthless. Our hold on each other may be the only thing keeping us both afloat.

"Can we trust him?" I ask on a breathy exhale, trying to hold in the tears that prick at my skull.

"We?" He pauses, waiting to see if I walk my word choice back again, waiting to see if it was unintentional. When I don't, a soft smile pulls at the corners of his mouth.

"Yeah, princess. We can trust him. But I need you to stay here, out of sight. We can't risk word getting to Marks that I'm doing anything other than gathering intel for what I might encounter in Emerald. We'll give him a day's head start and leave in the morning."

Even if Marks didn't have magic, he has the full force of the Corinthian military at his command. I don't like staying behind, and I don't like staying here longer than necessary, but Cal is right. We need the element of surprise on our side.

"Kieran rode off with Marks and rumor has it that Charles Rollins is sleeping off a hangover from hell, so you don't have to worry about them bothering you while I'm gone."

"It's Rollins who should be worried about me," I scoff. "Both of them."

Cal's thumb brushes across the tiny cut across my throat where Kieran held the dagger. The magic that usually flutters when his skin touches mine bursts into an explosion of light and sensation. His fingers tremble against my skin, a signal that our experience is shared.

I don't know who moves first, but when our lips crash together, the kiss is consuming. Neither of us able to fight the gravitational pull of the other. Cal's magic mixes with mine in a cocktail that could intoxicate even the most powerful of the gods. Every inch of me vibrates with the sensation, every nerve ending alighting with power. From the tips of my fingers to the tips of my toes, I am electric and thirst for more. He is an oasis in a desert and I drink him in.

Cal breaks the kiss, breathless and tense. Conflict is written across his features, clearly torn about his next move. Something hovers on the tip of his tongue and I decide to put him out of his misery.

"Go," I command. "Get information that we can use and come back to me."

He plants one last kiss to my forehead before stepping away.

"On one condition," he jokes as he retreats. "Try not to turn the entire manor into a greenhouse while I'm gone."

CHAPTER 24

The halls of the manor are eerily quiet. All of the servants are occupied with cleaning the ballroom from last night's revelry, tidying up guest rooms now vacated with the envoy's departure, or hiding after Marks' little power display in the dining room this morning. I climb the stairs, eager to retreat to the quiet, comforting escape of my silk-laden bed, when something stops me.

A magical, invisible rope wraps itself around my sternum and yanks. I dig my heels into the ruby runner that lines the floor in a futile attempt to resist. But its message is clear: follow the call or rip in two.

Resigned, I let the magic guide me down the third floor corridor, past the floor-to-ceiling windows that face the Facet Mountains and beyond the gallery walls lined with rich oil paintings and their gleaming golden plaques.

My feet stop of their own accord outside an intricately carved door. The swirls of clouds and rigid mountain peaks are identical to Rollins' throne-like chairs. Every detail is a perfect match, from the shape of the clouds down to the embedded rubies reflecting the daylight that pours in from the wall of windows.

You have got to be kidding me.

I trusted the magical pull in my chest and it led me straight to Kieran Rollins' bedroom. I take a deep breath and ready my magic to fight before I remember Cal's words: Kieran rode off with Marks. The doorknob turns easily, the click of the mechanism barely audible even in the empty hallway. I slip in, carefully latching it behind me lest I be discovered by a passing servant.

Kieran's bedroom looks exactly how I remember it. When it was Ruby's turn to host the summits, all of the heirs would hide out in here. At first with our nannies and then by ourselves when we were older. Long, boring weeks passed quickly over games of tables and chess played on the plush red carpet. Nights spent all pilled together in the large king-sized bed, heaps of exhausted limbs and childish innocence. We were closer than siblings.

But that was before. Before the sea beast touched me and unexplainable magic filled my veins. Before we were taught to see each other as competition. Before the boys grew into men and were conditioned to resent my recognized status. Before each of our mothers fell ill and passed away one by one.

A curse. That's what we believed killed them, once upon a time.

Anyone who loves a governor dies, Marianne would whisper to me in the dark. Foolish nonsense, likely, but I doubt I'll get the chance to find out. I'll be dead long before the others ever become governor of their own regions.

Bookshelves line the walls of the heir's room. Each crammed with books and loose papers and littered with broken quills and sentimental knickknacks. I drag my fingers down the gold embossed titles that decorate the leather tomes. These books are old, their spines cracked from days of endless reading from numerous heirs who came before Kieran.

The shelves are well stocked, topics ranging from science and art to history and politics. Titles on the history of Corinth, the lineage of the governing families, the detailed transcriptions of trade agreements. Everything a future governor—or future king— would need to know.

The pulling sensation in my chest tugs me towards the over- sized bed. Enthralled in the paintings that line the wall, I never notice the abandoned cloak that blends in with the red carpet. I stumble, banging my knee on the small nightstand as I crash to the ground in a heap.

A shadowy mass under the bed catches my eye. Instinctively I reach for it, my fingers wrapping around thick, leather straps. Moving to sit up, I lift the heavy bag and unbuckle the metal clasps. Gleaming gilded-edged pages catch the light, stealing my breath and further piquing my curiosity. Sliding the book carefully from the bag, I run my fingers over the embossed lettering and colorful illustrations that decorate its cover.

Tales of Provenance: Gods & Beasts of the Golden Pantheon

Magic sings in my veins, clearly pleased with my discovery. Delicately, I begin to thumb through the pages, growing more confused with each turn. Why does Kieran have a children's book about the gods hiding under his bed?

No one who truly knows him would consider him pious. One year, when the summit was hosted in Topaz, he could barely sit the entire week. Silas let it slip that Kieran had been whipped at school by one of the priests for openly calling Nobus a piece of shit. We were appalled at the time, but he wasn't wrong. The God King is pretty high up on my list of people that I'd like to punch in the face.

No, I doubt Kieran is reading religious accounts of the gods or fables of mythical beasts to fall asleep at night. So why does he protect this book like it's the only one of its kind? I pick up the tome and shake it—a little something I picked up during the library shifts dolled out as punishment at the hands of my school's overbearing headmaster.

On the third and final shake, I notice a worn scrap of parchment peeking out between the gilded pages.

No, not a scrap.

A neatly folded letter, its own edges so worn that they appear deckled. A single word is meticulously calligraphed in black ink across the front:

Son.

I flip the delicate paper over and inspect the ruby red wax that once held the missive closed. There, in the center of the seal, is the outlined image of a crescent moon. My breath catches in my chest, the image of my mother's drawing rushing back to me as I open the letter. It's not her handwriting, thank the gods. But it is the handwriting of another mother.

There is verity in fables, Kieran. Study this text. Dissect it and uncover the truths my people have tried so hard to hide.

He will need your help to defeat Mikais and get the others home. I can't tell you his name because I do not know what they chose to call him here, but you'll know him by her mark. Arcasia suffered for him and she marks all she sacrifices to protect.

The longer I'm away from my home, the more my power wanes. I have so little of it left now that I doubt I will live to see your birthday.

But know this, my darling. I do not regret the choices that brought me here because they brought me you. My only regret is that we took his choice. You must help him for all of our sake.

Look for me in the flames.

Mother

I neatly fold the letter back in its well-worn creases. How many times has Kieran read this? Dark spots smudge the 'r' in her signature. Tear stains from a boy who was left with a monumental task.

He was days shy of fifteen years old when she died, a marked turning point in the trajectory of the man Kieran became.

Magic pulls my attention downward to the open book in my lap. A single page, framed in golden filigree, and in its center, the black image of the sea beast stares back at me.

Holy gods.

I have searched the libraries of every governor's manor, every temple, and every major city in Corinth. Years of combing and questioning only to hit dead end after dead end.

But here it is.

In a dusty leather bag under the bed of the Ruby Region heir sits what might be the only written record of the serpent in our country.

I pour over every word with an insatiable scrutiny, examining every linguistic choice and analyzing the syntax of every sentence until my vision starts to blur. The tale of the sea beast unfolds before me in a haze of foiled pages, one story leading into another and another. Information stripped from our holy texts coalesces into a pantheonic history that the high priests would rebuke as sacrilege. The mere possession of this tome is enough to condemn someone to execution.

Legends, myths, fables—whatever they are, they are *damning.*

Page after page tells epic tales of a rebellion organized by Mikais that split the pantheon in half. Stories of the banishment that followed, bestowed by Nobus upon the gods and goddesses who sided with the Wolf God. An account of a mother's bargain to save her son and the punishment that befell her when the God King discovered she'd plotted to smuggle his heir away in the night.

The beast that marked me, the one that has haunted my dreams my entire life, isn't a demon after all. Not an omen or a creation of Death, but a mother cursed to live her days in the watery depths for the treacherous act of saving her son from a vengeful father.

Arcasia, the Goddess of Protection who marks all she watches, touched me. And I'm willing to bet she touched Cal, too.

I place the note in the drawer of the nightstand for Kieran to find when he returns. I may be stealing his book, but I can at least leave her words. I slide the volume in the leather satchel, but the flap doesn't close. Removing it, I shake the bag upside down and pause when something metal clangs against the floor.

An ivory handled dagger with runic markings running down its gleaming alloy blade lies on the ground at my feet.

That bastard stole my blade.

CHAPTER 25

T he leather satchel lands on top of the ruby-colored silk bedding with a muffled thud. The room is dark, the sound of my grumbling stomach from missed meals confirming the number of hours I spent engrossed in the strange book of tales that question everything being forced down the country's throats.

Everything we know about our gods is a lie. Entire lives have been devoted to teaching about the Golden Pantheon and none of it true. Years of being told to thank Nobus for his generous blessings and to blindly worship his divine justice. But just and fair kings rarely incite rebellions.

A rebellion that Kieran's mom somehow knew about. And if she knew about it, did my mother? Another book that leaves me with far more questions than answers. Answers that my gut tells me Cal has.

The soft, unexpected click of the door opening has me pivoting to face it. Cal offers a sad smile as he strides past me to the desk, setting down a tray filled with cheeses, meats, fruits, and ... oh my gods, are those chocolates?

"I thought you might be hungry," he says when he notices the way my mouth practically waters at the spread.

He pulls out the chair and motions for me to sit before he takes his own seat on the edge of the bed. His eyes assess me thoroughly, searching my facial expressions and body language to silently gauge how my day went.

"We need to talk," I say between bites of buttery crackers and salty meats.

"Eat first, princess. I can brief you on the situation in Emerald and, when you're done, we can talk about whatever you want."

I nod wordlessly, urging him to continue. My topic of conversation is likely to derail us for the rest of the evening, and I need to know what information he was able to gather.

Cal fidgets for a moment before inhaling sharply, his nerve mustered. "He's truly dead, Ivy."

I set the plate down, my appetite gone. Pain pricks the back of my head as tears well in my eyes again. I knew it was true, but hearing it confirmed is almost too much to bear.

"Marks didn't kill him, but he did order a raid on the capital city right after he died. The temples were already draped when the troops arrived. Emerald is under his control. For now."

My heart stops beating at his words, stalling for several seconds before summoned air fills my lungs and forces it to start again.

"No," I breathe out. "*No.*"

"Ivy..." Cal tip-toes around the rest of his news. "Lord Yarrow made a deal with Marks to spare the council, but ... fuck, princess," he groans. "He promised your troops in return."

Troops, *my troops*, promised to Marks. A promise Lord Yarrow had no authority to make.

The world tilts on its axis again, threatening to let me slide off its sloped sides into the numb abyss. Cal moves to kneel before me, taking my hands into his. Magic runs wild throughout my body at this touch, his emotions mixing with mine in a miserable symphony of pain and grief. Mists of thin black shadows dance along the wall, wisps that echo the ominous death that plays nightly in my dreams. The prize I can't decline in a game I never asked to play.

"Ivy." Cal moves his hands to cup my cheeks, forcing my eyes to meet his. "Do you still want to go to Amale?"

"I don't have a choice."

Tears burst from my eyes, no longer able to dam the flood that sweeps through me. Fate requires that I journey forward no matter how fast I want to run back to Emerald and retake my region from men who have no right to rule it. The Amethyst Throne burns in my nightmares, and I know in the depths of my soul that I am the cause of it.

I wanted to stop Marks before, but now I want his head on a fucking platter.

"You will always have a choice where I'm concerned. Marks deserves every ounce of your revenge and more, but I will never think you're a coward for choosing to go home instead."

"I can't go home, Cal," I confess, pulling away from him. Confusion tugs at his features as I extract Kieran's book from the leather bag and toss it on the floor in front of him with a resounding thump. "And I think you know why."

He trails his fingers over the embossed title in a way that feels eerily similar to my own movements hours ago. Cal opens the book, fanning through the pages in silence. A thousand questions and demands form on my tongue, but one stands out, more important than all the others. This first truth has to be shared so that all the others can be revealed.

"How many elements can you wield?"

Cal stands from the floor, gently placing the book on the desk before turning to me. His eyes close as he takes a deep inhale, physically bracing for what comes next.

"Three," he says. "Water, air, and fire."

Three. Cal can wield three elements. I knew he was powerful, could sense it in him, but this level of power ...

"Last night ... the blood ... how did you do it?"

"Blood is eighty percent water. If you isolate the element ..."

"Holy gods," I curse. The legend of the Captain of Corinth taking down an entire legion of Synalian troops must be true.

"No one besides you can wield the earth, princess," he adds.

"Take your shirt off," I command.

Cal's mouth pops open in surprise before pulling up in a playful smirk. "I've been waiting for you to say that to me since the first day I saw you."

"I'm not playing, Cal." I rush towards him, angrily jerking at the straps of his leather armor as I fumble with the buckles. "Show me your tattoo right now."

"I know, I know." He removes my fingers from his chest as he speaks. "I just wanted to take that look off your face even if it was only for a second."

He undresses from the waist up, stepping towards me until he stands side-by-side with the open book in my hands.

The drawing of the beast and the one inked on Cal's chest are a perfect match. Whatever pitiful glimmer of hope I had that they wouldn't be disappears.

Cal pulls a dagger from the sheath at his side and sits it down on top of the desk. My breath hitches at the sight. Running back to the bag, I extract the found dagger from the leather satchel. It's a perfect twin, from the runic carvings along its alloy blade to the polished ivory hilt that shines in the dim lantern light. Two identical blades further cementing the cosmic connection of this moment.

Using the pointed tip, I prick my finger. The runes glow a brilliant shade of blue as the crimson drop rolls down the carvings.

"The sea beast is Arcasia," I mumble, still clinging to a pathetic shred of disbelief that evaporates in my hands. "She touched me. She left this magic in my veins and she tied me to you."

"The magic is yours," he starts. "She may have connected us, but what I feel for you ... I see you in my fate, Ivy. There is no life for me without you."

Fire burns in his smokey eyes, the flames incinerating me without touch.

It's one thing to accept your fate, but another entirely to choose it. In a world that has denied me choice after choice, how can he be so brazenly resolute?

He steps closer to me, pulling me against his broad chest and into the inferno of our conjoined power. I breathe him in, the scent of leather and salty air clinging to him despite being more than a week's ride from the sea. I barely know him and yet my soul has always known his. His lips brush against mine, lingering only a second before he breathes against them, "When I meet Death, I'll do it at your side."

There's only one path forward for me, only one future that awaits me. I don't want to be the cause of Cal's death, but it's his choice to make.

"I have to kill Marks," I declare against his warm skin.

"I was wondering when you were going to say that out loud," Cal teases, pulling back to look at me fully. "I will help you, of course, but there will be innocents in the crosshairs."

"I know."

"No, princess, I don't think you do. That day on the battlefield, when my magic fully woke ... Ivy, they had Theo. The Synalians. They'd had him for days before I could get there. The broken, bloody shell of a man they pulled from that wagon ..." Cal's voice breaks, pausing to take a shaky breath before pressing on.

"Raw power consumed me and my only thought was '*kill them all.*' And it did. Every last Synalian on that battlefield died, and I didn't even have to lift a finger. Men who had no part in Theo's torture fell alongside those that did. Death feasted on so many souls that night that I expected him to appear in my dreams to thank me. What we possess … *this magic* … it's equal parts amazing and dangerous. It may do the killing, but we are the ones who have to live with those actions."

Wispy shadows flit through the air, wrapping us in a delicate, magical embrace. His pain overwhelms me, evoking more tears from my own eyes as his emotions wash through me.

The sea of despair that threatens to consume us is vast, and we cling together as if the other is the only rope that can moor us to the shore. Our only anchor in the neverending chasm of sorrow.

"How do you live with it?" I whisper against his chest.

"I have someone worth living for."

CHAPTER 26

Everything about my magic is different. What used to feel like a warm tingle is now a scorching river that roils in my veins. It burns with every pulse of my heart and every breath of my lungs.

I down the last of the water in the canteen that was supposed to last me until the end of the day, splashing the remaining droplets across my neck. Cal watches me, his gray eyes scrutinizing my every move as his magically summoned breeze attempts to offer a single moment of relief that never truly comes.

I need to release this burning power, to bleed off some of the magic that's running rampant through me, or I might spontaneously combust. I send little spurts of it out as we ride, planting seeds underneath the snow-covered ground to bloom in the springtime, but it's not enough to satiate it.

"Can we stop for a bit?" I finally ask.

It's only noon, but Cal doesn't deny my request. With a soft, knowing smile, he turns his horse off the road in wordless understanding. The sunlight catches his onyx hair in a glowing halo, the image so godlike it belongs on a temple painting rather than a forest in the Ruby Region. He leads us through the dense trees, winding around downed logs until we find a clearing ringed in snow drifts at least two feet deep. With a little magic, this place will be the perfect concealment.

"We'll make camp here. I'll go ahead and set up the tent if you want to meditate," Cal says with a wink before dismounting and pulling the large canvas out of his pack.

"Can you make it go away?"

Cal stops abruptly, turning to face me as the full implications of my words dawn on me.

"Not my magic!" I correct quickly. "The snow under the tent. It will be cold through the canvas and … I just want to see you do it."

"I can do that."

With a single swipe of his hand in the air, the snow under the tent evaporates, leaving nothing but dry, bare dirt behind. His mouth tugs up in a smile again as he stalks towards me, a hint of wicked delight sparkling in his gray eyes at the way my mouth hangs agape. Two tan fingers lift my chin and tilt it up until my mouth is inches from his.

"I can do a lot of things with my magic, princess. Would you like to see those, too?"

I absolutely would.

This close to Cal, the unrelenting power coursing through me is drowning out all logical thoughts. And if I don't use it soon, I fear I won't be able to control which side of it I use when I snap. Flowers, vines, or plants could be amusing, but if the decay came out instead …

"Does it get easier?" I ask. "The sharp edges and the need to use it?"

"You get used to it."

The magnitude of this power doesn't feel like something

anyone could ever get used to. Then again, I never thought I'd get used to the magic that possessed me at eight years old either. What felt gargantuan then pales in comparison to what flows in me now.

"You need to wield. Grow something, anything. Just focus on life." There's a slight tremble in his voice when he speaks, an echo of the residual pain somewhere deep inside.

On a steady exhale, for the first time in front of a living soul, I purposefully set my magic loose.

I start small, covering the brown patch of dead ground that Cal cleared in lush, verdant grass before moving to the snow drifts. Slowly, an assortment of flowers, the same ones I decorated the beds in the manor courtyard with, erupts. Purples, reds, yellows, and greens pop against the pristine backdrop, petals turned towards the sun directly overhead.

But the blade-like edge that cuts at my skin doesn't subside. Grass and flowers are not enough. Every side of this new magic demands more, even the side I want to contain.

"Spar with me," I command on a shaky breath. "I need to know that I can use my magic to fight. I'm tired of hiding it."

"Instinct will tell you to reach for your blades. Remove them so they're not a crutch."

Cal doesn't question my judgement or my motives, he just obliges me. I deposit the ivory-handled blade that I stole from Kieran into my saddle bag along with my cloak and the four other daggers I sheathed on my body before we left the governor's manor.

Please don't let me kill him.

I send out a silent prayer to Death—the only god I know for certain exists besides the one who has done a shit job at protecting me.

Power floods through me as I mirror Cal's stance, locking and holding his gaze while earth magic gathers in my fingertips. I never break eye contact as two vines snake upward from the snow and encircle his ankles. Squeezing my fists, the vines tighten around him, a second set springing to life in cuffs around his wrists.

Cal's eyes cut to the plants that wind around his extremities and back to me. His pupils dilate as the vines surrounding his wrists and ankles burst into flames. Green leaves turn to ash but the white-hot flames don't burn his skin.

"Marks will incinerate your vines before they've fully grown. You want to take him down? You're going to need more than party tricks."

"Party tricks?" I scoff. "Until two weeks ago, I thought I was the only person in Corinth with magic. I haven't exactly been to parties where people are growing vines from their fingertips."

"Do you even know what you're truly capable of?" Cal runs a hand through his black hair, tugging at the ends in frustration. "Ivy, you can cause the cliffs to crumble, the ground to tremble, and rivers to change their course! All you have to do is think it and the earth will obey, yet you doubt yourself."

I shake my head in conditioned disbelief even as my power rises in agreement. No one has ever taught me how to summon or wield. When my magic manifested, I was a scared child. So afraid that I would be used, exiled, or killed if anyone found out that I snuck into the woods alone at night to practice growing flowers until my fingers bled. It took years to master what control I have … or had until yesterday.

"I felt your full power in that dining room, but I understand if you're not convinced you can cause an earthquake yet," Cal says, resigned but not defeated. "Let's start small. Try something you've never done before. Why don't you shake the snow off those branches without moving them?"

The pine tree he's referring to across the clearing is massive.

There's no way I can move that, so this should be easy. Cal hovers, waiting for me to call to my power as I steady my breathing and try to focus on the individual pine needles. Like a burst of wind, the branches begin to shake, snow and pine falling to the ground in a quick blast.

"Stop." Cal's voice is commanding but kind. "You're moving the branches. Shake the ground under the tree."

Preparing to be embarrassed, I send my magic out quickly, half-heartedly shifting my focus to the base of the tree. My mouth falls open again as the large pine shakes at its roots. Cal plants his large hands on my shoulders, his breath tickling my ear as he speaks in a low, husky voice.

"The *ground*, princess."

My primed power explodes at his touch. I don't think about the snow or the tree or the ground. All I can think about is the heat that's overtaking me. I barely catch my breath before every tree in the clearing begins to shake.

"Easy, princess. Control it." Cal moves his hands down my arms in slow strokes, leaning down to punctuate each word with a light kiss. "Focus." He moves to the other side of my neck repeating the motions. "Feel."

Emotion and logic have been locked in a nearly two-decades long struggle for control over my magic. *Feel* isn't a command I would ever give myself. Power rakes its beast-like claws against the underside of my skin and I'll do anything to stop the agonizing pain, including following instructions that make no sense to me.

Resigned, I close my eyes and breathe in his heady leather scent. On the exhale, I focus on the threads of life that run through the earth and feel the ground tremble in reply. My eyes fly open to find the branches of every tree in the clearing now devoid of snow.

But I can't stop there.

The rush of magic intoxicates me, begging me to use more and more until I'm consumed, burnt and remade in its image. Power seers into my skin, obliterating every ounce of self-control I have left.

Magic swirls around me in visible shimmering viridescent bands as I drop to my knees. Fingers splayed wide against the cold snow, I pour every emotion that I have yet to shove into the iron-clad box that guards my heart into the ground: the sorrow for my region, the grief for my father, the fear for my friends. The flat land around me transforms into small, rolling hills covered in lush spring grass and dotted with clusters of godsbane.

Unsatisfied, my power searches the clearing for more, finding a sparkling cerulean mass behind me. Cal's magic—effervescent and brimming with potential, wholly invisible to me before.

The irresistible allure implores me to sample it. A single green band tugs gently at the blue, combining into a breathtaking shade of viridian.

The sky opens up, clouds releasing their watery contents in a sudden downpour. My magic flares out again, carving a serpentine trench between the newly-formed hills, a channel designed to hold his unrelenting rains. The riverbed cuts deeply into the new land-scape, a reflection of what his power threatens to do to me if I give it the chance. Each aquatic plant I seed within its silty bottom is a symbol of possibility—beauty only able to grow if attended to with care.

Black shadows commingle with the bands of green. The certain, inescapable death that awaits all life. I lift my hands from the ground, muscles trembling as I attempt to physically direct the decaying magic. Tears pour from my eyes as the flowers covering the clearing disappear into dust.

Focus on life.

Cal's earlier words are so clear that he might as well be speaking directly into my mind. I concentrate on the swirling colors, mentally separating the black until the smokey bands retreat inside of me. Magic bursts forth from the center of my chest in a screaming crescendo that rings deep in my bones. In this moment, I am the most powerful woman alive.

I am reborn.

I am remade.

I am a god.

Dark clouds block out the sun, thunder booming in the charged air. My chest heaves in short, gasping breaths as the burning power in my blood cools. Magic, now assuaged, settles like viscous paste, filling the cracks of my fractured body and fusing me into something new. A being transformed.

I am no longer the poisonous heir or the unwanted governor. The outspokenness that carefully concealed a delicate fear is gone. Bestial rage merges with unfathomable power in a deadly cocktail. The mixture alone is enough to shatter the realm if left unchecked, unbalanced.

And I will make them all pay.

The Lord General who mocked me, dehumanized me, and destroyed my home. The people who spread his lies and made me a pariah when all I ever wanted was what is just and fair. The gods who cursed me and abandoned me.

They underestimated me, but now they will fear me.

I rise to my feet and strip off the remnants of who I used to be. Soaked clothing too heavy, too restricting for my new body. Steam wafts off my bare skin, the rain dousing the fire that has consumed me. It purges every inch of me, cleansing me to my bones.

Callan Murphy kneels before me in worshipping adoration. My feet move without a thought, stepping towards him until I'm so close that he has to lift his face towards the heavens to look at me. The adulation in his ashen eyes turns to animalistic lust, a depraved sinner at my altar.

"Goddess."

A single whispered word drowned out by roaring thunder. Cal stands, his mouth crashing into mine with a hurried frenzy. With every press of his lips and sweep of his tongue, his magic melds further with mine until we're entangled so thoroughly that I cannot tell where mine ends and his begins. Our fused power is so charged it manifests in the sky as blinding, forked lightning.

Cal pulls back slightly, his forehead still pressed to mine as he speaks, "Rein it back in before you flood all of Corinth."

I step away from him, hoping the distance will help, but the rain doesn't relent. I close my eyes, focusing inward until I can visualize the viridian mass of our joined magic. I try to untangle the threads but I don't know how.

"Help me," I plead.

Cal's eyes go black again and I feel him inside of me, delicately unweaving the strands until a single blue one tugs free. An icy wind blasts through clearing, sending my wet, naked body into violent shivers. But the physical shock works. As the last bits of Cal's magic release, the storm comes to an abrupt end.

He rushes towards me, unclasping his cloak and wrapping it around my shaking body. Placing an arm under my knees, Cal sweeps me up into his arms and carries me into the tent. He places me on the ground like I'm made of porcelain. He disappears and reappears seconds later. Hastily, he rifles through the bags to locate a blanket to help stop the convulsing.

Cal removes his wet shirt and slides up behind me, tucking me tightly against his skin and covering us with the blanket. My blood warms immediately at his contact, the shivering finally ceasing in his hold. Heat radiates out from his chest as the leviathan inked across it sears into the scar on my back again.

He leans his head down, lips caressing my ear as he whispers. "Do you want to try it again? Using my magic?"

"Will you help me if I can't let go?"

"Always."

The single word, spoken into my hair, is equal parts heavy and calming. Terrifying and reassuring at the same time. I nod, slowly reaching out until I can grasp the threads of Cal's power. The urge to blend the bands with mine is tenacious, but I force myself to keep them separate.

"Water has always come easiest to me. Try that one first," he directs.

Tugging on the cerulean threads, I focus on the elements of life, the hydrogen and oxygen that are present in all living things. I let a single band of my power mix with Cal's until a small orb of water hovers just above my palm.

"Good girl," he praises against the nape of my neck. "Now try fire."

The liquid ball evaporates as I shift my focus from hydrogen to carbon. My hands tremble but no fire blazes. Cal traces circles with his tongue along the sides of my neck. Slow, agonizing swirls spark the magical kindling I've gathered. White flames ignite from my hand, the fire dancing between my fingertips as I wiggle them.

"Holy shit," I gasp in disbelief.

"Holy *you*," Cal corrects.

I clear my head until my only thought is oxygen—pure, clean air. But instead of the fire disappearing, the flames flare brighter. Again and again I try to summon the air, but nothing comes. Frustrated, I drop my hold on Cal's magic. A single tear leaks from my eye in defeat.

Cal's arms tighten around me in silent recognition. "You've kept your power subdued for years. You'll master it, princess. It just takes practice."

One question ricochets in my head, an answer that I need more than I need my next breath. I test the latch on the iron-clad box to make sure it's secure and steel myself for another piece of the puzzle that my brain is blindly assembling.

"Cal." His name is a whispered plea on my lips, a breathy appeal for the truth. "What are we?"

Whatever we are, whatever I am, it's more than a bedtime story about elemental magic wielders. The *aevus* of lore can't do what I just did—what we just did.

Cal's head falls until it rests against mine, his body tense in anticipation.

"Gods," he whispers. "We are gods, Ivy."

CHAPTER 27

T he world tips, spinning on a new axis that feels simultaneously strange and natural. There's so little oxygen that I can barely think straight. Power washes over me, slowing the blood racing through my hammering heart and filling my lungs with summoned air.

"How?" I demand.

How is any of this possible? How can we be gods in a world that keeps us powerless?

"The rebellion was real. The motive for it is still unclear to me, if I'm honest. Marks ... he told me that Nobus grew too powerful, but I don't think that's the entire truth. He and our mothers were exiled here for their part in it."

"My mother was a goddess?" I breathe in disbelief.

She never told me. Never prepared me. Maybe she hoped that magic wouldn't find me? Maybe she thought I'd be spared?

"The woman who raised me, Rhea ... she told me the story of the *aevus*. It's a mostly made up story," Cal continues, his words carefully chosen like an artist selecting the perfect colors for his masterpiece. "There was a sudden influx of magic in a magicless realm and the newly exiled gods needed a way to explain it. They created a myth, a false history to spread around campfires and taverns, and used their power to force humans to believe it."

Tears silently streak down my face as I process Cal's words. The revelation causes my body to shake again, nausea roiling in my stomach. It's too hot in this tent, too hot against Cal's body. His arms grip me tighter, panic taking root as magic races through me uncontrollably.

"Breathe, princess."

Two words.

One command.

Just like that, my power quiets, receding back into my core and curling tightly around my aching heart.

Cal's broad hands stroke my hair softly, rocking me back and forth in silence. His touch is intimate, more than a lover's, more than the heated passion we've shared. A comforting touch unlike any I've felt.

"I know it's a lot to take in," he says calmly. "I've had years to come to terms with it and it still feels unreal to be a *god*."

There's an understanding, apologetic quality in his voice. If this information came from anyone else, I wouldn't believe it. My magic wouldn't be chanting a resounding *yes* in my head to confirm every word spoken if they came from anyone else's lips.

I know it and yet I still want to yell at him, to call him a liar and harass him for attempting to fool me. But I can't. It knows—*I know* —with absolute certainty that Cal is telling the truth.

"If we're really gods, why can we only tap into the elements?" I ask.

I always imagined their power was raw, moldable into what-ever they were born to control, not limited to earth, air, fire, and water.

"This realm seems to subdue our true power. For me, it took a catalyst to force my magic to life here. I could wield a little as a child, but it wasn't until..."

His voice trails off, his pain barreling into me with the reminder of that day on the battlefield. Thousands of dead Synalian soldiers dropping to the ground in an image so vivid that it's as if I can see his memory.

"How old were you when ..." I can't voice the rest of the question, but I don't need to.

"Twenty-six," he replies.

Two years ago. Cal's power manifested on the battlefield two years ago when he was only...

"Wait." I sit up, turning at the waist to look him fully in the face. "It's not a coincidence."

Of course he's already connected the dots. Of course my full magic would also wake from its hidden slumber at twenty-six. Of course we have that in common, too.

"I broke Marks' direct orders to get to Emerald as soon as I heard about the king's death. I was never supposed to be there ... but if there was even the slightest chance your full magic might manifest on this journey, I knew I had to be with you. The Ascension Vote could have been that catalyst, and I would never have forgiven myself if you had been forced to navigate this alone."

The Ascension Vote could have been my catalyst, but it wasn't. Marks' raid on my home and my father's death were. They broke the chains I kept around my meager magic and propelled me into power.

And that will be Marks' fatal error.

His own inability to recognize me as a worthy opponent will ruin him. If he hadn't raided the Emerald Region, I might have shown up at the Ascension Vote unable to do more than *party tricks* and he would have his throne. But I have the power of a god now, and with Cal's help, I'll be able to use it to take him down.

A thousand questions fill my mind, but there's only one more that I have to ask tonight. One more answer that I have to have before I can begin to process this.

"Why?" A single word holding endless meaning.

"You know why, Ivy."

The ache in my chest opens into a cavernous hole. I've been avoiding this since the first moment he gave me his name. I have lied to myself over and over again, but my magic has always known. It ripples within his hold even now, undulating like waves from the places where our skin touches.

"Look me in the eyes and tell me that you don't feel it too." A single, tan finger moves to rest across my open lips. "And don't fucking lie to me."

Denial hovers on the tip of my tongue. The emotion I'm not capable of feeling is written so plainly across his handsome face that it steals my breath. We are dangling dangerously close to the edge of a cliff—and I can either run away with my tail between my legs, or I can leap off, face-first into the waiting arms of something designed by fate itself.

"No matter what you say, I am yours, Ivy. I will go to the ends of every realm for you." Cal grabs my hand and places it on his chest, my fingers splayed over the serpent twisting above his heart. "I—"

"Don't say it," I interrupt. Every fiber of my being knows exactly what words are about to fall from his perfect lips. "I don't want to run away from you."

His gray eyes darken with a possessiveness that causes my breath to catch. "You think I would let you run? There is not a path you could take that I would not follow, in this life or any other."

The heavy patter of rain sounds on the tent overhead as the hold on my magic dissolves in my grasp. Power sweeps over me in ethereal waves, the cosmic pull of Cal's blood to mine too strong to deny. He may very well be a siren song sent to tempt me, a poison created to control me, or a false prophet meant to pull me from my true path. Whatever the gods designed him to be, they designed him to be mine.

I should be stronger. I should distrust anything orchestrated by the gods. I should resist him.

But what if I didn't?

My entire life has been a resistance—against the magic in my veins, against the fated name from my dreams, against the gods forced down our unwilling throats.

What if I want to break all my rules? What if I want to deny the voice that tells me I'm poisonous, the voice that tells me that no one could love who I've become? What if I gave myself over entirely to the man from my dreams? If only for a single night.

The kiss we share is claiming, consuming, devouring, as if we're dying and our only hope for salvation is the other's soul.

This coupling is different. It isn't yielding to lust or giving in to insurmountable sexual tension. It's two destinies converging, two intertwined fates meeting at a crossroads and choosing to collide.

There is power in this choice, as pure and raw as the white-hot magic coursing at breakneck speed through my veins. And that power is hungry.

I push Cal backwards, lowering him onto the floor of the tent as I move to straddle him, my knees resting alongside his hips. I'm already naked and the blanket slips off my slick skin easily. I lean over him, pressing his wrists into the ground above his head.

Breaking the kiss, I run my lips across his jaw as I speak. "I choose to be yours for tonight. Don't make me regret it."

Cal moves to break my hold, but I don't let him. I call to my magic and a low rumble sounds in his chest as vines of ivy tighten around his wrists, securing him to the floor. His pupils flare, black overtaking the gray irises. Heated blood pulses through my flooded core and it only takes a moment for me to realize that he's using his magic on me in wicked ways.

"You want to play, princess?"

His sensual voice rumbles against my skin as his power sends another throb of need through me.

"Use me. Fuck me with every power you can summon. I am yours." His tongue slides up the column of my throat in a slow, tantalizing stroke.

"*You are mine,*" he growls into my ear, "and you will never regret it."

I slide my palms across the expanse of Cal's chest, pausing over the sea beast's head to take his nipple into my mouth. I suck gently, calling to the wind in an attempt to conjure a quick burst of air to nip at the delicate area. The guttural sound that escapes his lips quickly wipes away the disappointment I feel at my failure to summon the elusive element.

I drag my nails down the length of his tattoo, red scratches marring the inked skin. Claiming marks designating him as mine from his collarbone to the waistband of his pants. Pulling them down, my tongue finds the dip of the beast's tail and traces down-ward slowly to the base.

Cal's back arches off the tent floor, his eyes closed. His moan is louder this time, but still not loud enough.

"Look at me," I purr, my words vibrating against his length, "on my knees for a god."

I lick my lips, my mouth hovering over the tip until his gaze is right where it belongs: *on me.* One hand moves to grip the base of his shaft while the other curls into a fist beside me, magically tightening the restraints on his wrists.

I open my throat to take him deep, licking and sucking and twisting until the sound of his moans fills the tent. Cal's hands are in my hair the next moment, pulling my head up to meet his lips, the vines lying in a heap of ashes on the floor. We're a frenzy of tongues and teeth, exploring and teasing, playful and demanding.

I lower myself down onto him, my wet heat gliding sinfully until I'm seated fully. Cal's hands move to my breasts, each palm working in tandem to mimic the circles I'm now making with my hips. His fingers twist and pluck my nipples, causing gooseflesh to rise on my skin. A shudder of pleasure and magic ripples through me simultaneously.

"That's it. Show me what you can do, goddess."

I call out to the power that I know best and watch as a verdant vine wraps around the ivy tattooed on Cal's muscular thigh, the summoned plant a perfect match to the inky image. The free end snakes up his body in a serpentine climb as I ride him harder. His growl echoes through me as the green tendril finds its final destination: his throat. I squeeze it tightly and watch as his stormy gray eyes shutter.

"Fuck, Ivy."

"What was that?" I tease. "Say that last word again. *Louder.*"

Cal's large hands find my hips, one thumb making circles on my clit as my blood surges again under his touch in a wave of renewed heat.

"*Ivy.*"

"Louder," I breathe, my voice barely detectable over the thundering storm now raging outside.

I don't know if the downpour is my doing or Cal's, but I can't stop it. Everywhere our bodies touch is as charged as the air around us. I'm seconds away from bursting into flames and setting us both on fire.

Lightning illuminates the tent, cracking across the night sky as pleasure, blinding and absolute, slams into the magic within me. I feel Cal tighten inside me and I'm only vaguely aware of the sound of my name on his lips and the sound of his on my own. One moment I'm looking into Cal's stormy eyes and the next I'm looking down from above us at the near-celestial body of a woman glowing with power.

I blink and I'm back inside my body, my breath coming in heaving gasps. Cal sits up quickly wrapping his arms around me and pulling me tight against his chest. My scream fills the tent as sharp, hot pain sears through me.

"Breathe, princess."

His voice is commanding again and my body instinctively obeys. My magic, well and fully spent, finally retreats within me as the pain subsides.

"What was that?"

My throat is raw and strained as I lock eyes with Cal, afraid to look down at my own body. Pride fills his silver eyes as his hand moves to rest between the flare of my ribcage.

"Fate," he mutters, taking my hand and placing it atop his own. "Let me show you."

I nod still breathless and scared as he moves to get the compact from my belongings. The familiar scent of leather and sea salt air hits me as Cal places the mirror in my hand. His breath is hot on the column of my neck and his lips gently brush against my skin.

"Look" he whispers.

I lower my eyes, hesitant to see what I know now permanently decorates my skin. There, in the same place the red indention sat yesterday, is the image of the sea beast in obsidian ink. The tattoo pulses in time with my heartbeat, as if the serpent is a living, breathing thing slithering against the tender skin of my belly.

My fingers skim the dark brand. The image of the Goddess of Protection's cursed form is forever a part of me, much like the man who bears the replica across his broad chest.

"Is this what happened to you?" I ask him.

"I wish it had been this fun," he teases, placing light kisses along the column of my neck.

I shift the compact to take in his tattoo. The waves surrounding the beast glimmer for a moment in the dimming light, confirmation that his feels like mine. A living token of Arcasia's protection.

"We are inevitable, Ivy," Cal whispers reverently as he pulls me tight against him.

Happiness laces his every word, complete satisfaction as he holds the one thing he wants. But it's a heavy weight that settles over me as the euphoric haze of pleasure recedes.

I fear that giving into magic, lust, and a desire to be anyone other than who I am has led him to believe that he now has something I cannot ever hope to give. Something I'm not even capable of giving myself.

My love.

CHAPTER 28

Magic calls to me like the night sky yearns for the shining glow of the moon. I slowly slip out from under Cal's arm, careful not to disturb him. His deep steady breathing indicates the dreamless rest I covet that evades me yet again. The tug in my gut so intense that it pulls me outside before I even have shoes on.

I suck in a sharp breath at the first touch of wet snow on my exposed feet. With a sweeping motion of my hand, a clear path cuts through the snow, a runner of plush grass growing where I intend to step. The serpentine ditch I carved through the landscape earlier is overflowing now, rushing rain water threatening to spill over its shallow banks.

My skin is hot, so *fucking* hot. Even my thin shirt is too thick for the heat that wafts off me. For a moment, I'm tempted to strip down and plunge into the icy stream for relief before I think better of it. I don't know if hypothermia can kill a god, but I know they can die. They have to, otherwise my mother would still be here.

My mother.

I sit in the newly grown grass, the light of the full moon illuminating the fading crescent-shape sketched onto the first page of the worn leather journal that I slipped from my saddle bag, her piss poor attempt at an explanation.

Hold fast, my dark bloom, and destiny will come.

How was a scared, grieving eight year old supposed to understand her cryptic scrawling? Hell, I barely understand it now. Why couldn't she find the time to tell me any of this to my face?

'By the way, Ivy, if weird shit starts happening to you, it's because we are goddesses' seems like a pretty easy way to start.

But all it does now is fuel the anger I've held onto for all these years. I've tried so many times to make sense of her words without success, tried so many times to will the answers to light. The edges of the journal are still charred from the last time I fished it out of the hearth before it could fully catch fire.

I've let that rage consume me so much that I barely remember her any other way. There's only snippets, flashes of her singing, dancing, or painting. In every recollection, she is illuminated by a radiant light. Haloed in sunlight. Moonlight dancing on her porcelain skin. Firelight sparkling in her golden eyes.

I know I loved her before anger colored my memories, but I lost her and gained terrifying magic on the same day. And here I sit, eighteen years later. Another dead parent, another gift of power I never asked for.

Tears prick my eyes, threatening to spill onto the parchment pages. I knew I would likely never see my father again, but I thought I would feel him die. With my mother, it was as if we were a string being severed in two. I felt the moment her soul left this realm and crossed over.

But the man who raised me, the man who made me who I am, the man who gave power to a daughter where others would have cast her aside—that man slipped from this world days ago and I didn't feel it.

Questions I'll never get answers to race through my thoughts. Did he know what she was? Did he know what *I* am? Is he even my *real* father?

No. That one I will not entertain tonight.

His death is still too fresh, the grief still too raw for me to sully his memory with traitorous thoughts. Regardless of my parentage, he gave me more than any mortal father could. He gave me a title, a purpose, and a training to back it up—more than any female child in Corinth has had before.

An icy wind blows through the clearing, but it does nothing to cool me. I pull on the blue threads of Cal's magic again, eager to master the one element that still evades me. His magic filters into me slowly, my breath stilling as the image of my face pops into my mind.

I watch as silver rims my green eyes. Tan fingers grip my hand and splay it across the hammering heart that reverberates throughout this form. A haunted, pained look flits across my face as too sweet words flood my ears, a look that should have doused the fiery hope that burns in this chest, but doesn't.

It's easier to release his magic this time. Easier to let go of the emotions and memories that accompany it. I see how he looks at me, but to see it through his own eyes ... his steely gaze that threatens to cut through the iron-clad box that guards my heart, the metal so thick that nothing has ever pierced it without my consent ... that nearly breaks me.

Cal looks at me like he's been wandering the Synalian desert for two decades and I'm his idyllic oasis. Not the first drink he's found, but the only hydration he'll ever need again. There is no end to his want, no limit to what he'll do to have me. It's a look most women would kill to receive.

Dawn is nearly here, and in the last cold rays of night, I know

I've gone too far, entertained my own pleasure and whims for too long. Morning brings an end to the night I promised Cal. The end to the permission that I gave myself to give in to my own wants. Dawn brings me another day closer to the death that awaits me in Amale.

If the Dark God has any mercy at all for the man who has given him so many souls, he'll take me before I completely destroy Cal.

The weather becomes warmer the further west we go, leaving the last remaining dregs of winter in our wake. We travel slowly, determined to make sure Marks and his soldiers have already crossed the watery divide between the Ruby and Diamond Regions before we arrive at the port city. We don't leave camp until well into the morning hours, and when we ride, only the browns of the common folk adorn our bodies as we journey deeper into the heart of Corinth.

My magic hasn't quieted since the tattooed serpent appeared on my belly. It knows exactly where Cal's power is at all times. I can sense him without sight, without hearing. A mystical, infuriating sixth sense that I can't shut off or drown out no matter how much I try. It blazes with every delicate graze of his tanned fingers, sears me with every seductive wink of his gray eyes. It consumes my waking and sleeping thoughts, demanding I give it the one thing it desires: *him*.

But I'm a stubborn bitch, and I deny it with a renewed vigor. I don't let him get too close to me and don't dare to give myself over to him again, no matter how futile my resistance may end up being.

Quiet hours on horseback sneaking through the Godswood give me more time to think than I care for. Thoughts that start with denial and always end up in a state of *what if.*

What if I don't die in Amale? *What if* we have time? *What if* I *want* to have time with him?

But they're pointless questions. My nightmares only increase the closer we get to the Diamond Region, dreams that now include more blood than should be possible and the face of the man who rides alongside me.

Even cloaked in the common brown, every trace of his persona removed, he exudes power. Cal *is* power. Now that I know he's a god, I can't see him any other way. How he walked among us disguised as a mortal, I'll never know. He's a force to be reckoned with, and while all of Corinth may not know the true reason, they recognize it, fear it, and respect it.

Perhaps the most attractive thing about Cal isn't his honed physique or the downright sinful things he does with it, but the fact that he sees me as his equal. Not something to be used, extorted, or controlled. The first person to see my true power shattered the pretty little porcelain box I hid it inside all these years. He pulled the veil from over my eyes and gave me the first piece of my true identity.

An identity that still doesn't feel complete.

The revelation of my heritage does little to settle the decaying power that swirls in the shadows surrounding camp and lurks in the shade of the passing trees. The magic that claws at the under-side of my skin like a rough stitch. The constant reminder of the doom that awaits me.

We reach the port city just before nightfall on the third day. The last stop on the Ruby side of the Alloy River is especially dangerous. Marks has to believe I've returned to Emerald or we lose the one element we can't magically wield but have to have: surprise. If I'm spotted here, the plan we've managed to string together will unravel.

Soldiers, dressed in the gray and gold uniforms that signal their allegiance to Corinth, are stationed at the docks. Marks left his own men on this side of the river to replace the regional guard, a clear sign of the distrust we correctly anticipated.

Cal's face is too recognizable to these men, so there's no point trying to hide him. He exchanges his modest cloak for one in a striking raven hue, putting the first phase of our plan into motion. He'll secure passage for himself tonight, and in the morning, he'll bribe the same soldier to look the other way when he brings along a woman that he happened to meet in the tavern.

It's a ridiculous idea, but it'll work. A woman on the arm of a powerful man is rarely looked in the eyes. So I'll swish my hips when I walk, lay my head playfully against his arm, and swallow down my pride until we're in the safe cover of the Kingswood that waits on the other side.

"I'm not known for traveling with a … hired companion, so you're really going to have to sell this one, princess. You sure about this?" Cal asks.

"It'll work," I reassure him. "Go do your soldier thing. I'll meet you in the tavern."

I slink into the shadows and watch him stalk towards the docks. Cal dons his role as Captain of Corinth with expert ease, the mask of the menacing warrior slipping perfectly into place. There aren't many people milling about today, but those that are sidestep quickly to clear a path for him. The soldiers spot him coming, straightening to attention as he approaches.

He doesn't need me for this part.

Magic tingles across my skin before I can turn to make for the tavern. Slow, heavy footsteps sound on the cobblestones behind me, my hand instinctively drifting to the ivory-hilted dagger sheathed against my hip. The man stops beside me, the hoods of our cloaks concealing both of our faces, but I recognize him instantly.

"What are you doing here, Kieran?" I spit out.

"Same thing you are, Ivy. Securing passage to Amale."

"Why aren't you already across?" I turn to face him, taking in the brown roughspun of his cloak hood as he stares ahead towards the river, the ruby color of his region nowhere to be found.

"Don't worry, Marks and his faithful following have already crossed." Kieran meets my gaze, his russet eyes accentuated by a large, circular bruise covering his socket.

"You look like shit." The words escape my mouth before I think better of it.

"Yeah, well you told your boyfriend about what happened at the summit all those years ago and he decided to turn our performance for Marks' spies into a real fight."

"He's not my boyfriend," I correct. "What performance?"

"Of course he didn't tell you," Kieran scoffs. *"Don't say anything, Kieran. I'll tell her, Kieran.* Bullshit."

Finished with his mocking, he turns and heads into the weathered tavern. I follow quickly behind him, growing agitated at his lack of answers. Reaching out, I grab ahold of his arm and spin Kieran to face me.

"What the fuck are you talking about?"

"You're going to want a drink for this."

Kieran pulls from my hold and stalks to the bar, flagging down the barkeep to order two tankards of ale with a fake smile. Beers in hand, Kieran directs us to a large table along the side of the wood paneled walls. I pick a seat, pulling out the woven-bottom chair facing the door as he slams the tankards down and sits without removing his hood.

"Start talking," I command.

He takes a long gulp before wiping his mouth on the back of his shirt sleeve and motioning for me to do the same. I comply— only because the drink has never left my sight since Kieran acquired it —and I drink down the slightly warm, foamy hops without breaking eye contact.

"You might be," he leans in to whisper his next words, "a *god*, but you're not the only special person here."

I force my face to remain neutral and unfazed by his declaration. I don't know what Kieran knows—or thinks he knows—but he won't get any information from me.

"And I suppose you believe yourself to be special?"

Kieran reaches a tanned hand under the hood and runs his fingers through his tangled mess of wavy, auburn hair.

"Yeah, Ivy, I am. Believe it or not."

There's a pain in his voice that isn't normally present. He's unkempt, uncomfortable … un-Kieran.

"You're the heir to the Ruby Region. Of course you're special," I scoff.

"No. I'm special because my mother made me so. Just like yours made you."

Kieran tugs down the collar of his tunic exposing a small crescent-shaped birthmark just under his collarbone before lifting his tankard again. My composure slips at his revelation.

"Take another drink, Ivy. People are watching."

I lift the ale to my lips with shaky hands and force myself to take deep gulps of the hoppy liquid as I try to think. Kieran is *aevus*. Kieran is at the very least part-god, at the most, fully a god.

"We're on the same team," he says.

I don't trust him, but when I next meet his eyes over the rim of the tankard, my magic finds truth in them. He's not my enemy— not this time.

The door to the tavern swings open, and I know it's Cal before I even see the figure step through the threshold. His large frame blocks out the flickering light from the torches that line the village streets. The hood of his cloak covers his face entirely, but a hush falls over the patrons nevertheless at the menacing sight of the man in black. The magic in my blood sings in his presence as he lowers the hood and steps towards us.

"Holy gods," Kieran mutters, eyes going wide. "I sensed your power before, Ivy, but now ..."

"Now what?" I ask cautiously.

"It surged when he walked in. It wasn't like it was at the ball."

Cal pulls out the chair beside me, his knee brushing against mine as he sits.

"Does she know?" Kieran locks eyes with Cal, his face a mixture of hesitance and hope.

"There was kind of a lot to cover, Rollins. I didn't exactly get through everything." Cal chuckles and lifts my tankard of ale to his lips.

"Anyone want to clue me in on whatever it is you two are discussing?" I ask, annoyance lacing my every word.

"Ivy," Kieran starts, "before I say this, I need to remind you that there is a tavern full of people whose eyes are still on this table."

I feel Cal stiffen beside me, his broad shoulders squaring to appear larger. A quick glance around the room confirms Kieran's statement. All around us, patrons are pretending to sip on their drinks as if they aren't sitting on pins and needles waiting to see if the fabled captain will bring trouble to their doorsteps.

"Go on," I urge.

"Meet your newest travel companion. I'll be with you two the rest of the way to Amale."

I cut my eyes to Cal. There was plenty of time for him to warn me and yet he didn't, though this was a surefire way to make sure I couldn't stab Kieran. The dark purple bruising on the heir's face is another clue that we must need him alive. Cal would have killed him already otherwise.

"I am armed at all times, even in my sleep. And what I'm

capable of wielding is even more deadly than a blade. Do not fuck with me, Kieran."

I let the magic in my veins come up to the surface. I can't call to it here, but if he really can sense it as he claims, I want him to know that my threat is serious.

"He's not stupid enough to do that again. Are you, Rollins?"

Kieran meets Cal's challenging stare for only a moment before he swallows thickly. From the corner of my eye, I can see the corded muscle in the captain's forearm twitch. He's using his power on him again.

"That's enough of that, boys." I say flatly. Both men turn to face me, the air between them growing less tense as Cal's magic retreats. "From this point on, I am in charge. You will do what I say. Both of you."

Cal lets out an involuntary grunt, clearly pleased at the idea of being ordered around by me. Gray fire burns in his eyes as they boil the blood in my veins, the serpent on my skin slithering to life at the promise of his magic.

"Only if you two cut that shit out." Kieran rises swiftly and throws back the remaining ale before slamming the tankard on the wooden table. "I'll see you at sunrise."

Once Kieran stalks out of the tavern door and into the night, I turn to face Cal. I need a moment to tamper down my magic before I can speak.

"I can fight my own battles," I remind him.

"That fucker deserves worse than that. Lucky for him, we need him, otherwise he'd be dead."

I lift the tankard to my lips and take a moment to gather my thoughts as I finish off the warm amber liquid within. Soldiers from the docks, fresh off their shift, begin to filter into the tavern signaling the start of my role in this ruse. The part I tell myself is only for show.

"You'll explain his part in all this tomorrow?" I ask, taking his chin in my fingers and angling his mouth downward toward mine.

"I promise," Cal says on a breathy exhale.

His lips find mine, the first act in tonight's production that ends with me leaving this place clinging to his body while his hands roam over all the places he intends to thoroughly explore.

Prying eyes watch us with a curious intensity that tells me that I was right. Word of the captain's activities will be the talk of the port city by the time the sun fully rises over the Facet Mountains—and we'll be long on the other side of the Alloy by then.

CHAPTER 29

K ieran is waiting for us in the shadowed alleyway near the tavern at sunrise. He's dressed in brown again, the cloak hood fully concealing his identity.

"My passage?" he asks nervously.

Cal gives him a slight nod, never slowing as we pass. I cling to his side like he's a piece of driftwood in the middle of the Eastern Sea. Last night's performance was a success, but the addition of Kieran has me worried.

If the soldiers question us, Kieran is my brother. Cal drew a hard line at my suggestion of a very fake, very unserious three-some. The idea of someone else touching me drove him into a possessive rage that nearly made me break my self-imposed vow of celibacy.

Kieran pushes off the building wall and falls into a slightly slower pace several steps behind us. Cal's black cloak floats behind him as if it's carried on a phantom wind, a dark flag waving amidst shades of brown to signal his arrival.

The heir of Ruby would rather pretend to be a nameless, beaten brother than be seen boarding a boat in his own region, which can only mean one thing—he has made a very large enemy out of the Lord General.

The soldiers lift their hand in a salute as we approach the gangway. I lower my head so that loose hair and the edge of Cal's arm shields my eyes just enough to hide their distinctive color but not obstruct my line of sight.

"Captain," the tallest one says in acknowledgement. "All is as you requested. May the gods grant you safe passage."

"May the gods bless you, Private." Cal inclines his head at the man, placing a gold coin in his hand.

His hold on my arm tightens as we hastily board the ship. Kieran follows closely behind, his distinct red hair hidden safely beneath his hood.

Cal pulls us across the main deck, stopping halfway to lift a grated hatch. He ushers Kieran down the stairs first and then directs me to follow. We keep our heads down, avoiding eye contact with passing soldiers in the narrow corridor as we follow Cal's lead.

"Captain Murphy? Is that you?" someone shouts down the hallway.

Panic courses through me, the emotion not entirely my own this time. Cal turns, his large hands grasping the sides of my head before he lowers his to shield me with a kiss. It's quick and harsh, possessive and rough. Exactly how these men would expect him to treat someone whose time he purchased.

A door creaks open behind me, but before I can pull away, Cal is shoving me backwards into the open room.

"Wait here," he commands. "I'll be back as soon as I can."

The door closes quickly behind him, sealing Kieran and I inside the tiny room. The single bed against the wall takes up nearly the entire space, the only place to sit covered in haphazardly strewn, questionable bedding.

"You constantly surprise me, Ivy," Kieran chuckles as I push away the ratty blanket to sit beside him on the worn mattress. "I never thought I'd see you falling for Murphy."

"I never thought I'd see you hiding in your own region," I quip back, not bothering to lie.

Kieran goes still, the playful smirk on his lips falling. "When you disobey direct orders, it's usually best to hide your identity." The color drains from his face, his freckled skin turning to a sickly shade of pallor. "Especially if you just poisoned your father."

"You *what?*" I ask in disbelief. "Why?"

Don't get me wrong; I'm not sad that Charles Rollins is dead. He was a ruthless leader, a horrible misogynist, and somehow an even worse father, but I never imagined Kieran would take his life. Someone else who crossed him sure, but not his father.

"Old Charles felt snubbed after the last Ascension. He never could get past the hasty way the Diamond governor was crowned king or the mysterious way his former seat was gifted to the Lord General. Marks promised Father whatever he wanted in return for putting him on the Amethyst Throne. Cost and country be damned."

"And you wanted to stop him?" I ask. "You didn't want to join him?"

"You know how he was. His treatment of me when we were kids was just the tip of his cruelty. I played the dutiful heir in public, but I never stopped hating him in secret. What he made me do to you …" Kieran's voice cracks, the muscles in his jaw tightening as he whips his head away from me. "I couldn't sit idly by and take it any longer."

"When have you ever sat *idly by*, Kieran? He was an asshole, but don't make excuses for your behavior."

"You think you know everything, Ivy, but you know nothing." He faces me again, the faintest hint of silver rimming his russet eyes. "You don't know what he did to me. I tried to give you an out, a way for you to save yourself and your people despite the fact that I love—"

"You think marrying you would have saved me?" I interrupt. "Are you delusional?"

Marks wanted this marriage to secure the vote, but chaining me to Kieran was the cherry on top of the Lord General's fucked up little sundae. Living day after day in a region I couldn't control under the dictatorship of my enemy would never be torture enough for him.

"Marks doesn't want you to know what you're capable of. He can't touch you or he would have eliminated you from the game already. As far as he's concerned, the longer you're around Murphy, the bigger the risk of you finding out who and what you are. That's why he raided your region—to force you to go home. He doesn't want you to know about your own power, let alone that there's a resistance that has their own. And we're willing to do anything to stop him."

"A *what?!* A magical resistance … that you thought I wouldn't want to be a part of?"

A resistance with magic. A lifetime living in secrecy and fear of my own power while the people around me knew. They knew and never said anything. Pain pricks at my temples and I curse the weakness.

"Worse, you thought I'd just give up the title I've trained for my entire life? The one that made me Poison Ivy, the vilified heir? That I'd let you have my vote?"

"The plan was always to stop Marks before the vote. I knew you'd be upset when you found out, but I grossly underestimated how Murphy was going to react. From where I stood, leaving him and abandoning your journey to marry me was the only way you walked away from this, Ivy."

"I was never walking away from this, Kieran," my voice cracks on his name, magic rattling in my bones to be released.

Shadows creep to life in the corner at my rising emotions. Dark magic swirls, awaiting my command.

"I know that now, and for what it's worth, I'm not either. You can trust me, Ivy."

I don't want to. I want to push him off this fucking boat and leave him behind. For lying to me, for keeping secrets, for trying to poison me ten years ago ... but my magic trusts him and Cal must too. He wouldn't be alone in this room with me otherwise.

The cabin door swings open with a loud bang, Cal's form blocking the doorway from prying eyes.

"I've got the perfect opportunity for you to prove your loyalty, Rollins."

We both look at him quizzically. Nothing about this feels planned.

"We could use a little *push*."

"I've convinced the ship's captain to give us five more minutes before he calls for everyone to disembark and wait for more favorable conditions," Cal explains as we climb the stairs back up to the main deck. "I don't know what Marks said to him, but he's watching me like a hawk. I can't wield the wind needed while he's questioning me, so I need you two to summon it."

I follow Cal out of the hatch to find the air completely stilled. Not even a hint of a breeze lingers to move the thick clouds that hang motionless in the morning light.

"Cal," I groan as the captain snaps his head towards me in a hurried motion.

"Stay out of sight. Be quiet and be quick." His gray eyes echo the seriousness of his tone and I know this isn't up for discussion. I nod once in understanding.

Kieran, now above the hatch, grabs my arm and pulls me towards the railing.

"If we want to get across the Alloy quickly, we need a strong northeastern wind. How well can you direct?"

I pause for a moment contemplating my reply, but my silence gives me away.

"Don't tell me you can't direct," he growls lowly.

"Would now be a good time to tell you that I can't summon air?" I fake a smile to soften the blow, but it doesn't work.

Kieran's nostrils flare and his next words are spat through gritted teeth. "What. The. Fuck."

"I'm not a part of a *magical resistance*, you know? Until a few days ago, I had only ever summoned earth magic. I've been trying to summon air but there's only one time that I *might* have been successful. I'm still not sure if that was me."

"What were you doing when you *might have* summoned it? Can you do that again now?" Kieran runs a hand through his auburn hair, tugging it in frustration.

"I don't think you want me to answer that, Kieran."

"For fucks sake," he murmurs under his breath. "Take my hand." He extends a large hand towards me that I don't grab. "Seriously, Ivy, we are running out of time. Just take my hand."

I tentatively place my hand in his palm, swallowing down the bile that rises in my throat as our skin touches. There's no buzz or magnetic pull like there is with Cal, no connection between our magics, just good old fashioned loathing.

"Are you sure this is going to work?" I ask, eager to get away from his hold.

"No, but I'm not a strong enough wielder to summon a sustained wind on my own. We have to try." Frightened urgency laces his tone. Staying another night in Ruby is not an option for Kieran.

He points to the cliffs ahead, directing my attention to the rocky peaks that tower over the Alloy. "Focus your intention on that point and imagine the wind originating there."

Magic churns in my veins, ready to be unleashed. Dark magic—the opposite of what I need right now.

I swallow it down, willing the shadows that skate the edges of my vision to vanish. The tattooed sea beast slithers to life against my stomach, and somehow I know we've already lost one of our precious minutes.

Focus, Ivy.

I close my eyes and picture a hawk's nest amongst the southernmost point of the Facet Range. A platform of twigs and sticks filled with soft grasses, bark, and leaves. Sharp traces of broken, hatched life discarded around its edges.

A black-tipped yellow beak peaks above the rim of the nest just before the large bird emerges. She spreads her brown wings to the sun, the white underside of her plumage on full display. With a shrill, screaming "kee-ah," she leaps, plummeting down the cliff face until a burst of wind catches under her broad wings and carries her upward. The majestic bird soars from its haven, across the slope of the mountain, and over the now rippling current of the river.

Pride swells in my chest, my eyes popping open to see white sails hanging limp from their spars rather than billowing in the wind. None of it was real. The bitter taste of disappointment fills my mouth. I cut my eyes to Kieran to make sure he doesn't see the failure that is written on my face.

His eyes are closed, the muscles in his arms and shoulders tense with the strain of wielding. His grip tightens around my hand, his lips pursing as he increases his focus.

The Ivy I was when I left home would never in a million years believe what is happening right now. I'm holding Kieran's fucking hand while we try to simultaneously summon the godsdamned wind.

What the hell kind of game are the gods playing?

"Are you even trying?" Kieran spits at me through gritted teeth without opening his eyes.

"Are you?" I snap back.

A light breeze blows through the loose ends of my brown hair in response.

"Show off," I murmur.

The beast slithers again. Another minute down.

Familiar magic scrapes its claws across my neck. Somewhere behind me, Cal grows agitated. It's not directed at me, but I have the overwhelming urge to use it.

The glowing green strands of my power twist through the air searching for his. If anyone else can see them, they make no indication.

Magic spins in sparkling spirals, curling around Cal's dark form, prodding and teasing gently. A delicate knock to be let in. Cal's emotions flood me as he opens the door to his power. The verdant threads of my magic rush into the cerulean mass of his mixing into a shimmering viridian conglomerate of power. A rightness settles into my bones and I know I can easily wield his elements.

I pluck a single thread and pull it into me. One lifeline to help me ensure we leave the Ruby Region today.

Kieran's hand shakes in mine, drawing me away from Cal. There is no glow, no aura surrounding the new governor's power. Nothing that mine can mingle with or draw from. No element that I can summon and wield besides my own.

The faint wind that Kieran has summoned increases and I hear the soldiers around us start to murmur.

"Do you feel that?"

"The gods must be on our side today, boys!"

"If this keeps up, we'll be sailing soon!"

A sheen of sweat coats Kieran's brow, drops gathered on his temples beginning their descent to the column of his throat. He lifts his chin to the breeze, the cloak hood sliding backward and exposing a sliver of his curly hair.

The rising sun illuminates his auburn locks in a halo of fire. The steady wind he commands adds a dancing movement to the flames, and I wonder if his true calling should have been to summon that element instead.

The sea beast swishes her mighty tail across my tender flesh. Three minutes gone, only two remain.

I drop Kieran's hand, replacing his hood to disguise his hair. Disconnected from him, the wind slows to a barely perceptible speed.

Shit. That's the opposite of what we need.

I pull the thread of Cal's magic again, allowing it to fill my veins. I focus on the air moving in and out of my lungs, on the breeze that moved the ends of my hair earlier. His power mixes with mine, tangling together in a symphony that plays too quietly. Our joined magic sizzles in my veins as if it's waiting to be called to in the only language it speaks.

A realization settles into my bones as the serpent wriggles again. I can't summon the air. If we had more time, I could try to use more of Cal's power, but even that isn't guaranteed to work and we only have one minute left.

But I am not powerless. The depthless well of magic hasn't run dry, and I'm willing to try anything to get us off this dock.

With an unsure exhale, I push the unstable, raw core of my power directly into Kieran. It races across my skin, down my arm, and into where our hands are joined. His grip tightens, his eyes boring into me as I channel my power directly into him.

"What are you doing?" Kieran whispers.

"Just summon, air wielder."

A strong burst of wind cuts across the deck as my magic weaves into the faint red threads of Kieran's. His magic is weak, nothing like Cal's. No wonder he couldn't sustain it.

Shouts and heavy footsteps sound around us as the soldiers hurry to unfurl the sails, one loud voice booming over the others.

"Make ready, men! We might just leave this dock after all," a man who must be the ship's captain barks.

"Whatever you're doing, keep it up."

Kieran's voice is low and strained as he slowly increases the wind. His power, though weak, is sustained and controlled in a way that I haven't mastered. How many years must he have trained to accomplish this? How long has he been a part of this resistance?

The wind slows as magic rushes back into my body to soothe the ache that forms as self-doubt takes root. The sharp sting of pain replaces the power that surged through me only moments before. Time is running out, and I know the beast will signal the end of our window soon.

Cerulean washes over me in a comforting wave. The power that feels like second nature wraps me in a warm embrace that reminds me I'm not alone. Not anymore. The only thing that matters right now is getting off of this dock and across the Alloy River.

I gather our combined power, full of doubt and desperation, and push it all into the hands of a man I haven't trusted for ten years.

The heartbeat of the sea beast pounds through my body as a strong northeastern wind billows through the waiting sails.

"Underway! Shift colors!"

The men around us rush to carry out the captain's orders, a blur of Corinthian gray in my periphery as I lock gazes with Kieran. There's a relief that I don't share in the eyes that stare back at me.

"Holy gods, Ivy," he breathes.

If Marks finds out that I can funnel my power into someone else, he won't hesitate to use me in all the ways I've been so terrified of. And I've just handed that knowledge to a known enemy.

"If you betray me again, Kieran Rollins, I will kill you."

CHAPTER 30

The port city at the edge of the Diamond Region is swarming with activity. The docks are loaded with ships ready to make their way up and down the Alloy to trade with Topaz and Sapphire.

Kieran and I slip easily amongst the brown cloaks, melding into the bustling crowd that splits as the Captain of Corinth steps off the gangway. The black-clad god parts the throng of people, their faces colored with equal parts fear and disgust as they take in the creature who walks in their midst. Power surges in my chest, the sea beast undulating against my skin for an entirely different reason.

In another life, another fate, I walk alongside him. Not in hiding, but in emerald green. The feelings that warred within me only days ago as we rode through the streets of Gathe no longer battle for control. The urge to bring them all to their knees in submission takes root in my gut, and it requires a power stronger than magic to subdue it.

Keeping my head down, I set about securing a new horse. She's a pretty chestnut color, feisty and bold. Nothing like the docile caramel mare I left behind in Ruby, but everything I need for this leg of the journey. We follow the herd of people towards the city gates, riding until the cobblestones give way to a dirt road and the cover of trees thickens.

It's not long before Kieran arrives at our designated meeting spot on his own mount. He keeps his back towards the road, overly careful of being spotted by the white-coated Diamond soldiers that ride by sporadically.

"Looks like the road is off limits for at least a day," he mutters.

Cal arrives a short while later, dressed head to toe in brown atop a black mare with a glistening mane. We agreed that the Diamond port city had to be his last known location, but the clothes of a commoner can't conceal a god. There's a bulky bag secured behind his saddle that we didn't travel with, and I'm certain that I would find it stuffed with his leather armor if I opened it.

He gives me a once over, visually checking for any signs of trouble before spurring his horse deeper into the trees. We follow alongside the dirt road of the Kingswood, rows of trees concealing us from fellow travelers as we ride.

When the sun hangs low on the horizon, Cal leads us deeper into the woods to make camp. I've had hours of silence to stew in my own head, an entire day of waiting for Cal to uphold his promise for information.

"How much longer do I have to wait for someone to tell me what's going on?" I ask impatiently as Cal pitches our tent and Kieran builds the small fire.

A cool breeze stirs around us, air magically summoned to distort our conversation if listening ears happen by.

"Do you want to go first or should I?" Kieran asks.

"You're the one most likely to incur her wrath, so I'd start talking if I were you, Rollins."

Kieran sits with a huff beside the now lit fire, patting the space beside him. With a snap of my fingers, tree branches shift to camouflage our makeshift camp. His eyes go wide, startled at the sight of the earth bending to my will. The elusive element, if Cal's words are true.

"Unless you want to find out how I can use that magic against you, I suggest you tell me the truth."

Kieran's eyes meet mine as I sit, the awe completely gone from his gaze.

"I can pull the air from your lungs, Ivy. Your threats don't work on me."

"I don't think you can," I say flatly, "given what happened on the boat."

Cal pauses, the stake hammer still raised above his head as he turns to face us.

"What happened on the boat?" he asks, a tense strain in his voice that has nothing to do with physical exertion.

"Kieran couldn't summon the wind."

"Oh I could summon it just fine," Kieran starts defensively.

"Ivy." Cal sets down the hammer, walking cautiously over to kneel beside where I sit. "What did you do?"

"She funneled her godsdamned power into me," Kieran scoffs. "One minute I was commanding the wind and the next minute she was."

"Someone had to get us off the dock," I say, rolling my eyes. "You're welcome for the help."

"Help? More like theft! My magic wouldn't answer to me anymore."

"What?" Cal and I ask in unison.

"Are you some kind of amplifier? Is that even possible?" Kieran asks.

"I don't know." Cal shakes his head, running his fingers through his hair. "I thought you could use my power because of our—"

"It's different," I interrupt. "I didn't use Kieran's magic. There wasn't anything to use."

"There's plenty to use," Kieran huffs in agitation. "Just because I'm not a full god like you two doesn't mean I'm not powerful in my own way. I didn't see either of you coordinating a coup for the governing seat of every region in Corinth."

"You did what?!" I'm on my feet before my brain can process what I just heard. "*Every seat?*"

"As of today, every Governor in Corinth is *aevus*. You're welcome." Kieran beams.

"The resistance." I whisper in disbelief. "It's the heirs, isn't it?"

"Our mothers were exiled here, Ivy. It's Marks' fault that they're dead and that they were forced to live in the shadow of human men who believed his lies and wanted to make him a king. You can't blame us for wanting to change our fate."

I don't blame them for wanting change—I could never blame them for that. It's what I want too, even more so now that I know the truth.

But what stings, what cuts me to the core, is the realization that they all knew. Kieran, Silas, Micah, and possibly even Marianne knew what we are—*what I am*—and they never said anything. When did their powers manifest? How long have they been in this group, this resistance? And why did they never tell me?

"Besides you and Marks, the remaining governors of Corinth are all demigods. Four of the five ruling seats want to see the Lord General disposed of and they're on their way to Amale to make that a reality."

Cal's hand finds me, tanned fingers wrapping around mine to steady me as Kieran's words land. We have a real chance to change our country, and maybe even our world. There's no need for political strategies and negotiations, no necessity for the chess game that I've mapped out in my head. If this is true, we win the Ascension Vote in every scenario.

But I know in the hollow pit of my stomach that it can't be that simple. Magic scrapes its beastly claws under my skin again as I turn my attention to the pained expression on Cal's face.

"There's more, isn't there?" I ask tentatively.

Cal lets out a ragged exhale, the throb of his distress spearing me in the chest.

"There's more at stake than just the Amethyst Throne, princess. When Nobus exiled the rebellious gods here, Selene cut a deal with the God King."

The weight of both men's gazes slice into my skull at the mention of my mother. When I don't lift my eyes from the blade of grass I'm focused on intently, Cal presses onward.

"A mother's love runs deep. I don't know the terms, only that it gave the exiled gods a chance to go home again. Under the agreement, they will remain in this realm until the one with the power to unite us rises."

The one with the power to unite us rises—the prophecy from the strange, otherworldly woman in the streets of Eida, the words I easily dismissed now falling from Cal's lips.

"What does that mean?" Kieran asks.

"There's a doorway of sorts, a portal to the god realm. Marks wants it open—and he wants to be on the throne when it happens."

"That's why he's forcing the entire country to worship Nobus," I say on an unsteady breath.

"We're his offering to the gods," Kieran adds. "Fuck."

"The understatement of the century, Rollins."

Whatever part he played, Marks was definitely a member of the rebellion, an uprising that I'm beginning to think was more about stealing power than invoking change. And now half a million people are going to pay the price for his deeds with their lives.

We are his collateral, his sacrifice to the God King to reclaim his favor and return home, our own existences be damned.

I'm not aware that my hands are trembling until Cal squeezes them, the increased pressure of his magic against mine sending my traitorous heart skittering.

"Why don't we go get some water, princess?"

Kieran disappears into the tent, granting us precious privacy. Cal and I gather our vessels in silence before he directs us towards the water his magic detects.

He doesn't push me to speak while we walk to the small stream. He doesn't prod me as he takes the canteens and fills each one with the clear water. And he still doesn't question me as he sits on the bank and removes his boots.

I follow suit, letting my toes feel the biting cold of the flowing water and the thickness of the mud underneath before I speak.

"Kieran and the heirs are all demigods, but I'm not. My father … isn't Ansel Fellows." It's not a question anymore, but a fact.

"I'm sorry." He scoots closer to me, his shoulder pressing against mine. "I know this feels like a betrayal, but Ansel was still your parent in every way that matters. Rhea was Henry and Theo's mother, but she took me in and loved me like I was her own son. That's what makes someone a parent: not their blood but their heart."

Cal's grief mingles with mine, the shared wounds weeping with the endless, chasmic pain of loss. We sit in silence, the cold water numbing our skin until it matches the feeling that swarms within us at their memories. There's camaraderie in our commiseration, strength in the weakness that we both keep buried.

"Who is the prophesied one, Cal?" I ask on a shaky exhale, eager to feel a pain I'm more comfortable with.

As if his thoughts are my own, I know his next words before they ever leave his lips.

"Marks believes it's me, but I don't."

"What do you believe?" I ask cautiously, both wanting and not wanting to hear it said aloud.

"I believe it's you. Marks only knows about your earth magic …

which, while fucking incredible to witness, isn't what sets you apart. If he had any idea what you're capable of, he would have done far worse than villainized you. Poison Ivy was his attempt at controlling you, his personal revenge for your mother scheming with the enemy."

I would hardly classify negotiating a way home as 'scheming with the enemy,' but of course Marks would.

If my mother was pregnant with me when she was exiled, then he knows I'm capable of more than the other heirs. But rather than manipulating me to be his ally, he chose to belittle me and make the nation hate me. He wanted to make sure I never realized my own worth—and damnit if he didn't almost succeed. He crafted a narrative that I was a villain, and my words and actions proved him right. He created Poison Ivy, but I grew her thorns all on my own. I became what he made me and never realized I could be more. I wore the yoke the gods bestowed on me and never thought to remove it.

Until now.

"If we succeed and kill Marks ... if it's you who can open the portal ... will you?" I ask.

Silver rims Cal's gray eyes. I can't read him; his wants are muddy, like he's considered this question a thousand times and has never settled on an answer. He scoots closer to me, letting his arm drape over my shoulders and his head rest atop mine.

"If you want me to open the gates of the Under Realm and let Death's demons devour this realm, I will find a way to do it for you. Whatever you ask, I'm yours to command."

"Whoever sits the throne will command you, Cal. Not me."

"You sell yourself short, princess. You may not be the savior the people of Corinth think they want, but you are exactly what they need. Whether saving them entails killing a god or opening a portal to a different realm, you will do what needs to be done. You should be their queen."

I don't correct him. Letting him think that I want the crown is kinder than the truth: I won't be alive long enough to even cast my vote. No one can kill a god and live to tell the tale.

"Is there no limit to your delusion?" I joke, trying and failing to distract my aching heart.

"Limit?" he laughs. "I have no limits when it comes to you. There is nothing I wouldn't do, nowhere I wouldn't go for you. There is not a path you could take that I would not follow, in this life or any other."

A million tiny daggers slice my skin. Shattered fragments of what can never be rip me open in bloodless wounds. I slide backwards across the muddy creek bank to distance myself from his touch, from the magic that overwhelms every part of me.

I can't bear to hear him speak like this anymore, like I'm someone deserving of this kind of love when I am only every vile thing they have ever said about me. Even the gods believe me unworthy of happiness, or they wouldn't have dangled this in front of me while orchestrating my demise.

"Stop," I demand, cursing the tears that well against my will.

"Stop what?"

"Stop loving me!" I yell at him. "I am darkness and poison. I can't give you what you want."

"Can't or won't?"

My confession is little more than a whisper, the words shredding what's left of me on their way out. "Can't. There's too much at stake to get distracted now."

"How am I a distraction? We have the same goal."

The words I can't say hover on the tip of my tongue. The concession that I refuse to voice: *because you make me want to stay.*

"Because if it came down to it, you wouldn't choose Corinth and I will."

"Don't fucking lie, Ivy." Cal runs his fingers through his hair, pulling the ends tight in frustration. "You've never had a choice, not in your title or your destiny, and the very first one you get, you're going to pick the people who have loathed you over me?"

"How is this a choice?" I rise to my feet, lifting my shirt to expose the sea beast inked across my skin. "This is designed by the fucking gods. We didn't choose this."

"I did." Cal rises to his knees, tanned fingers gripping the fabric of his shirt as he tears open the buttons to reveal his matching tattoo. "We were always destined to find each other, but that could have been as enemies or reluctant allies. Our lives are connected, yes, but the only god who has a say in how I feel about you is *me*. My love is not fated; I willed it into existence. I alone chose you and I will do it every day for the rest of my immortal life whether you choose me back or not. Fuck destiny. Fuck the gods. Fuck the prophecy. All I want is you!"

"You don't even know me!" Black shadows dance at the corners of my vision as my dark magic rises in resistance.

Cal grips my wrists tight, pulling me down into the mud until we're chest to chest.

"Don't I?" he scoffs. "We are the same. If anyone can understand what it's like to live behind a moniker meant to dehumanize you, it's me. We are products of a cruel world and an even crueler god … but we don't have to be alone anymore." Rough hands find my face and force my eyes to meet his. "I want all of you, Ivy. There is no part of you too dark, too poisonous for me. No piece of you that I do not want."

I allow myself a brief moment to gaze into the depthless oceans of his gray eyes, eyes that I want to fall hopelessly into but can't. A life I want but can never have.

"You can't know that."

Magic barrels through me like a flash of lightning. The fathomless infinity of his devotion rushes through my veins, ricocheting between my bones and overwhelming my feeble soul. One look from him, one brush of his lips against mine and I will crumble into the dust that my decaying magic craves.

"I know you feel that. How can you possibly believe yourself reprehensible to me when the fabric of your soul denies it?" Cal shakes his head, a single tear threatening to break loose from the corner of his eye. "You can try to push me away all you want, but I'm not going anywhere."

"And if Marks kills me?" I ask, in an attempt to further sabotage the moment. Doom and ruin are all that await me on this journey, and I refuse to drag Cal down with me despite my declaration.

"I already said I'd open the gates of the Under Realm," he chuckles softly. "Who do you think will be holding them open for you when you get there?"

There's hope written into every line of his delicate smile, the sight of it demanding me to give in to his pleas, to forget every nightmare that's burned into my memory, and to let his cosmic pull drag me into blissful oblivion.

In a better world, we'd both walk away from this monumental task, both live to see the other side together. But that world doesn't exist. In this world, we're gods who have so little control over our power that we can't even choose our own ending.

No matter how much he may want to.

No matter how much I may want to.

"Do I want to know why you're both covered in mud and his shirt is ripped?" Kieran asks when Cal and I return to camp.

"Nothing to warrant that look on your face," I reply mockingly.

"Shame," the captain mumbles under his breath, gray eyes glinting in the moonlight that has fallen since we left the stream.

"I will take the first watch as long as you both agree not to do anything in that tent that I can hear out here," Kieran starts. "Your combined magic is already enough to upset my stomach, you don't need to make it worse."

"You can really do that?" I ask. "You can sense magic?"

"Sometimes I forget how young you were when your mother died," the governor replies. "Did your magic even manifest before she—"

"No," I interrupt.

Kieran swallows thickly, running a hand through his auburn hair as he replies. "Shit ... sorry. I can teach you if you want."

"I don't want anything from you," I spit back at him. "Least of all your pity."

Dark magic rises in my veins, shadows ready to strike at the source of my anger. A familiar blue power rushes out to subdue the black flames, a life preserver in the waves that threaten to pull me under.

"Ivy." Cal's voice cuts through the gloom, illuminating the way back to shore. "I need you to show me what you did to Rollins on the boat."

Funneling my power into Kieran right now may not be the smartest move, but there's a part of me that doesn't care if he's a casualty. Another wave of Cal's magic rushes out to wash away the remnants of the power we can't afford for me to use on our ally.

Reluctantly, I take a step towards Kieran, my hand outstretched to take his.

"On me this time." The captain takes three large steps back-wards, separating himself from the group. "I know you can use my power, but I need to know what happens when you funnel yours into someone else. I need to know if you're able to do that because Kieran is only a half-god or—"

"Or if she's able to take control of the magic of a full god." Kieran finishes the thought, taking several large steps away from us. "Let's see if you've got what it takes, Governor."

A deep, shuddering breath fills my lungs as I take a final look at Cal. Steel gray eyes lock onto mine, power pulsing in the air as I cast out the shimmering green bands of my magic. They swirl through the camp, the other governor blind to the power that circles him. But when they teasingly brush against Cal's cheek, he leans into them. All the confirmation I need that he's aware of their presence.

Incandescent tendrils of my magic tease the edges of Cal's power, green wisps glinting around his shining oceanic orb. Warmth washes over me as the colors begin to meld together, his power recognizing mine.

I push further, past the threads that beg to be woven. They part easily, welcoming me into the foyer of his refuge. I pour more of my magic into Cal, the sparkling blue aura of his power meeting mine in a thunderous crash of viridian that nearly steals the breath from my lungs.

His watery element cries out, tempting me to command the skies. The hair on my arms stands as the electric tingle of a thunderstorm becomes mine. The earthy petrichor that fills the night air around us gives way to the sulfuric smell of fire as I push deeper into him. The elements of fire and air fill my veins as I breathe in the essence of his magic. Each part of a beautiful symphony, strands of magic that I can wield individually or together.

The infinite, depthlessness I felt in Ruby rushes back to me. All-consuming, limitless power. Life and death. Every element in this realm mine to wield as I please.

I'm about to retreat, to call my magic back into my own body when a flash of black catches my attention. The beast on my stomach stirs, time slowing to a crawl. I tunnel into Cal, past the droplets of water, past the swirls of wind, past the flickering flames of fire.

Summoning this amount of power demands every emotion, every ounce of hurt and rage I can recall to pursue the darkness I seek. Water streams from my eyes, my entire body trembling as I latch onto the black core of Cal's bottomless power.

The sea beast thrashes wildly against my too hot skin. My knees give way first, violently crashing into the ground.

Cal's eyes are still locked on mine, the cool gray now replaced with white hot flames. His magic—raw immortal magic—is no longer his to wield. Veins protrude in his neck as he fights my hold, his own desperation flooding me. Black spots cloud the corners of my vision as I tighten my command on his body, holding him physically in place as I struggle to remain conscious.

I've overcome the first hurdle. I've grabbed the power of a god, but being able to hang on is another thing entirely.

Air grows thick in my lungs and I know I have to let go. Stubbornness pushes me to the limits of my power, digging its heels in and forcing me to hold on for a few seconds longer.

Pain cracks my head in two, time running out. My body collapses as lightning flashes across the sky and oblivion claims me.

CHAPTER 31

The glow of the midday sun is blinding. Salty air floods my lungs as my eyes adjust to my surroundings. I'm soaking wet, my green cotton dress clinging to my strange body. There's an unmistakable pearlescent sheen to my fair skin that glitters in the light as if I'm wrapped in the very essence of magic. My feet sink into sugary white sand as I struggle to stand.

Everything feels wrong, as if space and time no longer exist in this sliver of eternity. The seaside paradise of my childhood surrounds me, restored to the wondrous glory that colored it before Death's arrival.

"Arcasia!"

My stomach drops at the sound of her voice. The unmistakable timbre that fell silent nearly two decades ago. The voice that haunts my dreams and colors my memories. The rough-stitched wound of her absence rips open, the pain of her death fresh once again.

My hands ball into fists, nails biting into the tender flesh of my palm to stave off the tears as the outline of my mother steps into

GODSBANE

view. Her pale hair is haloed in a ring of golden sunshine, light pouring from her body as she glides atop the sand. The gauzy fabric of her emerald gown whips around her legs in the breeze as she approaches the water's edge.

The waves part easily for her, allowing her to effortlessly walk across the ocean's bottom. Black flashes in the water as she calls out again for the Goddess of Protection.

I move to scream, to warn her, but the sound dies in my throat. Iridescent scales sparkle in the sun as the head of the sea beast rises from the waves. Familiar silver eyes level their piercing gaze on Selene.

"It's done," my mother says. "The boy is safe here, for now. He can't find him." Her hands trail absently across her body, stopping to cradle the gentle swell of her belly. "Now it's time for you to uphold your end of the bargain."

The beast flicks her mighty tail in anger, causing the waves to roil around her. With a lift of her delicate hand, my mother casts the salty spray into flecks of pure light that pierce the blue horizon —new stars that will be visible in the dark fabric of night.

"I had to," she says in response. "Even in this form, you can feel what this realm is doing to our power. I gave them a way home ... but it only works if you seal *our* bargain. It has to be the both of them, Arcasia. I will not settle for less."

A grumble resounds from deep within before the serpent dips her head in submission, her giant tail twisting around my mother until she's fully in the beast's grasp. Light pours from their joining, magic rippling across the coast as their deal is sealed.

Pain sears into the skin between my shoulders, electricity sparking through the tattooed scar. Arcasia loosens her hold and soundlessly disappears into the depths of the Eastern Sea.

My mother turns from the water, the small slope of her abdomen glowing in a glimmering, viridian hue.

"Come."

A single word. A command I silently obey.

Endless white light lies ahead, but still I follow. The sand below my feet quickly gives way to wooden floors and plush rugs, the landscape around us transforming from palm trees to bookcases. The rich scent of leather tomes, salt air, and mahogany fills the air of the idyllic cottage library.

Selene stops, her golden irises glinting in the ethereal glow surrounding her immortal body as she turns to face me.

"It's time for you to finish what we could not. You have everything you need now. Use it wisely."

She tucks a strand of wet hair behind my ear, tenderly trailing her fingers across my cheekbone and the constellation of freckles that dust it.

My consciousness hangs somewhere in the space between the past, the present, and the future. Magic permeates the air, sweeping across her iridescent form. I open my mouth but my tongue can't form the syllables of her strange language, a language I understand but can't speak.

"You are approaching a fork in your fate. Each of the two paths were laid out before you were born, and both were paved by the wills of different gods. Which path you take is up to you, but you must hurry."

Selene's glowing form fractures, the image of her dispersing as she begins to fade into a ball of holy light.

"It's time to choose, my dark bloom."

Choose what? I try to scream the question, crying harder as the last bits of my mother fade away into the abyss that envelops me.

"Choose home."

I jolt upright, smacking my head on the lantern hanging from the ceiling of our tent. Cold air fills my lungs as I try to slow my frantic heartbeat.

"Finally," a voice groans. Kieran sits beside me on a rolled out pallet of furs, clearly agitated. "Holy shit, Ivy."

"How long was I out?" I ask, still fighting the panic rooted in my gut.

"Ten hours."

I gape at his response. What felt like only moments on whatever plane I ended up on was nearly half a day here.

I rip off the fur covering my lap to find myself not in a green cotton dress, but still in my muddy riding leathers. I examine my hands closely. They're drab and pale, no longer coated in a pearlescent sheen.

"Where's Cal?" I ask on a shaky breath. Did I drain him too? Is he sleeping off my magical assault outside in the cold?

"I finally convinced him to leave you long enough to take a piss. The bastard has been hovering over you like you're an egg that will hatch at any moment. It's a good thing you're awake, though. I was not looking forward to riding with your unconscious body slung over a horse."

"Your idea, I presume."

"Don't look at me like that." Kieran glowers. "The Ascension Vote is in a week and we have shit to do. Lover boy was content to stay here until you woke up, no matter how long that took."

"Good thing I woke before dawn, then." I scoff at Kieran.

He's always callous, but this time he's also right. We are on a schedule, and I would have been pissed if we missed our chance to take down Marks because of this. The *aevus* resistance is waiting.

My hands are still quivering, shaking from the otherworldly encounter. Kieran notices, his russet eyes freezing on them for a moment before moving upwards to my face.

"What you did out there," he says as he pulls out a pair of leather gloves from his pocket and passes them to me. "That was fucking incredible. This changes everything, Ivy. You're the weapon that ensures we all live to see the new Corinth."

I slip the sable-lined gloves onto my shaking hands, focusing on fitting each individual finger into its slot.

Weapon. The one thing I never wanted them to make me is exactly how he sees me.

But he's wrong about one thing—we won't all live. The fork in my fate approaches, the moment of truth when I make the choice I must no matter the personal cost. My mother bargained with multiple gods to give us a fighting chance. She sacrificed and now I must too.

"I know why my mother made the deal with Nobus," I murmur, eyes still focused on my gloved hands.

The canvas flap of the tent flips back. Cal's large frame in the entry blocks out the campfire on the other side, casting him in an eerie orange halo.

"Ivy."

Relief is thick in his hoarse voice but worry still colors his face. The dark circles under his eyes are obvious signs of his refusal to sleep.

"That's my cue," Kieran says, as he moves to vacate the tent. "You should talk to Murphy."

Cal quickly moves to take his place beside me, pulling my hands into his, squeezing them until they no longer tremble.

"Talk to me about what?"

I swallow, buying time while I decide my course of action. He patiently waits for me to continue, giving me the space I didn't ask for but desperately need. I want to tell him who I saw, but the words dry up in my mouth like sand. If I'm right about who he is … if I'm right, it changes nothing. Our mission, our fate is still the same.

"Hey." Cal's voice cuts through my clouded thoughts. "Talk to me."

"Your magic is limitless, Cal. Do you have any idea what you can do?"

"Me?" He asks with a half laugh. "Ivy, what *you* did … I've never seen anything like that. Marks is the most powerful god I have encountered and I don't think he can do what you did."

"You can," I say, pulling my hands from his. "You are powerful enough to take on any god. Why don't you?"

"I can't access it." Cal's hands snag in his disheveled mass of hair as his confession hangs between us. Shadows dance in his eyes, haunted memories that he doesn't openly share. "It's only ever responded to you."

My hand moves to his chest, instinctively splaying across the image of Arcasia's beast form that connects us and our power. The deal my mother struck with the leviathan to ensure my protection has led me to my end. And the more pieces of this puzzle I uncover, the more I'm certain of what I must do.

"Then we'll take him down together."

CHAPTER 32

The sun rises just like it does every day. The birds chirp and the crocuses open their petals to the morning rays as our strange threesome packs up our camp. Everything is as it should be ... everything except the atmosphere that hangs between us. The next time we stop will be on the outskirts of Amale.

Kieran has secured us a safe house just outside the capital city, a temporary respite where we can wait until the other governors arrive. He claims it belongs to a non-magical friend of the resistance, but he won't say who. Every question is met with an annoying *'trust me'* that makes it increasingly difficult to do so.

The only information he'll divulge is to confirm to Cal that this supposed ally is covertly acquiring a detailed floor plan of the palace. Considering I am not well-versed enough in its schematics to fully form an attack, I can't complain.

The time I spent in the palace over the years wasn't that of an overly welcomed guest, but that of an inconvenient pest that the council was forced to tolerate because of my title. The puppet king's council is the real pest, one that Marks likely has no intention to exterminate considering he already controls them.

Whichever of the *aevus* sits the Amethyst Throne next will have to disband them if they wish to make any progress towards changing Corinth. I wouldn't trust a single one of them as far as I can throw them.

Hooves beating on the dirt road are the only sound that's shared between the three of us as we ride toward Amale.

My magic is still barely at half strength. It needs to rest, and Cal was adamant that we stay for another day so I could sleep, but I refused. We need to get to the city. We need to strategize and perform reconnaissance while the palace is abuzz with activity in the days before the Ascension Vote. It will be our best chance to sneak in undetected and if we wait here, we might miss it.

Anxiety causes magic to dance to life under my skin. It seems emotions are the key to my power. Hurt, anger, and pain feed it like an accelerant on a dying flame. The roughness of my exposed soul like the bark of the tinder, my breath the oxygen that fans it.

Like a graverobber, I unbury my hidden emotions as we ride. I turn over secrets of heavy stone and dig through the dirt of heartache and lies, careful to avoid the iron-clad coffin that contains my heart—the one place I don't dare open. Power rises within me with each shovelful until it begs for release.

I summon the only element I can call my own, filling the empty ground alongside the road with clusters of deep purple flowers as we ride past.

Godsbane.

Poison.

Death.

All names for the dark blooms that effortlessly sprout from my fingers. All names I'm starting to claim as my own.

It will cost my lifeblood to unmake a god, but no price is too steep to save my home. And if I'm going to have even a sliver of a chance at that salvation, I need to hone my weapon.

Glimmering green bands of my still exhausted magic swirl from my body, drawn to the magnetic pull of Cal's aura. They tease and prod the edges until it parts for me. I bathe in the shimmering ocean of his power, letting it wash over me until I'm coated in it.

A ball of water forms in my hand, a multitude of magical droplets spinning in aqueous unison.

Cal's head snaps in my direction, tendrils of his dark hair waving in a breeze that answers to me. The element that has evaded me finally succumbs to my will. Air doesn't particularly care for my intrusion, but it recognizes me as the ally its master needs to live.

A prideful smile blooms across Cal's face at the way our power dances, entwined in a delicate waltz that only we can see and feel. The edges of Kieran's brown cloak ruffle in the wind but he pays it no mind. To him, it's not the conquered final element, but a natural occurrence.

I push deeper into the shimmering mass of Cal's power, ignoring the way my cheeks pink under the weight of his praise. I release the air and water in search of the final element he wields.

Even in my weakened state, the glow of our swirling viridian power could rival the sun. Tiny sparks sprout from my fingertips to form a single flame that hovers just above my palm. It's engrossingly gorgeous, the way the orange base gives way to a flickering yellow center before tapering off into a blinding white point.

Each of the elements is capable of sustaining life or ending it. Despite the constant growth, decay doesn't claw at me. The dark magic within me quiets in the haze of Cal's power, not kneeling to him but satisfied to hover at the edges while I take from the god.

The heated call of the magical fire sings to me in a familiar tune: *destroy, destroy, destroy.* I breathe it in, relishing in the temptation only for a moment. The smoldering sensation courses through me, the flame duplicating itself in my other palm until I hold the beginnings of our ruination in my hands.

A blast of icy wind cuts sharply through the trees, breaking my focus. The fire extinguishes, the ashes collecting in my palms tempting me to call it forth again.

"Burning the godsdamned Kingswood down is certainly one way to get Marks' attention, though I think that's the opposite of what we're hoping to accomplish," Kieran huffs.

"I wasn't going to burn the Kingswood down," I chide.

"I couldn't have stopped you." Cal's muttered confession settles over us like a wet blanket.

The call to lose myself in his power is strong, my inexperience too great to be trusted. I can practice on the demigods, on Kieran and other other governors when they arrive, but I have to resist the captain's pull.

When push comes to shove, when we finally face Marks and I attempt to pour every ounce of my magic into him, my only chance at saving everyone is if I don't know how to stop.

The closer we get to Amale, the more the weight of our monumental task settles over us.

The sun completes its arc overhead and disappears below the horizon, but still we ride. The moon never appears in the sky—a welcome relief for those who seek to traverse under the cover of darkness. The forgotten Goddess of Light grants us one small mercy at least.

The Starry Wolf and the Great Owl, constellations of the god-brothers Mikais and Nobus, stalk us on our trek into the heart of the Diamond Region. The clouds seem to deliberately move around them as to not block their all-seeing gaze.

The dirt road gives way to worn cobblestones as the dilapidated buildings on the city's edge come into view.

Decades ago, under a different, kinder king, the edges of Amale were bustling with commerce and industry. Talented tailors and dressmakers crafted highly sought-after fashions from shops that once lined these streets. Culinary masterpieces were created to fill the stomachs of the rich who often traveled to the far reaches of the city. But those hearths have long since grown cold.

As most trends do, the favor of the wealthy shifted in time, leaving the tradespeople without the income they relied on. After all, you can't covet something everyone has, and the Corinthian nobility are driven by their desire to be coveted by those they deem less fortunate.

Only the poorest of Amale's citizens reside here now. Weather-worn wooden planks make up the derelict homes and storefronts that line the streets. Instead of glass panes, long swaths of cloth hang from window openings and flit in the warm coastal breeze.

This late into the night, with no candles or fires burning to illuminate the shanties, the city feels inhabited only by the ghosts of those who once flourished here, the only noises the haunting whistle of the wind and the clacking of hooves on the jagged, cracked stones.

The ever vigilant military captain, Cal scans the buildings for any signs of soldiers or spies as Kieran leads us silently through the battered town. I memorize the path, three right turns and a single left from the city's edge. Halfway to the palace and the Port of Gems, the shining coastal port whose waters are said to be as turquoise as the gemstones exported there.

Kieran comes to an abrupt halt in front of a row of run-down homes, each blending seamlessly with the other identical buildings spaced only feet apart on each side. They look abandoned. It's been a long time since anyone looked too long at these houses, and I pray that doesn't change now.

The governor of the Ruby Region dismounts, carefully bouncing on his toes as he lands to soften the sound. Approaching the worn door, Kieran knocks four times. One long, two short, one long—a code that's immediately answered by two short and two long knocks. Whoever is on the other side wasn't just expecting us, they were actively standing guard.

The door swings open, revealing a large figure completely shrouded in a Corinthian gray cloak. Breath turns to stone in my lungs as two large hands reach forward and grip Kieran by the shoulders.

"Are you hurt?" the man asks in a husky whisper.

"No." Kieran's reply is quickly snuffed out as the hooded figure's lips find his.

Cal gently clears his throat, a reminder to the men of our presence, but also a cue for me to fix my steamed expression.

Trust me, Kieran said. A lot of fucking good that that did me.

"We weren't expecting you, Klein," Cal says.

Elias Klein, member of the former king's council and a loud advocate for a singular national religion, swings his attention toward us, letting the hood of the cloak fall back to reveal black curls and rich mahogany eyes.

"Captain," he nods, a wide smile plastered across his traitorous face as he takes in Cal and avoids me entirely. "Come inside."

Elias turns, never dropping his hand from Kieran entirely, as if his secret lover is an apparition that could disappear if he doesn't tether him to this plane.

"What the fuck?" I ask Cal when the others disappear inside.

"I don't know," he says, rubbing a hand gently across my upper arm. "Let's hear him out first and then we can decide if we're going to kill him."

The corner of his mouth turns up in a playful smirk that elicits an unexpected chuckle from somewhere within me. "Fine, but let me do the talking."

The home is small, the space crammed with a faded settee, a worn armchair, and a rickety dining table with four mismatched stools. Thick drapes cover the broken glass, all that remains of the window panes. The new, expensive fabric blocks out the candle light that illuminates the compact room.

"You all must be starving. I made stew." Elias Klein motions for us to sit at the table. A steaming cauldron hangs above the small fire, the smell causing all of our mouths to water. We sit at the table as he passes around a decanter of red wine and bowls of the hearty concoction.

"To Lady Ivy," Elias says, raising his wine glass in a toast. "May your endeavor here be successful."

"What are you playing at?" I ask boldly, dropping my spoon. The hot broth splashes onto the table as I push up to stand. "Are you here to sell us out? Is this foreshadowing to your fickle allegiance?"

"Ivy." Kieran grunts out a warning I refuse to heed.

"You were the most prominent member of the former king's council. You never once spoke up for me or spoke out against Marks' tyranny. You supported the crusade against Synal, for gods' sake. But here you sit, hiding me in your supposed safe house. Toasting my 'endeavors' and wishing me success."

"He is on our side," Kieran growls, his anger evident as he rises from the table to meet my challenge.

"You just believe that because you're fucking him. Elias Klein has only ever cared about saving his own ass."

Fury possesses me, magic building in my veins as I round the corner to come face-to-face with the man that I've debated more times than I can count. Of all the people in Amale who might be considered a covert ally, Elias Klein isn't one of them. He's not even on the list of possibilities.

"Only a fool would choose Marks," Elias scoffs. "Four *aevus* governors changes everything about Corinth."

If Cal notices that I've borrowed a thread of his magic, he makes no indication; he only watches intently, never interfering and letting me decide the fate of these men.

I don't use much, just enough to squeeze the water within Klein's blood. Not enough to kill him or to satiate the shadows that hover in the corners of the room, but enough to show him what I'm capable of. A small taste of the rage burning in my veins.

"Do you think I will spare you, Elias? That if by some miracle we manage to eliminate the Lord General, that I would what? Allow you to retain your seat on the new monarch's council instead of taking you out with the rest of the trash?"

Elias squirms uncomfortably as I increase Cal's power.

"Back. Down." Kieran spits each word through gritted teeth, his restraint fraying.

The air in the room constricts slightly, a piss poor attempt to use his meager magic. Bright red blood leaks from the councilor's nose as his panic-filled eyes silently beg for help.

"Do you think your lover can save you from my wrath?" A menacing chuckle escapes my lips. "He can't even save himself."

With a flick of my wrist, Kieran's blood coats his own face, a perfect mirror of Klein's appearance.

Cal grabs my arm, his fingers lightly digging into my skin. The water magic I'm wielding skitters under his hold, but it doesn't leave me. The captain leans in close, his mouth brushing my ears as he speaks low against my skin.

"I won't stop you from killing them if that's what you want." He pulls back, his gray eyes finding mine in a knowing stare. "But it would be advantageous for us to let them live."

In a single exhale, I let go of Cal's power, releasing the hold on Kieran and Elias. From my peripheral, I can see them rush to each other, but I don't hang around long enough to be chastised for my behavior.

There's an old wooden door off to the right that I'm almost certain leads to a bedroom. I rush towards it without hesitation, silently praying it's not a closet. Sweet relief fills me when I discover the cot-sized bed that nearly takes up the entire room. It's not a closet, but it's the size of one.

Flimsy shutters squeak open as I inhale the night air in a desperate attempt to clear away the anger that I let consume me.

Anger has always been my go-to emotion. It's the first to appear in every scenario, no matter the occasion. And when the irate wave recedes, tears follow in its wake. No matter how hard I will them to stop, my watery weakness shows up without fail.

The salty smell of the coastal air fills my nostrils as pressure builds behind my eyes. Every time I close them, the image of my pregnant mother walking into the ocean floods my vision. There's only one reason she would show me that. One reason that touching the ebony core of Cal's magic manifested it.

There's a hint of leather on the salty breeze and I know at once I'm not smelling the ocean anymore.

"I don't need a scolding." I say without turning around, swiping the evidence of my emotions from my cheeks.

"I know."

"I'm not sorry," I add with a bite.

"I know that, too."

The sound of creaking metal followed by two heavy thuds has me spinning around. The captain sits on the edge of the bed unbuttoning his shirt, his boots resting beside his sock-clad feet.

"What are you doing?"

"Going to sleep," he says matter-of-factly.

"Here?" I ask, looking at the bed barely large enough for one person. "In my bed?"

"We're attempting to kill a god tomorrow. I'd rather not sleep on the floor."

"It's the day after tomorrow, but I get your point," I sigh. "I guess you can stay."

Cal's presence will be a welcome distraction from the thoughts that haunt me. At most, I have two nights left in this realm. I know it's not right to lead him on, to let him believe that there's a future where we coexist, but underneath the callous exterior, the poisonous nickname, and the stubborn will, there's a person who just wants to spend her last moments pretending.

Cal scoots towards the wall, leaving room for me to sit to remove my own boots. He doesn't push me to speak, nor does he ask what overcame me at the table or at the window. He's just there. Solid and stable.

I inch under the thin blanket, careful not to press too close to Cal in the cramped cot. We lay there in silence, the only sound in the home the steady breathing of the man beside me.

But sleep evades me, and I can't quiet the question that sits heavily on the edge of my tongue. "You really wouldn't have stopped me?"

I didn't funnel my magic into him. I only borrowed a thread to use as my own. He can't stop the former, but he's stopped the latter before when I asked. I know he's capable of it even if he tries to deny it now.

"No." In a swift motion, Cal props himself on his elbow, his face hovering inches above mine. "Killing our allies may not be the smartest military strategy, but I will never deny you your desires."

I swallow thickly under the weight of his stare. "None of them? No matter how ill-advised my *desires* might be?"

"Not a single one." Thick fingers grasp my chin, forcing me to look into his sleep-heavy eyes. "From your holiest to your most depraved, all you have to do is whisper it and I will make it reality."

His thumb drags over my bottom lip as he removes his hold on my face. We're talking about murdering someone, about allowing myself to be overtaken by emotions and elements that have no business ruling me. I shouldn't be turned on right now.

My entire life has been a performance. The poisonous heir, the bitch heretic. Roles created to portray whatever version of me best served the narrative of others. But I don't have to perform with him, this truly powerful man who isn't just saying pretty words.

I know, without a shred of doubt, that his words are absolute truths. Whoever I choose to be in my final days—a rebel, a vengeful god, a murderer—Callan Murphy's devotion will not waiver.

"Have I told you how sexy you are when you're wielding my magic?" he whispers against my skin.

"It doesn't threaten you to know that I control it?"

"To know that *my* power is flowing through *your* veins? Fuck no. Every single part of me is yours, Ivy. Use me. Command me." Cal's lips brush delicately across mine, his next words a whispered prayer. "Destroy me."

Our lips crash together with a fervent hunger that no mortal could ever satisfy.

I cannot love him.

I cannot have a future with him.

But I can have this: one last taste of what might have been had our destiny not been written to end in destruction.

CHAPTER 33

The Amethyst Throne is on fire and the flames smell strangely like ...*breakfast.* Eggs, specifically. My grumbling stomach pulls me from the premonition. Another dream sent by the gods to remind me of my impending demise. An ending that is rapidly approaching.

I fumble around the small room for my clothes, but come up empty handed. Gnawing hunger urges me to abandon my search and simply wear the brown garment that hangs on the doorknob. Finding no other option, I slip into Cal's oversized shirt and out of the bedroom.

Standing in front of the fire wearing nothing but low-slung leather pants, the captain holds a cast iron frying pan with two perfectly cooked chicken eggs. Much larger than the ones he cooked for me in the woods, but no doubt equally as delicious.

"Good afternoon, princess," he says with a smile that could thaw even the most frozen of hearts.

"Afternoon?"

"Afternoon," he restates, motioning for me to sit. "It was nearly dawn before you fell asleep. Figured you could use your rest before everyone else arrives."

That explains why my stomach was so vocal. I didn't eat dinner and slept right through the morning meal. The table is set with mismatched plates, chipped cups, and tarnished silverware. An empty vase sits in the center. I wave my hand and fill the vessel with deep purple godsbane blooms while I wait for Cal to serve the eggs.

"I will never get tired of watching you do that," he says with awe.

"Party tricks, remember? I bet you could grow them if you tried."

There's so much raw power within him, if he can tap into it growing a few flowers would be easy.

Cal slides one of the eggs onto my plate. My mouth waters at the sight and I barely register his response. I'm too occupied suppressing the moan that nearly escapes my lips at the first bite of the perfectly cooked dish.

"I can't. Trust me." He fills the mug in front of me with a dark, aromatic liquid as I chew. "Klein may be a snake, but he did manage to decently stock the icebox and cabinets."

"Captain Murphy, did you make me coffee?" I smile over the mug, steam wafting over my face as I grasp the mug with both hands. I wasn't sure I'd get the chance to indulge in my favorite beverage again.

"I prefer the name you were calling out last night," he smirks.

I savor the taste of the coffee on my tongue. I sip it slowly, pretending the warmth spreading through my body is from the bitter liquid and not from the intimacy of this moment. It has to be. There is no time left for this.

Cal, reading my discomfort, clears his throat.

"I brought in a bucket of water and your saddlebag. There's no washroom, but there is a closet over there." He points to a door opposite the bedroom. "Closet is a generous word for that room, but it's private. The governors should be here soon. Wash up and I'll keep watch."

"Thank you."

I wash down the last bite of eggs with a final sip of coffee. The last moments of whatever false normalcy this is masquerading as disappears with them. My heart aches with every glimpse of what might have been, the meals shared over laughter and smiles, the kisses and pleasures shared in the dark.

I force the emotion and the longing deep into the iron-clad box, latch the lock, and hide the key somewhere that even I can't find it.

There's a broken spring in the dilapidated settee that creaks every time I fidget. The worn cushions, once upholstered in a pastel butterfly motif, do little to comfort me.

The governors should have been here by now.

I trace what remains of the insects with my fingers, imagining what they might have looked like before a cruel world stole their beauty. What might they have been if this place hadn't fallen into such disrepair?

Sweat slicks Cal's brow despite the lack of fire in the chipped stone hearth. He won't admit it, but he's worried. The boards below his feet might turn to dust if he paces over them for much longer. His restlessness only increases my own anxiety.

They should have been here by now.

I unroll the floor plan of the palace's main floor that Elias smuggled out of the archives. I commit each of the four entrances to memory, studying the path from the main gate to the throne room that will serve as my final runway.

"When Elias returns, we'll have a better idea of how many troops Marks has stationed around the palace," I say flatly. *If he didn't sell us out.* "And Kieran will be able to tell if any of them are secretly *aevus*," I add. *If he wasn't captured.*

Cal doesn't speak as he continues his pacing. The sun is starting to set, darkening the small home and the mood within at the same time. I light the candles that adorn the weathered mantle, sending up a silent prayer to Arcasia to ask her protection on those who claim to be our allies.

The sound of approaching hooves echoes on the cobblestone street, the clunking of wagon wheels following. Cal's posture goes rigid as he reaches for his ivory-handled dagger. Bodies shuffle in the dim light just beyond the door.

Too many bodies.

We're expecting four governors, but eight figures move in the shadows created by the fading sun. I reach for the matching dagger strapped at my thigh and ready my magic for a fight.

Cal raises a hand in silent command as a hooded figure approaches the door. A pale fist appears from beneath a brown cloak before connecting with the door four times—one long knock followed by two short and another long knock.

A thin wooden door is all that separates us from eight allies or eight more foes-in-disguise.

Cal, blade drawn, moves slowly towards the door, flanked by my swirling shadows of dark magic. He opens it only a crack, just enough for the candlelight to illuminate the face of a dark haired man with piercing sapphire eyes.

"Sorry we're late," the Sapphire governor nods. "We picked up a few stragglers at the port."

Cal opens the door to allow him to enter the safe house. Micah

Porter sweeps a glance around the already cramped space before locking eyes with me.

"It's going to be a tight squeeze in here," he says, "but we can use all the help we can get."

Behind him, Silas Wilson shakes hands with Cal before motioning for the rest of their crew to enter. The Topaz governor nods in my direction as he removes his hood.

"Good to see you, Ivy."

"What are you doing here?" Cal's stern voice severs our reunion, each of us directing our attention towards the doorway and the man in the Corinthian gray and gold cloak grasping the captain by the shoulders.

"Oh c'mon, brother. Surely you didn't think we'd let you have all the fun." Theo Murphy smiles slyly at me as he steps across the threshold. "Hey darling."

A mess of blonde hair stomps through the door behind him, her rage-filled glare pointed directly at the youngest brother.

"We didn't even make it out of the Bay of Jewels before this one started harassing me to let her off the boat," Theo mocks.

"The only reason I got on that boat in the first place is because you told me that Ivy was on it, you liar!"

A mixture of relief, gratitude, and dread courses through me as my magic attempts to calm my erratically beating heart. My whole body trembles as tears build behind my eyes at the sight before me.

"I keep telling her that I only lied to save her life, but she doesn't listen," Theo says in exasperation.

"Quinn," I breathe.

My best friend shoots another scathing look at Theo before turning her attention to me. "And you! I ought to kill you myself, Ivy Fellows."

Never in my wildest dreams did I imagine that Quinn Bartlett would be standing in the doorway of our safe house in Amale. And she can chastise me all she wants, so long as I get to hear her voice.

I step towards her, shaky palms face up in submission, a joyous smile plastered across my face.

"How are you here?" I ask with tear-filled eyes.

"Next time you're in danger, don't send a man to kidnap me from my bed." Quinn closes the distance, pulling my quivering body into her warm embrace as she jokes where only I can hear. "At least not without a little warning."

A giddy chuckle escapes my throat as I pull back to look into her blue eyes. They're so full of light and life, a sobering reminder that her very presence here may extinguish that forever.

"What are you talking about?" I ask.

"We made a visit to The Royal Jewel and made some friends over a pint," Theo explains. "Turns out, they cared an awful lot about you being alive. So, I, uh … well, I kinda snuck into Blondie's house and …"

"Kidnapped me," Quinn finishes. "But I would have come willingly, you know. You're my best friend. If you think for one second that I would hesitate to come to your aid, you are sorely mistaken."

"Quinn, you don't know what you're up against. This is bigger than anything we've faced before."

My best friend has been by my side for every protest, every demonstration, every deed of activism that has so thoroughly earned me my nickname. We were harassed and berated, but Death never waited for us there.

Not like now.

Quinn isn't a devout worshipper of the gods, but there's no way she can know what I truly am—what we all are. She'd call us heretics and liars. She wouldn't be here, wouldn't risk her life for pretenders.

"I do. All of it, truly." She takes my hands into hers before tipping her head towards Theo. "Lieutenant Kidnapper here filled us in."

I don't miss his scoff at the nickname that has undoubtedly

been used more than once. This all makes no sense. If she … *wait.* What did she say?

"Us?" I ask curiously.

"You didn't think I'd let her come alone, did you?"

Miles steps across the threshold, shoving past the hulking form that refuses to move to allow him easy entry. The room is silent except for Cal's low, barely perceptible growl as Miles sweeps me off the floor and into his embrace. Everyone stiffens in anticipation of the captain's next move as Miles whispers in my ear.

"My money was on irritating, but *you* … oh, Ivy Fellows, you little devil. I'm going to need all the salacious details on him."

He messes up my hair in brotherly affection as he sets me down on my feet, turning towards the group with his best courtier smile. "I hope you're all hungry because we brought dinner."

Kieran is the last to enter, arms loaded down with baskets. The smell of fresh baked bread and grilled fish fills the house. Everyone moves at once. Silas pulls plates from the crooked cupboards, Micah fills cups with a rich, honeyed wine, and Quinn hunts through drawers for forks.

I count the bodies that fill the cramped space. Only six have joined our original two. Cal has pulled Theo off to the side, and despite their hushed voices, it's obvious that the brothers' conversation is heated. I take a tentative step towards them, risking Cal's ire for information on the location of his other brother and our missing heir-adjacent.

"Marianne got word to us about the coup. Henry fucking lost it when he heard she was joining the fight. Revenge against the prick for torturing you was motive enough for me to—"

"Torture?" I interrupt.

Both men swing to face me. Rage simmers in Cal's storm-filled eyes, the emotion not directed at me but at Theo's careless words. Words that were never intended for me to hear.

"Theo," Cal scolds through gritted teeth. "You will stand guard outside until Henry and Marianne are ready to grace us with their presence."

"Cal, you're being ridiculous," the youngest brother refutes. "You know I couldn't stop him."

"What I know is that you shouldn't be here, yet here you are."

Every person in the small house pretends to be very interested in their current task, purposefully avoiding Cal's attention as he storms off for the tiny bedroom. The rickety door slams with a force that nearly knocks it from its rusted hinges.

"Give him a minute," Theo says, laying a hand on my shoulder to stop my forward motion. He squeezes it and motions silently for me to follow him outside instead.

Darkness envelops the streets of the skeletal town. Sticking to the shadows, he leads me around the corner of the house and into the small alleyway that runs in between the homes. Theo gives the space a careful inspection before sitting on a wooden crate and extracting a pipe from his pocket.

"Light this for me, will you?"

I tense, unsure if I should borrow a thread of Cal's power given his current state. The moment stretches between us as if it's a test I have yet to pass. With an exaggerated eye roll, I wield the tiniest bit of his brother's power, a single flame hovering above my finger.

"Thank you, m'lady."

"I told you not to call me that."

"Should I call you sister instead?" He laughs.

The spicy, woodsy smell of burning tobacco fills my nose as Theo takes a puff from the ornately carved pipe. He extends his hand, motioning for me to sit on the crate to his right.

"What is this?" I ask.

"Tobacco, darling. You'll love it."

"Not the pipe, Theo. What is *this*?" I ask motioning between us. "Do you think I'm not furious with you, too?"

The lieutenant takes his time exhaling smoke slowly from his mouth before he speaks again.

"We didn't have a lot growing up. My adoptive brother tends to get a little possessive of things that he considers his. Battles, victories … you."

"If you think he's mad because he's being possessive over this battle—"

"I don't," Theo stops me. "He's worried about me and Henry, but he's pissed because we brought collateral with us."

Collateral. I let the word sink in as I take the pipe from his outstretched hand and inhale from it slowly.

"Is that what my friends are to you?"

"That's not my opinion, darling, that's the truth," he says flatly. "Marks will use all of us against you both if he can."

"Then why are they here? Why are you here?" I demand.

The mask that has been carefully concealing Theo's true face drops, replaced by the face of a little brother terrified for his sibling.

"Marks created monsters out of the people we love the most. We want them back. Not the caricatures, the real fucking people. The ones who love and laugh and have a real chance at changing this godsdamned world."

"And if those people don't exist anymore?"

A sad smile turns up the corner of Theo's mouth. "Blondie said you'd say that. Do you really believe you can't go back to that person?"

"There is no going back, Theo. Not for me."

CHAPTER 34

Quinn sits alone on the worn butterfly cushions, her champagne hair pooling over the broken arm of the settee as she rests her head on her shoulder. I slide into the small open space beside her, careful not to jostle her in case she's asleep.

"Ivy," she whispers as she wraps her arm around me and pulls my head to her chest.

A million questions fill my head.

How was the wedding?

Do you hate me?

Can you believe that I'm a god?

Is Emerald okay?

Do you hate me?

I finally settle on "Where's Nick?" and immediately regret it.

"Hopefully keeping Lord Yarrow in check so we have a region to return home to. That's what my letter asked him to do."

"The letter where you told him you weren't going to marry him?" Miles jokes from his reclined position on the floor.

I sit up in disbelief. "The *what?*"

"I just told him that I needed some time to be certain. Someone that I trust very much reminded me that I shouldn't have to try to love him. And she was right, as she usually is." Quinn rolls her eyes playfully, a soft smile pulling at her lips.

"And you listened to her?" I ask. "You really took the advice of someone who knows absolutely nothing about love?"

"Oh, I think that someone knows a lot more about love than she wants to admit."

Quinn's eyes flick to the corner of the room where Cal stands around the kitchen table. Henry and Marianne, who finally appeared nearly an hour after everyone else arrived, along with the other governors and Theo, crowd around it, poring over the map of the palace and rehashing the attack plan we've been reciting for hours.

As if he can feel my gaze, Cal looks up from the rolled parchment, a determined fire burning in his gray eyes.

"You owe us stories, Ivy. Many, *many* stories, but let's start with him. Is the Captain of Corinth as menacing in bed as he is out of it?" Miles playfully squeezes my knee, leaning in close in hopes of sharing whispers of gossip.

"I am not even going to dignify that with a response," I say.

"That's a yes," he laughs.

"It doesn't matter," I sigh, turning my attention back to Quinn, whose eyes are still focused on the youngest lieutenant. "What's going on with you and Theo?"

"Nothing," Quinn answers, quickly snapping her gaze back to mine.

"Liar," Miles mouths.

"I'm not the one who's keeping secrets around here," she retorts. "Our best friend never bothered to tell us that she's a goddess. Can you believe it, Miles?"

"You'd think being best friends with a goddess would have had some perks," he jokes. "Remember that time Father Munding gave us stable duty for a month for taking Nobus' name in vain? You could have gotten us out of that, at least."

Of all of the things my friends could have requested from me, that's where they landed? A childish smile overtakes my face, a giggle breaking free at Miles' demand. This is why I love them. This is why I should have always trusted them with my secret.

"If I remember correctly, you were the only one who cursed, yet somehow all of us, even the heir who was normally assigned to library duty, ended up shoveling shit. And it was only a week," I clarify.

"You're both right. It was only a week, but you could have at least tried to get us out of it, Ivy," Quinn chimes in. "It's not like we asked you to kill Munding or something."

The atmosphere in the room drops at her careless words. "Shit," she stammers. "I'm sorry. That was … I'm sorry."

I sit up, untangling myself from her hold. "I'm the one who should be apologizing. We've been friends since birth and I didn't trust you—either of you—with my secret."

"You didn't know, Ivy," Miles excuses.

"I knew I had magic. I knew I could grow flowers and that my nightmares were haunted by a mysterious stranger and a mythical sea beast. I lied over and over about where I snuck off to and why I wasn't sleeping."

"There's no shame in having a secret. Your life doesn't have to be an open book for everyone who knows you. Especially not when your entire life is lived in the public eye. You haven't had many choices. Don't be ashamed of the few you've been given."

Quinn's hand trails through my hair, pale fingers combing through the brown locks. I lean into her comforting touch, savoring the moment that stretches between us. A gift from the gods to have one final evening with the people I love most in this world. If only I could share the biggest secret of all, the shadow of Death that looms over me.

But my confession won't change the outcome. They won't leave. They won't abandon me to my fate to save themselves. So I keep it closer to my chest than anything I've ever held before.

But my confession won't change the outcome. They won't leave. They won't abandon me to my fate to save themselves. So I keep it closer to my chest than anything I've ever held before.

And I have no shame in that choice.

One by one, everyone in our ragtag resistance begins to yawn until sleepy, restless bodies litter the tiny home. Ten people cram into a space barely suited for five. Every spare covering, towel, or scrap of clothing is serving as a makeshift pallet or blanket. There's not an inch of this home that isn't occupied by someone.

Ever the gentleman, Cal offered Quinn the space on the cot he occupied the night before. But something in the way her eyes cut to Theo at the offer gave me the impression that she didn't want to spend this night beside me.

I'm still awake when Cal enters the bedroom several hours later. I should have been asleep by now, but the suspense of what's to come resounds in the quiet like a pealing bell. Only a few hours separate us from the maw of fate.

We've decided to infiltrate the castle during the guard change just before sunrise, and Cal has made all of the arrangements to ensure his men are scheduled to take the first shift at all four gates. We'll use the waning dark of night as cover and face the full pressure of battle with the rising sun.

Cal stands in front of the small window. The moonlight pouring in from around the tattered curtain encircles his head in a halo that steals my breath. In an instant, I'm taken back to the night we met. For a moment, we're back in the dining room in Emerald, none the wiser of how thoroughly we're about to be destroyed.

Or maybe I was the only one unaware.

The more I let him in, the more I'm certain Callan Murphy has thought only of me for longer than I can imagine. I don't know what to do with it—this strange, unfamiliar feeling of being wanted so desperately that he's willing to take the barest of scrapes

301

that I offer him. I let him cross the threshold only to shut him out, never fully opening the door to my heart.

But he never wavers on his chosen path, an infuriatingly admirable quality that will make him a great ruler one day. I only wish I could be around to witness it.

"Come to bed." I scoot against the wall to make room for him on the cot but he doesn't move. "That's an order, Captain."

"I just came to see if there was an extra blanket," he says, dropping his head.

He wears the weight of what's to come like a yoke, personally bearing the responsibility for each of the lives that follow his command into battle tomorrow. Personally bearing the responsibility for my life, even though I never asked for such a thing.

"You know, I did see a spot on top of that sorry excuse for a table. I'm sure you'll fit comfortably. It's not like you need your rest or anything."

Reluctantly, Cal sits on the edge of the cot. He removes his boots wordlessly before slipping under the blanket. Tension radiates from him, his entire body taut. Before I can think better of it, I rest my head on his broad chest in an attempt to comfort him. My magic was on edge before, but touching him sends it skittering erratically. Uncertainty radiates from every pore and echoes in my blood.

"I can't shake this feeling," he confesses.

I feel it too. Death's silhouette lurks in wisps of shadows that hug the frames of my vision. The Dark God stands at the ready to claim my soul with the rising sun, but he will not take me without a fight. I need Cal at his best if we're going to have a shot at taking Marks out before Death collects his fated prize.

"You're the best military strategist in our nation and you said yourself that I'm powerful. Marks doesn't stand a chance." It's a pretty lie that tastes bitter on my tongue.

We lay there in silence, both simmering in the shared feeling.

Everything about tomorrow is wrong. Maybe that's how everyone feels in the hours approaching their destiny. Maybe fate is supposed to feel wrong just before it feels right.

"I know what you're doing, Ivy," Cal says with a bite that sends my stomach plummeting. "You might have everyone else fooled, but I see you. There is nothing you won't do to stop Marks, and as fucking admirable as it is, you're doing it for the wrong reason. Your people need you alive. *I* need you alive."

"Cal," I start but he doesn't let me finish.

"I'm not stopping you. Gods know that's a fool's errand. But I need you to know that I meant every word. You aren't alone. I know you don't want to hear this—"

"Then don't say it," I interrupt.

I know the words that hover on the edge of his tongue, but I can't bear to hear them. I've already allowed Cal to become too close. I can't change how he feels about me, but maybe if I can stop him from saying it out loud I can spare him from a fraction of the heartbreak that's in store for him.

We lay in silence listening to the chirping of the crickets outside the cracked window. The rhythmic sounds of his beating heart and steady breathing tug me closer to the sleep that has evaded me.

I'm just on the edge of unconsciousness, tipping head first into the abyss of oblivion when the words of his barely audible confession fill my head.

"I love you."

CHAPTER 35

Disembodied voices echo across the alabaster hallway as they call to me. Dark whispers propel me forward. I walk, slow and steady, towards the black mass that awaits at the end. Metal chains scrape against the cold stone with each step of my feet.

The voices pull me closer and closer to the golden door, shadows swirling from its hinges and pooling under the frame. Rather than a key, this door demands blood.

Powerful blood.

I raise Arcasia's dagger, slashing a diagonal cut across my palm. Crimson coats my hand. I turn it, inspecting the rivulet that decorates the white stone as it drops from my finger. A trail of scarlet trickles across the runes etched into the dagger's blade, each glowing a brilliant shade of blue as it comes to life.

Heat scalds my back, the sudden influx of pain causing me to spin to see its source. A blazing streak of fire races across the throne room floor, flames encircling the unoccupied Amethyst Throne. On its cushion sits a golden crown adorned with six sparkling jewels—a single stone each representing a precious region: Emerald, Ruby, Sapphire, Topaz, Diamond, and, in the center, Amethyst. It calls to me, singing in a language I can't speak, demanding I place the golden diadem on my head.

The fork in my journey is clear: use my blood to open the door to the god realm or stay and save my home.

The sea beast inked on my skin thrashes wildly, her desired choice evident in her desperate plea. The flames rise higher, the voices beyond the door screaming in an ear-splitting crescendo.

The time to make my decision rapidly diminishes; only mere seconds remain. A primal scream breaks through my lips, but it's not for me.

Something in the core of my being rips. My very soul splinters into two. One name forces its way into my head, my heart, and my throat: *Cal.*

CHAPTER 36

I t's a strange feeling to walk towards your death. The hangman's invisible noose tightens around my neck with every step towards the palace. My remaining words are limited, so I use them sparingly as we walk.

Cal blends seamlessly into the fading shadows. He's a fearsome sight. Dressed head to toe in black, from his cloak to his leather armor. The same armor he wore to my birthday dinner. He slips effortlessly into his role as both strategist and commander. No one, save me and his brothers, would believe this isn't his true nature.

Rather than our regional colors, we've all chosen to wear black today. Each of us secretly hoping that a fraction of the Captain of Corinth's infamous ruthlessness will rub off when we don his color. I've worn every shade of green, braved the ire of men while draped in amethyst, and disguised myself in the drab browns of the common folk, but I've never worn black before. Not until today.

Our ragtag army is divided into four groups in order to infiltrate each gate at the same time. Our plan is simple: push from all sides until Marks and his loyal men are forced into the throne room. Each group is led by an *aevus*, our power serving as a force multiplier against Marks' human soldiers.

Silas, along with his fire magic, is stationed with Theo and Quinn at the south gate. I begged her not to fight today, but my headstrong best friend wouldn't hear of it. We all agreed she was a liability to my focus if we were paired together. Theo, eager to join her, claimed he had sworn an oath that required him to go where she went.

With water magic at his call, Micah is stationed with Henry and Marianne at the east gate. No one was separating the twins, and only a fool would have tried to come between the lieutenant and his lover. With the addition of Marianne's air on their side, this group was chosen to infiltrate nearest the sea, the second most utilized entrance.

Elias Klein, the would-be traitor, surprised us all when he knocked on the safe house door moments before we departed. Miles volunteered to keep an eye on him and the air-wielding Ruby governor, and the others happily obliged him, no one else wanting the job. They're purposefully stationed at the least used gate to the west.

Cal and I comprise the remaining group at the main palace gate. Henry lobbied hard for us to be divided amongst the groups, and from a strategic standpoint, it makes sense. I am a liability for Cal and everyone can see it. He made it clear last night that he won't choose his own life if it comes to that—*when* it comes to that.

I made the executive decision to give the group the only evidence that would silence them. My ability to wield threads of Cal's power was met with gasps, but it was utter perplexity when I confessed how I can pour my magic into him. After that, no one could deny that we must remain together in order to launch a multi-elemental attack while we wait for the others to reach us.

I can grow flowers and shake the earth, but Cal possesses more power than all of us combined. I've seen the ebony core of it. I've felt its pull and touched its limitlessness. If he could access it, he could topple worlds. And that's exactly what we need him to do.

The first light of day dances across the horizon. The guard will be changing any minute. If everything goes as planned, Cal's men will be taking the place of Marks' soldiers and all four entrances to the palace will be guarded by men who will let us pass without question.

When the last body is carted away and the blood is mopped from the palace floors, the story of what happened here will spread. And whoever's atop the Amethyst Throne will be the author. They alone will have the power to craft the narrative. A generation of tall tales about victors and villains will be born today.

Dread settles deeper into my bones the longer we hide amongst the empty shipping crates that line the outside walls of the north gate. I scan the faces of every soldier who passes, attempting to discern friend from foe. There is no visual indication of their loyalty, so I wait impatiently for Cal to confirm their allegiance.

The clock tower chimes, signaling the end of watch for the night men. The beast inked on my skin swishes her tail.

One.

Two.

Two soldiers dressed in Corinthian gray and gold uniforms approach the guards. They exchange words, a post-duty debrief, a joke about the tall one's wife, and a card game challenge two nights from now in their favorite tavern. Their ease and casualness in the face of the chiming clock stand in stark contrast to the turmoil within me. It's a normal day in the lives of these men—and the very last day in mine.

Five.

The night guards finally depart, setting out for beds or women or ale. It matters not where they go, only that they do. The new guards look in our direction and panic grips me. We'll either be discovered and captured or we'll be granted entry. There's no going back now.

Six.

As the clock strikes the sixth hour, the soldiers turn their backs to the city in unison.

"It's time," Cal breathes. He's through the gate in ten long strides. My steps double trying to keep up with his pace as his hold on my hand tightens. My magic flips and frets in erratic spurts before it flares in alarm.

Something isn't right.

"Gods have mercy on our souls," one guard whispers just before a battle cry echoes off the stone walls. Squadrons of soldiers spring up from the hedges that line the interior and rush us at once.

Cal's power ripples through the courtyard in an icy wind. Soldiers drop to the ground, clawing at their throats for breath. My body barely recognizes what's happening before cold steel bites into my neck. Rough hands rip me from Cal's grasp, my back pressing against a broad chest. The gray and gold sleeve of my captor's arm is all I can see from my peripheral before he falls away convulsing, blood pouring from his nose and mouth.

My power strikes out, thick vines sprouting from the ground to wrap around our attackers. Inky shadows spread across the courtyard and pour into their open throats until they choke. Only dead bodies litter the grass for now, but more soldiers will be coming.

"Quickly," Cal commands, sprinting for cover.

I follow on his heels, drawing back the dark magic so I don't burn out too quickly. We skid to a stop at the edge of the palace wall, each hiding behind an ornate statue flanking the entryway. I can't see the face of the stone god concealing me, but I can clearly see its counterpart on the other side.

The stone effigy of the God King Nobus stoically guards Cal, a sight that nearly stops my heart's beating.

"Fucking bastards sold us out to Marks," Cal curses. "So much for loyalty."

Another wave of Corinthian soldiers sprints into the courtyard and halts at the sight of their dead comrades before them. At least two squads lay lifeless, easily eliminated with our combined magic.

But if squads were stationed at all entrances ... I shudder at the thought of how the rest of our resistance is faring. It's a risk they all willingly took on, but one I wish they were better equipped to handle.

Thunder booms overhead, drawing the soldiers' confused eyes to the clear sky above and providing the perfect distraction for us to slip into the palace unnoticed.

The interior is bustling with activity. Servants carrying pokers, tongs, and hand brooms rush by to light the morning fires. Maids scurry past with armloads of folded purple linens. Bedsheets, towels, tablecloths—every thread of fabric the color of royalty.

If they notice us, they pay us no mind. They're barely paid enough to live and not nearly enough to care if the duo standing in their midst is authorized to do so.

We walk, quickly and purposefully, through the open foyer and past the grand staircase. A booming voice echoes throughout the room, the alabaster walls and floors doing little to muffle the shouted command.

"Find them!"

Cal and I exchange a worried glance as we begin to sprint through the grand entrance hall. Unease radiates from him, but his composure never slips. Wordlessly, I follow his direction. Despite being discovered, despite knowing that the others in our crew are under attack, we stick to the plan.

The decorative suits of armor that line the long hallway provide cover for us several times as we stealthily make our way toward the throne room. Based on the commands and pounding of footsteps on the stone floors that cover the palace, there's at least six squads of soldiers hunting us now. A religious person would thank the gods, but I know what remains of Cal's embedded loyalists within their ranks are the only reason we haven't been found yet. They're leading their men on a wild goose chase, searching every corridor and hallway that doesn't lead to us.

Forty yards separate us from the throne room. Less than ten seconds stand between me and the culmination of eighteen years of nightmares. Barely more than a breath away from destiny.

I take a deep inhale to steady myself and prepare to run. It's now or never. Without sparing a look toward Cal, I dart out from behind the metal soldier. Black boots pound against the purple carpet runner, each footfall more sluggish than the last as time slows to a crawl. I don't stop to look down at them, don't bother to look towards the shouting coming from behind me. My gaze is locked solely on the intricately carved golden door in front of me.

A wave of magic washes over me, the world tipping as my feet no longer respond to my brain's command to move. I fall forward, unable to counter the momentum from my abrupt stop. The floor rises up to meet me in a white blur before black overtakes my vision and the palace fades away.

CHAPTER 37

I t takes a moment for my eyes to adjust to the morning light streaming in from the floor-to-ceiling windows that line both the eastern and western sides of the throne room.

No matter the time of day, the sun always shines on the King of Corinth.

A bullshit line fed to us in school by priests. Propaganda at its finest. The sun's only purpose in this room is to illuminate the throne, painting the monarch to mimic the glowing appearance of a god.

My chained hands slip in blood as I try to press up. My head is heavy and clouded. All I want to do is lay back down and sleep. The throbbing in my head is so loud it almost sounds like my name.

Ivy, Ivy, Ivy.

"For fuck's sake. IVY!"

The voice snaps me into consciousness and I force myself to turn toward it. Hair is matted over one of my eyes, and when I lift my hand to unstick it, I find a large gash at my hairline. A rivulet of scarlet decorates the white stone floor as it drips from my fingers.

"IVY!"

The voice draws my attention to a golden cage secured to the floor. Three bodies lay motionless in the square prison. Only their backs face me, each wearing black, rather than any color that could signify their identity.

"Ivy! Thank the gods! I thought you were dead." The governor of Topaz stands at the edge of the cell grasping the bars in his hands. Silas' blonde beard is stained red from the blood that streams from the wide cut that spans the length of his cheekbone.

"Wh...what...happened?" Words stick like honey in my mouth as I try to force them out.

"We were ambushed. They knew we were coming." Silas waits for me to continue with my questioning but I can't. My brain is foggy, barely able to form coherent thoughts. One name cuts through the haze, bouncing off the bony edges of my skull: *Cal*.

"Where?" I ask, the rest of the question not needing to be said aloud.

"They took the non-wielders to the dungeons and forced the rest of the *aevus* in here."

Mustering all the strength left in my mind and body, I force myself to my feet and lunge towards the cell. The heavy metal chain pulls taut in a dull snap, sending me tumbling back to the ground. I follow the links with my eyes, from the iron manacles around my wrists to the large bolt that secures it to the stone floor.

I reach out for my magic, desperately calling for vines to snap the chain or shadowy decay to eat away at the metal, but nothing answers. Power hovers in my peripheral, visible but just out of reach. It dances around the corners of my vision but never comes close enough for me to grasp it.

"Marks personally took Murphy."

Silas' words only increase the urgency at which I call for my power. Over and over I silently scream for it, begging any god who will listen to grant me access. Physically, I am no match for Marks or the army of soldiers on his side. My only hope is my magic.

Without it, I am nothing. Without it, Death will take me slowly and painfully. Without it, Death will take Cal too.

"Our magic is gone, Ivy." I snap my focus to the governor again as tears fill my eyes. "They forced a tonic down our throats."

"No. No! *NO!*"

My voice echoes through the room as I scream, each word more forceful than the last, as if my defiance alone could wake me from this nightmare. I yank at the chain and claw at the iron cuffs on my wrists, desperate to free myself. I look inward, hopelessly searching for the slightest sign of my power.

"It didn't have to be like this, Ivy."

My barely contained panic increases at the sound of his voice. The cold, icy voice that belongs to none other than Lord General Marks. Time stills again, stretching thin as soulless gold eyes lock onto mine.

"If only you'd stayed in Emerald like a good little girl. But don't worry, I will send your body back to your home … or what's left of it, at least."

"My home or my body?" I ask.

"Both."

Marks tosses two ivory-handled blades across the throne room, the rune-carved alloy clanking against the stone floor as they bounce beyond reach. The air between us grows thick and cold as he laughs, causing my lungs to contract at the loss of oxygen.

Anger courses through me at his patronizing tone. He couldn't stop at villainizing me; no, he had to ransack my region, destroy my home, and kill my people. All as revenge for my mother's deal with Nobus. With death a certainty, he thinks I will lay down and go quietly. He thinks I will submit, but he's underestimated me for the last time.

I try once more to call to my magic, squeezing my fists and eyes over and over to no avail.

"You have no power. I made sure of that. Not today, and not any day in your miserable life."

Marks flexes his magic again, forcing me to my knees as I claw at my throat for air. He kneels in front me, grabbing my chin to force my eyes to his.

"I thought turning your people against you would be the hard part, but you did that on your own. All I had to do was plant the seed and Poison Ivy grew herself. It was so easy to make you their villain and ensure you stayed powerless."

The golden doors of the throne room burst open, but Marks pays the intrusion no heed. He leans closer, his breath hot on my ear as I try to pull away from him.

"Your mother took me for a fool. She thought I wouldn't piece her little bargains together, that I wouldn't know you weren't half-human. She thought I'd hurt you, but I'm not the one who came here with the intent to murder, am I? I know who you really are, Ivy Fellows, but do you know who I am?"

Iron clanks behind him, the gray form of soldiers visible just over his shoulders.

"That will be all," Marks commands before releasing me and rising. He takes a single, deliberate step out of my line of sight, never taking his predatory eyes off of me.

A bloodied, beaten body lies chained to the floor across from me. A crimson trail paints the alabaster floor from the doors to his unconscious form. Something inside of me snaps, cracks in half at the sight of Cal.

I stand and lunge again, not learning my lesson from the first time. As the chain snaps taut and my knees slam into the stone floor, a deep and guttural scream breaks free from my throat.

"I've tried for years to get him to wield his full potential, you know. I've tortured him again and again, but no amount of pain could force it to the surface. So imagine my delight when I received word from Lieutenant Williams that the captain here had blackmailed him into being your little bodyguard. I had high hopes that proximity to you would naturally grant him access to the true depths of his powers, but," Marks clicks his tongue irreverently, "I guess I'll just have to force it out of him some other way."

Cal stirs slightly, his body twitching in the still expanding red pool. There's so much blood, more blood than should be possible for him to still be alive. I attempt to locate my magic again, searching for even a sliver of my power. But it's as if I'm digging in the sand with no end in sight.

I call and call, but nothing answers.

"Oh good, you're awake." Marks taunts.

Planting his foot on Cal's shoulder, he pushes down, causing the captain's back to hit the floor in a wet thud. Blood splashes up around him as his head smacks the stone. Deep gashes cut into his tanned chest, only tatters remaining of his black shirt.

The iron manacles cut into my flesh as I try and fail to slip my wrists from their hold.

Please, please, I beg to any god who will listen. *Give me my magic back.*

The gods don't answer.

Marks finds his favorite element first, constricting the air in the throne room until everyone but him is gasping for oxygen again. I crawl my way across the floor, inching as far as the chain will stretch before I collapse.

"Ivy." Cal's voice is strained, the single word excruciating.

Marks tightens his hold on the captain's air, his body twitching again as he struggles to breathe. The predator squats before his prey, forcing Cal's eyes away from me. A low, menacing growl rumbles through the chamber, an animalistic sound coming forth from the depths of Cal's broken body.

"Show me your true power and this will all be over, nephew."

Time slows again at the familial title that falls from the Lord General's lips. A single drop of blood leaks from the mouth of the sea beast tattoo, hovering just above the floor as it slides off Cal's chest.

Arcasia! I call out to the goddess, begging the one who sacrificed everything for him to help me save him now. *Help me save him, Goddess of Protection. Help me save your son.*

A single spark of magic flickers somewhere deep within me, illuminating the compound that makes up the plant-based poison in my system. The seed of power buries itself in the bonds and starts to leisurely unravel the tonic.

It works slowly—too fucking slowly. I need more time. I need to give it the life only my element is capable of—and I pray I won't be too late.

Focus on life.

In a heady rush, time returns to its normal speed. Flames burst forth in a circle around the base of the Amethyst Throne. The crown sits on the plush purple seat, each of its six jewels sparkling in the firelight. With a flick of Marks' eyes, the flames begin marching in a line across the stone floor from the throne to the bolt securing my chains in place.

I tunnel down, but the ember of power inside me is still too small to answer my call. Scurrying backwards, I pull the chain as far away from the bolt as possible. Once the flames reach the iron, I will have only minutes before the heat travels up the links to the cuffs around my wrists.

The sea beast on my skin twists in a slow, sluggish move. The beginning of the end.

"Your little ivy tattoo was quite the clue to the depths of Selene's treachery. But I'll let you in on a little secret—she wouldn't have needed to make a deal with Nobus if she hadn't helped your mother kidnap you in the first place. The portal was her attempt to get back in my brother's good graces. Dangling the carrot of his stolen son returning home one day. But I'm giving him something even better—an entire realm of devoted worshippers. And you two will be my greatest offering yet. The Wolf God will run free in the Great Wildes once again."

The traitorous brother of the God King pulls a golden dagger from the sheath at his side and slices through Cal's leather pants leg in a single swipe. Crimson spreads across the tattooed ivy leaves as the captain bites down a scream.

"Are you watching, Ivy?" Marks casts a look over his shoulder, menace shining in his golden eyes as he increases the speed of the flames moving across the floor. "Whatever pathetic emotion you think you feel for my nephew isn't real. Gods don't care about something as trivial as feelings."

Fire engulfs the bolt as I yank fruitlessly on the unyielding chain. I reach inward for my power to find the seedling of magic slowly spreading. It's still not enough to wield. I need more time.

Mark's maniacal laugh resounds through the throne room as I writhe on the ground to escape the encroaching flames. His eyes sparkle as his words hit, words that don't have their intended sting.

I may never have had a say in my fate's connection to Cal's, but I know, without a shadow of a doubt, that what I feel for him is real. And I'm ready to make my choice.

"Wield it!" he screams at Cal, kicking him again and again as the captain's body curls inward.

Circling him, Marks flexes his power, sucking the air from the room once more. He's so consumed with inflicting pain on Cal that he doesn't realize the fire banks at the loss of oxygen, buying me precious seconds to grow my seedling of magic.

The Wolf God runs the blade's edge up the backs of Cal's legs, blood pouring onto the white stone floors. I expect to hear Cal's hoarse scream, but it doesn't come. I see every ounce of the pain etched into his gray eyes, but his face remains stoic.

My heart cracks at the sight of him: a man who is no stranger to being on the receiving end of this kind of torture.

"Such a shame. Something as meaningless as the mortal realm shouldn't stifle the infinite power of the Prince of the Gods. You're weak, just like your father."

The storm cloud eyes of the Prince of the Gods search mine from across the floor. But they don't find shock or hurt or anger looking back at them in light of this revelation. My mother gave me his true identity days ago.

"Nobus thought sending me here would weaken me, but the only weakness here is you." I watch helplessly as Marks continues kicking, his boot now coated in his nephew's blood.

Cal's pain radiates throughout the throne room, ricocheting off the walls and piercing my dying soul. Pain that began twenty-six years ago when my mother helped kidnap him, when he was stolen in the night and taken to the human realm to live out his days, never to see his parents again.

The Prince of the Gods, fate-bound to me. A god who could have chosen to hate me for what my mother helped his family do but instead chose to love me. Not for what my magic could do, but for who I am in spite of myself.

The seedling of power within me spreads.

Marks loosens his grip on his magic and Cal flails at the sudden influx of oxygen, his whole body moving in great gasps. Fire resumes its ascent up the iron chain links as the Wolf God turns his attention towards me.

"It's me you want. I'm the one who can open the portal." I rise to my knees on the floor, willing my face not to show the panic coursing through my body.

"You?" Marks laughs again, moving across the room to stand over me. "You think you have the power to unite the gods? Oh, this is too good."

His heavy-booted foot meets my chest in a swift kick, knocking me backwards onto the ground.

"You wield a single element and some fancy shadows thanks to your father. That is not power, you fool. Callan here has power. The raw power of a king runs through his veins, and as soon as my nephew unleashes the magic that I know he's capable of, he will open the portal so I can return home and show Nobus what it looks like to truly rule a realm."

Cal's magic tingles in the air, weak and barely recognizable from the unimaginable horrors that have been forced upon him, but it's there. The Wolf God's chest constricts slightly as if something, or someone, is squeezing the blood pumping through his heart.

"Your magic cannot overtake me, boy," he bellows. "You have always been destined to die in this realm, one way or another. Do not waste your last moments fighting for *her*."

Marks grabs a fistful of my hair, hauling me to a seated position as the flames crest the final link of my chain. The cold steel of his blade bites my neck, warm rivulets of blood trickling down the column of my throat as my eyes meet Cal's across the room—despairing eyes pleading with me for forgiveness.

He can't save me and he knows it.

"What will it be, Prince? Will you wield your full power before or after I slit her throat?"

Fire engulfs the iron around my wrists, but I do not feel its heat. Not as my magic flares back to life within my veins, the full force of it overtaking me as I will it to calm.

Using the only element that Marks knows me to wield, I command the earth to tremble beneath our feet. Cracks spider web across the great windows as the walls of the palace shake under my command.

"That's it, boy. More!" he yells, pressing the blade deeper into my skin.

Even now, faced head on with magic that is undoubtedly mine, Marks denies the magnitude of my power, once again unable to fathom the endless depths of a woman. Layers of rage and love stitched together generation after generation to create seamless, exquisite beings.

The marble columns holding up the vaulted ceiling crack, chunks crashing to the floor as the brave soldiers of Corinth scream and run towards the exit. The smell of my burning flesh fills my nostrils as I dig deeper into my power. Death has come for me at last and I am ready for it.

"Cal," I call out on a shaky breath preparing myself to make one final choice.

When I am gone, there can be no doubt that this was for him. For the love that I denied because I believed myself unworthy, but the love I deserved all along. For the promise of what he will do for this world in my memory.

Death chose me, but I choose Cal.

I do not know what my first words were, but I know what my last words will be. "I love you."

With a final exhale, I open the floodgates within me to release every ounce of the magic that I have kept locked away for eighteen years. I rip open every wound, every scar to find any pocket of pain, hatred, or terror still hiding in my bones. Deeper and deeper I go, unburying graves and skeletons that I forced from my mind years ago. My body vibrates with power and I know I am primed to explode.

The outer walls of the throne room crumble as Cal calls out for me to stop. The Wolf God drops his knife and staggers back in shock as he recognizes for the first time what I am truly capable of. The woman he always underestimated will kill him even if it kills her too.

"You," he gasps, black pupils overtaking his golden eyes, a sign of his magic rising within him.

With that, Marks sheds his mortal persona, fully becoming Mikais, the heretical god he's hidden behind a human facade for so many years.

He doesn't have time to form another word before the column of my sparkling magic barrels into his chest. A scream rips from my throat as I push more and more power out of my body and into his. I call forth the fire in his veins first. Mikais falls to his knees, the smell of his burnt flesh mixing with mine as I roast him from the inside out.

But it isn't enough to kill a god.

I dig deeper, looking for any emotion that I can draw upon. I think of the man who raised me, the man I called a father, now rotting in a grave desecrated by the Lord General's soldiers. I think of my mother, a goddess who followed a misguided leader but still loved her people enough to buy them a way home. I think of Cal's mother, of the Goddess of Protection so afraid of Nobus' influence that she hatched a plan to have her son smuggled away.

I curl my fists into tight balls, finally allowing tears to fall. Blood pours from Mikais' eyes, nose, and mouth mirroring the salty liquid streaming down my face as I command the water in his veins.

Thick vines crawl their way upward, twisting around the god's body. Tighter and tighter they constrict, like a snake immobilizing its prey as it slowly suffocates to death. I force it taut, the magical vines remaining unburnt as Mikais fights for air. Shadows converge on his body, puncturing his skin with their pointed spikes and rotting the flesh from his bones.

But still he fights back. The living core of raw power inside of him still pulses.

I have to access it, have to force it to submit to me. That much power requires me to unlock the iron-clad door within my heart that I have been avoiding. The one that holds every ounce of self-loathing and unworthiness. The repressed emotions flood out of me, mixing with the most powerful feeling of all—regret.

Regret for how I treated Cal.

Regret for how I fought Cal.

Regret for how I denied Cal.

Regret for the time I didn't allow us to have.

The moment I first laid eyes on him, my soul recognized its counterpart. My magic practically screamed it at me every day since then, but still I fought it. I chose him for a night and felt whole for the first time in my life, but still I denied myself. Cal wanted to turn back but I rejected him, and now his life hangs in the balance because of my stubbornness, my unwillingness to walk away from revenge and my destiny to die here.

I take one last look into the depthless seas of his gray eyes.

Home. That's what we could have had together.

With my last moments, I will deny it no longer. He is the true owner of my broken, shattered heart. Cal is my home and I will choose him with my dying breath. There is not a path he could take that I would not follow, in this life or any other.

I push every last ounce of power coursing through my body into Mikais at lightning speed. The sea beast on my skin thrashes wildly, the last shred of her magical protection disappearing as the connection between us shatters. My body convulses, black spots creeping into my vision as my beating heart slows.

I have nothing left, no morsel or crumb of magic that I didn't give for him. I pray that it was enough to kill one god and spare another.

The sun disappears from the noonday sky, casting the throne room in total darkness as I take my final breath.

CHAPTER 38

CAL

An earth-shattering scream pierces the veil between worlds. It echoes throughout Corinth, Synal, and the island nations. It reverberates through the immortal lands of the god realm and ricochets between the dead and the living before settling into the crumbling walls of the Amethyst Palace.

A scream of agony unlike any ever heard by mortal ears. A scream formed in the depths of my soul, ripped from my raw and raspy throat.

I love you. The last words she spoke before sacrificing herself to save us all. To save me.

As quickly as it disappeared, the midday sun rises again, washing the throne room in daylight.

It's eerily still now. The earth has stopped its shaking, the walls have ceased their crumbling. The fire that engulfed the throne is now reduced to piles of ash. The once pristine alabaster floors are scorched with veins of godfire and stained red with blood.

There's so much fucking blood.

I can't see her over the mounds of my uncle's smouldering, rotting flesh that litter the ground between us. I try to stand but my broken, shattered body can barely move. She was chained to the floor and still she tried to get to me. Shredded muscles and gaping wounds won't stop me from getting to her. Death himself couldn't stop me from getting to her.

Using the sheer force of my will, I drag my mangled body toward her. Through the charred hunks of whatever remains of the god Mikais, over the unburnt vines that still bind what remains of his body, past the splintered gold bars of the broken cage where the four *aevus* stir.

Ivy's maimed body lies lifeless on the stone floor, the blood forming a halo around her brown hair.

"No. No. NO!" Each word is more desperate than the last. "Wake up, princess. Wake up!"

I feel their watching eyes on my back as they close in to survey the scene. I hear their silent exchange, their misplaced pity for the man who can't face what they believe to be certain truth—Ivy is dead.

But I can feel her magic inside of her, singing in a language only I understand. It's a song more beautiful than any ever composed for even the highest of gods. A song written for and heard only by my ears.

Ivy is alive. Barely clinging to life, but alive all the same. My stubborn, relentless goddess still fights. She is with Death now, but he won't keep her.

"Help her," I plead, but the gods do not answer, and neither do the *aevus*.

"HELP HER!" I demand louder, but still they do nothing. "Godsdamnit. She's alive, you idiots! She saved you all! Now use your fucking magic and bring her back!"

Kieran moves first, dropping to his knees in the coagulating blood.

"Murphy, look at me."

"No. Don't you fucking *dare* say it, Rollins. I am not giving up on her."

"Marks gave us all the same tonic, Murphy. We can't access our magic."

"She did!" I scream at him. Lies, pathetic excuses for denying their aid.

"Wilson, Porter. Release the others from the dungeons and fetch a physician." Kieran emotionlessly commands the other governors to do his bidding. Their footsteps on the stone floor indicate their obedience.

The adrenaline that pushed me across the floor fades as quickly as it appeared. Collapsing across Ivy's body, I pull her tight against my chest as if I can absorb her back into my heart where she belongs. Tears well in my eyes before spilling over my lids, the salty liquid mixing with the crusted blood smeared across her face before pooling into the open wound in her hair line.

If I could bring Marks back, I would, so that I could kill him myself. Not for what he did to me, but for what he did to her. I would choose another lifetime of torture and manipulation at his hand for five more minutes with her.

The large doors swing open. Heavy-footed marching indicates the arrival of the Corinthian soldiers now flanking the throne room awaiting orders. Twenty pairs of boots if my count is correct. I don't lift my head to confirm.

"Captain," Kieran says slowly. "What do you want them to do?"

The soldiers. With the Lord General dead, the responsibility to lead them now belongs to me. I am the heir apparent to the militant tyrant, the next in line to take up the mantle of my abuser and Ivy's tormentor.

I don't want to be the Lord General of Corinth.

I don't want to be the Prince of the Gods.

I don't want to be the son of Nobus.

I only want to be hers.

"Hen-ry." My brother's name is broken in half by the sobs that wrack my feeble body without shame.

Henry will lead them. Henry will know what to do.

The military was always a means of survival for me, a surefire way to stay out of the dungeons and put food on the table for my mortal mother and brothers. I never meant for Mikais to know my name, let alone know who I really am. For years I have wished that I could go back to that fateful day on the battlefield, wished there had been any way to save Theo other than putting my secret on full display. My uncle knew who I was after that, and he made sure the tales of my viciousness spread across Corinth.

If I had been able to tap into the core of my power, none of this would have happened. Emerald would still be whole. I would be alone, but Ivy would be alive. I would trade all of it, every second that I have spent with her, if only it would bring her back. I would damn the whole realm to the gods' wrath if it meant sparing her.

Time passes in a blur—seconds, minutes, or hours, I can't tell the difference anymore. Nothing matters without her here.

I love you.

The very words she refused to let me say are the last she spoke. Her final breath was meant for me. She fought us from the beginning because she thought she had to do this alone. And for some gods-unknown reason, she thought she wasn't capable of giving me what I wanted.

But all I ever wanted was her. Whatever fractions or bits she deemed me worthy of, I took them greedily. I was always left hungry, always wanting more of her. I could spend every year of eternity with her and it still wouldn't be enough.

The closer we got to the end, the more she withdrew into herself, the more I could feel that she wanted this, that she wanted me. When it came down to it, she gave me the one gift that meant the most to her. She chose me.

And I will spend every second of my immortal existence proving that she didn't make a mistake. That *I'm* not a mistake.

I don't need a throne or worshippers or even a god-family. She is all that I need. Everything that my soul aches for. She is everything to me. She is *home.*

"It's time to go now, brother." I turn my head to find Henry squatting beside me in the pool of our blood. "Let me help you."

He doesn't wait for me to reply before he wraps his arms around my middle and pulls me off of her. My entire body cries out in agony at both the loss of her touch and the pulling strain on my shredded skin. I can't leave her.

"Ivy!" I call out for her as Henry wraps my arm over his neck to support my weight.

"We've got her. We won't let anything happen to her, okay?"

His face is stoic, but his eyes give him away; they always have. Sorrow wells in them as he blinks away the tear that he would deny forms in its corner.

"This way!" another familiar voice commands.

Theo bursts through the throne room doors, two physicians following on his heels. The robed men stop and share a concerned look at the sight of my mutilated body, but their attention is misplaced.

"She's alive. Help her," I plead.

"But Captain, you need care," one protests.

"Help Governor Fellows first. That's an order," Henry bellows. His voice cuts through the commotion, causing every soldier in the room to snap to attention.

My eldest brother is a natural born leader. His skills on and off the battlefield should have been rewarded with the title of captain. And if the Lord General hadn't been a god with a vendetta, they would have been. I never wanted it. I only ever wanted her.

The room is a blur of motion as every available hand rushes to

Ivy's side. Black spots form at the edge of my vision. I don't have long.

"Take me to my mother's altar."

There's a temple just off the gardens in the Western Courtyard with a marble statue of Arcasia. It's one of the few in Corinth. Every time Marks summoned me to the palace before a mission, I left something for her in exchange for her gift of protection. And I have one final ask of her before I leave this world.

"You will see a healer first." I lift my head from Henry's shoulder to argue with him, but it's futile. "That's an order, Captain."

"I have nothing left to give but my life. Let me barter it for hers."

Henry kicks open a wooden door to a bedchamber where two robed physicians wait.

"No one dies today. Do you hear me, Callan?" The tear he tried so hard to hold in slips between his lashes and trails down his dirty cheek, desperation etched into his brown eyes. "No one."

The physicians herd us toward the bed, their assistants running to gather hot water, bandages, and needles. They survey me from head to toe, cataloging every cut. They clean the wounds excruciatingly slowly. Too fucking slowly.

I have to get back to her.

Impatiently, I rip the cloth from the assistant's trembling hold. Before I can attempt to stand, a large hand forces me to lay back on the bed.

"Prepare a calming tonic for him," Henry orders.

"Power is going to your head already, Lord General," I bite out with an exasperated huff.

"As soon as you're healed, I'm going to whoop your ass for putting that job on me."

"I'm counting on it."

The physician holds out a vial of green liquid, presenting it to Henry for approval before removing the stopper.

"Just something for the nerves, Captain," the weaselly man says as he grips my chin and forces the bottle between my busted lips.

The bitter liquid burns as it slides down my raw throat. An invisible heaviness weighs my body down as visions of Ivy dance in my head. A smile that outshines the sun, eyes that sparkle like the finest emerald, a ferocity that burns like a fire.

One thought fills my mind as my eyelids slip closed. One thought that will haunt me until I can say it to her face: *I love you; I'm sorry.*

CHAPTER 39

IVY

Death is an endless chasm of black.

I am another lost soul tumbling head-over-feet through an infinite void of darkness. The inky abyss is nothing and everything at the same time. I am weightless and heavy. Cold and warm. Alive and dead.

My magic is dormant, completely spent. Only a spark hides somewhere deep within me, a trivial flicker where a great fire once burned.

Not enough to take me back home.

Not enough to take me back to him.

Spots of light appear, tiny sparkling punctures in the obsidian fabric of space and time. The stars grow brighter, morphing into clustered constellations. They're gorgeous. My hand shoots out in a futile attempt to catch one of the passing orbs before sharp, sudden pain radiates from my right side.

My falling stops as I crash against the cold, polished stone floor. The darkness feels different here. Lighter, thinner, as if there's only a veil covering my face and if I remove it, I can see again. My eyes adjust, slowly taking in my surroundings.

The room emanates coldness despite its luxurious contents. Oil paintings and woven tapestries cover most of the walls, depicting headless men, faceless beasts, and women with blood trailing across their bare breasts. It's hard to tell if they're locked in battle or in the throes of carnal pleasure. Great streaks of white cover the spaces between. Walls made entirely of bone.

I suppress the shiver that tries to run down my spine at the realization, forcing my eyes to the large mahogany desk that sits in the center of the room. Used parchments, forgotten mugs, and a vase filled with wilted godsbane blooms litter the top, accompanying the black leather chair askew behind—all indicating the occupant's quick departure.

A massive fireplace crafted of exquisite black marble takes up the long wall behind it. Great onyx serpents with gleaming emerald eyes snake across the golden grate keeping the sweltering fire within. The crackling and popping of flames is the only sound throughout the cavernous space.

The ceiling overhead is made entirely of glass, the sparkling stars of night visibly dancing across the obsidian sky. But those aren't stars, not really. The last glimmers of desperate, seeking souls illuminate the room that I now stand in, and I feel their hopelessness in the pit of my stomach calling out for help. They want to be led and they seek me as their shepherd.

"What are you doing in here?" The voice is pure ice, stinging my ears and freezing the marrow in my bones. The hulking mass of a man steps forward, shadows covering his face. Glowing eyes in a haunting shade of green cut through the darkness, examining me from head to toe.

I am exposed, stripped bare before him as if he can see beyond my skin and is scrutinizing the fabric of my soul.

"Why are you here?"

My tongue feels heavy in my mouth as I try and fail to form words in his language—a language I have only heard spoken once before, yet I somehow understand every word. Ancient syllables and sounds that haven't been spoken to mortals in a millennia make perfect sense to me.

He moves towards me, stepping into the firelight to reveal a chiseled jaw more appropriate for a statue than a man. Stark white hair, a perfect match for the bleached bone walls, falls in effortless waves to his shoulders. He is devastatingly beautiful, so beautiful that a mere mortal might freely give over their life for a chance to look upon him forever. But it's his familiar eyes that hold my attention.

"Do you know where you are, girl?" He says it so casually, so lackadaisically. As if I could stand in the presence of my perpetual stalker and not recognize him. He is the source of the call that has beckoned me my entire life. Him I know—but how I ended up in Death's study is a mystery.

Unlike other souls, I guess I will not be ferried across the blood rivers to the Eternal Meadows after all. I killed a god, and the punishment for such an act is to face the Dark God himself.

The tiny spark of the destructive magic within me awakens in his presence, a single ember of power flickering to life. A shadow of my full power and not nearly enough to kill another god.

I don't mean for the huff of breath to escape my lips. The scoff was meant for me—for the absurd thought that I could kill the unkillable. Death's nostrils flare as he takes another step, scenting the blood that still coats my face.

"You smell like her." His voice is a growl now, his eyes narrowing to snake-like slits. He's more animal than man. An ethereal sheen coats his perfect porcelain skin.

Another step closer and my eyes catch on the black veins that spider across his forearms. Not veins—tattoos. Scrawling lines of magical ink swirl across his glowing skin, constantly changing shape.

"You smell like my wife."

No. No, no, no, no, no. I stumble back, reeling under the weight of his words.

Moving impossibly fast, a pale hand reaches out to grab my shoulder, hauling me upright effortlessly. My head smacks against his stone chest, causing fresh blood to leak from the wound on my skull. Ghostly hair covers my face as Death leans down and swipes his tongue through the blood running from the newly reopened gash on my temple.

As quickly as he grabbed me, he's gone again, reappearing behind the desk across the room in less than a half a second. Muscles strain throughout his arms as if he's physically holding himself back. He snaps his fingers and the heaviness of my tongue disappears in an instant.

"I ... I ... I ..."

Full languages flood my brain at once as Death's magic rushes through me, syntaxes and phonologies forming new synapses. My tongue rolls in my mouth trying to imitate sounds and inflections. Another snap of his long fingers and the lightning speed of linguistic knowledge stills.

"Speak," Death commands in the language of the gods.

"I can't be here."

Wetness threatens to spill from my eyes as the words in this new language leave my lips. Shadows writhe beneath my skin, eager to spring forth from my form if only I dare to whisper acknowledgement of my true parentage.

"Yet here you are, my child."

My child. The words slam into me with the full force of destiny as the origin of my taintedness is finally said aloud. The darkness that has always hovered right below my surface, the power of destruction within my veins. Growth and decay—balance of my true parents. Light and dark, life and death.

"Sit," Death commands.

The Dark God's voice booms through the room, bouncing off

the stone floors, the glass ceiling, and the bone walls. The distinct scent of sulfur fills the room, emanating from the pores of his pallid skin. Summoned by his magic, the leather chair swings forward as he sits in a single, fluid motion, the flare of his coattails rippling in an icy, magical breeze.

My feet magically move at his command, my movements not my own. A velvet, backless stool appears in front of the desk. I sit without remark, curiosity and dread commingling with the god's power that stirs within me.

In a blink, he reaches across the desk and swipes another boney finger through the gash on my head. Death lifts the blood-coated digit to his mouth, his all-seeing eyes weighing the truths and lies within my darkened soul.

"You taste of power. Some of it yours, some you took by force. You killed a god."

A wicked smile tugs up the corners of my lips at the memory of Mikais on his knees, the smell of his burnt flesh mixing with mine as I roasted him alive. Murder shouldn't make me happy. I want to believe that it's not the killing, but the man I saved that makes me smile. But that's not entirely true, and Death can sense it.

"The bastard had it coming," I mumble.

"Do you intend to absorb his power or relinquish it?"

"I can do that?"

The god tilts his head to the side, his knowing eyes snagging on mine. It's painfully obvious how very little I truly know about the gods. I barely grasp that I am a goddess, and I have no concept of what that entails.

"He may be a traitor, but the Wolf God has—or *had*, rather—great power. Power that I'm sure Nobus would be glad to have, if you don't want to keep it. Will you offer it to him? Or do you plan to make an enemy out of your king?"

My king. I don't hide my scoff at the title. A lifetime of religious indoctrination didn't make me respect him, and it damn sure didn't make me love him like the blind masses.

Regardless of the fact that she struck a deal with him, my mother played a role in betraying Nobus. She participated in Mikais' rebellion and smuggled Cal from the god realm. I am already Nobus' enemy—and if he plans to punish Cal for something he had no control over, I will be a ferocious one. Whether I choose to keep the Wolf God's power or not is of no consequence.

"I don't plan to tell him what I've done."

"The death of a god is felt in every realm," Death says. "The question is not *if* Nobus knows that his brother is dead, but rather if he plans to do anything about it. All power must have balance, *Godsbane.*"

"My name is Ivy Fellows, Governor of the Emerald Region of Corinth." I square my shoulders, rattling off the inherited title of a life I will likely never return to.

"You choose to lead with your mortal title?" Death scoffs. "You aren't just the governor of an inconsequential territory in an inconsequential realm. You are the Daughter of Light and Death. You are Ivy, Princess of the Under Realm and Goddess of the Umbra."

The dark power in my veins roars to life at the spoken acknowledgement of its true source. Shadows dance through the room in a frenzied jolt, no longer relegated to the walls and floorboards where they once thrived. Wispy black bands of magic skate across my skin, swirling into ever-changing shapes that mimic the magical ink on Death's skin. The daughter's mirroring the father's.

"You are the shadows, child. The eclipse. The product of the light of the full moon and the dark night of death."

"The decay that I crave … the destruction …" I stammer. "It's all from you. All this time I thought it was from the sea beast, but you were the one haunting me."

"I was preparing you. Selene thought it best to keep secrets, but your power hadn't manifested in that cursed realm and I'm an impatient god. Arcasia owed me a favor so I had her … *spur* you along."

"I almost died!" I counter.

"The mortal realm has made you so dramatic." Death rolls his eyes. "You'll have to unlearn that if you wish to exist amongst us."

"I don't," I reply without hesitation. "I want to go home."

"Home? The Under Realm is your home, and you are its princess," the Dark God says flatly.

"I have other powers—magic not from you that does not wish to live in a realm without life."

A realm without him, I think but don't voice aloud.

"Ah yes, your mother's gift to you. Earth-wielder in the realm you call home. The only one, if my spies are correct."

"I can do more than that." Hungry power washes through me again. The dark call of the magic I've only sipped from intoxicates me more with each passing moment in the Under Realm.

Death's low chuckle rumbles through the bone-walled chamber. His green eyes sparkle with delight in the dim firelight. "Clearly. But what will you do with it? Will you use it to aid your love-sworn prince? You already killed one brother, after all. What's another, future Queen of Shadows?"

"You are Death. If you want Nobus dead, kill him yourself." I try to stand but my feet won't move. Black bands of glimmering magic anchor me to the floor.

"It doesn't work like that, child. Nobus cannot be killed, only contained. Only one god has the power to do that and it's neither of us."

He doesn't have to say his name; I already know who that god is.

"But what will the boy prince decide?" Death tsks as he stands and rounds the desk. "Does power sing to him the same way it calls to you?" He leans down, his striking face only inches from mine as his eyes pierce new holes in my soul. "Is he able to resist it better than you?" he whispers.

A flare of rage sparks in my gut at his insinuation. The dark magic demands penance from the offender that it has no right to require. Death senses it, his nostrils widening in recognition as a predatory smile exposes each of his perfect canines. Beautiful and deadly, pointed and elongated to tear into the flesh of a man with a single bite.

"Embrace it and step into the depths of your true power. You have always been destined to rule, but which realm will you choose? You don't want this one, but your precious mortal realm also seeks a ruler. Will you claim that throne? After all, your beloved won't hesitate to claim the one that's rightfully his."

"Don't speak of him as if you know him. He's nothing like Nobus!" I try again to stand but the bands of magic only tighten their hold.

"How do you know?" Death taunts. "All he needs is your blood to open the portal. The God King will welcome home the stolen heir and grant him his heart's desire in exchange for his agreement to stay. What can you offer him? Shadows? Flowers? A broken, beaten heart that even you don't love?"

"Enough!" I scream.

The glimmering chains that hold me shatter, fracturing into a million shards that evaporate into black smoke. Shadows swirl around my exposed skin, wrapping themselves delicately around my limbs and throat like armor.

"Let me leave."

"I do not hold you here," the Dark God says. "Our magic is not like any other. You can traverse this realm with ease, coming and going any time you please. The shadows will always guide you home."

Home. My every thought turns to Cal.

Onyx hair. Crimson blood. A burning throne. Shadowy death. The

GODSBANE

images from my nightmares that were sent to prepare me—for Marks, for this moment, for him.

"He's not here." Death reads the question in my mind before the thought is even fully formed. "Mikais didn't use the god blades on him. His wounds will heal."

Cal is alive, and I must get back to him.

I focus all of my energy, all of my magic on him. On the memory of how his arms feel around me, how his lips feel on mine, how my heart skips a beat when my hand is in his. He is the north star to which I train my compass. He is home and I will return to him.

Amale was always meant to lead me to Death, but it's not the end of my story. It is simply the beginning.

I am Ivy, Governor of the Emerald Region, Goddess of the Umbra, Daughter of Light and Death, and the Bane of Gods. Nothing and no one can stop me.

Raw, immortal power shoots from the center of my chest. My eyes lock onto the emerald mirror of my true father's gaze one final time. The corner of Death's lip lifts in a half-smile as I levitate above the floor. Everything around me fades into nothingness, first the domed ceiling, then the bone walls and the stone floors.

Just before the Dark God fully disappears, his whispered voice fills my head.

"We'll meet again, my dark bloom. And next time, I'll bring your mother."

CHAPTER 40

CAL

I am losing my mind.

That's the only explanation I can come up with. No sane man would be staring so intently at a woman's left pinky finger. But I swear to the gods, Ivy's twitched twenty-seven minutes ago.

Twenty-seven minutes and ten seconds, to be exact.

No part of her has moved in the past eighteen days. Not an eyelid flutter, not a toe wiggle, and definitely not a pinky twitch. But it happened today. I know it did.

"Captain..."

A kind voice floats in from the bedroom doorway, but I don't break my stare. If I take my eyes off her finger for even a fraction of a second, I won't know if it moves again.

"Are you okay?" Quinn lays her hand on my shoulder to get my attention.

"Her finger moved."

"I think it's time for you to get outside again. Theo is waiting at the—"

"No," I interrupt aggressively, my eyes honed on the delicate fingers that lay in my palm. "She moved. I know she did."

"Captain, I know how desperate you are, how desperate we all are but ..."

"There!" I shout as Ivy's ring finger and pinky twitch in tandem this time. "Did you see that? It's real, Quinn! It's fucking real this time!"

This time. Unlike the other five times I've claimed to see it. Self-deprivation of sleep, food, and sunlight will do that to a person. I don't blame Quinn for not believing me.

Fifteen minutes later, her middle finger joins the others. Three fingers moving in the span of a quarter of an hour.

I lay my hands on her chest and push my magic into her as best as I can. More than two weeks practicing and I still don't fully know how Ivy was able to tap into the core of her magic, the locked away power that we shouldn't have in this realm. She did it though. My incredible, brave woman did the fucking impossible.

Tension hovers thickly in the air as we wait on bated breath for her next movement. Each minute takes twice as long as the one before it. Each second feels like a thousand years.

Ten excruciating minutes later, Ivy's entire left hand spasms in mine. I can't hold back the tears anymore. This is it. Everything I've been praying for. Ivy is coming back to me.

I push again with my magic, harder and faster than I ever dared to before. Her right hand twitches in answer, her left foot following less than five minutes later. I collapse onto the floor at the sight of it, burying my head into her side as I try to muffle my cries with the mattress.

So close. She's so fucking close and still so far away.

"Cal." A weak, barely audible voice squeaks out my name. Nothing has ever sounded sweeter to me than the way my name sounds as it crosses Ivy's lips at this moment. My arms are around her in an instant, my face moving to the crook of her neck.

"Ivy. Ivy. Ivy." Her name comes out broken in sobs, my entire body trembling in shock and relief.

This is real, I repeat to myself. *She is real. She is awake.*

"Water," she whispers.

Quinn holds out a cup, offering it to me instead of her best friend. There's a knowing smile on her face as she nods for me to take it. It's a testament to how much of her trust and respect I've earned over the past eighteen days. There's no doubt in her mind about the unending nature of my love for Ivy. She wants me to have this moment as much as I do.

Ivy drinks the cool, clear liquid in deep gulps. I have to pull the cup away from her face before she drinks too fast and aspirates. "Easy, easy."

Her emerald eyes stare into mine. They're even more fucking beautiful than I remember. She squeezes my hand, looking me over as if she's trying to discern reality from a dream.

Where has she been? Did the nightmares that plague her follow her there? Have the past weeks been torture for her? I tread slowly, praying that I'm wrong.

"This is real, Ivy. I'm here. You're safe."

"Marks is ..." she starts.

"Dead," I finish. "You did it. You killed him. You saved us."

"How long?" She doesn't have to finish the question. I know exactly what she's asking.

"Eighteen days." My voice breaks again at the sight of tears filling her eyes as realization sinks in. "But they haven't voted yet. I wouldn't let them."

"Cal ..." Ivy starts again with an unsteady voice. "I've been in the Under Realm."

"I don't know how much longer I can hold—" Theo's voice carries as he enters the room, his sentence halting abruptly at the sight of a conscious Ivy sitting up in bed. "Holy gods."

My youngest brother moves around the edge of the bed, laying his hand on her shoulder to affirm that she isn't a mirage. "You're awake. You're really fucking awake."

"Yes she is," Quinn says in a level voice that I'm not sure how she manages. "Go back in there and demand another hour. The Governor of the Emerald Region will be attending the Ascension Vote."

"She just woke up." My voice comes out in a near growl. Those godsdamned animals have been chomping at the bit to vote for days. They owe their lives to Ivy and they can't even wait for her. "Give her time to—"

"I want to be there." Ivy's voice is feeble, but there's a fierce determination in her eyes. "I need to finish this."

"An hour, Theo. Go."

My brother jumps like a dog at Quinn's command. I haven't left Ivy's side long enough to investigate what's going on between them, but it's evident that something has taken root. She's gotten comfortable ordering everyone around, always making sure that Ivy and I had anything we could need.

Never once doubting that her best friend would be attending the vote, she even ordered a dressmaker to custom create gowns for Ivy to wear. Four gowns in various styles and colors to allow her to choose what statement to make. Quinn understands Ivy deeply, in a way that I will spend eternity trying to replicate.

"Captain." It's my turn to be on the receiving end of Quinn's orders now. "Give Ivy a kiss, go take a bath, and, for the gods' sake, please shave what's growing on your face."

"I'm not leaving."

"Yes. You. Are." Quinn tugs my arm, forcing me to face her. "Look at me. You've barely left this room for weeks. You have done your part and now it's my turn."

She easily reads the torn expression on my face and adds, "I've got her."

"Hey." Ivy caresses my forearm, her cadence perfectly matching her gentle strokes. "I'll see you in there, okay?"

Reluctantly, I do as Quinn commands. I kiss Ivy's forehead delicately, reverently, as if she might split into a thousand tiny pieces if I grab ahold of her face and kiss her the way I desperately want to.

"One hour and not a second more," I promise.

It feels unnatural to leave her when I've just gotten her back. The walk to my brothers' rooms to clean up is a blur. My body goes through the motions, muscle memory guiding me through bathing and shaving. The only thought that echoes through my mind is her name on repeat: *Ivy. Ivy. Ivy.*

There's a gray and gold uniform in my size laid out on the bed, one final offering from Henry. One last chance to take the position that is mine by right. But I'm even more resolved in my decision today than I was the day I made it.

The position of Lord General is better suited for an ambitious man, not one who has already found everything he's been searching for. My place is at Ivy's side, not at some war room table or on a battlefield without her. I serve no ruler but her.

I dress in a suit of solid black, feeling more like a jester than a soldier without the comforting embrace of my leather armor. Marks' men cut it from my body, and while there's an armory full of pieces I could seek out, I don't. The menacing presence of the Captain of Corinth is not needed. Today, I take a page from my beloved's book and choose to make a different sort of statement.

Theo, the secret romantic that he is, managed to gather Ivy's magically-grown godsbane blooms from the throne room and has been keeping them alive. I pluck the largest bloom from the vase on the dressing table and secure it to my lapel with a gold pin—a tiny emerald encrusted sword. If there is any question as to where my loyalty lies, these touches will make it abundantly clear.

I can feel the tension before I step foot into the council room. It radiates from the empty chair at the head of the rectangular table, the large amethyst embedded in the carved back sparkling in the light from the obnoxiously large chandelier. Each chair has a similar, smaller, jewel indicating the region its occupant represents.

The governors don't try to hide their disappointment when they see me enter the room. Sapphire, Ruby, and Topaz are present, but Emerald is not. She hasn't arrived yet, and her hour is up.

But any chance of them starting without her just evaporated. They'll have to kill me first, and they wouldn't dare try.

The Diamond Region's chair, the one reserved for the Lord General, is also notably empty. Henry, decked in full military regalia, hovers beside it with Marianne's hand gripped in his own. She's a vision in blue, and it's written all over his normally stoic face.

It dawns on me that I never asked if he wanted it, the promotion that he is overqualified for. I never stopped to consider if he would be willing or able to leave her. His eyes meet mine, his head bobbing in a solemn nod, and I know for sure then. My brother is a man of duty and honor. This is his chosen path and Corinth will be better for it.

I hope the same can be said for the rest of them. The governors who sit around this table, clothed head-to-toe in the colors of their region, certainly look the part. And no one can deny what they've done to earn their seats. They overthrew their own fathers and risked their lives for a chance to change Corinth. But their sacrifices pale in comparison to Ivy's.

"Captain," Silas begins, "We are pleased to have you join us today. There is a matter we need to—"

Whatever bullshit is about to spill from his mouth is silenced by the opening of the heavy wooden door.

Every governor rises to their feet as Ivy steps into the room. From my vantage point, I see the pointed toe of her high-heeled shoe first, a shiny black that elongates the pale leg peaking through the slit of her dress. My eyes follow it, tracing the outline of emerald silk that perfectly hugs the curves of her hips and the swell of her breasts before it disappears over her delicate shoulders.

Ivy commands the room, no sign of the fragile woman that lay unconscious only an hour ago, and instead, every bit the goddess she truly is. She makes her way to the chair reserved for the Emerald governor, offering me a soft smile as our eyes lock across the room. When she turns away from me, my knees nearly buckle.

There, embroidered across the back of her dress in black thread, is the sea beast. The large, serpentine form takes up the entirety of the gown, from the top hem to the end of the flared train. It's a near perfect copy of the leviathan inked on both our skin, the symbol of our connected fates.

Ivy takes the long way to her seat, passing by each of the governors and offering only a silent nod as they bend at the waist.

Bowing. They're fucking *bowing* to her.

It takes every bit of restraint in my body to stay upright, to resist the overwhelming urge to hit my knees in her presence. When she passes the chair inlaid with a large amethyst and it becomes clear that she doesn't wish to occupy it yet, I rush to pull out the Emerald Region's chair for her.

Ivy is many things, but a tyrant will never be one of them. If her rule is dictated, she's no better than the men who came before her.

"Nice flower." Her whispered words are just for my ears.

"Nice sea beast," I reply in the same hushed tone.

"Emerald and onyx. Quite the pair, don't you think?"

Her green eyes lock onto mine, and the air in the room thins though no one commands it. The only magic here is what is uniquely ours, and I will gladly spend eternity worshipping the goddess before me.

"I speak for all of us when I say how truly overjoyed we are to see you here, Ivy," Kieran speaks as the governors sit. There's no trace of the usual sarcasm or taunt in his voice, only sincere reverence for the woman who saved us all.

"Out of respect for the diplomatic process, if you are not a voting member of this council, we ask you to leave at this time."

At Micah's words, the servants who flitted about filling goblets and passing out canapés exit the room. I scoot Ivy's chair up to the table and make my way towards the door when the Sapphire governor stops me.

"Are you certain about your decision, Captain? Corinth would be lucky to have you as its Lord General."

"Corinth is already lucky," I correct. "Lord General Henry Murphy is the most qualified soldier for the role, of that I am more than certain."

Without another word, I stroll confidently from the room, out of the palace, and into the city of Amale. While the future of Corinth is being decided, I have urgent matters to attend to that will decide my own future. And Ivy's, if she chooses it.

I follow the pull of her magic down the alabaster halls, past the empty bedchambers and the empty council room to the golden doors of the throne room. The one place in the palace I can't fucking bear to go. But I told her that there was no path I wouldn't follow—so I open the doors and face my worst nightmare.

What happened in this room has replayed in my head a thousand times: Ivy's final words, her lifeless body on the ground, the seemingly bottomless pool of her blood that covered the floor. They're all stars of the nightmares that have haunted both my sleeping and waking hours.

I take a steadying breath, swallow my fear, and push open the gilded door. Ivy stands in front of the Amethyst Throne, the train of her gown cascading down the steps of the dais. From this angle, the maw of the beast looks poised to attack any who approach her.

She's a fucking vision.

Regal. Royal. *Mine.*

I focus on her alone, ignoring the pink stains and charred veins that streak through the otherwise flawless stone floor. Blood and godfire, evidence of the battle for those that come after and each its own lesson.

Ivy's magic rises up to meet mine in a familiar, playful dance. It warms my blood and soothes my rapidly beating heart.

"Admiring your new seat, my queen?"

"It's not my seat," she replies, her attention solely focused on the Amethyst Throne before her.

"Tell me who voted against you and I'll cut out their tongues."

I unsheathe the ivory-handled dagger at my side for dramatic effect. She doesn't need me to fight her battles and I'm positive that whatever happened in that room is exactly what she wanted.

"You'll have to cut out mine then."

"Never mind," I say, tucking away the blade. "I'm fond of it right where it is."

She turns to face me with the sweetest, sad little half-smile on her perfect lips. "We both know I never wanted the throne. I just wanted to stop Marks from ascending, but then he attacked Emerald, and my anger felt endless. I let it consume me. I became the kind of ruler Corinth wouldn't survive. Fury is a blinding mistress and a cruel queen has no loyal subjects."

I take her trembling hands into mine, unable to resist the urge to touch her any longer. "They bowed to you in there," I whisper. "That looked pretty fucking loyal to me."

"Now we all bow to another," she says in a steady voice. "Our Sapphire King."

Leave it to Ivy to accomplish exactly what she set out to do despite all of the odds being against her. The very nature of the game and all the players on the board changed, but her mission never waivered.

And now, every region in Corinth is governed by strong, allied leaders. Leaders who won't hesitate to check the monarch if they overstep. That was the original intent of our structure, after all. Before puppet kings and dictator Lord Generals, before politics and the egos of gods overshadowed knowledge and skill.

"Speaking of kings," she says, squeezing my hands. "You're a *prince*."

"I should have told you, but I was so scared you'd hate me if you knew."

"Because your dad's a prick?" she laughs. "Turns out mine is too. But unlike me, I don't think you're anything like yours."

"You can't possibly know that." She's not like him, the Dark God who feasts on souls and relishes in the demise of everything around him. She is not the pitch black of night. She is the caressing shadow on the sunniest of days, the cool reprieve from the scalding summer heat.

But am I like my father? My uncle called him weak and spineless. The holy texts, scriptures filled with lies, call him an all-seeing, just, and fair god. I can't know who he truly is or how much of him I possess until I meet him—something I'm eager not to do anytime soon.

"I'm glad you didn't tell me who my father is, Cal," Ivy says, her emerald eyes shining in the dimming light. "Someone very wise once told me that some things are better experienced. You could experience meeting yours too, you know. You could open the portal, if you wanted to."

Leave it to Ivy to brazenly broach the one topic everyone has tiptoed around for weeks.

"I want to do what you want to do," I smile. "It has to be both of us. It was always meant to be both of us."

"Your family is on the other side of that door, Cal."

"My family is right here." I lay her hand across my heart, across the tattooed beast that matches the creature on her dress and her skin. "I go where you go, Ivy. Whether that's back to Emerald or to the god realm, it is your decision."

Tears well in her eyes. I may not have been forthcoming with my heritage, but I never lied to her. When I said I would follow her anywhere, I meant it. I know that Ivy's path leads back to Emerald, to the place where her version of our story began, and I'll be right beside her.

"We can't outrun him, Cal. Nobus will come for us—for *you*. It's only a matter of time."

"Let him. Let the God King come into our realm and try to take me from you. I fucking dare him." Magic scrapes its claws against my skin at the threat. I may not have been able to take down Marks, but I will rip Nobus apart if he even thinks about separating us. I don't know if existence can survive the death of a god that powerful, but we can certainly fucking find out.

Ivy smiles again, despite the tears that streak across her pinked cheeks. Her fingers trail sparks across my face as she wills my magic into submission. It kneels at her feet like a godsdamned house cat curling around a fireplace.

Safe. Warm. *Home.*

"Then we go home first," she says. "Together."

"Home," I smile. "Let's go home, princess."

Ivy winces at the use of the pet name, and I'm filled with instant regret for my carelessness.

"Call me something else, please … anything else. I'm not ready to face what I'm the princess of just yet."

"What would you have me call you?" I ask.

"You'll figure something out." She smiles, the words from our first day together sounding ten times as delicious the second time around. "I'm sure of it."

ACKNOWLEDGMENTS

Godsbane has been a labor of love and a rollercoaster of self-doubt. The fact that you're holding this book in your hands today is a testament to the incredible support system that surrounds and uplifts me without fail. I hope you'll humor this author and allow me to gush about my people for a moment.

First and foremost, this book wouldn't exist without you, Wil. I can only write about the kind of love that shatters realms because I found it first with you. Thank you for supporting me through the late nights and early mornings and encouraging me to never give up. Thank you for being the best husband and father around and not complaining about your wife living in a fictional world for over two years. You never miss a chance to tell people that I wrote a book, and it's there, in the warmth of your praise and admiration, that I feel the quiet depths of your love. Forever and always, my love.

To RK and WC, my tiniest supporters. I hope when you finally read this book (in ten-plus years), you'll be able to see how much of my heart and soul I left in these pages. You two are the reason I get up every morning and keep pushing even when I want to stop. Always know that you're never too old to chase your dreams. To the moon and back, my babies.

To my friends and family who have been my cheerleaders, thank you for every like, share, comment, phone call, or text message of support. You were proud of me without reading a single word—and I hope you're even prouder after reading this book.

To my parents, in-laws, grandparents, and elementary school teachers, I am so sorry about chapters 18 and 19 ... and 27. Forget you read them.

To my Shadow Baddies, this book wouldn't have an ending without you. Thank you for helping me plot, forcing me not to kill off a very important character (looking at you, CB), and hyping me up always.

To NS, thank you for playlists and friendship bracelets, for being a sounding board for my ideas and never being afraid to tell me when something wasn't working. Thank you for keeping all my secrets and celebrating every milestone with me.

To HR and VR, thank you for pouring your time and talent into editing and designing the perfect grammar and art for Godsbane. I'm so thankful CHS brought us together all those years ago. Your talents are unmatched and I'll forever hype them.

To my BookTok and AuthorTok community, I'll never stop being grateful for finding you. Thank you for the advice, the hype, the laughs, and for humoring my unhinged videos.

To my alpha and beta readers, thank you for investing your valuable time into helping me make Godsbane the story it is.

And to you, my readers, thank you for taking a chance on an unknown indie author. Your support means the world to me. I can't wait to continue this journey with you!

ABOUT THE AUTHOR

Lindsey Richardson is a self-proclaimed book dragon and lover of all things fantasy and romance. When she doesn't have her head buried in a book, you can find Lindsey at home crafting, spending time with her family and pets, cheering on the Tennessee Vols, and forcing her impeccable music taste on anyone who will listen.

Lindsey has dedicated her professional career to making a positive impact in the world through her favorite nonprofit organization. She is also an avid supporter of the Panhellenic experience.

Discover more of Lindsey's work and subscribe to her newsletter at www.lindseyrichardsonauthor.com